PRAISE FOR THE DAMAGES

"In the 1990s, women were going to university and joining the workforce in record numbers. Why, then, do many of us have conflicted feelings when looking back? This is one of the first novels I've read that does a brilliant job of unpacking the duplicity and dishonesty of the era. An intelligent and intense read about how power structures are passed on—*The Damages* held me, riveted, in a tight, icy grip."
—**Claire Cameron, author of *The Bear* and *The Last Neanderthal***

"*The Damages* is a probing, courageous work—a dance along the tightropes of memory, justice and love. It explodes the myth of the innocent bystander and ultimately celebrates the lifelong moral challenge of learning who you really are."
—**Sarah Henstra, author of *The Red Word,* winner of the Governor General's Literary Award for Fiction**

"*The Damages* is an eerily sharp depiction of being self-conscious, self-obsessed, and eighteen in the late nineties, and just how painful it can be to face the past and question why one makes the choices they do when they're young. Packed with insecurity, embarrassment, jealousy, and shame, each page made me anxious in the best possible way. Heart pounding, I couldn't stop reading!"
—**Cedar Bowers, Scotiabank Giller Prize-longlisted author of *Astra***

"There is a skillful irony in a character so courageously honest about her lies. Genevieve Scott offers a view inside of a complicated woman from young adulthood to middle age, in refreshing and deceptively clean prose. *The Damages* takes a critical look at truth and perspective in a (post-) #MeToo era, calling into question the ways our personal truths are shaped by our pasts."

—Fawn Parker, Scotiabank Giller Prize–longlisted author of *What We Both Know*

"*The Damages* led me into a maze with a thread—and then just never let me go. This story builds with thrilling intensity through moral knots and human dilemmas, led by a brilliantly complex protagonist as she navigates her way through betrayal, guilt and culpability."

—Charlotte Gill, author of *Almost Brown*

"*The Damages* is the most honest novel I've read in a long time. A propulsive story about the complexities of trust, the cruelties in relationships, and the space between meaning well and doing good. Genevieve Scott is a fresh, brilliant voice in fiction."

—Leah Mol, author of *Sharp Edges*

"Genevieve Scott is a sophisticated writer, and *The Damages* is a sharp, multi-layered story about truth, lies, history and memory. I stayed up late to finish it! I was not disappointed: this is a complex and satisfying novel."

—Sarah Selecky, author of *Radiant Shimmering Light*

THE DAMAGES

Also by Genevieve Scott

CATCH MY DRIFT

GENEVIEVE SCOTT

THE DAMAGES

RANDOM HOUSE CANADA

PUBLISHED BY RANDOM HOUSE CANADA

www.penguinrandomhouse.ca

This novel contains discussion of sexual assault that may be sensitive to some readers.

LIBRARY AND ARCHIVES CANADA CATALOGUING IN PUBLICATION

Title: The damages / Genevieve Scott.
Names: Scott, Genevieve, author.
Identifiers: Canadiana (print) 20220488460 | Canadiana (ebook) 20220488487 |
    ISBN 9781039004924 (softcover) | ISBN 9781039005075 (EPUB)
Classification: LCC PS8637.C68615 D36 2023 | DDC C813/.6—dc23

Text design: Kate Sinclair
Cover design: Kate Sinclair
Image credits: Tim Alex / Unsplash

Printed in Canada

10 9 8 7 6 5 4 3 2 1

Penguin
Random House
RANDOM HOUSE CANADA

For my mother

PROLOGUE

Spring 2020

What I remember best about that week in January is trying to keep track of all the lies I told. Still, they want to hear from me.

Elaine Ng called it *a conversation*. We could meet whenever it suited me. Nothing to bring along, just my memory.

I haven't met Elaine Ng, but I have studied her photo on the Burton Jafari LLP website. She is attractive, a year younger than me, if I've calculated her age correctly from LinkedIn. Two years ago, a Canadian legal magazine named her a "Top 40 under 40." I'm sure her personal and professional choices have been, on balance, more impressive than mine, which is the main way I size up women now. At one time, the time period she wants to discuss, I considered only prettiness, thinness, and some ever-evolving coolness factor, indexed from aesthetic choices like cut of jeans and hairstyle (though even by this standard, Ms. Ng scores high). Ms. Ng is probably good at what she does, but I don't understand this whole system, her system, that puts so much stock in the reliability of memories.

Back when I lived with Lukas, he said he didn't need to remember things like our dry cleaner's name or our friends' food sensitives because my memory was a spiderweb, nabbing every detail. At dinner parties, I was proud to supply whatever got lost at the tip of a storyteller's tongue—the name of a child actor, the year of the Albertville Olympics, the author of a book I'd never read. Early in our relationship, Lukas brought me to lunch with his agent, and years later, he marvelled at what I could still recall about the evening: the Weimaraner she waved at through the window, her tendency to repeat the phrase "Let's face it," the fleck of taramasalata on the sleeve of her white caftan. I liked being the person who could turn up scraps like these—it was a party trick. It was also, I see now, a distraction. A way to seem clever and observant while avoiding anything of substance. I don't remember much of what the agent said about Lukas's book that night or why they stopped working together several months later. My memory may nab more details than most, but these details don't form a complete picture; more often, they obscure what's there.

I could describe to Ms. Ng, for instance, the shirt Megan wore to the bar on the night she went missing. It was borrowed from Sue, white with a ruffle over the chest. I once read a teen magazine article on swimwear that described flattering bathing suits for various body types: "Not much on top? Reach for a ruffle!" Megan tried it on at the full-length mirror on Sue's closet door. From the way she bit her lip, I could tell that she liked how it looked. But I don't think this is the sort of detail Ms. Ng is seeking.

I searched Regis University online and found a news clip from this past March, a segment on students who were refusing to social distance despite the COVID outbreak in the town of Creighton, Ontario. It was the first time I'd seen the campus in over two decades. The kids were crowded in front of a reporter's microphone, jackets open, glittery hats jauntily askew, green beer sloshing in frosted glass mugs. One pretty girl narrowed her eyes at the camera. "Are we *not* allowed to enjoy our lives?"

They sounded so dumb. Were we that dumb?

If that week in January had happened even a decade later than it did, this conversation would be easier. I would have photographs, videos, all kinds of documentation. There would be hashtags: *#Pray4Creighton, #CreightonStrong*. But we didn't have cellphones or social media in 1998. I didn't take pictures, hardly used email. Ballpark is the best I can do for Ms. Ng, if I talk to her at all.

The few things that I'm certain of are the things that everybody knows. Megan Main, my roommate, went missing from Alice Cole Hall on January 9, 1998. Though there were 250 people sleeping in a dorm built for 115 that night, no one saw her leave. It was in the middle of the biggest ice storm in Creighton's history.

On the first night, the storm was magical. Our campus was like the atrium of a shopping mall at Christmas: trees dripping with tinsel-fine icicles, rime-crusted windows, sparkles of moisture under the streetlamps. But freezing rain fell for days. Thick layers of ice accumulated on trees, windshields, hydro poles and wires. People lost their homes, their farms; livestock froze to death. Nearly all of Creighton's forty thousand households were blacked out.

As students in residence, we were ignorant of the devastation; we didn't want the chaos to end. An ice storm was a dream come true for us—classes were cancelled, there was nowhere we had to be, no responsibilities. And we weren't afraid of falling on ice. If anyone was going to die, it would be from drinking. A different sort of blackout.

Alice Cole Hall, the dorm where I lived, was the centre of the party because we never lost power. People said we had power because we shared a generator with Creighton General Hospital. Maybe that's right, I don't really know. I didn't understand anything about power then.

PART ONE

Winter 1998

1

It is practical to put borders around this story, fuzzy as they are. So let's say that the story begins the day we returned to campus from the Christmas holidays: Sunday, January 4, 1998. My dad drove me to school in the Jaguar he'd bought himself as a retirement gift on Boxing Day. I spent most of the drive pretending to be asleep, not because I didn't like my dad, but because I didn't really know how to sustain a conversation with him for three hours. We didn't have a lot of common interests. He was seventy-one, which was older than some of my friends' grandparents. Growing up, he never knew the names of my friends or teachers. He wouldn't, for instance, have known the name Megan Main, even though she was my roommate. At eighteen, I was self-doubting, self-obsessed and a follower. But my dad had his own ideas about me, ideas that made me a credit to him, and it was easier to be who he thought I was, easier for both of us. On his desk at home, he kept a single photo of me; it was taken at Swiss Chalet when I was five, and it captured everything he felt he needed to know. Under the haze of a yellow-and-brown hanging lamp, I'm contemplating a structure built from creamer cups, sweetener packs and condiment bottles, my chin resting on my hand. Thoughtful, focused, independent. I was quiet around him because I wasn't prepared to challenge that image. My dad was old, impatient with people, and had an unshakable sense of how things should be. I often worried that I'd say or do something stupid and reveal too much of myself.

I was eager to return to school that January. At that point, Regis was home. In August, my parents and I had moved back to Toronto after a five-year stint in L.A., but the new condo felt to me like their space, not mine. I was a college student now, on my own, on to the next thing. I had spent most of the Christmas holidays watching TV while my mother suggested ways to brighten up my north-facing bedroom. I said, "Do whatever you like. I don't really live here." This was also an excuse not to lift a finger.

My dad was a Regis alumnus, and he was pleased to see that I'd taken to the school. He'd whistled along to the radio for most of the ride there, but once we arrived, I didn't want him to linger because I didn't want anyone to see his Jag. Although family wealth was common at Regis, it was best to downplay it. When people knew you had a lot of money, you got judged more harshly. There was a girl on my floor whose highly recognizable surname linked her to a major Canadian grocery store chain. Behind her back, her presumed wealth was used to minimize her generosity ("I'd give you a ride, too, if I had Daddy's Saab") and to barb any criticisms ("You'd think she could afford to wax her moustache"). At Regis, being broke was *de rigueur*. It had been the opposite in L.A., where everyone exaggerated their status whenever they could get away with it. At Regis, if the subject came up, which it didn't very often,

I told people my dad was an artist. It wasn't totally untrue, he was an architect. A fairly famous one.

Before I pulled open the heavy wooden doors to Alice Cole Hall, Dad whistled at me from the sidewalk. I turned to face him, and he grinned in the same proud but embarrassing way he had when he pointed out that I was wearing mascara at eighth grade graduation. "Do you own this place or what?"

I forced a smile, looked around, hoped to God no one was watching us.

"Let me get a picture," he said. "For your mom."

Among my dad's various false impressions was the idea that my mother and I were close. This assumption that all daughters are tightly bonded to their mothers must have come from his first marriage: my half sister, Val, was close to her mother. But my mom and I were not friends. Unlike my father, she didn't view me with rose-coloured glasses—quite the opposite. Nothing impressed her. I suppose the upside of this was that it was also hard to disappoint her. She knew a few more of the basic bullet points of my life than my dad did—my room-mate's name, for instance—but she didn't know anything about how we got along. She never asked.

I stood stiffly in the cold, duffle bag slung in front of me, while my dad fumbled with the camera.

This wasn't the last time I saw my dad, but I think it's accurate to say that this was the last time he saw me, or at least the version of me that he'd never previously had to question. The last time I was his bright, uncomplicated youngest daughter, with her best years ahead of her.

"You probably noticed I like horses."

This was the first thing Megan Main said to me. The first thing anyone at Regis ever said to me.

The week before I started at Regis in September, I got my dorm assignment in the mail and was devastated. Since receiving my acceptance in June, I had daydreamed about living in the Ex—James Exeter Hall, the huge coed tower I'd seen in the housing brochure—next to a long-haired, guitar-playing film major with a name like Hugo. I'd rehearsed the conversation that Hugo and I would be forced to have when, after several months of tension-filled, late-night talks about our childhoods and favourite movies, we admitted our feelings for each other and had to decide whether sex would ruin our friendship. It was very fashionable then to have guys as best friends and to worry, or fake worry, about ruining the friendship. Getting assigned to Alice Cole Hall, which was girls only and the least cool dorm at Regis, was a pretty major blow to my fantasies.

Long before I arrived, people had been shortening Alice Cole Hall to AlCo Hall, which would be an obvious joke for a normal dorm, but AlCo Hall was for girls who wore French braids for fun and volunteered at hospitals. It was the only dorm with "dry" floors, which made it considerably more boring than the other two women's dorms, all of which sat in a row on the same cul-de-sac at the edge of campus.

When I moved in, my dorm room had two cut-out construction paper hearts on the door with a cupid in between. One heart said Megan Main, Woodstock, NB; the other said Rosie Fisher, L.A., Calif. The idea that someone on this floor thought I'd shorten my name to "Rosie," like some '50s girl in a poodle skirt, was a good summation of the problem.

Megan was the first to move into our room. She wasn't there when I arrived, but her bed was already made up with a dust ruffle and a horse-print duvet set. On her desk, there were two framed pictures: one of her with her parents at graduation and one of a guy in a backward ball cap posing in front of a Grand Am with his arms outstretched. Above her desk was a poster for the Penfield High School production of *Anything Goes*.

I saw that horse decor, the cheesy boyfriend, the poster, and whatever hope I still had for my cool university life began to fade. Back then, I saw my peers in only two columns: "cool" or "loser." Megan's things confirmed that she was a loser. And I was pissed. There are confident, charismatic types who are considered cool no matter where they are or who they're with, but I was not one of them. For average people like me, coolness is contingent. If you're saddled with too much baggage, like a dork roommate in a dork dorm, coolness can slip completely out of reach.

Regis University was about a hundred years old, small, and elite. The campus spanned several blocks of scattered turn-of-the-century limestone structures, undifferentiated midcentury expansion buildings, and muddy playing fields. It was a hard school to get into, and the admissions team valorized the "well-rounded": preppy, high-spirited, class president types. Leafing through my dad's issues of *Alumni Quarterly*—chock-full of kids in fleece vests and canvas backpacks—I was heady with the idea of being a big fish in a small pond. The kids in the photos were nothing like me, but they weren't *better* than me, either. There was a chance that I might impress them. At my high school in West Hollywood, where beautiful kids were literally *creating* youth culture on a weekly basis, it was impossible for me to impress anyone. I was background, plain rice. But at a provincial place like Regis, it seemed to me that I might convince people otherwise. Regis was a shining second chance; it was my first-choice school.

Megan and her uncool things, however, were a threat to my potential. Before even meeting her, I decided that if I didn't want to be dragged down, the best strategy was to keep a distance from her. But a problem with my plan cropped up right away—Megan was an extremely kind person. When she eventually came back to our room that first day, carrying a stack of leaflets from the Student Activity Centre—*I got double of everything!*—I quickly realized I couldn't just ignore her. In our first ten minutes together, she offered me stick-on hooks for my closet, a sachet of her mother's homemade potpourri, and a roll of paper for "lining my drawers." When I sliced my index finger cutting the paper, she gave me a Band-Aid.

Megan was a dream roommate. She vacuumed both sides of our floor every Sunday, made us tea, and let me use her printer whenever I wanted, even though I never once paid for replacement toner. And lucky for me, Megan's hectic schedule made her exceptionally easy to avoid outside our room. She had two jobs: regular weekday shifts in the cafeteria and a weekend gig at a stable on a professor's farm. She was also an active member of both the equestrian and musical theatre clubs. The rest of the time, Megan was at the library, trying to get ahead. She had grown up around horses and wanted to be a large animal vet, which would eventually mean grad school. Megan was the first in her family to go to university, which is not something I could appreciate then. To me, university was not "the big leagues," it was just somewhere to spend four years because that's what everyone did. My choices at Regis weren't linked to any particular career ambition.

Of the two of us, I considered myself to be the sophisticated, world-wise one, but I must have seemed so lazy and immature to Megan. I didn't have a job, I barely studied, I took no special care of my personal belongings. But at the time, it never seemed like Megan thought anything negative about me. She was just very capable and responsible while managing not to be smug about it.

So I led a double life. Behind our door, I reaped the benefits of being Megan's roommate, and we enjoyed each other's company. I ate the day-old desserts she brought me from the cafeteria, and I helped myself to her economy-sized bottle of Outrageous shampoo. Megan ironed my dress before the semiformal, and she helped me get puke stains out of the carpet the next morning, but it wasn't all one-sided. I made her laugh. I liked to amuse her by drawing pictograms on her whiteboard when I took phone messages. Kyle, her boyfriend, might be represented as a tall drink of water, while the cafeteria could be a hot dog. If she guessed that the hot dog was Kyle, I'd tease her that she had a dirty mind. We were friends, more or less, but we weren't often seen together outside of our room. Until she disappeared, I considered her a footnote to my life at Regis. That fall, if anyone asked me how I got along with my roommate, I'd say, "We're not close."

The person I wanted to be close with was Supriya Verma. Sue.

I noticed Sue in the common room at our first floor meeting in September. She was sitting with her legs up on a faded velour armchair, painting her toenails with Wite-Out. There were more chairs available, but all the other girls sat on the hardwood floor, too humble or too afraid to take up any space. Bev, our resident assistant, briefly paused her speech on the street names of various drugs—most of which, like *grass*, were embarrassingly outdated—to stare directly at Sue and say, "Those fumes can kill brain cells too, Supriya." Instead of apologizing, Sue looked up dispassionately and said, in her English accent, "Well, holy fuck. I had no idea." And then she got up and wandered away, still barefoot. Sue glowed with a natural-born confidence; I wanted to be close to her not just because that glow was dazzling, but because it was so abundant that others might mistake me as part of its source.

A few hours later, I had my first real encounter with Sue. I was taking my contacts out in front of the bathroom mirror when she came in wearing flip-flops and carrying a plastic bucket of toiletries. Megan, at the sink next to me, said, "Your eyes are all red, Ros. You, okay?" I met Sue's glance in the mirror. "Yeah," I said, all casual. "I ran out of *grass* so I had to get high on school supplies."

Sue snorted, and I felt a door nudge open for me. I would have traded all of Megan's kindness for Sue's approval.

In a normal dorm, Sue probably would have just ignored me, but in a nerd dorm, I was her best option. By mid-September, we were regularly knocking on each other's doors. She told me she thought I was funny. One way I knew how to get her to laugh was by being a little bit mean, and the dorks in our dorm were sitting ducks. I didn't feel like a mean person in my heart, but I was very talented at mocking people behind their backs.

Like me, Sue was somewhat of an outsider. She was born in Canada but had gone to boarding school in the UK since the age of ten. She didn't fit with the Regis brand, but she didn't aspire to either. She mocked the intramural sports, the theme nights at the bar, the endless loop of U2 and Counting Crows playing in the hall. The Regis leather jacket was the mainstay of this brand, and she called the girls who wore them "leatherettes," copycats. Why would anyone *want* to be one of the many? Another pony-tailed, poli-sci major with an unironic passion for Jewel. Sue listened to Jane's Addiction, had a lip ring, and smoked hand-rolled cigarettes. She went to classes swaddled in a moth-eaten cardigan but would later show up at the bar wearing a genuine Hermès scarf as a top. On Sue, scruffy looked stylish, and expensive looked effortless. She was all over the place, hard to figure out, and that gave her status at Regis without having to follow leatherette code. In my greatest flights of vanity, I believed that I was also different and interesting. That Sue recognized something special in me. But now I think what made me interesting was only my connection to Sue.

That January, the first thing I did when I got back to school was head for Sue's room. Her rare single was at the end of the hall, just above the entrance to the cafeteria. From Sue's window, we would watch other students come and go before deciding when to head down for meals. I liked to come up with nicknames for the people passing by: Skeletor for the tall, bony guy with a shaved head, Suicide Spice for the gothy girl in the dog collar, and—Sue's personal favourite—Jesus Christ Superstar for the girl who wore long Laura Ashley–esque skirts and homely blouses.

When I opened the door to Sue's room, she was looking at a spread of photos on her desk. She turned toward me and smiled. "About fucking time!"

Sue was updating her corkboard. Up to that point, the board had been a braggy collage of her cool pre-Regis life: pretty, kilted girls with coloured streaks in their hair and moody expressions; Declan, her gaunt-cheeked Irish boyfriend, with a guitar on his lap; a group of shirtless, long-haired boys on a beach somewhere in India, dancing with flaming torches. But now there were new photos going up. A shot of our friend Dutch had been added to the outskirts of her board. In the photo, he was lying on her bed with his head propped on his closed fist, staring right at the camera.

Dutch had been my friend first. We were in the same orientation group during frosh week. When our group leader got to him on roll call, he said, "Van *Kampen*? Like Van Halen?"

"Like Van Kampen," Dutch said with a look of waning patience.

"I'm going to call you Eddie," the guy said, baring his teeth and playing air guitar.

"People call me Dutch," Dutch said.

I was in awe. You could just decide your name? I was wearing a hard hat then because the same group leader had made me put it on; he'd said my name for the week would be "Hard-head frosh," and if anyone asked why, I was supposed to shout, "Because I like to give head, *hard!*"

Over lunch on day two, Dutch told me to lose the stupid hat and then suggested we bail on parachute games to get drunk together and walk around. He said he noticed me mouthing the words to the song "Vienna" earlier before "some asshole" switched the track. "Fly" was blaring at that moment, as it would be for much of the fall.

"Billy Joel is our generation's soundtrack. It's practically primordial," Dutch said, leaning back on his chair and staring at me. "Think of what was playing during carpools, at the bowling alley—"

"Orthodontist visits," I offered, remembering Dr. Arkin's schmaltzy radio, loud enough to be heard over drilling.

"Never had one of those, but yes." He grinned; he did not need dental work. "Not everyone will admit to liking Billy Joel. I respect you for that. Very genuine of you. I'm not saying the guy's cool, he's not. But he's part of us. Not like this Billy Ray shit."

I never said I liked Billy Joel. I hadn't even known "Vienna" was a Billy Joel song before he said so. But I nodded in a way that attempted to convey, *Yes, Billy Joel's not cool, and yes, yes, I deserve your respect.* I did not correct him that "Fly" was by Sugar Ray, not Billy Ray—not knowing the name of the band you hated somehow seemed cooler.

Dutch wasn't someone I would have bothered to have a crush on— he was too good looking for me, I could see that—but I did want his attention. I took off with Dutch after lunch, waiting nervously outside his dorm room in Herbert Hall—Regis's boys-only residence, generally known as Pervert Hall—while he filled a water bottle with rye and ginger ale.

We walked away from campus, cutting through the student housing area to get downtown, and that was my first time on Heritage Street, Creighton's famous main drag of dilapidated Victorians, all student rentals. Sitting proudly on their front porches, upper-year students sipped from Solo cups and beer bottles. Girls ran barefoot into the street to consume their friends in full-body hugs. Up on a roof, two dudes were hanging a banner that said: Grads '98, Check Us Out & Masturbate!

Heritage Street had none of the overly eager smiles and jumpy, nervous energy of the dormitories; everyone seemed convinced of themselves, like they belonged exactly where they were. I was entranced.

Maybe it was the rye, but looking up at the sunlit trees, I was overcome with such a dizzying sensation of having found what I was searching for that when I looked down again, I was afraid that somehow I'd already lost it.

"Do you play guitar?" Dutch asked, noticing the Band-Aid on my finger as he passed me the bottle.

Without really thinking, I nodded. It wasn't a total lie; I'd taken three lessons in tenth grade with a dick named Donald, who cringed when I asked him to teach me "What's Up?" by 4 Non Blondes, shattering my confidence in my own musical taste, perhaps permanently. But I felt like someone who *could* play guitar.

"So we'll jam sometime?" he said.

"For sure." I'd figure it out later.

Dutch didn't ask me too much more, to my relief, but I learned a lot about him. He was from Windsor, had no siblings and had spent the last two years surfing and working in Tofino. He was older than most first years, which at least partially explained why he looked more mature, more *mannish*. He was tall with a stubbly face and lightly creased forehead, but there were subtler aspects to what made him seem older. That fall, most first-year guys were into trends like frosted tips, Vans, Oakleys, but Dutch's style was more classic, in my opinion, more sophisticated. That afternoon, he wore Birkenstocks, Wayfarers, and a white button-down with the sleeves rolled up. His hair was neatly overgrown, no product.

We went as far as Eddy Street, the major retail strip in Creighton's small downtown. Every window advertised back-to-school sales. We stopped for chips and cigarettes at the 7-Eleven, and then Dutch bought a Talking Heads CD at Radio Gaga, the used-book-and-music store. I flipped through the store's ramshackle offerings, making sure to seem interested, but not interested enough in any one thing to have to talk about it.

Returning to campus down Heritage, we passed a group of girls sitting in a circle of lawn chairs on a driveway. One of them called out to Dutch and then came bouncing toward us. She said she knew him from Citizens of Insanity, his high school band back in Windsor. Apparently, his band was good enough to perform at actual bars. I wished, then, that I hadn't told Dutch I played guitar. This girl had a tattoo of a daffodil on her forearm and an unopened beer bottle tucked jauntily into the pocket of her jean shorts. She had a natural, Noxzema-girl face that lit up with Dutch's hug. Her curly, damp hair smelled like fresh cedar wood, and that fragrance seemed somehow connected to her beauty. Even if I used the same shampoo, I felt certain I could never emit that scent.

What would it be like to be her? Her best friend? How magical it would feel to simply exist in the easy company of someone like her. When Dutch introduced me, she glanced in my direction but said nothing.

Back at the dorms, as soon as I had the chance, I introduced Dutch to Sue. I knew they would like each other and that my association with each of them would raise my stock with the other. The first night we hung out, Sue spent forty-five minutes reading Dutch's palm—fortune-telling was a skill she purported to have. I'm not sure what Dutch believed, but he liked the attention, her fingers tracing his palm.

Dutch and Sue were always flirtatious with one another—massaging each other's feet and "falling asleep" in the same bed—but they weren't a couple. Sue was still technically involved with Declan back in London, and Dutch had an on-again, off-again girlfriend who was tree planting out west. But they were—I can still hear Sue say it now—*such* good friends. Whenever anyone suggested there was something going on between them, Sue would bark with incredulous laughter. But I'm sure they thought about fucking each other all the time.

I liked to think of us as a trio, but Sue and Dutch were king and queen. They called themselves the "2PAC" after Tupac Shakur. Even though that made me feel left out, I still felt special to have brought them together. And it was easy to maintain my spot in the triangle because I had plenty of access to both of them. Sue and I had AlCo Hall in common, and Dutch and I were both English majors, sharing three classes. When Sue and Dutch did 2PAC-only things—like watching *Twin Peaks* in Dutch's room after Tuesday night econ—I don't think they were looking to exclude me, they just didn't think about inviting me.

As the early January dusk settled outside Sue's window, she turned on her desk lamp and handed me another photo of Dutch for consideration. "Doesn't Dutch look like such a nerd here?" she said. Sue had taken the picture at his twentieth birthday party in December, at a karaoke bar. I had baked him a cake in the common room kitchen and decorated it like a twenty-dollar bill. We'd stuffed ourselves on the walk to the bar.

"He just looks like Dutch," I said, handing Sue back the photo. Where I considered my own looks to have significant bandwidth— washing my hair and putting on concealer was the difference between looking like a rundown teen mom or a perky girl next door—truly good-looking people like Sue and Dutch didn't seem to vary all that much to me.

Sue considered the photo again, and I bit my tongue. I'd been surprised at how much Dutch sucked at karaoke that night. The worst part was that you could tell he thought he was good. His version of "Creep" was so earnest and intense that I figured it was a joke at first. He shut his eyes, stooped over the microphone, convulsed at the beginning of the chorus. Some people in the audience laughed, but he was too into himself to notice. I tried exchanging a pained look with Sue, but she was swaying and biting her lip, taking Dutch's spitty, interminable performance just as seriously as he was. I wanted to run out the door. About fifteen minutes later, while his roommate, Stefan, was screeching his way through "Zombie," Dutch puked—green, from the cake frosting—all over the urinals and got us kicked out.

"He gave me the sweetest phone call on New Year's," Sue said. "Declan was off his head on coke, and I was feeling so neglected. We just talked and talked. Then Declan was all mad. I was like, *What right do you have?*" She grinned mischievously. "I was *going* to punish him with no sex, but it's just so bad for his ego. And anyway, the makeup sex is too good."

What Sue could possibly have known about good sex at that age is a mystery to me now, but I was a virgin then, and I was rapt. I don't think that I've personally experienced any sex as titillating to me as the sex I imagined other people were having back then.

Sue reached up high to put the second photo of Dutch on the board. Her T-shirt crept up, revealing her narrow waist. To me, Sue had the best body: long limbed, slim, streamlined. Her body was efficient. Mine, in contrast, felt loose and messy. My height and weight were average enough on a doctor's chart, but my stomach wasn't as flat as I thought it should be, and although I didn't feel weak, my arms and legs were anything but sculpted. My body was unremarkable: a neutral, basically unnoticed entity. Sue liked to point out that my boobs were on the bigger side, like that should be a compliment, but I knew they weren't great boobs. I'd been failing the pencil test since ninth grade.

Sue handed me a photo of the two of us taken right before the Christmas semiformal. I was doing the smile Sue taught me: fold your tongue up behind your teeth and giggle a little bit. Sue had one knee kicked up in a mock sexy pose. Although it *was* sexy. We'd done a lot of takes with her tripod. "I hate how I look here," she said. "And you're smiling like an asshole." Of course I couldn't pull off that smile. Sue gave me the photo, and I would later put it up in my room, asshole smile and all. It was the next best thing to being on her corkboard.

"What do you think about me bringing Queenie over next year?" she said, heading over to the window with her bag of Drum tobacco. "You love cats, right? When I saw Miss Q at Christmas, I was like, *Absolutely not, I can't leave you again!*"

I didn't love cats, didn't even like them, but this request was the best thing that had ever happened to me. In December, people had started making plans for where they would live next year. Everyone was trying to reserve a house on or around Heritage Street. Even Megan had gone to see a place with some girls from our floor. I wanted to live with Sue, but I hadn't wanted to be the first to bring it up in case Sue wasn't into it. Some days, I couldn't think of any reason why Sue would say no to me—we hung out all the time. But on other days, when I saw Sue from a distance around campus talking with other people, I imagined her getting many offers, and I'd think, If she wants to live with me, won't she just ask? Then, right before the holidays, Sue told a story about a friend at some college in England whose housemate regularly sterilized her dildo in the kitchen. At the end of the story, Sue turned to me and said, "Please tell me I'm not going to find out you're a nympho next year?" It wasn't exactly an invitation to live together, but I took it that way. Buoyed, I sent Sue an email over the holidays about a family friend who would be vacating a two-bedroom apartment in September that I described as "not right on Heritage (sorry!), but practically touching." Did she want me to inquire? When Sue didn't write back, I couldn't focus on anything else and fretted to the point of immovable irritability. I spent most of Christmas day rereading the email I sent, wondering how I could pass it off as a joke.

"I'm down with cats," I said. I had to keep cool, try not to show her how elated I really felt. This was the hardest thing about being friends with Sue and Dutch. I was constantly watchful, continually looking for approval and trying to anticipate and adjust my tone and facial expressions to match theirs.

"And yeah, I like the sound of being off Heritage," she said. "No one wants to be right on it."

"Totally."

Sue handed me a cigarette and rolled another for herself. I opened the window and leaned out into the moist winter evening, watching a crowd of leatherettes make their way to the cafeteria. I wanted them to look up at me, framed in the buttery glow of Sue's window. I felt like taking a bow. Supriya Verma would be my roommate.

The ice was coming, just hours away, but you couldn't feel it yet.

2

It was that first Sunday dinner in January when I learned that Megan might be considered cute. It wasn't something I was open to noticing on my own, mainly because Megan's fashion sense was so oblivious. Regis was no L.A., but people still paid basic attention to styles and brands. It was one thing to eschew trends, which was its own kind of cool—something Dutch could pull off—but Megan wore things that you could tell she thought were nice and that just made you feel bad for her, like pleated jeans that puffed out at the hips. She curled her bangs right up to the day she went missing.

Normally, Megan worked the dinner shift, but that night she had a tray like any regular student and came up to where I was sitting with Sue, Dutch, and Stefan. Megan's presence in social situations made me self-conscious in two ways. I worried about the optics of being connected to a loser. But I also cared how I came across to her. On the one hand, I wanted her to know that I had status within an intimidating, good-looking crowd, but I didn't like her to see me acting too exclusive or unkind. Even though people said otherwise later, I *did* care about Megan's feelings. I cared what she thought of me. It was just that the opinions of Sue and Dutch mattered to me more.

"Who's this chick?" Stefan asked, lifting his chin to indicate Megan. Dutch knew Megan because he was on our floor so often, but Stefan didn't.

"Christ, Stef. *Chick?* Evolve, why don't you?" Sue said. She made a gesture for Megan to sit. "Stefan, Megan." I was relieved that Sue took care of the introduction. Having a connection to a loser wasn't a threat to Sue because she was never at risk of being mistaken for one.

Megan sat down. She had a steaming plate of shepherd's pie, which made me a little embarrassed for her. Beef-based entrees were not something girls ate in the cafeteria. We chose things that were odourless, clean and spare—it came down to a lot of green salads, turkey slices, and bagels with a bit of cream cheese.

Before Megan came along, the four of us were discussing a guy who'd been kicked out of Pervert Hall for using another student's credit card to download internet porn. Dutch and Stefan knew the thief and were sympathetic to his situation.

"Thing is," Dutch said, looking at Megan to bring her into the conversation, "it's an easy mistake to make. He didn't think there'd be any charges."

"Why would there *not* be charges?" Sue asked.

"Because you need a credit card to even get the free stuff, just to prove you're eighteen or over," Stefan said. "And they make it very easy to click on the wrong shit."

I nodded along, but I didn't really understand. I had never seen porn online before, had no idea how it worked. Back in September, Chris, a guy I dated for three weeks over the summer, sent me a black-and-white video to download of a woman giving a horse a blow job, but I didn't think that counted. I deleted it instantly. It made no sense to me why anyone would want to see that, or show it to someone, especially someone who had once tried to give him a blow job and gagged. Hard-head frosh, I really was not.

"Whatever. I don't feel sorry for him," Sue said. "Watching porn isn't, like, a basic human right."

"It should be," Stefan said.

"Okay, so what I'm hearing is that you guys download a lot of porn?" Sue said.

"Not, like, habitually," Dutch said.

"I just don't get the appeal," Sue said, moving into a cross-legged position on her chair. "What's sexy about static chicks on a computer screen?" She looked at me, and part of me wanted to back her up, but I also wanted to seem like the type of girl who was relaxed about porn, who maybe even liked it. I didn't say anything.

Stefan made a clucking noise. "You should be glad guys jerk off. Otherwise, we'd be like dogs on the dance floor." He stuck out his tongue and panted in Sue's face. Sue shoved his shoulder. She had a habit of touching men in easy, teasing ways. It was not something I would have attempted; I didn't know what sort of pressure to use or where exactly to touch.

"I'll lend you my Mastercard anytime if it means I never have to see that face again," I said to Stefan.

"Master-*bate* card?" Dutch said, grinning at me across the table. "What do you think, Rosie? Can I work with that? Make that funny somehow?" Dutch was the only one who ended up calling me Rosie, and I didn't mind when he said it.

"You can do better," I said.

Dutch wrote for the *Ragged Regis*, a weekly humour paper. He was one of two first-years on the writing staff, in charge of dorm gossip and other "frosh topics of interest," and he liked to bounce ideas off me. He did a popular series of imagined dates between profs:

"I like a good cocktail," said Professor Winifred Christie, Women's Studies. Professor Lou McNeely gestured down at his lap. "Lucky for you, Winnie, I've recently been named the very—ahem—endowed chair of Public Affairs."

Stefan started panting again, now in my face. The stereotype that guys were all horn dogs was a bit of a sore spot for me. Girls were supposed to act irritated and exhausted by all the men who couldn't keep their hands off them, but no guy ever acted like he couldn't keep his hands off me. It's not that I wanted to be groped, but I felt I was missing out on something, some part of the whole experience. Maybe I wasn't attractive enough for male attention.

"Stefanimal's just saying that guys have needs," Dutch said.

Then Megan spoke up. "Everyone does, right?"

I don't want to overstate, but this might have been the comment that changed everything.

Stefan turned to Megan with a greedy smirk. "Go on."

But Megan didn't go on, or not in the direction he wanted. "The problem isn't the pornography," she said. "It's the theft. The violation."

"Allegedly, he found the guy's card number in the computer room trash," Dutch said. "It's not like he went into his wallet."

"Whose card was it?" I asked.

Stefan shrugged. "The details are all hush-fucking-hush. No one's allowed to tell us who the 'victim' was. Some dink, probably."

"Really, Stef? Not wanting to cohabitate with a pervert who steals makes you a dick?" Sue said.

"I said *dink*."

Sue held up her hands in a well-excuse-me gesture.

"No, it's totally different. A dick is a *diiick* . . ." Stefan drew out the word. "Dicks have, like, leadership skills. They take control of a situation. A *dink* is just a little bitch who only *wishes* he could be a dick." Stefan sat back with the look of someone who would be totally fine, happy even, being called a dick.

Stefan was the kind of guy who prided himself on being shocking, particularly with girls. Earlier in the year, Sue had encouraged me to have a crush on him, but I said he was too immature. More to the point, I knew I was definitely not *his* type. He was a "skater" with shaggy hair and baggy pants, and he thought his aesthetic made him counterculture and edgy. I pictured him being into a beanie-wearing girl with heavy eyeliner, multiple piercings, and tattoos. He regularly rated the girls who passed us in the cafeteria with either a one or a zero. A one was fuckable, a zero wasn't. "It's binary, so you can't think too hard about it," he explained. "If you catch yourself needing to think, she's a zero." If a "one" went by, he held up one finger. I was afraid to ask what number I was. Once, he'd referred to me as "a poor man's Jennifer Grey," which was more confusing than insulting because my hair's not even curly, but I didn't probe further. Over the summer, I'd made the mistake of asking Chris if he thought I was pretty, and his response had been, "You *can* look good."

Sue had grown bored of all the dick talk and dismissed it by turning away from the guys and asking me, "Are we going to Phantoms tonight?"

One problem in our friendship was that Sue loved dancing and I didn't. I didn't think I was good at it; I never knew what to do with my arms. But I also didn't like the ritual of it—the dressing up, the display. Sue said that if I wanted to find a guy to make out with, I needed to "green light" more, smile, make eye contact. "Guys are stupid," she would say. "There's no room for subtlety." Still, the idea of putting out signals felt desperate to me. At 2 a.m., when I saw so-so girls all tarted up in tube tops and miniskirts shivering in the line outside Burger King with everyone else, to me, they looked like a pack of ugly stepsisters, and I felt embarrassed for their efforts and failures. I thought the best thing to do in my position, the position of an average-looking person, was to play it low-key, to act like I had no skin in the game. Turning up at the bar in hiking boots, a pocket tee with a sweatshirt around my waist, and not dancing—or only joke-dancing—made me the kind of girl who didn't need boys' attention. The twisted part is that I hoped this persona would make me more attractive to boys. I wanted to make out as much as anyone, I wanted to lose my virginity, and weirdly, I tried to accomplish this by acting like I didn't give a fuck. So I stood at the bar with the guys, drank, trashed the competition: *She looks desperate, bad hair, maybe she should try not moving her arms.* The media taught me that some guys went in for this sort of chill, disaffected Winona Ryder–type. But maybe they only liked Winona Ryder because she was hot?

"I'm too tired," I told Sue. "Let's just hang out here."

Sue let out an exasperated sigh. I knew this side of me disappointed her. "You've just had two weeks holiday. You literally can't be tired." She looked around the table. "Anyone else?"

"What's it like? I've never been there," Megan said, too polite not to respond to a question, or too oblivious to know it wasn't directed at her.

Stefan looked at Megan in bewilderment. "Why not?" Stefan said. "Don't you have ID?"

"Actually, I turned nineteen on New Year's Day," Megan said.

I'd forgotten about Megan's birthday. Other than Dutch, she was now the only one at the table who was legal drinking age. Not that being underage mattered much for the rest of us. Sue and I both had fake

IDs—our foreign licences, unfamiliar and inscrutable to your average Creighton bouncer, had been easy to alter.

Stefan was the first to clue in and say happy birthday. Megan blushed as she thanked him. When she cleared her tray and left the cafeteria, Stefan looked at her, then the rest of us, and held up a finger. "One."

3

The storm began a few hours after dinner that Sunday. I Googled weather records to confirm the accuracy of my memory. We were drinking Jack and Coke in Dutch and Stefan's room, listening to Dutch play Radiohead on guitar at Sue's request.

Stefan was grilling me about Megan. "What the fuck, Ros? How have I never met your roommate?"

"We're not close."

"Why don't you ever bring her out?"

Stefan's curiosity about Megan ran counter to all my beliefs about him and about how attraction should work. Megan was a dork; she shouldn't—couldn't—be desirable to him.

"She's not your type. Megan's idea of a wild time is watching *Party of Five* in the common room with a bottle of Fruitopia," I said.

"She is my type. She has *needs*," Stefan said.

No girls I knew discussed sex in terms of biological drive. That was the wrong way to talk about sex in the '90s, at least at Regis. It's not that we were prudes—sex was a mark of desirability, and we wanted to be having it. But in front of guys, most girls at Regis, including Sue, acted like sex was something mainly men wanted, something we gave to them because we were generous and chill, not actually horny ourselves. We didn't talk frankly about sexuality—not with guys, not with other girls—because the only people who did that were Dr. Ruth and a handful of embarrassing hippie moms. I had a vision of Megan forty years down the road, the kind of woman who said, "Don't be shy, we're all girls here!" before rolling off her one-piece bathing suit at the Y.

"Back off, Stef. She's so innocent," Sue said.

"Not so innocent," I said. "She actually masturbates all the time."

Stefan was wide eyed. "Really?"

I had heard her. Once. It was late after a theatre rehearsal, and she must have thought I was asleep. I recognized the catches in her breathing, the rustling of sheets, a barely suppressed moan. But I hadn't intended for the story to turn Stefan on. It never occurred to me that guys would want to imagine this. Maybe it was naive of me, but I thought masturbation was in the same league as taking a shit: something guys could joke about, but not girls. Changing direction to something that might intimidate Stefan and keep him away from Megan, I said, "She has a boyfriend back home. He's training to be a cop, so."

Kyle and Megan had been together since tenth grade, and he went to community college somewhere in New Brunswick, but Megan said he was thinking of transferring to a police academy. Most girls I knew in high school with long-term boyfriends had broken up with them before university so that they wouldn't be tied down. Staying with your high school sweetheart was something I associated with uncultured people from small towns. Well, except for Sue.

"Do they have phone sex?" Stefan asked.

"They fuck like rabbits," I said.

"That's how I like to fuck," Stefan said, undeterred, jutting out his top teeth.

Even though I was extremely curious about the sex lives of everyone I encountered, I didn't actually know whether Megan and Kyle had any sex at all. In October, I'd accompanied Megan to the Student Health Centre when her cramps were so bad that she could hardly get out of bed. The doctor put her on Tri-Cyclen to ease the pain, and later Megan told me that she'd have to hide this from Kyle because he was very old-fashioned. She said it as if the subtext were obvious, but I wasn't sure I got it. Did *old-fashioned* mean no sex until marriage? Or was it just that he viewed the pill as a gateway to sleeping around? In any case, I'd had enough discussion of Megan's sex life—or how Stefan might improve upon it—so I said, "And her feet stink."

That wiped the pervy look off Stefan's face. And I felt bad about saying it, but it was also a little bit true.

Sue, displeased with our decision to stay in that night, made a show of falling asleep on Dutch's bed by eleven. I left Pervert Hall alone, stepping outside and into a glittering Narnia. The sidewalks shimmered with ice, and the tree branches blinked in the lamplight like giant crystal chandeliers. I hadn't spent a winter in Canada in six years, but my slow, deliberate steps across the slippery path came as second nature, even with a buzz on.

When I reached the sidewalk, I heard my name and turned around. Adam Linsky, a guy I knew from first-semester French, was coming up behind me. Adam was in a category of guys that I liked to be a little more prepared to see. He was cute in a sweet, bespectacled way, with an attractive margin of freckles under his eyes. I had a low-grade crush on him, one that had sprung up after he attempted to rescue my lacklustre French presentation on "La cuisine et la société Française" by asking me a lot of questions, as if what I'd said had been thought provoking. Although I had put almost no effort into my presentation, I actually knew a fair amount about French cuisine. Reading my parents' mostly decorative cookbooks had been a hobby of mine since childhood. Adam asked me what made the perfect baguette and then apologized after class because my response that it should be very long and quite firm had made the class explode with laughter. About a week later, he was waiting behind me while I photocopied someone's entire binder of English notes page by page, and after several minutes, he politely said, "Do you know about the feeder?" When I looked back at him, flustered and helpless, he took the pile from me gently, his fingers brushing mine for longer than seemed necessary.

I hadn't told Sue about Adam, mainly because Adam wore a Regis leather jacket. Knowing Sue might disapprove of Adam kept me from fully committing to the crush. I couldn't even fantasize about something—not a guy, or even what colour I should paint my nails—without immediately wondering what Sue would say about it.

Adam was wearing his jacket that night, his major and expected graduation year in fuzzy lettering on the back: Commerce 2001. When he asked if he could walk me home, I hesitated. I wanted to come across as breezy and independent, not the type who just expected this from a guy. He reddened a little before saying, "I don't think girls, like, need escorts or anything, but I just saw a cab on Heritage Street spin out and hit a parked car. So, unless you're really opposed, it would make me feel better."

"All right," I said.

"If I slip," he said, "it's because these shoes have zero tread." I noticed, then, that Adam was wearing weird shiny shoes and formal pants. He noticed me size him up. "I'm volunteering at a conference thing," he said. "Do you know WILD?"

"No. Sounds wild though."

He chuckled a bit, I think to spare my feelings. "Women's Ideas for Leadership Development. That's what it stands for." Regis was obsessed with committees and acronyms, and people threw these around self-importantly like they were interns at the White House. It didn't occur to me, then, to be offended by this particular acronym, which appeared to sum up the notion of women in business as something outlandish, uncivilized, out of control.

The idea that anyone would want to attend, much less volunteer for, a business conference was *wild* to me then. It still is. Adam must have noticed the look on my face and said, apologetically, "They needed a guy on the exec." He didn't say why.

Adam asked what I was doing at Herbert, and I told him I was visiting Dutch and Stefan. "They're some of my really good friends," I said, glancing up at him to see how this landed. I wondered whether he would be impressed or intimidated by their names, though he seemed to have no reaction. Maybe he didn't know who they were, but I doubted that.

As we approached my dorm, he skimmed his hand along the top of a frozen hedge, crispy with ice, then wiped his fingers on his jacket. "It's like tempura."

Japanese food wasn't something everyone had tried back then, at least not in Creighton, and I considered our shared knowledge of tempura to be notable, a spark of connection. "I love Japanese food!" I said.

"Yeah? I could eat, like, fifty avocado rolls. We should go sometime."

"But here in Creighton?" I didn't know how to greenlight.

Then neither of us knew what to say, and in the awkward space that followed, I brought up the Herbert Hall gossip, the porn guy.

Adam exhaled slowly. "It's not really out yet, but it was my credit card the guy stole."

"Oh shit. So *you* reported him?"

Adam shook his head. "Not exactly. Just before the holidays, my parents got a couple hundred dollars in Visa charges from"—he paused, cleared his throat—"anyway, somewhere clearly pornographic. I swore to them it wasn't me, and when they finally believed that, they got Visa and the school to do some kind of investigation."

"Jesus."

"His mom was here to clear out his room today and was, like, basically hysterical. They saved a lot of money for him to come here, first in the family to go to college and all that."

"That doesn't make him a stand-up guy or anything."

Adam shrugged, but in his face, you could tell he felt genuine concern for him. "He isn't really a bad guy, either."

"So now he's getting kicked out of school?"

"There's going to be a senate hearing, apparently."

"Whoa." I didn't know what that meant, but it sounded bad.

We walked past a guy pulling two girls along the ice-lacquered sidewalk with a scarf. All of them wore Regis jackets.

"Are you taking the second French unit?" Adam asked, changing the subject.

I told him I wasn't. I didn't tell him that I hadn't gotten a high enough grade to move to the next unit.

"That's what I thought you'd say," he said, and I wondered what it meant that he had contemplated my response to this question, and when exactly it had been on his mind—only just then, or had he thought about me at some other time?

We were crossing the lawn in front of AlCo Hall, and I was thinking about who might be looking out the window and what they'd make of Adam and me, when we heard the snapping sound. There was a crack a few seconds later, and then Adam grabbed my wrist as he pulled me toward the dorm's main entrance. We were still holding hands, sort of, as a heavy cluster of tree branches crashed onto the sidewalk, maybe twenty feet from the door.

"Fuck," Adam said, looking up at the maimed tree. "Just missed the wire." I looked at the power lines above us: one thick, one thin, both sleeved in ice and bowing badly. Adam let go of me. "I saw a downed wire once in a parking lot in Montreal. It was totally surreal, like some giant, fire-spitting cobra in an arcade game."

A few lights came on in the windows above us. I fumbled in my jacket pocket for my keys. "Walking me home almost killed you," I said. "I feel bad."

"I feel bad" was probably one of my top ten most used phrases in university, though it was rarely an accurate articulation of how I felt. Generally, when I said it, I was just seeking assurances *not* to feel bad, because I already didn't. Other times, I was just confused by how I felt, or I couldn't explain myself, so "I feel bad" was a low-risk thing to say when an awkward situation demanded I say something. But in this case, what I wanted to say and should have just said was thank you.

I asked Adam if he'd be okay getting back. It was a stupid question, how could he know? It crossed my mind to invite him in, but I knew I couldn't for a few reasons. There was Megan, for one. But mainly it felt too embarrassing. I'd already decided I wanted to be more than just slightly drunk the next time I saw him, to loosen me up. I told him to send me a message on ICQ when he got back. I loved ICQ because it was easier to flirt online than in person. He said he would, and then we both looked desperately at the road. After he set off, he looked back and waved the hand that had been grasping mine. If anyone had been watching, they definitely would have said that we were holding hands.

———

Megan was in bed when I got back to my room; she had apparently slept through the crash and was making the *pff pff* noises she did when she slept. I thought about Adam as I brushed my teeth and got changed for bed. I positioned my IBM ThinkPad at the edge of my desk, where I could reach it from bed to receive his ICQ message.

My screensaver kicked in, and for what felt like a long time, I watched the phrase "Regis '01" bounce against the borders of my screen, maddeningly never reaching the corners. After about twenty minutes, I was worried—for Adam's safety, but mostly for my own ego. This was a downside of ICQ: the anxiety of waiting. I was working up the courage to do something I never did, message a guy before he messaged me, when I finally heard the cartoony, computer-generated chime: "*Uh-Oh!*" A fluorescent green flower blossomed in my contact list, opening itself to me.

Adam: *ICY-Q!*

I tried for too long to think of a good ice joke to send back. *N-ICE to hear from you!* was what I came up with.

I waited a moment for a response. Soon, a white bar appeared over his green flower, which meant "away." Sue told me that she used "away" to avoid conversations with people she didn't feel like talking to. But did Adam do this, too? Was Adam avoiding me? I felt special knowing Sue's secret, and when I saw her on "away," I'd often message her to say, *Are you really away or just pretending?* I typed to Adam: *So, you're putting our convo on ice?*

I was proud of that one, and I waited twenty minutes, nerves buzzing, before I finally shut the laptop down, my face hot with humiliation.

4

The next morning, I woke early to the sound I now recognized as another crashing tree limb. Rain thrummed the windowpane, which was already coated in a thick layer of ice; I couldn't see the broken tree through the blurred glass, or see anything at all.

I figured Megan was at the caf at North Campus, where she normally started work at five thirty, but she came in from the shower while I was still in bed. Her shift had been cancelled, she said, because the power was out on North. I think it was the first time since September that Megan had a free morning. From bed, I watched her organize and file her first-semester notes, then wipe down her desk with some kind of spray. Our desks alone were a crash course in our differences. Megan's was a gleaming expanse of honey-coloured wood, no random papers, sticky spots or crumbs swept to the edges. Just a computer, a horse-themed desk calendar, neatly stacked textbooks, the two photos I'd judged her on back in

September. My desk showed my laziness and indecision: loose papers, glasses of stale water, used tissues. But I did have one personal touch that I hoped said something about my taste. A *When Harry Met Sally* poster hung above my desk, which I bought because the coolest girl at my high school quoted the movie in our yearbook.

As Megan worked, she hummed loudly along to *Evita* on her Discman. Andrew Lloyd Webber musicals were a thing that Megan and I bonded over. In the privacy of our room, we sometimes sang together. There'd been a time in my early teens when Andrew Lloyd Webber meant something to me. During our first spring in L.A., my dad had the idea to rent a weekend house out in the desert for a season. It was a failed experiment because he could rarely take a weekend off, but on Fridays after school, my mother and I would drive up together—arguably just to reassure my dad that his money wasn't being wasted—and we listened to two cassettes on repeat: the *Beaches* soundtrack and Andrew Lloyd Webber's *Premiere Collection*. I'd sing the songs to myself and stare out the window, thinking about the guys I liked and about them finding out what a great voice I had. By the time I got to Regis, I knew that my voice wasn't special, but I still fantasized that some charming ability of mine would be discovered and considered irresistible by men every-where. I knew that Andrew Lloyd Webber wasn't cool, but neither was Megan, and we were hidden in our room, so what did I care? Some nights, if we were getting ready for bed at the same time, we sang verses from our favourite numbers ("Take That Look off Your Face" for me, "Memory" for her) and praised each other's talent. She often said that I had perfect pitch (is that just what you say when there's nothing else?) I critiqued her rendition of "Poor, Poor Joseph" before she auditioned to be the Narrator in the December production of *Joseph and the Amazing Technicolor Dreamcoat*. I meant to go see her in it—she played one of the children—but I never made it.

That morning, Bev came around to the rooms to let us know that classes were cancelled and that there would be an emergency floor meeting at ten. I checked ICQ for messages from Adam, but he was still "away."

Megan wanted to do some laundry in case our power went out, so I went along with a heavy bag of dirty clothes that had been sitting in my closet since before the holidays. After dumping my stuff in the first available machine, I watched Megan carefully sort her garments. She had an elaborate system with many rules for which colours and fabrics got washed together and at what temperatures. She actually took the time to decode the hieroglyphics on the labels and follow them, even hand-washing as necessary. Laundry was just one example of Megan's "suburban skills," a term I made up to mock her behind her back. I also referred to her as Tony Micelli, the housekeeper from *Who's the Boss?*, to make Sue laugh. I thought Megan's skills were retrograde and a waste of time. If one of my shirts got a stain, I stopped wearing it. I thought this made me laid back and focused on more important things; I didn't understand the aspect of privilege in being reckless and wasteful.

While we waited, I looked at Megan, trying to see what had gotten Stefan's attention. Her eyes were big and denim blue but, I thought, a little too buggy. Her face was round and babyish, but she was slimmer than me overall, smaller busted and fitter. Her arms looked better than mine in a T-shirt, probably from shovelling shit every weekend. But I also thought she had too much arm hair. *Teen Wolf* was how I might describe the situation to Stefan if the subject of her sex appeal came up again.

Despite the conditions outside, the atmosphere was festive at the floor meeting, and people passed around bags of Smartfood and SunChips, only these "healthier" options were popular at the girls' dorm. You could hear the wind howling through the ancient walls.

I found a spot next to Sue and Courtney Davis, a girl I liked to keep tabs on. I was wary of Courtney; she was the only girl in AlCo Hall who reminded me of L.A.: blond, pretty, aloof. She had gone to private school in Vancouver, had several friends in cooler dorms and a third-year boyfriend who she knew from "skiing." Sometimes, she would come up for a smoke in Sue's room after their night class, and for a while, I worried that Sue might start to like her more than me because she was prettier, but recently Sue had proclaimed her a leatherette. This kept me from agonizing over the time in the cafeteria when Courtney fixed me with a cold stare and said, "Do you know that your earlobe is black all around your earring?" I ignored her, tried to pretend like, *So what?* but when I got back to my room, I took my cheap gold hoops out for the first time in weeks and found that the area around the piercing was the gunky black-green of a bathtub plug. I cleaned my earlobe with rubbing alcohol and hoped that Sue hadn't noticed.

Bev was in fine form at the meeting. Emergencies were her favourite—she shone. In her pink denim overalls, she paced around in front of us, the colour high in her cheeks. I hadn't seen her as animated since the flu outbreak in November.

"Go, Beef, go," I whispered to Sue. Looking back, my meanest Regis nicknames were blatantly fatphobic, and Bev was—I would have said then—an "easy target." I referred to her only as "Big Bev" or "Beef."

"I guess you've all figured out why we're meeting," Bev said.

Sue glanced at the window and yawned. "Icebreaker games?"

"This is serious," Bev said.

Bev may have been annoying, but I realize now how dickish we were to her. She was a physics major, only a couple years older than us, and yet she was responsible for our well-being. She moderated tearful roommate conflicts, helped at least one girl schedule an abortion, cleaned up a maggot infestation in the bathroom after someone threw a sandwich in the sanitary bin. Her job was hard.

Bev turned to face the others, ignoring us. "Power's out on North Campus and almost all of downtown Creighton. Men are working their butts off out there." She gestured at the window as though we'd see scores of technicians outside, but the view was obstructed by ice.

"*Men's butts?*" I repeated, feigning terror. "Are they allowed to be this close to us?"

"Power lines are down, trees are falling, garages are collapsing," Bev continued. "These are major causes of injury and death."

"God, yeah. I know *sooo* many people who have died in collapsed garages," Sue said.

I cackled at this, adding, "That's how we lost Meemaw."

But Bev soldiered on. "We have to stay safe and stay together. We're asking you not to leave the dorm unless it's absolutely necessary."

"What if I just have to get something from my garage real quick?" I said.

"Stop it!" Now Bev turned to look at me. She had pink-framed glasses with a seemingly sky-high prescription because at certain angles her eyes looked like billiard balls. "People are cold and scared and dozens will die. Some are dead already."

Sue and I couldn't repress our laughter. Megan tsked, but I wasn't sure if she was tsking Bev's unsubstantiated statistic or our reaction to it.

"There's absolutely no reason to visit other dorms, or go downtown, or wander around and looky-loo," Bev said. I pinched Sue's arm, and she pinched me back, and I knew we both were saying *looky-loo? What the fuck?* Then Bev held her hands up. "But please don't panic, either. No matter what, we'll get through it, okay?"

A girl called Simone shot up her hand. "Is there anything we can do to help?"

I hated Simone, a nosy friend of Megan's who hung around our room. She was always talking in indignant tones about boring transgressions, like people not pulling their weight in group projects. Megan, to her credit, listened. She seemed to be very patient with her friends. Really, it's a shame that I was too insecure to be closer with her. But I want to clarify: Megan wasn't falling all over herself trying to be my best friend, either. She didn't cling, she didn't ask much of me. She made her own friends.

"I'll look into it," Bev told Simone.

Bev said that the administration was instituting a buddy system effective immediately. Roommates were buddied together, and singles were paired. You needed to know your buddy's whereabouts at all times. If you lost track of one another, you were to report this to Bev immediately. Sue, to my dismay, was paired with Courtney.

"Are we going to lose power?" someone asked.

"We're connected to a generator," Bev said. "Thank goodness."

I was definitely not feeling thankful. If anything, I felt like AlCo Hall was missing out. Growing up, I was the kid who secretly wanted the bus to break down on the way home from a field trip, who fantasized about being locked inside the mall with friends after hours. I dreamt about the romantic possibilities of a wildfire evacuation centre. All I saw in this ice storm was potential for fun, to shake things up. I didn't think we were in danger.

The time between Monday and Thursday is a blur. And those days were also, literally, a blur. Grey, grainy, wet. Freezing rain continued to fall hard in Creighton, and a huge swath of land east of us into Quebec and New Brunswick. Hundreds of the city's trees came down, bringing the power down with them. The cover of the *Creighton Standard* showed a line of collapsed hydro towers along the highway, hulking piles of steel and wire like giant arthropods from a science fiction paperback. The city declared a state of emergency, and classes were cancelled indefinitely.

All dorms, with the single exception of AlCo Hall, eventually lost power. They remained open for a day or two in the dark and growing cold, converting into zones of unchecked, all-day parties. If you walked into almost any room on Dutch and Stefan's floor, you could join a round of never-have-I-ever, century club, or—while there was still some heat—strip trivia. But Sue, Dutch and I spent most of the time lying in a pile of blankets on Dutch's floor, eating snacks and drinking Jack and Coke. I wasn't an experienced drinker before Regis, but by January, I could hold my own pretty well, and I liked how alcohol took the edge off my insecurity, made me bolder.

The three of us would have been more comfortable in AlCo Hall with its warmth and electricity, but we didn't want to miss the chaos, even if we liked to hold ourselves a little separate, a little superior. And talking under those blankets, it felt as if we were finally coming together as a trio. I listened more than I talked—I didn't have interesting stories—but I felt central to the flare of new intimacy among us. Sue confessed that she kissed her father's business partner, a married man in his early thirties, at a music festival over the summer. Dutch showed us his favourite books, one for each year of high school: *Lord of the Flies*, *A Separate Peace*, *The Stranger*, *The Unbearable Lightness of Being*. He read us his autobiographical short story about stealing a rotisserie chicken from a grocery store when he was fifteen just to see what he could get away with. His mom, a music history professor, didn't even punish him. In the story, he chalked this up to her being a "nutjob," though he admitted to us that it was probably from her that he got his artistic sensibility and "perspicacious" nature—a word I didn't know but asked Megan about later, back in our room. I also found out that week that Dutch was at Regis on a full-ride merit scholarship. He shrugged after telling us this, as if to say that without the scholarship, he wouldn't have bothered with school, which made sense to me. It seemed that Dutch was already so smart, so sure of his value in the world as an independent thinker, that he didn't really need to be at university at all.

We took turns picking CDs to play in Dutch's room until the batteries in his stereo died, and then he played guitar for us. Dutch refused all campfire classics, giving us acoustic new wave instead. I was grateful that he didn't ever seem to remember my saying that I played guitar. Or maybe he never mentioned it because he liked hoarding the attention. He played Roxy Music, Yazoo, Echo & the Bunnymen, bands I didn't know. I felt that he was teaching me things, things I could repeat later and call my own. But what I remember best about those shadow-filled hours are the tingly whispers of my own pride: *Just look at your cool friends.*

Still, even during those easy, cozy days, there were reminders that Dutch and Sue held more power. One morning, the two of them, but not me, received handwritten invitations to a "hickey party" on the top floor of Herbert Hall. I didn't really know the organizers, but neither did Dutch or Sue, and my feelings were hurt. To my relief, Sue and Dutch didn't go, calling it seriously middle school, which only proved their superiority: the only thing cooler than going to the "it" party was *choosing* not to go. But dozens of pretty girls—though not all prettier than me—showed up at breakfast the next morning with purple bruises all over their necks. I pretended to be above it all and agreed heartily when Sue said, "How desperate can you be?" but I felt left out.

One night that week, walking home from Herbert, Sue and I stopped to help a girl who had dropped to all fours on the ice and was holding a plastic bag filled with her own steaming vomit. We led her to AlCo Hall through a back entrance, proceeding right past Bev's open door. Bev wrote us each an Oops Report because we weren't with our buddies. Oops Reports were for minor violations, and even that name—*Oops!*—made you not take them seriously. I'd already received a few during first semester for things like playing music with the door open after 10 p.m. or drinking beer in the hallway.

Wherever I was that week, I was looking for Adam. In my opinion, the only downside of the power outage was that Adam couldn't use ICQ, so I hadn't been able to sharpen my read on him. When I finally did see him again, it was at the cafeteria. He said hi to me as he passed my table with a group of friends. It was a quick hello, but Sue noticed.

"How do you know him?" Sue asked.

"I don't really know him," I said. "He was in my French class, I think?"

Something about my interaction with Adam caught her attention. Or maybe it was the unconvincing way I pretended to forget how I knew him. Whatever it was, she was on to me, and her eyes followed Adam to his table. When Dutch and Stefan came and joined us a minute later, she brought Adam up before they even sat down. "Doesn't that tall guy over there live on your floor?"

Dutch looked over at where she gestured. "Linsky? Yeah, why do you ask?"

"I think he's Ros's new boyfriend." I made a give-me-a-break face, maybe a little too theatrically.

"Huh. I just heard a rumour that he's the one who ratted out the porn guy," Stefan said.

"Don't keep that confidential or anything," I said.

Sue looked back at Adam, nodding her head from side to side, considering. "He looks like a boy scout. Why is he dressed like that?"

"In a suit? He's part of the WILD conference," I said, trying to make it sound like something they should know.

"What the fuck is that?" Sue said.

"Business School thing," I said. "He's on the exec."

She smirked. "You know a lot about him."

"What? No, I don't."

"Did you know he's vegan?" Dutch said.

"He puts orange juice on his cereal. And at our floor party, he needed his own *special* pizza." Stefan said this in a whiny, childish voice.

"So what?" I said.

"Pizza isn't pizza without cheese," Stefan said.

I looked over at where Adam was sitting. "I thought vegans didn't wear leather," I said. "He has a leather jacket." I avoided saying Regis jacket; I didn't want to give them more reasons to judge him.

"Maybe he's not that hard-core?" Sue suggested.

"Unfortunately for Rosie, I heard he's pretty hard-core," Dutch said. "He only dates vegan girls." He shook his head ruefully at the folded turkey slice on the edge of my plate.

"How do you know?" Sue asked.

"Just staying on my beat."

"You're going to write about the kind of women he dates?" I asked.

"It's called gathering the facts," he said. "I might write *something* on the great porn scandal, so I'm casing him out. What can you tell me about him?"

"Nothing. I'm not remotely interested in him," I said, simultaneously considering the relative hotness and likelihood of veganness among the girls eating next to him. From what I could see, they were mostly eating bagels, so it was hard to say.

Dutch dug a fork into his baked potato, releasing an avalanche of sour cream and bacon bits. "The vegan thing is not your main problem."

I did my best to laugh. "Tell me my main problem, please, Dutch."

"He's a classic underdog-overdog."

I looked over at him again, not sure if I was supposed to know what that meant.

"So he's a nice guy, right?" Dutch continued. "Smart, whatever. But he's not, like, *extra* hot, so girls think he's, like, this undiscovered secret. They think they have a chance because no one else will notice him. But really, there are so many girls thinking the same thing that he's not an underdog at all. He's an overdog."

Dutch's description, unfortunately, was precisely my read on Adam.

I thought I had a chance. But maybe he helped every girl on campus at the photocopier, and maybe they all thought it meant something.

"He has a harem," Dutch continued. "All these commerce girls follow him around. They're always in the common room playing euchre and listening to shit music."

"What shit music?"

Dutch gave me a disappointed head shake, unwilling to lower himself to respond. "Just know that a lot of commerce girls are gagging for him," he said. "Plus, you can do better."

I was bummed that Adam dated only vegan girls, and I felt stupid for misreading his attainability. But I also felt myself become even more interested in him in that moment, and that had everything to do with Dutch saying I could do better. For a second, I burned with confidence. If someone like Dutch thought I was better than the guy I liked, that meant everything.

It was either late Tuesday night or early Wednesday morning when the toilets backed up at Herbert Hall and shit-water leaked onto the bare feet of people having a drunk, coed shower. Stefan was one of them. The next morning, all the dorms without power were ordered to evacuate. Any student from anywhere west of Creighton, which included Toronto and the surrounding area, was pretty much ordered to go home on Greyhound buses arranged by the school. The students who couldn't leave, either because home was also in the area where the storm hit or because they came from far away, were assigned a spot in AlCo Hall or in the campus gym-turned-shelter.

Many people seemed relieved to get out, but I couldn't have wanted anything less. When Bev came around on Wednesday to do an inventory of available space and to ask which bus I would be getting on, I told her

I hadn't made any plans. "Think of the ethics of that," she said. "Literally hundreds of students *can't* leave, and they need food and shelter." I told Bev I couldn't get a hold of my parents. Bev said, "You'll have to keep trying," before she left in a self-important huff.

"Your parents will be glad to see you," Megan said. "Mine are freaking out. They want me to go to my aunt's place in Toronto."

"You should." I felt some level of antipathy toward Megan, who got to stay, while I was basically being ordered away from the fun.

"I'm not working this week, so if the school needs the space, it's an option," Megan said. "If it gets really bananas around here, I guess I'll go. The issue is that my aunt and uncle are in the middle of a separation right now, so it's kind of uncomfortable."

Did Megan and I have this conversation at precisely this moment? Was all that critical information condensed and conveyed in exactly that way? I can't say for sure. But she did tell me all of this. I know she did, because it gave me an idea.

Bev's room smelled like Pizza Pops. When I knocked on the open door, she looked at me in the startled, vacant way that she often looked at people when they surprised her, as if she needed a second to unscramble their features. She was sitting on her bed, putting the finishing touches on a sign that said, Look Twice. Beware the Ice!

I closed the door and sat myself on the edge of her desk. "So I'll just come right out and say it," I said. "My parents' marriage is falling apart." I could feel my blood vessels expanding, warmth spreading over my neck and face. I tried to make heartfelt eye contact. Bev just gazed at me, confused. "Christmas was really difficult. Actually, hell, to be honest. My dad got caught cheating."

Bev put the cap back on her marker and set it down on her desk. "That's not easy," she said. I had Bev in the palm of my hand. She loved to put her training into action.

"With a much younger woman," I continued. "So you can just imagine."

This really wasn't the most far-fetched lie. What I was describing was Val's story, my half sister. She was about my age when Dad left his first wife, her mom, to marry mine.

"When school starts again," Bev said, "I can definitely help set you up with a counsellor in Student Services."

"Sure," I said. "That would be so great. But for now, I'm just wondering if maybe I could be, like, exempt from going home?"

Bev didn't say anything. I picked up a lump of Blu Tack on her desk and rolled it around between my thumb and finger. Someone knocked on her door. "Two minutes!" Bev called. She looked back at me. I was running out of time, and I could tell I hadn't quite persuaded her.

"If it's okay with you," I said, "maybe I could just stay here in the dorm and help out?"

"I don't know," Bev said. "I understand your problem, but we need every bed we can get. Higher-ups are really pushing for you guys to go home. It's not really up to me."

"It must be at least a little bit up to you." I made my voice crack a little when I said, "I don't think home is actually a safe place for me right now? I can't get into it, but it means so much to me that you're listening. I don't know what I'd do if your door wasn't always open."

I would have faked tears, but it didn't come to that. Bev just let out a heavy breath. "Stay another day or two, okay? But if things get nuttier, we might not have a lot of choice."

"That really helps. Thank you so much, Bev," I said.

"And, Ros," she said, "no more Oops Reports."

I said thank you again and turned to open the door. It was Megan on the other side, probably coming to help with Bev's posters. I don't know what she heard, if anything, but I avoided eye contact and passed her with a quick hello.

6

Exciting news came to AlCo Hall on Wednesday afternoon. The remaining boys from Herbert Hall were moving in. Megan and I carried extra cots up from the basement, and room assignments were reshuffled to create space. Courtney moved to Sue's room, and Dutch and Stefan got Courtney's room. By dinnertime, guys were making themselves at home by hooking up PlayStations in the common areas and exploding Cup-a-Soups in our microwaves.

I ran into Adam in the hallway as he was coming out of the showers, a towel draped over one shoulder. His T-shirt was damp and pressed against his skin. "Looks like we're neighbours now," he said.

"Cool," I managed to say, lost for words and trying for nonchalance. I avoided looking at his wet shirt, the outline of his chest.

"Which is your room?"

I pointed at my door, and he read the names on the hearts. "I think

Megan Main is in my accounting class." Megan studied science, but she also took management classes in case she needed the background to run her own vet clinic someday.

"I wouldn't know. We're not close."

We looked at each other. For no obvious reason, he pulled the towel off his shoulders—did he want me to look? "I hope you girls don't mind us crashing your dorm," he said.

"We don't really have a choice, do we?" Was I pulling off pretending not to care? Was it too much? "Aren't you supposed to be at a conference or something?"

"Cancelled," he said, looking disappointed, though I was delighted to hear it. "Apparently we gave the delegates a pretty icy reception."

I laughed. "Did they expect dry ice?"

He smiled, though I think maybe we both wanted out of this pattern of jokes. "Want to get dinner?" he asked.

I didn't tell Sue I was going to dinner, even though we'd had every meal together since the start of the storm. I felt disloyal, but also giddy about the possibility of Sue running into us. I thought Adam looked cute with his hair all messed up, or at least he looked less like a boy scout. I also wanted Adam to see me with Sue because, well, everyone liked her.

Adam took a heaping plate of pasta and red sauce with a side of bean vinaigrette salad—I'd always wondered who ate that salad. He led us to one of the few two-seater tables at the back of the caf. Sue and I called this area the "seductions section," and we made fun of the couples who sat back there as if they were on dates. I tried not to read too much into Adam's choice. Maybe to him, it was simply reasonable to sit at a two-top with one other person.

"California Dreamin'" was playing, a song I found a little dirge-like, creepy, but Adam said he liked it, and so I agreed that it was great.

"I bet you wish you still *was* in L.A.," Adam said.

I was surprised he remembered that I was from L.A. I couldn't think of when that had come up. It was usually me who knew things about people that were out of proportion to how well I knew them, and this reversal made me feel powerful. "My family moved back to Toronto," I said. "So there'd be nowhere for me to go in L.A."

"Does that mean you're going home then?" I thought I saw disappointment flicker across his face, or maybe I just hoped I did.

"I'm exempt," I said. "My parents are in the middle of a divorce, so." The lie was second nature now.

"That sucks," Adam said. "They moved and then decided to get divorced?"

I realized that this was a flaw, or at least a curious aspect of my story. "They can both start over now, I guess."

"My parents were separated for a bit," Adam said. "When I was a lot younger."

"I'm sorry."

"It's okay now. My dad had this midlife crisis and wanted to quit everything and move to Guadalajara. But my mom isn't the adventurous type."

"So what happened?"

"My dad went to Guadalajara for a few months, and then he just came back, and it was like nothing had changed."

"Happily ever after?"

He squinted. "Hard to say."

It occurred to me that we'd not only moved past the ice quips, but that this was the longest stretch of conversation I'd had about relationships in a long time without everything regressing into some kind of sex joke.

"I don't think I'll ever get married," I said, abruptly.

He paused before sipping from his fountain drink. "Really?"

I'd just said it to try it on. I'd created a scenario in my brain where, if I were the kind of girl who didn't want to get married, he would think of me differently—not your typical needy girl, but someone he could just date casually so it wouldn't be a big deal if we didn't share the same fundamental beliefs about stuff like meat. But the comment didn't seem to land with the offhand or lighthearted effect I wanted. He seemed actually disturbed by it.

I arranged cucumber slices on top of my plain bagel. "Well, who knows? That's what my sister said, too, but then she met some guy on an ashram at twenty-one and married him pretty much immediately."

I didn't make that up. Val met her ex-husband, Paul, in India in 1979, the year I was born. She'd gone to the ashram on a lark, but stayed a year, withdrawing from architecture school and then getting married before returning home. Now she was divorced, and for my dad, the word "ashram" had become synonymous with reckless misadventure. But mentioning the ashram to Adam now, I saw an opportunity.

"When they came back from the ashram, the whole family started eating differently. Just like vegetables, tofu, lots of seeds. It's so much better for the planet." I tried to give him a significant look.

"That's cool." I noticed him glance at my plate. He didn't ask for more details, but I thought, Great, he can make whatever assumptions he wants, that's really not my problem.

The beginning I chose for this story may not be the right one. The truth is, I was a liar before I even got to Regis.

The first time I was caught lying was in middle school, a little after my family moved to Los Angeles. In my first week at my new private school, I was buddied with an impossibly pretty ice queen called Nicola

Driscoll, who was assigned the task of helping me make friends. I sat silently at the far end of her clique's bench in the cafeteria for five straight lunches. I learned that Nicola had recently been on an episode of *Wings* and that her uncle was directing a movie starring Tom Hanks. Her best friend, Kelly, was absent once that week because she "had to be an extra in *Star Trek: The Next Generation*," which seemed to strike everyone as an ordinary hassle on par with getting your braces tightened. Everyone at the table teased a kid in seventh grade for his role in an embarrassing Pop-Tarts commercial. "He will never get out of commercials," Nicola said, rolling her eyes. I thought there was no way I could survive this new school, and by week two, it was clear that I couldn't. Nicola was relieved of responsibility for me, and for the rest of the month, I ate alone in the bathroom.

Several weeks later, in geography class, a girl finally started a conversation with me that felt both voluntary and warm. I was so grateful for the attention, even though I could tell—without knowing the term then—that Robin was an overdog. She was nice to everyone, and everyone seemed to like her, too. Robin got the record number of Cupid-grams on Valentine's Day: thirty-seven, mostly from guys. (For the sake of comparison, I got a total of two: one from her and one from her best friend, Cammie, who she'd probably made do it.) I had to work to stay in Robin's sights, memorizing her class schedule and fabricating a regular after-school piano lesson that gave me a reason to walk home in her direction.

The lie that my dad was designing Will Smith's house wasn't premeditated, it just came out one afternoon when Robin mentioned that she babysat for an actor from *Designing Women*. I couldn't take being on the outside anymore. Pretending to have my own access to celebrity gave me confidence. And it wasn't a *huge* stretch: we had moved to L.A. so that my dad could work on a major architectural project, it just happened to be a boring museum. I regaled Robin and Cammie with all the features of Will Smith's new Brentwood mansion, so much better than the home on *Fresh Prince*: basketball courts, three swimming pools, a sculpture garden. We could maybe go check it out one weekend, I found myself saying.

Cammie always seemed skeptical of my Will Smith connection, and I think she had been investigating my story for a few weeks before she outed me. Maybe she didn't like me moving in on Robin.

The confrontation came at a sleepover at Robin's in the early spring.

"Hey, Ros," Cammie said as we laid couch cushions out on Robin's floor for me to sleep on (of course, Cammie got the trundle bed). "Is your dad *really* Will Smith's architect?"

My heart pounded. I said, "Yeah, of course, what do you mean?"

Cammie pulled a magazine from her backpack, flipped to a page, and passed it to Robin. I could see the glossy shot of Will Smith, the aerial view of a mansion that probably wasn't in Brentwood. She picked up Robin's phone. "Do you mind if I just call your parents to ask?"

First, I said go ahead, casual as could be, but a film of perspiration was gathering under my sleep shirt. When Cammie started to dial, I broke down. I began a complicated story about how the project had fallen through, how we weren't supposed to talk about it.

"See?" Cammie said to Robin.

"Just don't," Robin whispered to me when I tried again to protest.

Robin and Cammie decided not to be friends with me anymore, and I didn't fight it. A rumour went around that I didn't wash my hair, and although I didn't see the connection between my hygiene and the Will Smith story, I was glad that this was as bad as things got. My luck should have improved in high school when the student body doubled and Cammie moved to Kentucky, but I missed half of ninth grade because I got mono, the "kissing disease"—I wish I'd gotten it from kissing!— and for a few months that gave me a new reputation as weird and contaminated. Not pretty enough for the standard popular crowd, I angled, self-consciously, toward the more vibrant fringe groups—the ravers, the grunge kids, the hippies. But my attempts failed pretty much across the board; dying my hair lime green was not enough to convince the ravers that I was one of them, and no matter how many Jerry Bears I doodled on my binder for the benefit of the bubbly hippie girl who shared a desk with me in chem, I was never invited to one of her legendary parties in Topanga. I did, eventually, find a crew of kind bland girls to get through the next four years with, but what I really needed was an opportunity to reinvent myself. And it seemed that I would have to be patient. People in high school just didn't know me as I knew myself. Hiding inside me was the kind of person everyone wanted to have around, to hear from, to confide in.

On Monday mornings, I'd listen in the hallways, sweep up gossip from the cool kids' weekends and imagine myself as one of them. When I got to university, I would be a native speaker of their language. I wouldn't need to lie.

1

The night before Megan went missing, just before midnight, someone organized a game in our dorm called manhunt. It was, essentially, a combination of hide and seek and capture the flag. Girls hid, guys hunted. Some guy made the point that girls were smaller, so they could hide more easily, and no one argued it. If you got found, you were thrown in jail—the third-floor showers—and in order to get set free again, you had to either wait for another girl to come along and jailbreak you or perform some kind of dare.

Normally, I would opt out of a game like this—Sue and Dutch weren't often joiners—but Sue was on a boring call with Declan, and Dutch was playing *Final Fantasy*, so I went along with it. I was found right away in my first spot behind the vending machines and escorted to the showers by a guy I liked to call Casper the Friendly Ghost because of his pasty complexion.

Courtney and another girl were already in the showers.

"So what do you want us to do?" I asked him.

"Hmm." Casper rubbed his nearly see-through temple.

"Want us to serenade you?" Courtney said.

"Truly Madly Deeply?" the other girl suggested. She was a big-haired redhead who wore a ton of makeup; I remember telling Sue that she got her beauty tips from Peg Bundy on *Married . . . with Children*.

"Please, no. Not that," he said.

"You want, like, a blow job or something?" I said.

"Jesus, no. I have a girlfriend."

I didn't believe him. "Relax," I said. "I'm not serious."

Courtney gave me a look of revulsion and then turned back to him. "You're not allowed to guard," she said. "You have to leave us alone so we can get jailbroken."

"You guys just go," he said, waving his arms around. "Be free." Freedom only meant getting to hide again.

Casper smacked my ass as we were leaving and said, "Bad girl." That was a first for me, and it surprised me too much to say anything back.

My second hiding spot was in the laundry room, wedged in a gap between two counters. The occasional sound of laughter or eruption of footsteps from above made me feel lonely. After it had been quiet for a while, I thought maybe the game had ended, and then I wondered how long it would take for people to realize that I never came back.

My hiding space was cramped and uncomfortable. Dryers tumbled and vibrated just a few feet away. I was contemplating a jailbreak attempt when I heard someone step into the room. My heart seized for a second, but when the lights snapped on, I could see through the crack between the counters that I wasn't being hunted and that the person who'd come in was Adam. I watched as he gathered his laundry out of the machine and piled it into a cracked plastic hamper. He turned a blue T-shirt around in his hands and then quickly pulled off the one he was wearing, replacing it with the fresh, clean one. His naked chest was slightly hairy and a little concave.

Right as he turned out the lights again, in my best imitation of Ghostface from *Scream*, I said, "*Do you like scary movies?*"

Adam jumped, knocking over an ironing board next to the door. The crash startled me, too, and I banged my head on the countertop. I had wanted to be funny, but now it was awkward. Whenever I tried to do spontaneous, teasing things, I usually got it wrong. Maybe it had something to do with being a de facto only child. He flicked the light back on, and I stood up so that he could see me over the countertops. "It's Ros," I said, rubbing my head. "Fuck, I'm sorry. I didn't mean to scare you."

"That's the second time you almost killed me," he said. Then he smiled as if to reassure me that he wasn't mad. "What are you doing?"

"Hiding," I said. "I'm— It's a game."

"Did you win, or did I?"

I felt my cheeks redden. "I meant the dorm's playing manhunt." I wasn't sure whether I should keep standing or go back to the hidden, crouching position. I decided it was less strange to stand.

"Ah. I tried to come in earlier, but there was a couple making out in here." He blushed just slightly. I wanted details, but Adam didn't seem like the type to get into that sort of thing.

"You must have scared them," I said.

He looked away. "Honestly, I've been a little jittery since that tree. Do you keep thinking about it?"

I nodded, though I hadn't thought about the tree very much at all. I'd thought about that night, about Adam holding my hand, but that was it. Still, I was delighted that Adam had been thinking about the tree. It meant that I had been somewhere in his thoughts.

"It's scary out there," he said, and I realized he was trying to prolong our conversation.

"Most people seem to be doing okay," I said. "Like, in reality, everyone is fine."

He shook his head. "My friend's family has a dairy farm in Belleville. There's no electricity for milking or anything. It's like financial free fall."

This didn't interest me much. But I pretended to care, sort of. Mostly, I wanted to know if the friend was a girl. "Is she a really close friend?"

He leaned toward me. "Your hair smells like Outrageous."

"Good nose," I said. My body tingled.

"My ex-girlfriend used that shampoo." I couldn't tell whether this made the smell good or bad to him. Either way, I liked that he mentioned an *ex*-girlfriend—it felt like a stepping stone to telling me he was single now.

And then Stefan burst into the room, ruining everything. "Got you," he said.

"We're not playing," I said.

He looked at Adam, winked at me, and then backed out of the room with his palms held up. "I *heard* you were giving out free BJs," he said. "I just didn't believe it was true!"

My face burned. I could have killed Stefan.

After Stefan left the room, I noticed that Adam looked embarrassed. Was he mortified by the suggestion that we'd been making out? Did he think maybe I was some kind of slut?

"Stefan and I are good friends," I said, trying to defang the comment.

"Cool," Adam said. Then he took a step toward the door. "I better get going."

I said goodnight, and although I could have left with him, I was too crushed about the interaction to move.

8

The fourth day of the storm was the last day Megan was seen on campus.

Normally Thursday was the main going-out night in Creighton. Phantoms, the Love Shack, and the Worm all put on special deals: half-price pitchers, dollar drinks, two-for-one shooters. The Worm even ran a free shuttle bus between campus and the bar. None of those bars had power that Thursday, but we learned sometime in the afternoon that electricity had been restored on the east side of Eddy Street. The east side had the town's main movie theatre, some restaurants, the shittier grocery store, and one bar: the Old Vic. The Old Hick, as we called it, was popular with Creighton townies. Despite its pubbish name, it was known for electronic music and light shows, which were like second-rate raves. Sue and Dutch had gone once in the fall, proclaiming it a 2PAC night when I asked about it afterward, as if that were a real thing and a completely sound explanation for not extending me an invite. Stefan let it slip that Dutch and Sue had tried ecstasy there. To me, this felt like a secret kept only for the sake of exclusivity, and so I thought of the Old Hick as a site of betrayal.

But people were excited about getting out that Thursday, even if I wasn't. Electronic music meant dancing of the worst kind for me: no lyrics to make joke actions to, just sweaty, embarrassing body movements. I was also enjoying the novelty of being confined to the dorm. AlCo Hall was like one of those red spots on a weather map, a hot concentration of possibility. Anything could happen, and I wanted to hold onto that, not let that energy disperse. But Sue was eager to go, and because I didn't want to be the source of her disappointment again, I blamed Megan for holding me back. I explained that Big Bev's espionage levels would be heightened on Thursdays, so if I went anywhere, Megan would need to come with me, and there was no way she'd go to a bar.

"Did you even ask her?" Sue said. "She seemed curious at dinner the other night."

I told Sue I'd ask, but I didn't have any real plan to talk to Megan about going out, at least not until I ran into Adam after dinner at the vending machines.

Seeing me approach him, he said, "Do you know a kid got crushed by one of these in a dorm a couple years ago? He punched the thing in frustration, then boom."

"Wow," I said. "You're really obsessed with things falling on you."

He laughed. "I guess it's just not the way I want to go."

Adam told me that he was headed to the Old Hick with the WILD crew. "The place is gross," he said, "but everyone's bummed about the conference and wants to go out, so I have to be a good sport." Being a good sport was definitely the correct way to be a Regis student. It was annoying, but it occurred to me that I could also use it to my advantage. Megan was a people pleaser.

"I'll probably see you there," I said.

———

When I got back to my room, Megan was talking to Kyle on the phone. She was lying on her side, facing the window, and eating from a bag of microwave popcorn, her favourite. She was saying something to him about her Aunt Lisa. I still didn't know if she'd overheard the excuse I gave to Bev for staying. I busied myself by putting up the photo that Sue had given me, along with another photo I'd found over Christmas and brought back: a snapshot of Val and me that my dad had taken years ago when she visited California. Val was twenty-one years older than me, and we didn't grow up together. We weren't at all close, but I liked to pretend that we were. I thought she was beautiful, and I liked to advertise our connection. At that point, I still held out hope that I'd grow into looking like her. We shared many of my dad's pointy facial features, but while they were striking and elegant on Val, the chin and nose were harsh and beaky on me.

"How's Kyle?" I asked after Megan was off the phone. She never stayed on the phone for very long when I was in the room, even when I put my Discman on. Maybe this was because she was private, but I think it was mainly out of consideration for me.

"Worried," she said. "The images on the news are pretty shocking. He's having dinner with my parents tonight, so hopefully, they'll calm each other down. I promised I wasn't going anywhere outside."

"That's nice that your parents like him."

"They like him more than they like me." She laughed, and I could tell it wasn't the first time she'd used that line.

"Do you wish Kyle was here?"

"Sometimes. But I don't know if he'd like it. He loves home."

"That's sweet," I said. "Do you think he'll visit?"

She shrugged. "Probably not. It's a lot of money."

"Sure," I said, as if I were the kind of person who was sensitive to these things.

She smiled. "I bet he'd like to meet you. People from home can't believe I have a roommate from Los Angeles."

"Well, technically, I'm from Toronto."

"Still. No one else in my family has been to Upper Canada."

"What's Upper Canada?" I asked.

"Well, Kyle would call it Onterrible?"

"Onterrible? What's so terrible? It's extremely varied."

She shrugged. "People from home are like that. Either they can't wait to leave, or they never will."

"Which are you?"

She seemed to think about this. "Getting into Regis was my dream," she said. And I knew it was true; she'd saved up all semester to buy a Regis jacket. "But I couldn't live in the city forever. I want to have horses."

It was laughable to call Creighton "the city," but I let this go. I needed to cut to the chase. "Can I tell you something?" I said quickly. "Like, in confidence?" I knew how flattering it was to have someone trust you with a secret.

Megan's expression showed more concern than eager anticipation. "Is everything okay?"

I hugged my knees to my chest. "No, everything's fine. I'm just a bit sweet on someone." I'd never used that expression before, but it seemed well-suited to Megan—what I imagined someone "from home" might say.

"Really?" Megan said. I think the curiosity in her tone came more from the fact I was confiding in her than from any specific interest in the details.

"Maybe you know him," I said, though I was pretty certain that she did. "His name's Adam Linsky. In commerce."

"Oh. Adam's a good-looking boy," she said. "And he has good politics."

I wasn't sure what she meant by that. Did I have good politics? Did she think I was good enough for him? I waited for her to say more, and when she didn't, I said, "Anyway, he invited me to come out with him later." I felt a pang of guilt because, of course, he hadn't. But telling me where he was going, unprompted, seemed close enough.

"You're going to go out?" The note of surprise in her tone was discouraging.

I smiled and lowered my voice conspiratorially. "There's no actual law against being outside, Megan. That's just a Bev rule. I thought maybe you'd want to come with me?"

"Where exactly?"

"Do you know the Old Vic on East Eddy?"

"I've heard of it."

"Come!" I said. "We're buddies. We should stick together."

And here's the thing. She did want to go out. Sue *had* detected something in Megan that night at dinner. I didn't drag her to the Old Vic. Later, people all said that I did, but she wanted to come. Sure, she was conflicted because of the storm. But I saw her interest immediately in the way she hesitated, as if she wanted me to provide reasons why she couldn't say no. So I did. I told her I'd pay for a cab, adding that it was also good to support the local businesses when the storm was destroying livelihoods left and right. I said that we could *finally* go out at night together since she didn't have any work in the morning, as if her schedule were the reason for our separate social lives. And then I said, "We need to get you to a bar! You just turned nineteen. Bring Simone or whoever and we'll celebrate."

"I don't think Simone would be interested."

"But you'll come, right?"

She looked at the window and didn't say anything.

"Nothing bad will happen."

She shrugged her shoulders gamely. "I guess you would do the same for me."

Happy as I was, it made me a little sad to hear her say that—I never did a thing for Megan.

When we got to Sue's room, I saw that Courtney's cot was pushed up against Sue's bed in an L-shape. Sue was lying on Courtney's white duvet, flipping through her CD album. I hated that.

Although Megan was already dressed to go out when we arrived to predrink, Sue called her Northern Reflections sweatshirt and puffy jeans "a snowsuit" and then threw an arrangement of tops on the bedspread for Megan to try. Courtney produced a caboodle of makeup, suggesting that Megan use her pearly lip gloss and metallic eyeshadow. I wondered if Megan's feelings would be hurt by my friends' fixation on making her over, by their big-sisterly condescension, but she seemed to like the attention. I was the one who didn't like it. I couldn't stand the way Sue and Courtney banded together like Cher and Dionne from *Clueless*, taking Megan on as their little Pygmalion project. I felt left out, too unstylish and gunky-eared to be asked for input. It was easy to turn things around in my mind and to feel like I was the one doing Megan a favour by hooking her up with this free makeover, this free confidence boost. I smoked by the window and tried not to let this little moment dampen my spirits. I was itchy to see Adam.

When Courtney asked Megan what she liked to drink, and she answered, "Spiced rum and Pepsi," I looked at Sue and rolled my eyes. I said, "Did you just turn nineteen or ninety?"

Sue and Courtney laughed, but Megan's expression was so painfully puzzled that I felt guilty. I still needed her; it didn't make sense to freeze her out.

"You know what," I said. "Sue has Goldschläger. It's like cinnamon hearts, you'll love it."

And Megan did like it. She drank the shots no problem. She put on Sue's white ruffle top, and we all told her how great it looked, but I didn't think she looked *that* great. Her feet were too small to borrow anyone's shoes, so she wore her own clunky brown heels that looked better suited to a piano recital than a nightclub. But I told her that if she didn't have a boyfriend, she could definitely pick up in that outfit.

Sue took photos that night, but I never saw them. By the time the roll would have been developed, we weren't on speaking terms. Still, an image is frozen in my mind. There is Megan, brushing out her hair in front of Sue's mirror, those dirty blond waves puffing out like cotton candy. Courtney is on the edge of Sue's bed, filing her nails. Sue is doling out Goldschläger in waxy cups.

And where am I in the picture? I can't quite see myself. But I know what I wore: a light-blue spaghetti strap tank that belonged to Sue but had been in my drawer since November. "That's where that went," Sue said when I showed up in it. "Keep it. Just don't put a sweater over it like you always do, please!" And I thought, All of next year will be like this, our lives merged, her stuff in my drawers, mine in hers.

The wait for a cab was long, so we did a few more shots down in the foyer of AlCo Hall. We played a few rounds of would-you-rather that got increasingly ridiculous: *Would you rather have spaghetti for eyelashes or mushrooms for ears? Would you rather write three letters home to your parents every day of your life or braid Bev's pubic hair once? Would you rather have sex with Dutch or Stefan?* We all picked Dutch, except Megan, who abstained.

Our cab driver remains clear in my head, probably because I was later

THE DAMAGES   67

asked to describe him several times. He had wispy hair, round red cheeks and didn't look to be more than a decade older than us.

"Good-looking bunch," he said as we piled in the cab.

"I only cavort with the best," Sue said, climbing into the front seat.

"Go as slow as you need to," Megan said.

He chuckled. "I know what I'm doing, sweet tits." Megan glanced down at her open jacket, her cheeks tinted with shame.

The cab ride was the first time I understood the severity of the ice. The usual route to the bar along Heritage Street was blocked off by a fallen hydro pole wrapped in yellow caution tape. We followed other cabs through a maze of dark neighbourhoods, their headlights bouncing off the glassy road and illuminating the scattered flotsam of the storm: cars riveted to the curb, abandoned shovels, dam-like clusters of tree branches.

"It's a fucking war zone," Sue said. She unbuckled her seatbelt to improve the position of her camera against the window. Sue often brought her camera out places, and it got on my nerves. To me, it was a bulky, pretentious prop that was often in the way. I thought of it as an affectation, another thing that would draw guys to her.

Sue unrolled the window, letting in a cold, wet slap of air.

"Fuck that," the driver said, powering the window back up from his side. That made one guy who wasn't impressed by her camera. "By the way, I was in Kuwait in '91. This isn't a war zone."

"Military man," Courtney said. "Sexy."

I caught his eye in the rear-view mirror, looking for Courtney. "Air Force," he said.

"What's your name?" she said.

"Mike."

"Air Force Mike," Courtney said.

He grinned. "You like that, eh?" We all exchanged looks, mouthfuls of laughter puffing our cheeks. I felt sorry for him that he couldn't distinguish mock flirtation from the real thing.

Sue turned on the radio. We all sang along to "The Freshmen"; it was "our song," and we sang loud, even Megan, our eyes squeezed shut during the chorus, for passion's sake.

When we arrived at the bar, Air Force Mike handed a business card back to us, and Megan eventually took it. "Give me a shout next time you need a ride," he said.

"I will definitely call you for a ride," Courtney said, then squealed with laughter as she got out of the cab. Megan just thanked him.

We walked around to the front entrance and joined a line on the sidewalk. A bouncer kept herding the line away from the wall, where icicles as large as traffic cones clung to the eavestroughs. Steam rolled out each time the bouncer opened the door. When it was our turn to go in, he barely glanced at our IDs.

The Old Hick had once been a theatre, and the dance floor had a stage at one end. There was also a second-floor balcony overlooking the main level, which served as a lounge. Coloured lights from the ceiling zigzagged across our faces as we pushed our way through the dense tangle of bodies. Megan tripped halfway up the steps to the balcony, and I caught her by the arm. I felt a twinge of sympathy for her. I wasn't sure what Megan had expected to find here, but I didn't think it was this. Maybe something more like a high school dance.

Megan looked back down at the dance floor, and I followed her gaze. The erratic pulsing of bodies reminded me of a science video I'd seen on particle diffusion back in high school. "The dance floor is in Brownian motion," I said to her. I thought a nerdy joke would make her feel more at home.

But Megan didn't hear me, and Sue turned around instead. "What?" she yelled. "Who's here?"

"Nothing," I said. "Never mind."

I offered to go to the bar for us, and Megan followed me while Sue went to find the boys. I leaned my arms on the sticky countertop and ordered four vodka limes, making the local hand symbols: a peace-sign *V* and a backward *L*. I wanted to show Megan that I fit in here, that I knew what I was doing.

"I've already had plenty," Megan said when I handed her a cup. She tried to give it back to me.

"We're just getting started," I said.

"I thought warm-up drinking was so that you didn't have to buy drinks at the bar?"

"Don't worry about buying anything," I said, like some big shot. "It's your birthday."

The balcony was just as rammed as the main level. I spotted Dutch looking out over the railing, surveying the dance floor. He was smoking a cigarette, slowly inhaling and exhaling, Sue's camera hanging from his shoulder. This was their arrangement: if he held her camera, she wouldn't pester him about dancing. He turned and gave me his inverted smile—down-curved like a frown but unmistakably a smile, at least to me—which always made me feel in on a secret. He alerted me to Adam's presence a few feet away with a little chin wag. Adam was the only guy in a group of girls, all of whom were dressed in a safari theme: zebra stripes, leopard spots, catsuits. Which ones wanted Adam? Maybe all of them? He appeared to be exempt from their dress code.

I walked over to Dutch, and he leaned into me. "You going to go for it, Rosie?" I looked over at Adam, and we made eye contact only for a second before breaking it. My heart was racing as I turned back to Dutch. I reached for his cigarette, and he put it between my lips. This was the best-case scenario, the perfect tableau to present to Adam: popular, sexy, desired. When Megan came over, blocking me from Adam's view, I turned to stay in his line of sight. I smiled at Megan, touched her arm and tilted my head back in laughter when she asked where the bathrooms were. I was a breezy, fun person.

"Nice shirt," Dutch said to Megan.

"Thanks!" Megan looked down at it.

"We chose it for her," I said. If Megan was being noticed, I wanted the credit. There was only so much attention to go around.

"I'll show you where the shitter is," Dutch said. "But don't count on any toilets working." He dropped our cigarette onto the floor and stubbed it out before leading Megan to the washrooms.

Sue and Courtney went down to the dance floor. I told them I'd wait for Megan, but it was really Adam I was waiting for. Left on my own, my body became highly attuned to Adam's across the room. The air between us was charged, humming. I was certain I could feel the vibration of his laughter above the din of techno music. When Megan returned and the two of us headed downstairs to find Sue and Courtney, it was like my body already knew that Adam would follow us.

We'd been dancing in the sweaty mob for several minutes before Sue made her way to the stage and climbed up on one of the speakers. Although it wasn't like me, I followed her up, leaving Megan with Courtney. Sue squealed with delight, grabbed my hand and waved it high up in the air. The lights flashed around us in quick, dusty beams. I wished I could see myself from a distance; I wanted to look up from below and get a load of myself. I had done it now; I wasn't plain rice. I was on a fucking speaker.

Down on the dance floor, Stefan was grinding with Courtney from behind, her hair pushed over one shoulder. Where was Courtney's boy-friend from skiing? Did they break up over Christmas? And just a short distance away from them, I spotted Adam. A short girl in cat ears grabbed his hand and spun herself around, pulling him this way and that while a bunch of other WILD girls formed a protective circle around the two of them. The cat-ears girl caught me staring, and a cold energy passed between us. *What are you looking at?* her face seemed to say, but she didn't seem sure of her position.

I could feel the hair on my arms react. My usual don't-give-a-fuck attitude was not what the situation called for. I needed boldness, self-assurance. I tried to catch Adam's eye, and the moment I did, I looked away quickly, grabbed Sue around the waist and swung my other arm around like a lasso above my head. Confidence was supposedly attractive, I'd read it in *Sassy* a million times. The critical thing now was to appear vibrant and empowered, to put on a show.

Then the room went black. There was a hush at first, followed by a couple of *woot woots*, but when the power didn't immediately come back on, everyone panicked. The crowd scrambled in various directions, look-ing for the exits. The speakers rocked beneath us. I grabbed Sue's hand, and together we climbed down to the floor. I felt myself land hard on someone's foot; an elbow smacked me in the temple. I kept hold of Sue's hand as we pushed toward a door, my other arm up protecting my face.

When the power came back on a minute or two later, it felt violent. Sue and I ducked from the blast of music, the shock of light. But seconds later, everyone cheered. The crush of bodies reversed, turning away from the doors and back onto the dance floor. People were laughing, whooping, kissing like it was midnight on New Year's Eve.

I felt a hand on my back and whirled around. It was Megan, her face red and sweaty. She glanced at the exit. "Do you think we could go soon?"

"Let's stay a bit." I searched the crowd for Adam.

"Someone grabbed me," Megan said. She touched my arm again to get my attention. "Up top." She gestured over the ruffle.

"Sorry, that sucks," I said. She bit her lip; I thought she might cry. "Hey, it's okay. The Old Hick is a meat market. That stuff happens to me all the time."

"I think I need to go."

There was a limit to my sympathy. I needed to stay. "Another hour?"

"Let's get you a drink," Sue said, straightening Megan's top at the shoulders. "I'll buy."

"Listen. It was so dark, it was probably accidental," I said to Megan, gently steering her toward the bar. "Come on."

Megan was obviously unhappy, but she didn't resist. Out of the corner of my eye, I saw Adam being pulled back onto the dance floor by Cat Ears. Megan followed my gaze. "Have you talked to him yet?" she asked. I was pretty sure that she knew I hadn't, she'd been at my heels all night.

"Not yet," I said.

"Didn't he ask you to come?" I detected judgment in her voice, though it seemed that she was judging him for being a bad date, not me for failing to get his attention. There was no suggestion that I lied about being invited. "You must be frustrated."

"He's got a lot going on," I said. "He's on the WILD exec."

At the bar, I bought Megan a rum and Pepsi. "Your favourite," I said when I handed the drink over. She looked down at it gloomily.

Several minutes later, I spotted Adam again, this time without his entourage. He was coming out of the washrooms, a goofy, drunk look on his face. I broke off from the group and went right up to him. I had something to prove, to Megan perhaps most of all.

Adam smiled broadly when I cut him off. He said something, but it was hard to hear. He said it louder, and I moved my ear closer to his mouth. "I'm drunk!" His spit misted the side of my face.

"Me too," I said. Then I gestured toward Cat Ears. "Is that your girlfriend?"

"What?!"

His face was inches away. I felt like I was standing at the edge of a high diving board, heart hammering, everyone watching. In a burst of courage, I pushed off, grabbed Adam's cheeks and kissed him on the mouth. Greedily, he went along with it, steering me around so that my back was up against the wall. I was really on fire now; I was someone making out in a club.

I can't remember how long after that we left, or who said, *Let's go*, or the mechanics of how we got our jackets and slipped out into the night. I know that at some point in the minutes before leaving, he asked me if I thought Megan was okay. I don't think he even knew about the buddy system—boys didn't appear to have buddies. I looked over at Megan by the balcony rail next to Sue; she looked back at me, but her eyes weren't asking for anything. She could have been a little unsteady, there was a pink stain on her shirt, but she wasn't a total mess. I was uninterested, and maybe even a little annoyed by Adam's concern. I didn't want to think about her. There was nothing extraordinary about being drunk, getting wasted was the goal. Unless a girl was on all fours on the ice, vomiting into a plastic bag—and let's just be clear that Megan wasn't that, very far from it—she didn't need my help.

"She'll be fine," I said.

We must not have been able to find a cab because we walked back home over the icy sidewalks. Did we hold hands for real? I can't say. I wasn't very present, both because I was drunk and because I was preoccupied with imagining what was going on in Adam's head. Trying to guess what someone else was thinking came so much more naturally to me than processing any thoughts of my own. I was accustomed to being in the background, never the focus of something exciting. I have a general recollection of giddiness, a feeling that the best thing to ever happen to me was about to happen. But I wonder now, is that accurate, or is it just convenient to remember those feelings? Time doesn't just delete details, it can also invent them. We pad our memories with facts and feelings that make our decisions easier to narrate, or to make them seem more clearly motivated. If I was as distracted about going home with Adam as I remember being, then it's a little easier to forgive myself for what happened later.

That night, I didn't feel any guilt for abandoning Megan. I didn't really think of her as abandoned—she had Sue and Courtney. I thought about Megan again only when Adam and I walked into AlCo Hall because I hoped to hell Bev wouldn't see me without her. After overcoming that obstacle, I just hoped Megan wouldn't walk in on us. I stuck a Post-it on the door, over the paper hearts, that simply said: Knock.

My single bed was unmade, but at least my sheets were recently washed. Adam took off his glasses, and then our clothes came off in a rapid but respectful order: shirts, then pants, then bra. When he took off my underwear, I was embarrassed by how wet I was. I wasn't sure if you were supposed to be that wet, whether it was good or bad to be so obvious about what you wanted. I didn't know how to touch him, so I didn't.

He said, "Do you have condoms?"

I said I did. One. A giveaway from Student Health Services during orientation week.

I rolled over to get it from the milk crate next to my bed and handed it to him. I could feel his heartbeat when he pulled me close and our chests touched.

"Have you done this before?" he asked.

"Yeah," I lied. "Have you?"

With a sharp intake of breath, he said, "Yeah."

I have returned to this moment frequently in my life. Despite everything that happened later, for a long time, just remembering *Have you done this before?* could light a small fire in me.

When Adam asked if everything felt all right, I really wasn't sure—I was uncomfortable at best—but I said yes, totally fine. I wanted to be having sex right then, and with him. But my head swirled with things I couldn't ask: How much should I wiggle around? What was the right amount of noise? Did I feel approximately the same to him as his ex? Once I'd heard Stefan dismiss a girl he'd taken home as "too cavernous inside," and I hoped that wasn't what Adam was thinking about me.

Adam closed his eyes tightly, the way people close their eyes when they're trying very hard to picture something. I wasn't sure whether his need to concentrate was a good or bad sign, so I was relieved when he came—I knew, at least then, that whatever I did worked.

Megan did knock. I don't know how many times, but I heard her, eventually. I wanted her to give it up and go to Simone's room or something, but she kept at it, and I had to answer. My clothes were tangled up at the foot of the bed, and Adam was asleep, wearing only boxers. I wrapped myself in a towel and cracked the door open. I had no idea what time it was.

"Can I come in?" Megan asked. She leaned heavily against the door frame.

"I have company," I whispered. "Would it be okay, just this once, if you slept at Simone's?"

She just stood there, staring at me.

"Please? I'll do the same if Kyle comes." Even though she had just told me that Kyle would probably never come.

"I'm going to the bathroom," she said. She raised her eyebrows in a way that I took to mean that Adam should be gone when she returned.

After closing the door, I looked at Adam's sleeping body and decided not to try to wake him. It was uncomfortable but not uncommon to have to share a room with someone your roommate hooked up with, so I decided Megan would just have to deal with it. I found my underwear, a T-shirt that might be cute enough to wake up next to someone in, and got back in bed. I waited for Megan to come back. But she did not. And feeling only relief about that, I fell asleep.

9

The next day was the day I saw *Titanic* twice.

The first viewing was a matinee. I was hungover, but getting out meant that I could put off running into Megan and stumbling through an apology.

The stormy weather was as dangerous as ever, but we were a few days in now, and we were over it. I met up with Sue and Dutch outside the front doors of AlCo Hall to walk to the movie. It was like, suddenly, no one gave a shit anymore about being seen without a buddy. Dutch was smoking, and Sue was crouched down, taking pictures of the dead grass; each blade was sheathed in ice, like clusters of glass test tubes. She stood up when she saw me, her mouth twisting into a wry smile. "So what happened to *you* last night?"

"To me? Nothing." I did my best to sound bored yet surprised by the question. But actually, I was thrilled, finally, to be the subject of sex-related gossip. I wanted to draw out the moment.

"We all saw you leave with him."

"Let me guess," Dutch said. "You took Linsky back to your room, stole his Mastercard, and downloaded a shitload of porn while he was passed out in bed?"

"That's it."

"Sounds like a better night than mine," Dutch said.

"Did he sleep over?" Sue moved her eyebrows up and down.

"Maybe." It took everything to keep from grinning.

"Slu-*ut*." Sue clapped her hands. "Was he good?"

Was he? Was I? "Can't complain."

"He seems very sweet," Sue said. I wasn't sure whether seeming sweet was an endorsement or not coming from Sue.

Dutch clicked his tongue. "What did your roommate have to say about all this?"

"We haven't discussed it yet."

Sue put her camera into its case. "By the way, thanks for ditching her with us last night. *Soo* fucking wasted."

"Really?" A stab of guilt. "I'll apologize to her later." I decided I would try to smooth things over by bringing Megan my leftover movie popcorn.

"Is she still sleeping it off?" Sue asked.

I winced. "I feel bad. I pretty much told her to get lost. I made her sleep at Simone's, so I haven't seen her yet."

"We could hardly get her in and out of the cab, Ros. I knew you were with lover boy, so we carried her to Courtney's room and left her with a barf bucket." There was a note of annoyance in her voice.

"Oh shit, I'm sorry. Did she barf?" I looked at Dutch to gauge how real or widespread the annoyance was.

"Don't look at me," Dutch said. "I wasn't with them, I walked home early."

Sue tightened her scarf. "She passed right out on the bed. Then we smoked a bowl with Dutch upstairs—did you know this asshole was hoarding pot?" She made a face at Dutch, then looked back at me with a wicked gleam in her eye. "By the way, you weren't the only one *gettin' jiggy wit it* last night." We still weren't mature enough to discuss hookups in nonironic language.

"Who?" I looked from Sue to Dutch as if to say, *You two?*

Sue made an offended face. "Please. Court and Stef!"

"What?" I didn't like this development at all. I'd already had enough of Courtney. I wanted her out of our lives as soon as the ice storm was over.

"Let's just say there was lots of heavy breathing coming from her cot when I woke up to piss," Dutch said.

"Did they *do it*?" I was obsessed.

"Court was like, *I don't know—I was so wasted*. So, like, she obviously did and doesn't want to say." *Court*. When did she become "Court"?

"It happened," Dutch said. "Stef told me."

I was disappointed to see that Courtney and Stefan were getting more airtime than Adam and I. "I thought Courtney had a boyfriend."

"He's on exchange in Sweden this semester," Sue said. "When the cat's away . . ."

"Stefanimal will play," Dutch said. "Lucky bastard."

"She's not *that* hot," I said.

Dutch rolled his eyes. "Incorrect."

"But don't they sort of look the same?" I said. "Blond, tiny heads, those rosy cheeks. It's just, like, a little *Flowers in the Attic*."

"Ouch, that's cold," Sue said. I was confused. Sue normally went in for this type of dis. Did she *like* Courtney now?

"No Ros without a thorn," Dutch said.

"So will this happen again with Adam?" Sue asked, moving on.

"I don't know," I said, like I'd be content with it going either way, like this hadn't been the only thing on my mind since he left my room. "It's funny, though. I'm pretty sure he thinks I'm vegan. Maybe we'll get married after all."

Sue furrowed her brow. "Why does he think that?"

I shrugged, held my hands up like, *Not my problem.*

"You told him you were vegan?" Dutch said. "Nice."

"Not *exactly.*"

"What, then?" Sue said. Her expression seemed sort of annoyed.

"Just—" I tried to think. Dutch chucked his cigarette onto the frozen lawn. Sue looked at me warily, and I couldn't think of what to say. "Don't worry about it. Tell me more about Court and Stef."

"They're still upstairs," Sue said. "We're giving them space."

"*I* need space. How about we get the hell out of Creighton?" Dutch said, looking at me. "Maybe we could crash at your parents' place? Would they be cool with that?"

Sue seemed to want to go, too; she gave me a puppy dog look. Had they been discussing this? I hadn't told Dutch or Sue the reason I'd given Bev for not going home. Everyone had just accepted that I wasn't going anywhere—or they hadn't bothered to think it through. I never considered that people might eventually get bored and want to leave. I would have given Sue and Dutch anything, but I didn't want to leave right then—I wanted to see Adam again.

"I don't think so," I said. "My dad is ancient. I don't have cool parents." This was the other problem. I couldn't let them see my parents, their cars, their fancy new condo. I didn't want them to look through my high school CDs, expecting to find something good. I'd planted too many impressions with Dutch and Sue; I was still building an image, and I needed absolute control of the component parts.

"Your dad's an artist," Dutch said. "He can't be that uncool."

"She doesn't want to let Linsky out of her sight," Sue said.

"That's not the *only* reason," I said.

She and Dutch exchanged a look. The look said I was a wet blanket. Something had shifted, but I wasn't sure when or why.

"We should get going. I want to go by that house I was telling you about for next year," I said, hoping to change the conversation.

Dutch lit another cigarette and kicked at the ice on the lawn. "You guys go ahead. I think I have too much self-respect for this movie."

Sue made a sad face. "Aw, Dutch's afraid he'll cry in front of us."

"You got me," he said, winking. "But actually, I started *Finnegans Wake* last night, so maybe I'll just finish it."

"Today? Impossible," Sue said. "It's a million pages and unintelligible."

He squinted, took a drag off his cigarette. "I read eleven books over Christmas."

"Good for you," Sue said in a mocking tone. "Don't forget to stop by the library and collect your badge."

Dutch smirked and gave her the finger.

Sue sucked on her lip ring. After a moment, she said, "Are you seriously not coming? You have to—what if *I* cry?"

"You have Rosie."

I did not feel like a prize.

Sue took pictures on the walk to the theatre, and I tried to say interesting things about her subjects: a bicycle frozen to a pole, a newspaper trapped under the ice, a toppled steeple lying in a church cemetery. She was clearly irritated with Dutch for bailing, and she seemed pissed at me, too, but I wasn't sure why. Maybe because of the Megan thing, but I'd already said sorry for that. I wanted to talk more with her about Adam, but Sue clearly wasn't in the right mood.

I felt tense as we approached the house, wondering whether Sue would acknowledge our proximity, but she stopped right in front without me having to point it out. She must have remembered the address from my email. It was a red-brick duplex with a wide front porch and second-floor balcony. The string of Christmas lights hanging from the roof, each bulb pointed with ice, made me think of a diamond necklace. A cardboard sign on the front door read Cold Beer, Dark Rooms, Hot Girls.

Sue pointed her camera at the balcony. "We'll get patio furniture," she said. "Vintage." With those words, the tension broke. I imagined us sitting up there in September, shouting down to our friends on their way to the bar.

"Go stand in front," she said.

I nearly skipped into position, struck a pose with my hands held out to one side like, *Ta-dah!* "How do I look?"

Sue clicked. "Freshly fucked."

Even Sue didn't know I was a virgin—had just been a virgin. I never suggested I had a *lot* of experience, but I did imply that I'd done it with my summer boyfriend, Chris. (I also implied that *boyfriend* was the appropriate term for Chris, though I doubt *he'd* have called himself that. We worked together at a funnel cake shop on Santa Monica Pier and hooked up three times.)

"I'm so tired," I said to encourage more conversation about the cause of my exhaustion.

Sue yawned. "Was it awkward with Adam this morning?"

"Not really."

But it had been, a bit. When I woke up, Adam was fully dressed. I didn't get out of bed, just pulled up the sheets and tried my best to appear like a very alert and together person. Adam said he needed Tylenol and a jug of Gatorade, and he squeezed my shoulder before leaving the room. The squeeze was tender, but no more romantic than a squeeze from a soccer coach or a kind doctor.

I got out of bed a half hour later, realized I was very hungover, and microwaved Megan's last bag of popcorn in the common room. There was a message on my answering machine when I got back to my room, and though I couldn't imagine why Adam would call rather than message me on ICQ, my heart pounded with hopefulness while I waited for it to play. But it was Megan's Aunt Lisa, asking Megan about her plans. *Still thinking of coming down? There's a warm bed waiting.* I summarized the message on Megan's whiteboard—a sketch of Lisa Simpson + the CN Tower—and then I drew a big smiley face to be conciliatory.

My main reaction to this call was that it would be great if Megan went to Aunt Lisa's because then Adam and I could have the room to ourselves. Looking in Megan's mirror, I noticed that my face and chest were flushed. I also saw a new inspirational sticker on the glass, the kind of thing you might find in a Christmas cracker: "A smile is the prettiest thing you can wear!" Sue would definitely be hearing about that one. I imagined the mocking way we'd repeat it to one another when we got ready to go out. I smirked at my reflection.

Sue breezed right past the concession stand, so I didn't stop to get Megan anything. In the stuffy warmth of the movie theatre, I let my shattered, hungover body melt into the seat next to her. My head was swimming with Adam, with what would happen next, and I fell asleep five minutes into the film. When I woke up, the actors were shouting and getting on lifeboats. I wanted them to shut up and let me sleep, but then I heard Sue crying softly next to me. *You have Rosie*, I thought. I wanted this to mean something. I leaned my head on her shoulder and pretended to cry too.

———

Did I think it was weird not to see Megan in my room when I got home that evening? Whenever I tell this story and get to this point in the timeline, I like to emphasize that I *had* seen Megan in the hallway about twelve hours before. We'd had a conversation. Plus, I'd been out all afternoon, and I figured she was avoiding our room because she didn't want to be around me. In any case, there wasn't a lot of time to think about her. I had a message on ICQ from Adam: *Want to go see Titanic?*

I didn't tell Adam I'd just seen the movie, but I don't really count that as one of my lies. Since I slept through the first round, I hadn't truly seen it.

The vibe between Adam and me was stilted on the walk, though the weather didn't help. We kept our heads down and collars up, charging through a fresh burst of icy rain. Seeing my disheveled reflection in the mirrored lobby of the theatre, I was reminded of a phrase I'd heard my mother use: ridden hard and put away wet. My hair looked feral, and my jeans were soaked all the way up to the backs of my knees.

I did think of buying popcorn for Megan again, but I wasn't sure if vegans could eat movie popcorn, so I just followed Adam into the theatre. Minutes before the movie started, a girl a few rows ahead of us stood up to let someone pass down the aisle. She was the same height, with the same frizzy blond hair as Megan. I felt some anxiety about Megan being at the theatre, about the encounter the three of us might have in the lobby, but mostly I felt relief. I was finally able to acknowledge some creeping concern about her whereabouts because now everything was fine, here she was. I relaxed into my seat.

When scenes got tense during the movie, Adam fidgeted with the zipper of his fleece, jiggling it up and down. Boldly, I leaned against his shoulder to comfort him; I didn't pretend to cry this time.

At the end of the movie, when everyone got up, the blond girl in front of us made her way into the aisle. It wasn't Megan. A niggling worry came back to me as we followed the crowd to the fluorescent lobby, but feeling Adam's hand at the small of my back, that fear was easily overpowered.

10

When I stuck my key in the door an hour later, it's hard to say what I was dreading more: finding Megan in the room or not finding her there.

She wasn't there. The telephone's message button flashed red in the darkness. It was Megan's Aunt Lisa again: *Curious if you've made any plans. I'll pick you up from the bus stop, just let us know what you've decided.* Before that week, I had never heard of Aunt Lisa. The sudden surge in Aunt Lisa activity, combined with Megan's absence, wasn't a red flag to me— it all fell together into a kind of logic. Megan said she would go back to Toronto if the dorm ran out of space, if things got "really bananas," and it was fair to say that what happened the night before—the escapades at the bar, passing out, getting kicked out of her own room—would, by Megan's standard, be bananas enough. I thought, Okay, Megan packed while I was out of the room, then she got on the bus to go to Aunt Lisa's. This all could have happened while I was at one of the *Titanic* screenings.

And either she forgot to call Aunt Lisa to confirm, or Aunt Lisa hadn't gotten the message yet. Her deadbeat husband probably forgot to pass it along. Megan would arrive at their doorstep any minute now.

There has always been a lot of speculation about how I could have jumped to this conclusion concerning Megan's whereabouts so quickly. What I can say about myself now, twenty years later, is that *an* explanation, however flimsy, can be enough to chase away a disquieting feeling for a good amount of time. And the Aunt Lisa thing really was a rational explanation. If it even occurred to me to check with Bev, I dismissed the idea because it would have gotten me in trouble. It would have been admitting that I'd lost track of Megan, my buddy. But just because I was aware that I could get in trouble doesn't mean that I fabricated the Toronto thing to cover my ass. People thought that, and I get why they did—I might have thought that about someone else. But it wasn't quite like that. Megan never communicated any solid plan to me, it's true. But I believed that the conclusion I had reached came from enough evidence that she *might as well* have told me the plan herself.

But none of this matters now. I'm not the one on trial this time.

The second time Adam and I had sex, it went on for much longer than the first. I was worried that I was doing something wrong because it was taking so long. I was so tense and anxious that it felt impossible to breathe until it was over.

Afterward, as we lay facing each other, his stare made me insecure. It felt like he was trying to decide whether I was pretty or not. "I've only had sex with one other person," he said suddenly.

He was trying to look me in the eye, and I wanted to come clean. I wanted to feel close to him, to tell him that he was the first person I had ever slept with. But I couldn't. I didn't want him to feel bad about the drunk way it had happened, or to think it was fucked up that I lied before. "Same," I said, hoping that pretend sameness could bind two people just as much as honesty. I took his hand, laced our fingers together. "So, no worries."

He kissed the back of my hand. I wanted to ask about the other girl. Had she been his girlfriend, or was it a situation more like this? Or was this a girlfriend situation? That was a bigger question that I definitely wouldn't ask. I wasn't sure what to say to follow up my dorky "Hakuna Matata," so I just turned to look out the window, still too thickly coated to see through.

After a moment, Adam said, "Do you know there's ice in Antarctica that's a million years old?" I guess he wasn't sure what to say now, either.

"That's so interesting," I said, though I was only interested in what he thought of me, what would happen next with us. I also had to pee, but I wasn't sure how to say that without ruining the moment.

"They say the internet will be like that in the future. Just like layers over layers over layers of human history," he said.

"Huh."

He flipped onto his back; I'm pretty sure he sensed my incuriosity. "Sorry," he said, "I feel like I should know this, but what's your major?"

"English. But I don't love it." I'd been decent at English in high school, back when I didn't have much of a social life and relied more on school work for self-esteem, but I felt no special connection to books or writing the way people like Dutch did. I would never choose *Finnegans Wake* over *Titanic*.

"Do you know what you want to do after this? Like, career-wise?" he asked.

Was this a test of some kind? I wanted to impress him, say something appealing and original. "I wouldn't mind being, like, a baker?" I was surprised to hear myself land on that, but it wasn't *untrue*. I'd gotten a lot of compliments on Dutch's cake in December. It was, quite possibly, the only project I had felt proud to accomplish all semester.

"Really?" Adam said. "Can you study that here?"

"Not exactly," I said. "But I worked at a funnel cake place last summer, so I have experience. We had to design all kinds of different cakes, all different styles. We could do mermaids, butterflies." He seemed curious, as if I should say more. "That's why I took French," I said, throwing in some glam. "In case I want to study in Paris someday."

"Wow," he said. "Sounds like you know what you want to do."

I liked the person I was becoming in his eyes. But then I remembered I was supposed to be vegan. "What I'd really like to do," I said, "is, like, animal-free baking?"

Adam looked perplexed. "What's that?"

"You know, so that people with different political views—people against cruelty to animals—can still eat great desserts."

"Oh," Adam said. "That's cool."

Another *that's cool*? I'd been hoping for more reaction.

"Like, what would you want me to make?" I asked.

Adam combed his fingers through the ends of my hair. "I have a ton of respect for your beliefs," he said. "But I still probably couldn't eat any of it." He flipped onto his back. "I have severe food allergies. Like, a lot of them. Processed meat, shellfish, dairy, eggs, nuts. It was a nightmare when I was a kid, especially birthday parties. No pizza, no cake."

So much for Dutch and Stefan's facts. "What happens if you eat those things?" I asked.

"Well, it's not pretty. Milk makes my face balloon. Shellfish could kill me."

"My cakes won't have shellfish," I said. "I promise."

He smiled, but it didn't seem like he wanted to talk about his allergies anymore. I wasn't sure what else to say, so I asked him what he wanted to do when he grew up.

"That's the thing," he said. "Everyone else in commerce already has a top five list of companies they want to work for. Until two months ago, I didn't know the difference between Price Waterhouse and Fisher-Price." I laughed, but I didn't know the difference. "I took one of those aptitude tests at the career centre before the holidays," he said. "They told me I should consider a future in social work."

"I did that test. Did they make you fold a paper square into a box?"

"I gave up after step four."

I scored in the 99th percentile on paper folding, but I didn't tell Adam. "The counsellor told me that I should be an architect, but I was like, *No fucking way*. My dad's an architect—actually both my parents, but only my dad really worked as one—and he's talented, I guess, but he's never made it seem even slightly fun." It felt strangely good to say something true about my parents. But what if Adam became my boyfriend? Would it somehow slip out in front of Dutch and Sue that my dad wasn't who I'd said he was? The good feeling started to evaporate.

"But baking is sort of like designing, right?"

"Right!" I said, feeling good again, because I'd never considered the connection and was glad it came to him so quickly.

But for the first time, I also considered this: maybe Adam's observation was an obvious example of the *thing* about him that had pulled me in. He was literally interested in me; he was trying to connect the dots, he wanted to learn more. Before, I thought being interested in a person was more of an egocentric thing, like you thought they'd look good on you, that they'd somehow enhance your image. Maybe Adam had truly been intrigued by my baguette presentation in the fall, maybe his questions weren't only a kindness. I put my head on his shoulder, he stroked my hair. What was happening felt grown-up.

"I think you'd be perfect for Price Waterhouse. Or Fisher-Price," I said.

He tilted my chin up and kissed me. When he pressed his hips into mine, I thought my bladder was going to burst. "Um, would it be okay if I—"

Adam rolled away again, too fast; he seemed wounded. "I should get going, huh?"

"No, no. I just have to pee."

"But what about your roommate?"

"She went to Toronto." This was the first time I said it out loud.

"And they didn't move someone from the gym in here? Lucky you."

It hadn't occurred to me that someone should have been reassigned to my room, but I was happy for the oversight. "I guess not."

11

Everything unravelled on Saturday.

The phone woke us up. I didn't answer it, but Adam got up anyway. Before leaving, he squeezed my shoulder. He'd done that twice now. Was it a move he'd learned with his ex? Did she find it sexy?

I listened to the message after Adam left. It was for Megan again, this time from Kyle. This did register to me as weird. I could understand why Megan hadn't gone out of her way to communicate her plans to me, but Kyle?

After I showered and was back in my room, the phone rang again. I bit the bullet and picked up.

"May I please speak to Megan?" It was a woman's voice.

"Megan's not here right now." I hoped my tone sounded normal. "May I take a message?"

"Do you know when she'll be back?"

"I'm not sure."

"Could you have her call Lisa, please?"

Suddenly flustered, I managed only to say, "Okay."

"You're Megan's roommate?"

"Yes."

"You're holding up okay over there?"

"Yep. Thanks for asking!" I just needed the call to end.

When I understood that Megan wasn't at her Aunt Lisa's, maybe I should have panicked. But I had already convinced myself that Megan was in Toronto—I'd made that true, it was too late to make it untrue. I just needed to figure out where *specifically* in Toronto she'd gone in case anyone else asked. Then everything would be fine. I went to Simone's room.

Simone's roommate, Claribel, was cleaning her trumpet, all of the brass pieces laid out on a towel on her bed.

"Hey," I said, trying to sound casual, like we were friends. "Is Simone here?"

Claribel shook her head. "She went back to Toronto yesterday afternoon."

So there we go, I thought. Megan was most likely at Simone's. They were pretty much best friends. Plus, it made sense that Megan wouldn't call Kyle long distance from Simone's house, didn't it?

"So Megan went with her?"

"I didn't see her."

Although I asked Claribel the question, I didn't put much stock in her answer. If Megan wasn't at Aunt Lisa's, Simone's place was where she was, a perfect explanation.

I don't remember much about the rest of that afternoon, but when Bev came looking for me, I was in Sue's room with her and Dutch watching

VHS tapes of *My So-Called Life*. Sue was wearing a fitted white sweat-shirt that said "Whistler." It was definitely Courtney's, and I felt a cold shiver of jealousy.

Sue and Dutch were debating the imbalance in Jordan and Angela's relationship. Sue was arguing that Angela was dating down by being with Jordan—he was dumb, whereas she was hot *and* smart. But Dutch disagreed. He said Jordan was a talented musician who knew who he was, whereas Angela was an overprivileged proto-yuppie, just playing at grunge. I normally had a lot to say on this kind of topic, but I couldn't focus on them or the TV.

When Bev opened the door, Sue said, "Courtney checked out the VCR for me, I swear." Sue had received several Oops Reports about the VCR, but I knew, even before Bev spoke, that this wasn't why she was here.

"There you are," she said to me. "I've been looking for Megan. Where is she?"

"She went back to Toronto," I said, glancing up only for a second.

"She did?" Bev said, alarmed. "She didn't sign out. Which bus?"

"She didn't sign out?"

"Could you turn that off, please?" Bev said.

Sue huffed as she crossed the room to pause the VCR.

"You get that you're her buddy, right?" Bev said to me, hand on her hip. "You're supposed to know where she is." Bev was wearing plaid PJs and one of the buttons had come undone around the middle, exposing a roll of pink flesh.

"I'm aware," I said. "But I assumed that was if we were both here. If she's not here, how can I possibly know where she is?"

Bev flared her nostrils. "Were any of you going to tell me she left? Because her parents just called, and they have no idea what's up. They've been trying your phone for the last couple hours."

"Sorry," I said. My tone conveyed a shrug, but my pulse felt like a fist opening and closing around my neck. "Did you try Simone's house?"

"She went to Simone's?" Bev asked.

"They're best friends."

Bev gave me a piercing look. "Simone left yesterday. Are you saying Megan was also on the four thirty bus?"

"I think so, yeah."

"Seriously, Ros?" Bev said, with a dubious glare.

"What?" I looked at Dutch and Sue, but they were also staring at me.

"When was the last time you spoke to her?" Bev asked.

I wasn't quite sure how to answer that. Sue piped up in my place. "She was at the Old Vic with us Thursday night."

"That was the last time?" Bev's face was pure stress.

"We came home together," Sue said.

"I've seen her since then," I added quickly.

"When?"

"The next morning."

"But it's Saturday!" Bev said, voice raised now.

"Call Simone, seriously. She will know," I said.

"I will," Bev said. "And I suggest you check your phone, too."

After Bev left, I went over to the radiator and picked a cigarette out of Dutch's pack on the windowsill. "Sorry, guys," I said. The show was still paused. "Overreaction city."

Dutch spoke first. "Do you actually *not* know where Megan is?"

"I'm like ninety-five percent sure she's at Simone's."

Dutch glanced at Sue, then back at me. "Are you worried at all?"

"No. I saw her yesterday." But yes, I was worried. Because by *yesterday*, I really meant sometime after the bar on Thursday night, only *technically* Friday morning. My hands didn't feel right; I couldn't light the cigarette.

"Maybe you should find out what's going on," Sue said.

"Guys, it's fine," I tried to sound convincing, but I knew I wasn't, and I put the cigarette back in the pack. I left the room feeling watched, and I assumed they were whispering about me when I didn't hear the show turn on again.

Back in my room, there were two messages from Megan's parents. There was also one from my mom, saying Bev contacted her, that they'd had a "weird" talk, and asking me to call to confirm that everything was okay. I hoped it wasn't obvious to Bev during the call with my mother that my parents weren't on the brink of divorce.

When Bev came by my room, she was visibly pale. "Megan's not with Simone," she said. "Simone hasn't seen her since Wednesday."

"Thursday," I corrected. "Megan slept there Thursday night."

"Simone said she saw her on Wednesday."

"That doesn't make sense," I said.

"I need to call campus security."

"She said she was going to Toronto. It's fine." I was hardly aware of what I was saying.

"You're the one who is supposed to be in Toronto, Ros. I'm going to get in trouble for that, too."

"Sorry," I said under my breath. And then, "Is that why you called my parents? Do I have to leave?"

Bev rubbed her forehead. "No. Just—please don't go anywhere, Ros."

I remember getting into my bed and going under the covers. But what was I actually thinking then? If I'm sure of one thing, it's that I didn't want to think too hard. If I avoided thinking too hard, if I kept certain scenarios out of my head, they couldn't exist. But there was one big thing that I had to face: Megan wasn't the type not to think of other people. It was unlike Megan not to sign out, to create this rising level of panic in others. She would not have dashed out and dropped all responsibilities in order to avoid some minor awkwardness with me. For a time, I must have turned Megan into someone else in my mind. Someone more reckless, more thoughtless, more like me.

My conversation with the cops happened a few hours later. By that point, we already knew that Megan had not been on any buses the day before, at least none organized by the school. Campus security had contacted several girls on our floor who'd taken the buses home, and no one could recall seeing Megan aboard. The local Creighton Greyhound drivers had also all been given a photo and description.

While one cop talked to me, a second one was poking around Megan's side of the room. I watched him slide the photo of Megan and her parents out of its frame and put it in a clear plastic bag.

I was worried about Megan, I must have been. But so long as there were cops in my room, my main concern was self-preservation. If I was about to get in trouble, I wanted to minimize the amount. Maybe I'd been wrong about a few things, but I hadn't *done* anything wrong. Whatever bad thing had happened to Megan—if anything bad had even happened—it wasn't something I did to her.

The cop talking to me had dark corkscrew curls. I can't remember for sure, but I think her name was Officer Danes, though maybe it was Daniels and I'm just remembering it as Danes after watching *My So-Called Life*. She sat at my desk and moved a hairdryer aside to put down her notebook.

The questions she asked were variations of the same ones that I would be asked over and over again. I described going out to the Old Vic with Megan but then leaving ahead of her because I was ready to go first. I told her what Sue had said about taking her to Courtney's room, and that the last time I had seen Megan was when she knocked on the door.

"But she didn't come in?" Officer Danes said.

"She went to the bathroom across the hall," I said.

"How did she seem to you then? Was she obviously drunk, stumbling, slurring her words?"

Sue had made Megan sound like a mess. It was possible she'd been a little unsteady against the doorframe, but I hadn't noticed her being that weird. "No," I said. "I don't think so."

"You don't think so," Officer Danes repeated. "And she never came back from the bathroom?"

"If she came back, I was sleeping."

"You told Beverly you saw her in the morning?" Officer Danes wrote something down.

"Right. But night was really morning. I mean, it was after midnight."

She gave me a long look. "So that was the last time then, when she came by 'after midnight'?"

"Right."

"And you weren't worried about this? Not seeing her since then?"

"I wasn't, no." That was mainly true. "We have all these extra people here now, and everyone is kind of sleeping all over. I thought she slept at her friend's."

"What friend?"

"Simone," I said. "I don't know her last name."

"But why not just sleep here?"

I made a face like her guess was as good as mine. She smirked; I wasn't sure what that meant.

"And all day yesterday, you didn't see or hear from her?"

"No."

"And you didn't think to tell anyone?"

"I assumed she was in Toronto at her Aunt Lisa's."

She cocked her head to the side. "And why was that?"

I looked over at the whiteboard and gestured at the pictogram I'd drawn the day before: Lisa Simpson, the CN Tower, the smiley face. "See up there?"

She squinted. "What?"

"Lisa. Toronto?" I said.

She kept studying the drawings. It was convenient, for me, that Megan's whiteboard said "To Do" across the top. Easy to suggest that the pictogram was Megan's own enthusiastic note to self. But it was also just a pictogram, subject to interpretation. I tried to look calm and confident for Officer Danes—*What more evidence do you need?* I didn't mention Lisa's calls.

She leaned back in her chair. "But she didn't go to her aunt's," she said. "She isn't there."

"Yeah, I heard," I said gravely.

Officer Danes narrowed her eyes at me. "When did you hear?"

I had to think about this. I was getting mixed up between the truth and the story I was assembling on the fly to make me sound better. "Um . . . just a little while ago?"

Officer Danes clicked, then unclicked her pen. "Lisa Phillips said she talked to you earlier this morning."

"Right, that's right," I said, trying to appear composed, appreciative of the reminder.

"She says you told her that Megan was here?"

"Here?" I felt a sickening jolt. "I never said that." And I hadn't. I'd simply told her that I would pass along a phone message. I never said when I'd deliver that message; I made no promises about *when* Megan would call her back.

"But meanwhile, you told Bev that Megan was at someone called Simone's?"

"Yeah, that's what I thought."

Officer Danes exhaled. "You'll need to go over this for me again."

"What part?"

Across the room from us, the other cop interrupted. "She keep a diary or anything?"

"I don't know. We're not really close," I said.

"And what about this? This hers?" He pulled her green canvas suitcase out from under her bed.

"Yeah," I said.

"You never checked if her suitcase was still here?" He glanced at Officer Danes. His glance implied that I was both stupid and criminal.

I was proud of my next response. I used it whenever this question came up. "She told me she was going," I said. "I didn't have any reason not to believe her, so I didn't go checking for her suitcase."

"You didn't send her any emails or anything?" Officer Danes asked. "Just to make sure she arrived in the city safe?"

I shook my head. "Like I said, we're not that close."

"Ms. Main is missing," she said. "As far as we know, you are the last person to have seen her in thirty-six hours. Do you understand?"

"Yes," I said. But maybe part of me didn't get it, not totally.

"If you have any idea where your roommate is, any idea where she might have gone, you need to tell us."

"I definitely will."

The other cop spoke up again. "This her purse?" He lifted a black leather purse off a hook on the closet door. "You wouldn't leave town without your purse," he said. "Would you?"

"That's a going-out purse, though."

He looked confused. But in that moment, an important detail clicked: it was the purse Megan had at the bar.

The cop dug around inside the purse, pulling out cash, a few cards, her licence. "This is the main ID she uses?" It was.

I appealed to Officer Danes. "That's Megan's *going-out* purse. She had it with her on Thursday at the bar. So she must have come back to the room after I saw her in the hall. She must have come back and hung it up."

"You're sure she didn't drop it off when she knocked?"

"She never came inside. She must have come back later," I insisted.

"Who is Mike Merritt?" the cop asked, holding up a little white card that I recognized as Air Force Mike's.

"A taxi driver."

"What is their relationship?"

"Um. He drove our taxi to the bar?"

He put the purse and its contents in a plastic bag.

Officer Danes made me run through the details of Thursday night again, looking to integrate the return of the purse into the timeline, even though I had no information about when the purse was put back. After that, I went through a list of people who Megan was in regular contact with. There was the cafeteria manager, who Megan might have advised of an upcoming absence in case the power came back on. Professor McClanahan, who lived on the horse farm where Megan worked, although he was out of town. I named other girls from our floor, shared what I knew about the clubs Megan took part in. They also wanted more on Air Force Mike. Did I think she would have contacted him? I didn't think so. Definitely not. He was just the driver.

I never mentioned Adam in this interview. I had avoided bringing him up for too long, and I thought it would look suspicious to suddenly add him to my story. I wasn't embarrassed to tell anyone that we slept together, that wasn't it. I just wanted to keep things clean and simple, and I didn't think his presence in the narrative made much difference. But mainly, I didn't want the cops to talk to Adam—I didn't want him to think that I'd done something wrong. I'm ashamed to admit that how Adam would view me after finding out what happened was on my mind at least as much as Megan's whereabouts. Because although terrifying scenarios were beginning to worm their way into my head—Air Force Mike with a knife and a ski mask in the bathroom stall, Megan pinned under a tree somewhere—finding her purse in our room brought me great relief. Even if something terrible had happened, it was not all my fault. It was not a direct consequence of me kicking her out of the room. She had come back. At some point, while I was out of the room, she had returned with her purse.

But I couldn't keep Adam out of the story for very long; the story couldn't be contained by how I'd answered the cops' questions. Over the next several hours, they talked to a whole whack of people in AlCo Hall. It got to be sort of a status thing, who the cops had talked to, who was closest to the drama.

Before the cops left my room, Officer Danes said, "I hope you're taking this seriously, young lady. You had a duty of care for this young woman."

I wasn't sure what she meant by that. Could I be charged with something? It was only Bev's stupid buddy system that I had violated. But that didn't stop me jumping whenever the phone rang, and for a long time afterward.

Around eight that night, every first-year student still on campus gathered in the cafeteria. We all knew why we were there: the whispering-turned-hysterics had been going on for hours by that point. We sat at tables facing the adults up front: Officer Danes, someone from Campus Security, a fortysomething administrator named Nancy Calandra.

I was sitting between Sue and Courtney. I was getting a lot of attention because Megan was my roommate, and people, up to this point anyway, felt especially sorry for me. I looked for Adam, who I saw sitting two tables in front of us. The room was very quiet, and outside it was almost black; I kept glancing at the large glass windows, reflecting our group. I could see Adam better in the window than from behind.

Nancy thanked us all for cooperating with the police that afternoon and for taking the matter of a missing person seriously. She told us that Megan was top priority for the Creighton police and that we needed to do everything the cops asked. She kept emphasizing that it was very common to find missing people in the first seventy-two hours. I calculated that it had been only forty hours and whispered this to Sue, but she just stared straight ahead at Nancy.

Nancy distributed copies of a timeline detailing Megan's whereabouts in the six hours before she went missing, pieced together from conversations over the last several hours. "If you have any details that aren't reflected in this timeline, anything that you think is important that you haven't told me or the police, please speak up," she said.

THURSDAY, JANUARY 8—FRIDAY, JANUARY 9, 1998

· *9:30 p.m.*—Main leaves Alice Cole Hall in a taxi with Rosalind Fisher, Supriya Verma, and Courtney Davis. Taxi driver is Capt. Mike Merritt.
· *9:45 p.m.*—Main enters the Old Vic bar on Eddy St.
· *12:45 a.m.*—Main leaves the Old Vic Bar with Verma, Davis and Stefan Scobey.
· *1:00 a.m.*—Main arrives at Alice Cole Hall with Verma, Davis and Scobey.
· *1:15 a.m.*—Main is visibly inebriated. Verma, Davis and Scobey put Main to bed in Davis's Room, #219. Davis, Verma and Scobey go to room #248.
· *3:30 a.m. (Approx.)*—Fisher and Main talk at the door of Main and Fisher's room, #243.

· *3:31 a.m. (Approx.)*—Main tells Fisher she will visit restrooms. 2nd floor, east.

Description: Megan Main is 19 yrs old, approx 5'5", 130 lbs., with shoulder-length blond to light-brown hair. Last seen wearing jeans, a white top with a white ruffle, and a Regis leather jacket.

At the table in front of me, Claribel spoke out without raising her hand, perhaps a first in her life. She said, "Wait. When the cops told me before that no one's seen her since Friday morning, I thought you meant a normal time on Friday morning. You're saying no one has seen her since the middle of the night?"

Nancy crinkled her eyes, acknowledging this with compassionate concern. "Yes, as shown on the timeline, we are estimating her last sighting at three thirty a.m."

Claribel whipped around to face me. "You didn't see her in the morning or all day yesterday, and you didn't report it until *now*?"

Nancy cleared her throat. "Let me just say straight away that there was some misunderstanding about Megan's plans."

"Like what?" Claribel said.

I looked at Claribel. "As far as I knew, she was in Toronto." I turned to Nancy and repeated what she'd just said. "It was a misunderstanding."

I would come to rely on that word, *misunderstanding*. Through the following weeks, I maintained that I *misunderstood* Megan's plans. That wasn't quite honest. But I also don't think it's true to say that I made everything up, either. Yes, I misled the cops with the whiteboard, but that was only because I didn't have any other evidence to support what made sense to me. And what made sense to me was that she was in Toronto.

"Did she sign out?" Claribel asked.

"No," Bev confirmed.

"So you ditched your buddy at the Old Vic and didn't even care if she never came back?" Claribel said.

"She came back with them," I said, indicating Sue and Courtney next to me.

"They just dumped her in a room," Claribel said.

Next to me, Courtney made a noise like she was going to be sick.

Nancy put her hand up to quiet this line of conversation. "The main thing is, I need to hear from anyone who saw her, or thinks they might have seen her, *after* three thirty Friday morning."

"Her purse is in the room," I said. "So she definitely came back later." I was mainly looking at Sue. She needed to know this was not my fault. But Sue still wouldn't look at me.

Courtney stood up then. "I just want to say"—she was trembling— "I just want to say that I came back with Megan, like it says on the sheet. We were all really drunk, but yeah, we shouldn't have left her alone. I should have checked on her. I just want to say—" Courtney broke down then, sobbing into her hands.

Sue stepped around me to comfort her. "It's not your fault," Sue whispered, wrapping her arms around Courtney. I wasn't sure whether I could join the embrace or if I was already too late.

"Courtney, thank you," Nancy said. "This is a very emotional time. We're trying to understand what occurred. We're not assigning blame."

"I took photos," Sue volunteered. "From before we went out? Shots of what Megan was wearing, that kind of stuff. I can get you the roll if it helps."

"Thank you, Supriya," Nancy said.

Peg Bundy raised her hand. "Did you try Professor McClanahan's? She works for him on the weekends."

"Thank you, yes. The cops have been in touch. Professor McClanahan is out of town, and Megan was not scheduled to work this weekend," Nancy said.

Another girl broke down in tears.

Peg Bundy turned toward me. Loudly, she asked, "What did you guys talk about at your door, Rosalind?"

Everyone looked at me then, eyes greedy for information. "Nothing," I said.

"Nothing whatsoever?" Peg Bundy's voice was heavy with suspicion.

"She didn't have her key, or she couldn't find it, I don't remember. She just knocked, and then, when I answered, she said she was going to the bathroom." I glanced at Adam in the window; like Sue, he was looking ahead, not at me. People were either staring or avoiding my eye completely. "That's it, pretty much."

Peg Bundy wouldn't let it go. "Couldn't you see she was too drunk to be on her own?" She looked around the room, inviting reaction from the crowd like a talk show host.

And then I was flooded with questions:

"Wasn't Megan your buddy?"

"Why did you leave her at the bar?"

"Why didn't you look for her when she didn't come back from the bathroom?"

"Why didn't you look for her in the morning?"

"Why didn't you look for her, period?"

I stared desperately at the adults at the front of the room, wondering when one of them would take control, stop letting all these people harass me with their accusatory questions. But they let it go on. What ended it was Claribel standing up. She looked like she might start to hyperventilate, like someone ought to get her a paper bag. "You *did* look for her," she said. Her voice sounded constricted, the utterances of someone with no experience speaking up. "This morning, you asked me if she went to Toronto with Simone. And I told you I didn't think so. I *told* you. You knew that before Bev found you this afternoon."

"Is that true?" Nancy asked. Her tone was gentle, but I wasn't sure why. I expected her to be concerned and pissed off, like everyone else. Was she just trying to get me to trust her so that I would confess things? But I didn't know anything, that was the problem.

"Not quite true," I said.

Claribel rushed from the room, like someone about to vomit. The security person got up, but it was Sue who followed first, with Courtney trailing.

"It's not my fault," I called out to the backs of Sue and Courtney.

"Everyone calm down," Nancy said. "It's not about fault. We all need to stay calm and think clearly."

The meeting ended with half the room in tears. Nancy came over to me. "Go back up to your room," she said. "We need to know where to find you, and you don't need this right now." She gestured at a gathering cluster of sobbing girls. She told me Megan's mother was coming to town that night and would probably want to talk to me in the morning. I really hoped she wouldn't. Until that moment, *sad* wasn't the word for how I felt, but the idea that Megan's mom's first visit to Ontario would be to look for her missing daughter, that shattered me.

I ignored Nancy's warning and stopped by Sue's half-open door on my way back from the meeting. Dutch was sitting on the radiator, and Sue and Courtney were on pillows on the floor. The three peered at me through the smoke that filled the room. My hands shook; I jammed them in the pockets of my cardigan.

"How's Claribel doing?" I made a sympathetic face.

Sue looked up. "Bad, obviously. This is pretty fucked up, Ros."

"I know."

"We were just talking, actually." She glanced over at Dutch. "Did you mention to the cops that Adam was in your room that night? Did you tell them you told Megan to get lost?"

"I didn't tell her to *get lost*," I said.

"That's pretty much exactly what you told us," Sue said.

"Come on. I was kidding."

"Mmm hmm." She tapped her cigarette ash into a soda can. "Well, it was hilarious."

"It was more like I made a suggestion," I said. "I didn't force her to go anywhere."

"But what I'm asking is, did you tell them Adam was there?" She tilted her head, narrowed her eyes as she took another drag.

"Yes," I lied. "Of course." I could feel the line they were drawing, the side of it that I stood on.

Courtney looked up and said, "We find it kind of weird that Adam wasn't on the timeline. He might know something, right?" *We*? Since when did Courtney speak for Dutch and Sue. I glared at her.

"Adam was asleep." I looked over at Dutch as I said this; I didn't see him as a panicker. He was reasonable—he'd been fair-minded about the porn thief, for instance—and he'd been mostly quiet so far.

Dutch crossed his long legs in front of him. "So, if we talk to the cops, they won't be surprised to hear about Adam?"

"No," I said. I was in middle school all over again. "Go ahead." Dutch just stared at me. "What?" I said, in a tone not even close to playing it cool.

He raised his eyebrows, showed me his palms like, *Back off*. "Look, I think like a reporter, okay? And I'm just saying we have to consider every scenario, including one where Adam might be involved," he said.

"Involved how? He didn't do anything to her."

"Maybe not," Sue said. "But, like, maybe that's something for the cops to decide?" She ground out her cigarette. "But another thing is bugging me—us." She looked at Courtney, then over to Dutch again. "Yesterday, you said you were going to apologize to Megan, but how were you going to do that if she was in Toronto?"

"I meant when she got back from Toronto."

Dutch and Sue exchanged a look.

"Stop looking at each other," I said.

"Whoa," Courtney said, making wide eyes at Sue.

Sue sighed. "We just think you're being kind of sketchy."

"I'm not being sketchy."

"Oh my God, yes, you are," Courtney said as she looked up at me. She'd never liked me, that was now plain to see. "Do you think maybe you could just go?" She turned to address Sue. "Otherwise, I'm going to have to leave. I really can't deal with her right now."

Sue put her hand on Courtney's arm. "No, Court. You stay."

I was twitchy with anger. "I want to find Megan, too," I said. "Why is everyone mad at me?"

"We're not *mad*," Sue said. "We're worried. Something really terrible might have happened."

"I know that," I said.

"She could have been raped," Sue continued. "And left for dead."

Courtney covered her ears. "Stop." She was being so overdramatic; it took all my strength to not roll my eyes.

"Courtney is super upset, and *she* definitely didn't do anything wrong," Sue said.

"*I* didn't, either."

"Except not tell anyone she was missing," Dutch said.

"I didn't know she was missing."

"That makes no sense," Sue said. "You live with her. You should have known."

When I turned to leave, Sue did not get up to follow me down the hall. I waited for five minutes after slamming my door, but she didn't come.

I called my parents. I couldn't put that off any longer.

"Thank God," my mother said. "Were your phone lines out? We kept trying." It was a reprimand disguised as a question.

"I'm sorry," I said, avoiding the question.

"I was going to send your father out."

"Don't do that."

I wanted to leave, I wanted my dad to pick me up. But now I wasn't allowed to go. I felt guilty for saying that my parents' marriage was falling apart; maybe they were the only people on earth who liked me.

"Beverly called us. It was very awkward not to have any idea what was going on," Mom said.

"Sorry."

"Is everything okay?"

"My roommate's missing."

"But what do you mean, *missing*?"

"Like, she's a missing person."

"Oh my God, Ros."

As a parent now, I can imagine how petrifying a call like this would be. But at the time, I was so unaccustomed to sharing any aspect of my personal life with my parents, I couldn't begin to anticipate their reaction. I tried to backpedal and downplay the severity of the situation as soon as I said it. "They don't want us to freak out about it or anything yet. She was in the dorm yesterday at some point, so . . ."

"Her poor parents," my mother said. "But in a storm like this, who knows? She may have snuck off to meet a secret boyfriend, probably a professor, and with no power to contact anyone . . ." This was a very odd scenario to leap to, and it also revealed how little my mom knew about Megan. The idea that she would have an affair with a professor was ludicrous. Yet it's clear where I got it from, this tendency to look for a quick explanation, however unlikely. And, at that moment, I was also willing to latch onto any theory that assumed Megan was safe and that I was not to blame.

"Exactly."

"But who would go out in weather like this? Not too bright." My mother also tended to blame people for their own misfortunes. Back in high school, a friend of mine had to be hospitalized for an allergic reaction to sesame oil after eating at our house. My mother's response? *Well, if you have that kind of deadly allergy, what are you doing eating at other people's houses?* If bad things happened, it was because of people's own carelessness. My warm feelings about my parents were fizzling out; I wanted to get off the phone.

"Are you sure I can't send your father up?" Mom said. "He'd feel a whole lot better getting you out of there."

"I'm going to stay here in case they need my help."

"That's good of you," she said.

"Yeah. But I should go now."

"Please keep us looped in," she said. "I'd prefer not to hear from a panicked mother next."

When someone knocked on my door a little later, I figured it was Bev or Nancy, but it was Adam. I was so relieved to see him.

After letting Adam in, I sat on the edge of my bed, leaving him room next to me. He took the chair at my desk. "Are you doing okay?" he asked as his gaze shifted across the room to Megan's side.

"Not really," I said.

"Everyone's lighting candles on the steps. Do you want to go?"

I didn't. I was afraid to see anyone. "Do you want to go?" I asked him.

He shrugged like, *What's the point*. We sat quietly for a minute. He rubbed his eyes, lifting his glasses. "I never knew she came back here that night."

"You were asleep."

"She didn't stay because of me, right?"

"It's not your fault."

"I feel like it is."

"It's not. Plus, it's pretty normal to go somewhere else if your room-mate has a—has a guest, or whatever."

I'd said it to make him feel better, but he looked at me funny. "So that's normal protocol for the two of you? You bring a guy over and she goes and finds another bed?"

"No," I said. Again I wanted to tell him he'd been my first, but it was long past the appropriate moment for that.

He was looking down at his feet, swivelling the chair gently from side to side. "How come you didn't tell me she was missing?" he asked.

"There was nothing to say. I thought she went back to Toronto."

"People are saying she never told you that."

"People can say whatever they feel like saying." I turned to face the ice-sealed window then, hiding my trembling chin. I couldn't bear for Adam to think I was sketchy.

"It's just all so weird," he said.

I kept my back to him. I didn't know if Adam was waiting for me to say something more. I couldn't think of anything, but I didn't want him to go.

I heard the chair roll closer to me along the carpet. "I didn't mean to make you feel worse." He moved onto the bed and put his arm around my shoulders. I crushed my face into his armpit.

I couldn't tell whether he wanted to stay or just felt as if he should, but he stretched out on the bed, and I curled into his side. He turned the lamp off.

We may have whispered a few things in the dark, but I don't remember what we said. I don't think he asked more about Megan. He didn't accuse me of anything. He stroked my back, and I fell asleep in my clothes on top of the duvet. When I woke up at six in the morning, he was gone, and the duvet was folded over my body. If he squeezed my shoulder when he left, I didn't feel it.

12

The two or three people I saw on my way to the shower the next morning avoided looking at me. The hallways were lined with Missing posters that showed the photo of Megan and her parents smiling at graduation. After my shower, I decided to hide out in my room as long as I could, but I still got dressed and made my bed. If anyone came by, I wanted to come across as responsible, not like someone who just lazed around in bed all day while her roommate was missing. I folded the laundry from a few days ago, cleared off my desk, and used Megan's cleaning spray to wipe it down.

When Bev came to my door, her hair was greasy, and her face was all blotchy. "We found her," she said quietly, stepping inside, closing the door behind her.

The pounding in my ears made it hard to hear my own voice. "Like—alive?" I asked.

"She's safe," Bev said.

I hugged Bev; she stank like sweat and coffee.

"She was at the McClanahans' farm," Bev said.

"I thought they were out of town?"

"They are. Look, I don't know, it's all a bit unclear. She's a little confused."

"Is she okay?"

Bev dipped her head from side to side. "I'm not sure—I don't have many details. There's going to be a lot of questions. Her mom's going to take her back home for a little while." Bev looked around the room. "Could you clear out for a bit? She'll need to come by to grab some things. I'm not sure she's ready to see anyone." I wondered if *anyone* specifically meant me.

"When?"

Bev looked impatient. I didn't deserve people's patience anymore. "Now would be good." She opened the door to leave and tapped the front as she walked out, poking her head back in to say, "And maybe get rid of this?"

After Bev left, I opened the door and saw that someone had written "BITCH" over my paper heart in dark-red lipstick. I ripped my name off the door and threw it away.

Sue's door was closed when I went by to tell her the news. I could hear Dave Matthews Band playing inside, definitely not Sue's pick, and I heard Courtney say, "She pretty much sucks." She could have been talking about anyone, but it didn't feel too paranoid to think that she was talking about me. The most upsetting part was how comfortable Courtney sounded saying it, like Sue's concurrence was just assumed. I didn't try to listen for Sue's response.

With nowhere else to go, I walked downtown. I figured an hour or so would be enough time for news to spread about Megan's return; after that, everything would be fine. The ground was starting to look dirty, the old snow the colour of cigarette ash. The caution tape everywhere made all of Creighton look like a crime scene. Now that I could breathe easy about Megan, the weight of all that could have happened to her was finally hitting me. I was extra vigilant on my walk, taking care to stay in the middle of the street, out of the way of laden branches and power lines. What was Megan doing at Professor McClanahan's farm when they weren't even home? It made no sense. And if it turned out that something bad happened to her there, how much of that was my fault?

I bought a coffee and doughnut at the Jumpin' Bean. A man at the counter was reading the newspaper, and I could see Megan's face in the lower corner of the front page. A sick feeling whooshed through me, and I had to get up and rush out, just like Claribel the night before.

I killed the next hour looping around my future house. Smoke rose cozily from the chimney. Was I already mourning it? It's hard to say.

When I returned to AlCo Hall, a cab was parked outside. Megan saw me before I could react in any way to seeing her. Her mother, who looked younger and prettier than she did in the photo, was holding Megan's suitcase, the one the cop had made such an issue of. I gave them a tentative wave. Megan stopped what she was doing and waited for me to approach.

I kept about a ten-foot distance from Megan and her mother. "Hey, you," I said.

Megan put her hands in the pockets of her jacket. Her eyes were looking past me; I turned to see what she was looking at, but the road behind me was empty.

Megan's mother gave me a polite smile. She put a hand on Megan's shoulder, leaned in and said something to her that I couldn't hear, and then went quickly to load Megan's suitcase into the trunk.

"We're so glad you're okay," I said cautiously.

"Who's glad?"

"Everyone," I said. "Everyone is glad."

Megan looked down at the sidewalk.

"Do you mind if I ask . . . why did you go all the way out there?"

"I needed to check on the horses," Megan said.

I had no idea how to respond to that. "How were they?"

"Fine." She briefly glanced over at her mom. "Aurora is expecting a foal. It's very stressful for her in weather like this."

"I'll bet." What else was there to say?

"I need to go," she said. Then, after a pause, "You can call me at my parents', if you want to. Bev has the number."

"Sure."

She wiped her nose with the back of her hand before turning back to the cab.

"I'll see you soon!" I said.

I didn't try to hug her; it didn't feel allowed.

I thought that since Megan was found safe, everything would go back to normal. But that's not what happened.

In a conversation with Bev several minutes after returning to the dorm, she told me two things. First, that Megan's family and the school administration had decided that we should be vague about where Megan had gone—*a friend's place off campus* was what we were supposed to say, rather than naming McClanahan's farm. I guess they didn't want anyone to jump to the conclusion my mother had. But I don't know what world Bev thought we were living in that *friend's place* was going to cut it in a dorm full of scared, nosy girls. Second, Bev said the administration was very concerned about inconsistencies between my story and Megan's account of what occurred in the last few days.

"She went to check on the horses," I said. "How could I possibly have known that?"

"It doesn't matter *where* she went. You didn't tell us she was gone."

"*She* isn't mad at me," I said. "She told me to call her later."

"There's something going on." Bev pointed to her head. "She's not okay."

"Right. That's not my fault."

"There's more to the story."

"One of the horses is pregnant, I guess?"

"Ros, she walked all the way there. That's hours in terrible weather and total darkness."

I thought of Megan's piano recital shoes on the ice. "No one made her."

Bev shook her head. "You knew better. You need to take responsibility." She was furious at me, I could see it in her face. I figured she was worried about losing her job over this. But I didn't really care what Bev thought. Bev was a loser. Megan was safe, and eventually, this would all be behind us. I was exhausted, so I walked away from her and slept for the rest of the afternoon.

It was another day before I approached Sue. I think I was hoping she would come to me, maybe even apologize, but she didn't. Then on Monday morning, my contact at our future house called me back. She said the landlord was coming that afternoon to check out the storm damage, and it was a good time to meet her if we wanted to settle things up for the following year. I messaged Sue on ICQ about getting together at two thirty to walk over. I didn't hear back, so I knocked on her door at two fifteen.

Sue said to come in. She was sitting at her computer, still in her pyjamas, which were hospital pants and a ribbed white tank top. She looked up at me vaguely, then back at her computer.

"Did you get my message?" I sat on her bed while she continued typing. She chuckled at something on the monitor. "About the house?"

Sue kept grinning at her computer.

"What's funny?" I said after a long moment of just sitting there, talking to myself.

"Pardon?" Sue said.

"We should probably get going. I told them three." Sue didn't say anything. "Or whatever," I said, trying to hide the hurt from my voice. "If you're busy, I can call and ask about going another time."

"Yeah," Sue said.

I nodded, waited a moment in an effort to be casual, then said, "So when do you think?"

Sue stopped typing. She touched her fingers to her temples, then swivelled her chair to face me. "Actually," she said, "I'm going to pass."

"What do you mean?" But I knew.

She let out a breath. "I don't want to live with you."

I wasn't sure what to say. I felt stupid sitting at the edge of her bed, bundled up in my jacket and scarf with no place to go. I suddenly got very overheated. "Are you going to live with Dutch?" I asked.

"I don't know."

"Were you going to tell me?" I bit my lower lip in an attempt to redirect the pain in my chest.

"I am telling you."

"It's just that I thought we had a plan."

"It was an idea. It wasn't a plan." She looked back at the screen and responded to someone on ICQ. "I need roommates who are more . . . consistent."

"What do you mean?"

"Ros, you know what consistent means." Sue flipped her hair to one side. "Or maybe you don't. You're not who I thought you were."

This pronouncement knocked the wind out of me.

"I need to live with people who think about other people once in a while," Sue said.

Didn't Sue know that all I did was think constantly about other people—think about her, mainly?

"I need a housemate who'll look out for me," she continued.

The idea that Sue thought of herself as someone who needed looking out for didn't feel real. But I understood what she was saying. It was over. I knew I was supposed to leave her room, but part of me hoped that if I stayed there long enough, if I stayed near her, we could somehow find our way back. Back to a few days ago, to hanging out under blankets. "I'm sorry," I said.

Sue shook her head. "That's just a selfish apology. You don't care about Megan. Or the rest of us. You're . . . I'm not sure you're a good person."

It was too much. I started crying then, I had nothing to lose. "What am *I* supposed to do?" The real question was, who would I hang out with? I only had Dutch and Sue; currently, Sue hated me, and even though Dutch was my friend first, he belonged to Sue now.

Sue pushed at her lip ring with her tongue. "I don't feel sorry for you, Ros," she said.

"Are you going to live with Courtney?"

"Oh my God, Ros. What I do is none of your business."

Later that night, I heard "Freshmen" playing in Sue's room, the song we scream-sang in the cab. I pictured Sue and Courtney inside, refusing to feel sorry for me. Or more likely not thinking about me at all.

13

Power was restored on most of the campus the next day, and the boys moved out of our dorm. I only saw Adam one more time, and it was the following weekend. There was a parade to celebrate the end of the storm, to recognize everyone's resilience and their efforts to clean up in its wake. I certainly wasn't seeking the parade out, but I bumped into it on my way to buy shampoo in town. Megan had left her Outrageous behind, but the smell had started to make me feel sick. A crowd was gathered outside the Civic Centre, listening to the mayor give a speech from the steps. Behind him, an ice-glazed portico blinked in the late afternoon sun. The Regis marching band was there, red cheeked and wearing their tartans. The mayor's voice was hoarse, and his words came out in white bursts. "We've sustained real damage here in Creighton," he said. He held up a finger. "But we've also experienced something incredible. Because in our time of difficulty, we stepped up, we banded together. We looked out for our friends and neighbours, and we kept each other safe. You make me proud to live here."

I kept my head down as I worked my way around the throng, but when the band started, I looked up reflexively. I noticed Claribel first, standing at the front of the brass section. Next to her was Adam, holding a trumpet. I had no idea that he was in the band, no idea he was musical. No idea why he was studying business when he didn't even seem to like it. I knew so little about the first person I had ever slept with.

Adam acknowledged me with a flat-line smile before immediately looking down at his instrument. It was the kind of look I might give an unstable-looking stranger on the street after accidental eye contact: *I see your struggle, but I don't know you, and I won't help.* I didn't fault him for that.

I thought things might get better when Megan returned to school, but she never came back, and that made things worse. People kept their distance from me, and I did them a favour by keeping mine. I timed my meals to avoid Dutch and Sue, and when I did run into them once at dinner, they got up from their usual table and moved to the seduction section.

At the end of January, Bev told us that Megan was withdrawing for the semester. People were saying that she had a mental breakdown. Who but a mentally ill person goes to check on horses in the middle of the night? The truth about where she'd been leaked somehow, but not because of me. How could it be me? No one spoke to me. You'd think that since Megan's mental health was cited as the reason for her disappearance, I'd be let off the hook, but the way people talked about it, it was like I'd caused the breakdown: I'd callously kicked her out into the street in the middle of a storm. Looking back, I think that people were afraid. It scared them that someone as bright and chipper as Megan could just lose her mind like that, and they needed someone to blame for what happened. And I wasn't entirely blameless.

On the last Friday in January, after enough dust had settled, a new issue of the *Ragged Regis* came out. The back page had a comic drawing of Bill Clinton on the prow of the *Titanic*, pants down. "Question of the Day: Did more women go down on the *Titanic* or on President Clinton?" The news about the Clinton-Lewinsky scandal had just broken; the two became the butt of all jokes practically overnight.

The front page of the *Ragged Regis* that week, however, had something else. The headline was "Couple Crowned Frost Queen & King" and featured a quarter-page picture of Adam and me leaning into each other at the Old Vic. My face looked shiny with sweat, even in black and white. My posture was terrible, hunched. I looked so much worse than I thought I had that night.

The piece ran without a byline, but of course, I knew who wrote it:

Thank you for your nominations for the worst frosh on campus. We're delighted to name this year's Frost King & Queen.

And this couple is COLD as ice.

How did they find each other?

King & Queen were first spotted together in the AlCo Hall laundry room during the ice storm. Witnesses report that Queen was offering free blow jobs (yes, before Monica made it trendy!), so we guess that's what broke the ice. But the laundry room wasn't quite private enough.

And here's where the tale gets chilling . . .

Early in the morning of January 9, the Queen locked her roommate out, making her fend for herself in the worst storm in Creighton's history. Queen was having such a rollicking time at the tip of her King's iceberg, she didn't tell anyone when her roommate NEVER returned!

A natural partner in crime, King has been making frosh disappear since December. Curious what happened to that nice kid in Herbert 211? Ask the King. (He refused to comment.)

And while you're at it, ask him if Queen fakes her orgasms as convincingly as she fakes her ethics*!

*Sorry, King, she lied about being vegan to get <u>your meat</u> in her mouth.

It wasn't a big school, and even if you didn't read the story, you heard about it. I didn't think it was possible for people to stare and whisper more than they already had been, but they showed me. Still, it was Adam I felt the worst for; he hadn't done anything wrong.

Eventually, I stopped going to class, didn't go to the cafeteria, and only left my room at odd hours to buy meals from Subway off-campus. In the first week of February, I got a letter from the Residence Disciplinary Committee of the University Senate. The letter was a summons for a hearing in two weeks concerning my status as "a resident of Alice Cole Hall in good standing." The letter referred to a possible breach in residence community standards, endangering the safety and security of fellow residents. The letter also listed six Oops Report infractions.

I showed up to the hearing in a white blouse and black slacks; I thought I'd appear serious and responsible, but I looked more like a stressed-out waiter. The committee was not just university faculty, as I had expected, but also included a handful of smug students. It was the first time I heard the actual details of where Megan had gone, what she had done that night. Because I never did call her; I had no idea what to say to her. And I was intimidated by the possibility of her mental breakdown. I had no experience with that.

In the hearing, a student read out a report from the police: Megan had walked nine kilometres from Alice Cole Hall to the farm. She had let herself into the house at some point, but it was in the stables, sleeping next to the horses, that Professor McClanahan's son found her on Sunday morning.

As my defence, I simply continued to insist that Megan had told me she was going to Toronto, and that communicating this to Bev had been Megan's responsibility. Only fifty minutes later, the committee presented a recommendation: a six-week residence suspension beginning at the end of the reading break, just a week away, until the end of the semester. I was welcome—and expected—to file an appeal. Nancy Calandra told me my chances of having the sanction reduced were very good, especially given that my father was a major donor, but I did not want to involve him. I did not appeal.

I also didn't look for somewhere else to live. I was unwanted at Regis, and I didn't want to be there. The night before the break, the last day I could withdraw without academic penalty, I dropped all my classes. I packed two duffle bags of clothes and left everything else behind. I bought a train ticket and decided that I would come up with a story to tell my parents on the ride home. Val was a college dropout, and I'd seen how upset and annoyed it made my dad. At some point in my teens, Dad said that, compared to Val, I was "sensible as hell." I liked him thinking that about me, even if he was just taking note of a dissimilarity to Val. I didn't want to disappoint him, destroy his dreams for me at Regis—it was the only thing we had. And I had no idea what to say to my mom, who I hadn't spoken with since the day Megan was found. In all likelihood, she was going to assume I was quitting because I'd had an affair with a professor as well. Would that be better?

I slept through the three-hour journey and had to be woken by my seatmate when we reached Union Station in Toronto.

14

This is not the complete picture. Memory is slippery, and I've tried to be careful, but there are surely details lost to time, and some that I never grasped in the first place—I was too self-focused, self-conscious, self-absorbed.

Recalling this time, it's been hardest to know what to do about Dutch. Have I hidden things, have I overcorrected?

I could tell Ms. Ng that I hated him when I left, and that would be true. But that was mainly because of the article. It is also true that I would have done anything to be his friend again—his and Sue's—even though they had hurt me.

But there is one more detail that feels relevant now. I saw Dutch leaving Sue's room the morning I moved out. I was carrying the two duffle bags, and he said, "Let me take one, at least let me do that." *At least*.

Dutch shouldered the bag and carried it down to the cab that would take me to the train station. I don't remember what we said to one another once the bags were in the trunk, maybe nothing other than, *Thanks, see you.* We hardly made eye contact, which I would have said was due to my own discomfort. I would have said that because I knew nothing about the discomfort Dutch was feeling at the time. That was long before Dutch would start to go by his real name, Lukas. It was nine years before I ran into him again at a Starbucks in Orange County, California. Before we began a relationship, before we had a child together. Before he was famous.

But it was not before he was—at least by one account—a sex offender. According to Main v. Van Kampen, an action filed in the Ontario Superior Court on March 3, 2020, he became a sex offender at about 2:30 a.m. on the morning of January 9, 1998.

PART TWO

Summer 2020

1

In the photo on TV, Megan looks like her old self, but possibly not so much her old self that I would recognize her on the street. She has lines on her cheeks, lines on her forehead, loose skin along her jawline. I'm pretty sure that, objectively, she looks more haggard than I do. Cute wouldn't be the word for her anymore, though she has a certain pluck.

Mom turns to me. "What's with the pink hair?"

"For the kids. To be accessible, I guess?"

"I thought you said she didn't have kids?"

"She works with them. Can you please be quiet?"

This summer, the world is slowly reopening, and apparently, this means the reopening of Megan's story, too. Megan's lawsuit against Lukas, filed in Toronto in early March, was quickly eclipsed by COVID. I thought maybe he got lucky—Lukas is often lucky, despite how it looks now. But then Dr. Bella Andersen ("Bella"), "Canadian women's favourite morning show host," announced her program's return after a four-month pandemic hiatus. No live audience, guests on video, but all the "up-close examination" her viewers have come to expect. Megan Main is the first guest in her reopening week lineup.

This morning, Bella is testing our patience. She kicked off with a segment on how to make reusable face masks from old T-shirts, followed by an interminable video tribute to health care workers to the tune of Natalie Merchant's "Kind & Generous." (I noted at least a half-dozen pictures of Bella herself in the mix.)

When the camera finally returned to Bella in her studio, she said, "Over the last few months, I've had the privilege to connect with *so* many wonderful women doing brave and important things across the country. Throughout the summer, I'll be bringing you their stories. Even when"—she paused—"*especially* when they deal with hardship."

And finally, the picture of Megan. Now a statistic slowly types itself under her chin: "30% of women age 15 or older report experiencing sexual assault."

Bella says, "The impacts of sexual assault are lasting. And devastating. The good news is that open conversation can help. Stay with us for more after the break."

A colourful photo collage of Bella spins past as the show transitions to commercials: the doctor crouching to speak with an old woman in a wheelchair; the doctor as activist in a hard hat, helping a team of folks lift a wooden housing frame; the doctor as down-to-earth animal-lover, chucking a frisbee to a three-legged dog.

"What kind of doctor is she again?" I ask, as a Febreze commercial begins.

"Women's?" Mom says, like it's not a real thing.

To avoid more conversation, I respond to a text message from Ginny, who is down at the dock watching the kids. *Nothing much yet*, I type. She sends back a bulging bicep. Mom also looks at her phone, holding it an inch from her face.

I get up to peer out the window. Benji, my eleven-year-old, and Ginny's daughter, Alex, are jumping off the dock onto a giant inflatable poop emoji, one of Benji's birthday gifts from last month. I hadn't expected to still be at the cottage in June, and now July; when we arrived from Orange County at the end of March, the ice on the lake was just beginning to break up.

Benji and I didn't come here because of what was going on with Lukas, we came because Mom was hit by a car while jaywalking and broke her leg. All my life, Mom has crossed busy streets with impunity. She is not particularly fast and does it with a kind of terrifying arrogance: the cars *will* stop. When the accident happened in the very same week that the lawsuit against Lukas was announced, it felt as though every part of my life were coming home to roost.

I was too overwhelmed to fly to Toronto right away after the accident. Instead, I arranged a six-week stay for Mom in an exorbitant convalescent facility near her condo in Forest Hill. For her own safety, she was released ten days later after a COVID case popped up among the nursing staff. I flew to Toronto with Benji and then made the decision to stay during lockdown when schools—including mine and Benji's—went online. We came out here to the cottage to avoid the stairs in Mom's condo, and I found a local physiotherapist to help with her rehab. None of it was ideal, but I thought it was a good temporary arrangement. It was good for Benji to be out in nature during a pandemic, away from our SoCal neighbourhood's disconcerting number of overprivileged, science-distrusting parents. Good for Benji to spend time with his grandmother, who was just short of an alien figure to him. Good for me to demonstrate the importance of looking out for an aging parent, since I, too, will one day be old. Good for us both to have some separation from what is going on with Lukas.

What I didn't properly account for was how much my mother would drive me nuts.

A cheerful splatter of music pulls our attention back to the TV, but then a warning appears that the content and language in the segment to follow may be disturbing to some viewers. Bella says a few words, and then a clip from Megan's press conference in early March begins to play. I watched the whole conference in real time: the cramped meeting room, the clambering reporters and photographers. And here it is again. Megan is in front of a bouquet of microphones, and her lawyer, Elaine Ng, the one who contacted me a few weeks back, is at her side.

A reporter asks Megan, "Why now?" Megan leans into the microphone, face flushed. "This has been a difficult decision," she says. "But women all over are being courageous in the face of adversity, and I need to be courageous, too."

Another reporter jumps in. "Lukas Van Kampen is considered a national treasure. Children look up to him. What do you think the impact of your allegations will be on his career?"

Megan rubs her arms up and down like she's cold. "We can't protect a predator just to protect someone else's ideas about them," she says. She looks at Elaine, who gives her a nod of encouragement. When she starts again, her jaw wobbles. "I'm not doing this to destroy his future. But you know what? *I* was destroyed." She taps her chest. "Without any consideration for my future."

Bella is now back on the screen, and she faces the audience. Her skin sags at the cheeks, and she has a large nose. She doesn't look like a celebrity, which is perhaps her appeal. "In March, Megan Main filed a lawsuit against acclaimed author Lukas Van Kampen, who is best known for the Billi Bean book series for young adults. Main is accusing Van Kampen of a sexual assault that took place at Regis University just over twenty years ago. I want to note that Lukas Van Kampen has not been convicted in court, but Miss Main's allegations are fuelling very important, often difficult conversations across the country."

Megan's face, now live on video, appears next to Bella's on a split-screen. Bella turns, as though facing Megan, and welcomes her to the show. Megan smiles. "Thank you so much for having me."

"Megan, I'd love to share a little bit about you with our audience," Bella says.

Bella begins by discussing Megan's current work as the executive director of RideOn, a horseback riding nonprofit aimed at underserved teen girls. The screen shows a series of shots of adolescent girls on a farm in Vaughan, just north of Toronto. Girls carrying saddles, pushing wheelbarrows, crouching determinedly on horseback. Then there's a photo of Megan dressed in jodhpurs and a half-tucked white blouse, posed against the side of a red barn and laughing heartily at something off-camera.

"RideOn is your passion project, and you've been at it for how many years now?" Bella asks.

"We just celebrated our fifteenth season," Megan says.

"Can you tell us a little bit about what RideOn offers teens?"

"We're giving girls from all kinds of backgrounds a chance to ride and care for horses in a fun and empowering environment," Megan says, as if she's reading from a script. "It's really just a lot of fun."

It feels disingenuous to me when people refer to their work as "a lot of fun." I've heard Lukas say it in countless interviews, but most of the time, his work just seems to make him agitated and depressed. I imagine that Megan's job is probably extremely stressful—a constant battle for funds, underpaid staff, teens with behaviour problems, volunteers who don't show up.

Bella lets her smile fade into a line. "Did you always want to work with animals, Megan?"

"I did," Megan says. "One of my uncles bred horses in New Brunswick, and I wanted to be a veterinarian for as long as I can remember."

"But you never finished your degree," Bella says darkly.

Megan shakes her head. "No, I never did."

"Can you tell us what happened?"

"In my first year of university, I was sexually assaulted."

Mom sucks in a breath. "She's not wasting any time."

"Shh," I tell her.

"That was twenty years ago," Bella says. She squints with thoughtfulness. Watch out, I think, or your face will stay that way. "What made now the right moment to speak up?"

Megan twists her earring. "In the work I do, I tell young women to stand up for themselves. I preach all this bravery, but I haven't been brave. The MeToo movement has helped make it easier to discuss sexual violence, but it's still very hard to step forward as a victim. I want young women to know that I understand what they're going through. And I'm in a position to be a role model, not just for speaking up but also for—"

"Helping to overcome?" Bella suggests.

Megan shakes her head. "No, no—I don't think that's right. I don't think we ever *overcome*. We may hope for that, but I'm not sure that's even healthy, you know, as a goal. It's more a matter of learning how to live with this trauma as part of your story." She nods at her own point. "Being assaulted didn't kill me, I didn't die that night, but some of me did. Part of me was erased. I tried to put that behind me for years, but at some point, I started to feel very bitter about the fact that I never got to have the life I was supposed to have. School was ruined for me. Relationships were ruined for me. Sometimes I'd wake up in the middle of the night, totally terrified, not even sure of who I was. I was depressed for a long, long time."

A photo of Lukas on stage at the Robur Awards this past January pops up on the screen. The Robur Award for Young Adult Fiction was Lukas's third major literary prize in five years. I was in the audience with Benji. In the photo, Lukas is dabbing sweat from his forehead with a Kleenex. He looks stressed out, guilty, gross.

"I think I would speak up whether Lukas Van Kampen were famous or not," Megan says. "But does it make a difference that he's famous? Probably. He shouldn't get to hide behind that."

"Absolutely," Bella says. "We are seeing this too much—this misuse of power."

"For fuck's sake, he wasn't famous back at Regis," I say to the TV. But Megan doesn't address this conflating of narratives.

"You say relationships were ruined for you?" Bella probes.

Megan looks away. "I was in my midthirties before I really felt comfortable being intimate with someone again."

I feel an ache in my sternum.

"Were you afraid?"

Megan considers the question. "In part, yes. But there was another part of me that thought I just didn't deserve a happy relationship. That someone could treat me like such garbage that night . . . it impacted how I saw myself."

"At the press conference, I heard you say it was the night that defined all of your life decisions afterward," says Bella. "Can you tell us what happened?"

Megan takes a sip of water. "I was in my first year of university. I had just turned nineteen, and I went out to a bar with friends one night to celebrate. I didn't have a lot of experience drinking, and I drank too much because that's what everyone did, that's what it seemed like I was supposed to do. Regis was like that. Kids would clink glasses and say, *Here's to what I won't remember!*"

That is not something I ever remember saying.

"Lukas Van Kampen was one of the people I was out with," Megan continues. "I didn't really know him, but I guess we were flirting a little. It was interesting because that sort of thing, being hit on, that didn't happen to me a lot. I guess I found it exciting because he was handsome. But I had a boyfriend back home, so I wasn't . . . I was having fun talking to him, that's really all it was."

"And there's no shame in that, not at all," Bella jumps in. "Dancing, flirting, drinking alcohol, these things are never, never ever, an invitation to assault."

"No, that's right," Megan says. "But I drank too much that night, and that made me lose my grip on things. Drinking does make us more vulnerable. I'd tell any young woman that. And that night, I got drunk." She hesitates for several uncomfortable seconds. "And these people, these friends, they took me home and put me to bed in a room that wasn't mine. I fell asleep, but when I woke up a little later, Lukas was getting into bed with me. He said there was nowhere to sleep, so I didn't stop him." Her avoidance of context irritates me: It was *the ice storm*. There really weren't any places to sleep, and that bed—Courtney's bed—had been assigned to Lukas. "I passed out again," Megan says, "but I woke up to the feeling of his body rubbing up against me." She takes in a sharp breath. "He was saying stuff like, *You like this, right?* And he was touching me and"—her voice quakes—"it was confusing. My pants were off, but I wasn't sure when that happened. Did I take them off? Did he?" She exhales and looks back at the camera. "I froze. I didn't know what to do. He just kept rubbing up against me."

"I'm so sorry, Megan," Bella says. "We can feel so powerless in that kind of a situation."

"Is that all he did?" Mom asks. I don't respond, I don't know the answer. This is the first time any of us have heard details. If Lukas knew them, he has consistently pretended otherwise.

"When he was done," Megan says, "I got up and got out of there as fast as I could. I remember feeling that there was nowhere to go that was safe. So I walked nine or ten kilometres through an ice storm that night to the one place I knew I would be okay."

"And where was that?"

"A farm. Somewhere I worked part-time. The family was away, but I slept in the stables with the horses."

"You could have died," Bella says. "How long were you out in the cold?"

"Well, at some point, it occurred to me to go inside the farmhouse. I knew how to get in. There was no power because of the storm, but I found blankets to keep warm."

"And you were missing for over forty-eight hours." Megan's Missing poster, the one that was up everywhere on campus, comes on the screen. "How were you found?"

"My employer's son found me," Megan says. "He'd come to check on the horses. Obviously, he could tell something was seriously wrong with me. He called the police."

"And when the police asked you what happened?"

"I just told them I wanted to see the horses." Her voice on the sidewalk that afternoon comes back to me: *Aurora is expecting a foal.*

"So you never made a formal complaint?"

"No."

"Did you ever tell *anyone*?"

"I told exactly one person. My boyfriend back in New Brunswick. He was someone I thought I trusted. But after the way he reacted, I never told another soul."

"How did he react?"

"He called me a slut," Megan says, straightening.

"Oh, Megan."

Megan waves this away. "I'm not making excuses for him, but he was young, he was upset. I think he thought I was making up a story because I felt guilty for fooling around."

I thought of Kyle's cheesy smile in the photo on Megan's dresser. How I said they fucked like rabbits.

"I thought it was my fault, too," Megan says. "I shouldn't have had so much to drink, I shouldn't have gone to sleep in a stranger's bed."

"Women who have been assaulted so often blame themselves," Bella says. "On this show, we know we shouldn't 'should' ourselves, but it's not always that simple."

Megan laughs uneasily and takes another sip of water.

"What did your parents make of what was going on?"

"I think they just thought I'd cracked under the pressure of school and being so far away from home. I think it was easy for them to just think it was too much."

"And you let them think that," Bella confirms.

"I didn't want to frighten them. I wanted us to have our regular lives back." She pauses for a beat. "And you know, I thought that I *had* cracked. I mean, Lukas even sent me a letter after I got home, asking if I was doing okay. It made me second-guess everything."

This is news to me. He sent her a letter? Why and when exactly did he send her a letter?

"What did the letter say?"

Megan sighs. "Not much, really. It was short, just a 'get well soon' kind of thing. But, you know, it was confusing. Sending a note is kind, right? I thought, Did I misunderstand something?"

Bella nods and, after a respectful pause, moves on. "Why is this not a criminal case?" she asks. "Why aren't you seeking criminal charges?"

"Can she even?" Mom says. "For a thing like that?" I give her a please-shut-up look, though I am wondering the same thing. Can you give someone a criminal record for grinding against you? Make them register as a sex offender?

"I've learned a lot about our criminal justice system," Megan says, "and it is very hard on victims because you have to convince a jury that your side of the story is true, beyond a reasonable doubt. And this happened to me more than twenty years ago, and that alone creates reasonable doubt. But what happened to me, happened to me. I hope a judge will see how it's impacted my life."

Bella leans back. "I'm a doctor, not a lawyer, but what Megan is describing is the difference in the level of proof required for criminal and civil cases. In a civil suit, which is what Megan is pursuing, she needs to prove that it was more likely than not—in other words more than fifty percent likely—that she was assaulted in the manner she claims. She may be awarded damages, which is financial compensation from the accused, but Lukas Van Kampen will not face jail time."

"Money is not what I'm after," Megan clarifies for the audience. "What I care about is that Lukas Van Kampen be held accountable."

"Now I should say that Mr. Van Kampen is denying these allegations," Bella says. "And Megan, I know this may be difficult to discuss, but this morning there have been viewer comments online questioning your story."

"Calling me a liar," Megan says.

A series of tweets scroll up the screen:

$$$

THAT'S NOT RAPE.

She should have came out 20 yrs ago if this really happened.

And this is why these places should not allow ladies and men living together.

Megan sighs. "I expected this. People will say all sorts of things when they don't understand something. This is why women don't feel they can speak up. Who wants to be called a liar on top of everything else? But what I want to do is thank everyone who *is* supporting me. They are the ones who need to be acknowledged. Women *can* come forward when they have support."

Bella nods enthusiastically. "Well said."

As Bella thanks Megan again for joining the show, I contemplate, as I have a few times since March, how it would feel for me to learn all this if Lukas weren't involved. I would feel sorry for Megan, but would I mostly feel relieved? Absolved? Megan was clearly saying that *I* was not responsible for her breakdown. Some guy was.

Would it be as straightforward for me to see what I see now? That I betrayed Megan twice that night—at the bar, at the dorm—with far worse consequences than I ever imagined? It's hard not to wonder what Megan thought when she discovered that Lukas and I were—had been—a couple. Was it salt in the wound? Did she pity me? Did I disgust her? Did she think we deserved each other?

Bella lists a number of resources for victims of sexual violence before introducing her next guest, a social worker who would walk the audience through the steps involved in reporting a sexual assault.

Mom turns to me. "Why this next lady? Do you think they're expecting more women to come forward?"

I hand Mom the remote control. "I have no idea. I'm going for a swim."

2

The circumstances weren't ideal for answering a call, especially a life-altering call.

I was in the parking lot of Whole Foods, loading groceries into the trunk, when I felt my phone vibrating. I assumed it was my dean calling about an email he'd sent that morning about a student complaint—*What does it mean for a student to call you a "Karen"?* I was pretty sure that I knew the student in question and that she was pissed at me because I wouldn't let her submit her essay by text message. I'd been fuming all morning because I didn't think I was old enough to be called a *Karen*, and as much as my students could get on my nerves, I thought of myself as patient and generous. But indignant as I was, my fear and paranoia were stronger. Eventually, inevitably, people turn against me. I know how quickly it starts. I know how fast it spreads. *Karen* would be a difficult label to shed.

But the voice on the phone was young, female. "Good morning! Am I speaking with Rosalind Fisher?"

"Yes, this is Rosalind."

"This is Stephanie Seyburn from *Punchline*," the voice said. I searched my brain for the name, came up with nothing. "I'm wondering if you'd like to make a comment about the situation concerning your husband and Miss Maine?"

I held the phone in between my shoulder and chin, closed the trunk. "I'm sorry, what is this regarding?"

"Do you have any comment to make about Miss Maine's allegations against your husband?"

I genuinely didn't know who Miss Maine was, but from the word *allegations*, I had a good idea of the territory we were in. I did not clarify for Ms. Seyburn that Lukas had never been my husband, nor did I add that we'd been living apart for two years. "I'm going to hang up the phone," I said, and then I did.

I can't say I was shocked to receive that type of phone call. It wasn't that I was necessarily waiting for it, I hadn't prepped myself in any particular way, but ever since the MeToo movement caught fire, my stomach pulsed with awareness of how exposed Lukas was. He was a bestselling author, a writer for young adults, which somewhat intensified the pressure to be morally pure. And yet, by his own admission, Lukas had slept with over a hundred women in the last decade, the vast majority while we were together. It seemed reasonable that one of these paramours might have a thing or two to say about how he treats women. Managing multiple affairs, even among consenting adults, is messy, and someone is bound to be offended at some point.

While the call shook me on some level, I was still calm enough to get home without crashing the car. Not that I didn't feel sick, I did. But I got the frozen fish sticks and waffles in the freezer before doing anything else. And while I was doing that, I was imagining telling Julianne, my therapist, about the call. She'd say, *Oh my, it sounds like you really have it together, considering!* And I'd say, *Yeah, well, Lukas can't surprise me at this point*, all the while wondering if I was her best client. As in, her easiest, most unflappable client.

I texted Lukas: *A reporter just called me?*

As I waited for a reply, I Googled "Van Kampen + #MeToo." I tried "Van Kampen + Sex" and got a book review from the *New York Times*:

> *We've become so preoccupied with "correctness" in young adult literature that we risk not discussing sex at all. Van Kampen takes the plunge and is frank on sex and sexuality. The Billi Bean book discusses sexual relationships with the emotional shorthand that kids understand.*

What was emotional shorthand?

Lukas had gone to Bangor on his book tour a couple of years earlier, so I got it in my head that Miss Maine must be the Miss America contestant for the state of Maine, and they met somehow during his trip. I figured he'd had sex with a twentysomething beauty queen while touring his "frank on sex" book—which, from that moment on, I began to think of as his "Frankensex" book—and that she'd publicly called him out on it. I Google-imaged the last ten years of Miss Maines. The majority still looked under thirty. Had the Miss Maine in question been an erstwhile Billi Bean reader? That was a shuddering thought.

On the *Punchline* website, I found a picture of Stephanie Seyburn, who looked young enough to be a Miss Maine. Her lipstick was too purplish for her pale skin and thin lips, giving her the look of a child with a grape-juice-stained mouth. Her latest piece was about a Danish DJ accused of groping a woman at a music festival two years ago. MeToo was her beat.

"Miss Maine?" I said to Lukas when he finally returned my call. "Can you tell me exactly which Miss Maine, because there are a surprising number of them."

He was quiet.

"Tell me."

"It's Megan, Ros. Remember? Megan Main?"

I hadn't heard the name said out loud in over a decade. But when had he seen Megan Main? Did he graze her ass while posing for a photo at some book event, her kid grinning in the foreground?

"When did you see Megan Main?" I asked.

"Did you say anything to the reporter?"

"No."

"Don't," he said. "If anyone else calls, don't talk."

"Can you answer my question?"

"I haven't seen her in twenty years," Lukas said. "More than that."

My next thought was that this was about me. Maybe an unstable Megan Main had told the press the ice storm story—about my betrayal and her subsequent breakdown—and now Lukas was being slammed for his connection to me. "What is she saying?"

"She is filing a lawsuit against me."

"You? Why?"

"It's a bullshit story."

"But what?"

"She's saying I sexually assaulted her. Basically."

"What do you mean *basically*?"

I am constantly telling my students to avoid the word *basically* in their essays. A sentence like "Pablo Picasso basically founded cubism" leaves the reader unsure of the fact while also making them feel like they've been judged too dumb for the details. Thinking about my students, it occurred to me that no matter the outcome of this lawsuit,

Lukas's name would be tainted and so, by association, would mine. That would, *basically,* seal my reputation as the campus Karen.

"Back in first year, apparently," Lukas said after a moment. "It's not true."

"But why would Megan make something up about you?"

"Again, Ros, I don't know. Didn't she have some sort of mental breakdown or something?"

"When were you going to tell me?"

"I just found out myself yesterday. I'll shoot you the media bit."

My phone chimed. I clicked the link and read it quickly:

Media Advisory: Sexual Assault Lawsuit Filed
Against Lukas Van Kampen, Author.
TORONTO, Ontario. March 3, 2020.

Today a lawsuit has been commenced against young adult author Lukas Maarten Van Kampen. The plaintiff claims that she was sexually assaulted by Van Kampen in January 1998, when they were both students at Regis University in Creighton, Ontario.

"This courageous lawsuit is a pivotal action in holding Mr. Van Kampen accountable for a terrible wrong that has had devastating consequences in the course of my client's life," said Elaine Ng of Burton Jafari LLP, counsel to the plaintiff.

The plaintiff will be holding a press conference on March 4, 2020, to discuss her claims. The press conference will take place at the offices of Burton Jafari LLP. See location details.

"This isn't a lot of info," I said.

"It's a load of crap."

"You had no idea?"

He breathed out slowly. "Rosie," he said calmly. "I'll take care of it."

———

I spent most of the afternoon digging. There wasn't much to find yet, but I did track down Megan on Twitter. I found two interesting tweets. In January, alongside a link to a photography exhibition on climate change at the Art Gallery of Ontario, she tweeted: *Bracing work by @ sueverma.* To this, @sueverma replied: *Thx. Memory lane, huh!* Megan tweeted back: *@sueverma Bad memories, solid art.* Just a couple of hours later, Megan tweeted the link to the Robur Award: *@roburaward Your prize is a joke!!!* But none of these tweets mentioned Lukas directly.

As I have also done several times over the years, I Googled Supriya Verma. Like Lukas, and pretty much no one else I know, Sue has been successful in the arts. Her photography was included in the Venice Biennale a few years ago, and she's shot covers for *National Geographic.* Sue's website listed a handful of past events, including a group show on climate change in the fall of 2019 at the Art Gallery of Ontario, featuring her "early work." I suppose she is famous enough now for people to care about early work.

I found a review of the show in the *Globe and Mail* with prints of Sue's ice storm–era photos. The first showed a girl kneeling on frozen ground, her mouth wrapped around the tip of an enormous icicle that hung from the Herbert Hall dormitory sign. The second photo was a silhouette of a man standing in front of the window in Sue's dorm room. You could tell he was half-nude, just a white towel around his waist. I recognized Lukas, but only barely: the curve of his butt in the towel, the length of his hair. Raindrops beaded the windowpane, and beyond the glass, you could make out the faint shape of a power line, slack as a summer hammock.

Had Lukas known he was in Sue's show? He never said anything about it. It occurred to me that if Sue and Lukas hadn't achieved such public visibility since Regis, Megan's story might never have emerged.

———

A few days after the press conference, Lukas's publisher shared that they were rethinking the spring book tour for Billi Bean book six, but it was the pandemic that ultimately forced the decision to cancel. The outbreak of COVID pulled attention away from the allegations, but it didn't neutralize the story completely. There was a bad week on Twitter when people started calling for Lukas to be cancelled. A former student tweeted: *LVK is a woman-hating monster. Don't try to defend him.* Benji's former babysitter tweeted: *RIP Billi Bean. U used to be my safe place.*

Not everyone turned against him, though. His fan base was huge and mostly loyal. For some parents, Lukas's books were the only ones they could get their kids to read, and they weren't prepared to cast him out just yet. And Lukas's publisher was waffling, saying they would do their own thorough investigation. I've never understood what that means.

Lukas came out with a statement, widely shared:

These allegations are very painful for me and my family. But I believe in taking all allegations seriously, and I will not stand in the way of any process that will follow. I welcome the overdue cultural shift that is making it easier for women to speak out against their abusers. I want to say clearly that I did not abuse Megan Main. That is not who I am. I wish her, and all women who have faced abuse, hope and healing in their journey toward recovery.

When I said that I expected Lukas to eventually be brought into the MeToo line of fire, I was not expecting this. I thought he might get called out as a pig, something of a womanizer. I didn't expect assault. But after years of no one accusing him of anything, I started to believe that maybe his philandering had only ever hurt me.

3

"Going for a swim" is the only reliable way to escape my mother at the cottage. She is moving around fairly well now, but she hasn't yet attempted the steep wooden stairs down to the dock.

My parents designed this cottage together in the early '80s, their only ever joint architectural project. The structure was inspired by a modern cliffside home they saw on their honeymoon in Laguna Beach, coincidentally enough, not far from where I live now. It's a box of concrete and glass, perched atop a steep chunk of bedrock that overlooks Kendrew Lake. Inside, wood flooring and panelled walls warm up the austere modernity of the exterior. My parents named it Swallows' Point for the birds that swooped in our first summer, making their nests under the deck that hangs over the rockface. After we moved south to L.A. in 1992, the name took on new significance. Like the swallows, we came back every June, flying up thousands of miles from the south. In August, we left again.

I, however, have never called this place Swallows' Point. It's pretentious to name a house, but especially *this* house, which already commands too much attention on a lake of cheerfully painted, rough-hewn timber lodges, mostly original builds from the first half of the last century. Kendrew Lake is not a fashion runway for cottages like the old-money Muskoka lakes south of us. We're a little too far north, the cottage boonies.

Ginny is still supervising the kids from the dock, and I join her on a deck chair. Benji and Alex seem to be trying to knock each other off the poop inflatable without using their hands. Benji swings at Alex with a right-side kick, and she dives into the water, avoiding contact.

"They've been doing this for over an hour," Ginny says.

"Whatever. They look happy." I watch Benji help Alex back up. A gentleman, I think. My stomach turns at the thought of the conversation we still need to have, now more urgent.

Ginny squints at me. "And how are you doing?"

"*Comme ci, comme ça.*"

Ginny's family has owned the cottage next door for decades, and her parents handed it down to her last year when they decided they couldn't handle the upkeep. I knew Ginny when we were kids, but she is two years younger than me, and I only played with her when I was desperate for company. In the background of my lonely summer memories, she is a skinny, sunburned fling-a-ling in a life jacket. After she arrived with Alex in April to escape rising COVID rates in the city, we eyed each other for a day or two and waved politely. She knocked on the door on day three, gestured to a giant box on her driveway and asked for my help assembling a basketball hoop in exchange for unlimited play time for Benji and a cold bottle of wine. Four hours later, we were friends. Ginny's another single mom, a better listener than my therapist, and she never seems to get bored of hanging out. As for the kids, Benji and Alex are seven months apart, and they get along very well and have so much space to run around between our two properties that sometimes we wonder if they even realize that their wings are clipped.

"I think I caught most of the show on Twitter," Ginny says, picking up her phone.

I closed all my social media accounts a couple of months ago. Absolutely the healthiest thing. "What's the hot take?"

"Believe her. Believe women. The usual." She looks at me. "Was it what you expected? The details?"

I try for phrasing that is more sensitive than my mother's. "I guess I didn't realize the whole thing was just dry humping? I'm not saying that forcible grinding is remotely okay, I just thought it was something more."

"More what?"

I can't find the word. "I mean, it sounds stressful. I just want to make a clear distinction between that and—"

"And rape? She isn't accusing him of rape. She's just saying that what happened to her was also not okay."

"I get that. But I just wonder if something happened to her before Regis? Something in her childhood, maybe. Not that what she described isn't bad on its own, but is it—life destroying?"

"Depends, I guess. The whole thing made me remember this camping trip in the summer after high school grad. I woke up to a friend of a friend using me as a personal rubbing post. Of course, *he* pretended to be asleep when I sat up."

"Yuck. I'm sorry."

"Yeah, it wasn't great. But to be honest, I didn't really think it was that big of a deal. I should have been more pissed, but it was just kind of a gross story to tell later." She looks at me, pauses. "I mean, the guy gave me his number the next day, as if I might actually want to hang out again. That was fucked up, but at the same time, I don't think it crossed his mind that I might be upset about what happened."

"Did you say anything to anyone?"

"Yeah, totally. Any friend who would listen. I was like, *Hey, want to hear a gross thing?* People thought it was funny, like, what a dirty little perv. But nothing really changed for me. Maybe I became slightly more reluctant to pass out in a tent with strangers." She leans back in her chair a little. "But I could see someone else feeling differently. I mean, it sounds like Megan was pretty drunk and disoriented, which would be scary."

"Right, but that could also make the particulars a little fuzzy, no?"

"Hard to say. But now that you know all the details, do you feel better or worse about the whole thing?"

"I don't really know," I say, honestly.

Ginny has been listening to my vacillating point of view on the whole thing since the spring. My first theory, when the story broke, was that there had to be some mistake. It was the same feeling I had when my car was stolen in downtown L.A. last summer. I walked up and down the block, scanning the sidewalks, as if it were possible that the car had simply rolled away, slipped behind something. I just couldn't accept the worst-case scenario. I didn't think that Megan was lying—I thought it was quite possible she'd been assaulted, but maybe not by Lukas? I'd never known Lukas to be physically aggressive with anyone. What seemed plausible to me was that Megan had seen the ice storm photos at the AGO, including the image of a half-naked Lukas, and it had been triggering. She seized on the idea that *he* was her assaulter. I didn't know if this kind of thing could happen to someone with PTSD, but it seemed consistent with portrayals of the condition on TV.

Lukas's position was that Megan was unstable and made the whole thing up. For money, for attention, for whatever. But even setting aside the fact that false accusations are extremely rare, I had trouble wrapping my head around the idea that she was lying. In fact, the assault I'd just heard Megan describe struck me as quite a *likely* explanation for her bizarre behaviour that night. Plus, what incentive did she have to lie? Lukas had some money, but he wouldn't make her rich. And the Megan I knew—though it was possible she had changed—just wasn't a liar. And if she *were* going to make something up, wouldn't she go with something bigger? Something more clear-cut? Something any reasonable person with a shred of morality would agree is unforgivable?"

"We forget how different things were in 1998," Ginny says. "The world was super gross for women, like, even grosser than now, but I don't remember thinking so then. During frosh week, our leaders made the girls on my floor pretend to give head to a Teddy Ruxpin. I thought, Okay, I guess this is what adulthood is like."

"During Regis frosh week, there were signs on the turnoff to campus that said, Fathers, thank you for sending us your daughters!"

"Exactly. And I'd never heard of affirmative consent, no one had," Ginny says. "Seriously, most of my hookups involved a minimum of discussion. When I was in undergrad, the default was that the guy kept on trying stuff, and it was fine until you said stop, right? Until then, you were basically consenting."

"And she didn't tell him to stop," I say.

"Well. She was basically passed out."

"Alert enough to let him in the bed."

"It's definitely assault, Ros," Ginny says. "It isn't any less painful for the victim because it happened in 1998. But—" Ginny looks at me to fill in a blank.

"But what? It's less bad for the assaulter?"

"It's *bad*. It was always bad. But it's also conceivable to me that— well, in *that* time and place—Lukas may have thought it wasn't that bad.

You know, because it wasn't sex. Remember all the blurry shit that used to happen? At Dal, we drank our faces off, and then people would come home from the bar and just sort of pass out together and—I don't know, but how many times did you hear girls on your floor say stuff like, *I think we might have hooked up? But I'm not sure. Ha, ha. Oh my God!* If you heard that kind of shit enough, you could start to think that *accidental* fooling around was some no biggie thing. Both sides could be confused about how exactly that transpired."

I think of Courtney's account of what happened with Stefan that same night in January. How she acted as if she couldn't remember, and couldn't care less, whether they had sex or not. But I am also thinking of Adam. Adam had understood what to do. Strictly speaking, *Have you done this before?* is an insufficient stand-in for asking for consent, I get that. But still, he was looking for signals that I was okay. And either he was ahead of his time, or he was a good person while Lukas was not.

Ginny turns to me. "What was that about, anyway? Did it make you seem like less of a slut if you pretended you couldn't remember a hookup? I'm honestly trying to remember why any of us would have acted that way."

"I think so," I say. "Guys were definitely supposed to want sex more. It was always supposed to be their idea. If the woman was seen to be leading the charge, that was slutty. Remember how dirty we did Monica Lewinsky? And she was a powerless intern, and basically a kid. He was the fucking president." I see the cartoon on the back page of the *Ragged Regis*, so clearly stamped in my mind.

"So dirty. *Vilified*," Ginny says. "I dressed up as Monica for Halloween in a short skirt with toothpaste smeared all over it and a cigar tucked behind my ear. It was definitely seen as not okay to be the one pursuing sex. But even once you were in bed with a guy, the idea of acknowledging what you were about to do was still too embarrassing to contemplate. I was constantly struggling to find the line between being a slut and a prude. And for whatever reason, it seemed like the guy's job to lead that process."

Before the pandemic, my college ran a mandatory training day for staff on sexual assault. A consultant explained the new affirmative consent standard as a continual process of asking permission: *Can I kiss you now? Can I kiss you here?* I remember an older colleague, Don, pretended to get up from his desk at one point, saying, "You're telling me I've never had above-board sex in my life? Excuse me while I go do some damage control!" We laughed, because he *was* joking, but it also broke the ice. We were all quietly reexamining our past conduct. But the consultant was very gentle with Don, with us. "I don't know your history," she said, "but I want to reassure you all that despite what you may hear out there, most people are not looking to recast previous sexual experiences that they *willingly took part in* as assault." She continued to explain, however, that anxiety about this sort of thing goes away when we agree with our partners on what's okay. "Think about how it was before they added the traffic signal to the crosswalk on Dowd Avenue," she said. "There were accidents all the time. Kids got hit. One died last year. Some of those accidents happened because people were legitimately confused about who had the right of way, but we also know that some drivers turned the lack of clear signals into an excuse not to stop. With affirmative consent, we not only avoid genuine misunderstanding and accidents, but we also stop protecting 'misunderstanding' as an excuse for just doing the wrong thing."

Over the last few months, "misunderstanding" was the third scenario I considered. The idea that something did happen between Megan and Lukas, but that Lukas hadn't genuinely grasped—at least then—that it was harmful. Maybe he misunderstood her signals. Maybe he misunderstood the line. Maybe he forgot exactly what happened—or that anything of note happened at all, and now he was as surprised as anyone to see the events presented as something traumatic. But maybe this was why "misunderstanding" was something the consultant was so worked up about: it was a throwaway label that could hide within it all manner of delusions, misinterpretations and misremembering.

"It doesn't matter anyway," I say now. "Having some sort of flawed '90s approach to consent is not Lukas's defence."

Ginny nods. "Right. He's not dumb."

But I don't think his total denial is just strategic; if *anything* happened between Lukas and Megan, it feels impossible that I wouldn't have known about it. Some couples never discuss their sexual histories, but Lukas and I weren't like that. We talked about everything. We went to therapy specifically to do that. In the end, I knew much more about his partners than I ever wanted to know. Plus, Megan wasn't some random woman to me. If something had happened between them, and if the experience hadn't been particularly transgressive from Lukas's perspective, I couldn't see how the subject wouldn't have come up.

"If something did happen, I still think I would know."

"Ros, he hid a lot from you." Ginny's tone is not unkind.

"I know how it looks. But when he was confronted about those other women, he always told the truth. And in detail. He slept with his agent's twenty-two-year-old assistant for Christ's sake, did I tell you that? That's so bad, and I know the whole fucking play-by-play."

"You told me."

"And none of those other women have come forward with anything."

Not yet, anyway. Before this, I would never have considered Lukas's lifetime of cheating to be a credit to him.

"What's his lawyer saying?" Ginny asks.

"They're still hoping to settle."

"Why is settling the best-case scenario here? If he didn't do it, doesn't he want to prove that?"

I'd had the same question early on, but I tell Ginny what Lukas told me. That a trial will cost a ton. And the media will find reasons to attack him no matter the outcome. "She's a victim, right? And he's just a cocky famous guy. It doesn't matter what he did, people are going to act like he's a monster anyway. He can't win, even if a judge decides in his favour. Better to let it quietly fade."

Out on the sun-striped lake, Alex and Benji are laughing, still going at it. I feel a stab of loneliness. One day, I think, Benji will be forced to take part in conversations about what his dad did or didn't do. Megan's words come back to me: *You can't protect a predator just to protect someone else's ideas about them.* But what if that someone else is your kid? Shouldn't you do everything to protect your kid—at least while you can? And what made a predator? Who got to decide?

"Five minutes," Ginny calls out to the kids. Then she turns to me. "I think Benji wants to come along to check out the dog down the lake with us this afternoon, okay with you?"

"Is it okay if I don't come?"

"That's what I was thinking. You need space."

Ginny's been talking about staying at the cottage into the coming school year but says she'll feel safer with a dog around. I'm not sure how serious the plan is, but Ginny's pretty decisive. She didn't, for example, need a whole decade to think about leaving her husband after *his* affair. She cashed in her half of their two frozen yogurt franchises, took a year to update the graphic design skills she'd fallen behind on since college, and then landed a full-time job in the creative department of a "big five" bank. She also allows herself to hate Carl, her ex, with a depth that I can't even pretend to match when I'm talking about Lukas.

Ginny hands me a photo of a midsized copper-coloured dog on her phone. "It probably won't work out," she says. "The guy on the phone asked me if there were other dogs living nearby. I was like, *What, to play with?* But, no. Apparently, this dog's a scrapper."

"Well, good thing I don't have a dog then."

"You could also get one?"

"We live in California, so that won't happen." She shrugs like this is a minor technicality. "Why are you even considering an aggressive dog?" I ask.

"Well, the guy says he's great with kids. And apparently there's this thing called the fight-to-bite ratio? If your dog fights a lot but doesn't generally injure other dogs, he's probably not *that* dangerous, so you just keep him away to be safe. This cutie's only ever bitten one dog, so—" She shrugs, takes back her phone. "I'm not ready to rule him out."

Ginny gets up and shakes out her towel. The kids are making their way toward the dock, swimming underwater, coming up only for air and to check who's ahead.

To answer Ginny's question, I think I feel worse now that I know the details. Megan's story, unfortunately, makes the whole scenario easier to imagine. It would have been better if Megan had said her attacker had a knife or something—some detail that was so out of character for Lukas that I could easily eliminate him from the mental picture. Because I have to eliminate Lukas from the mental picture. If I am ever going to truly believe Lukas's side of the story, I have to believe that he wasn't there—that he wasn't part of the story at all.

4

The first time I saw Dutch after Regis was at a Starbucks in 2006. I was interviewing to run the Writing Center, a resource for students at a large community college in Orange County. I had recently finished my BA in English at Cal State Long Beach, and I was working as a literacy tutor at a Sylvan Learning centre. An old professor of mine had given me a lead on the job at the college.

I had driven in from Long Beach for the interview, and my anxiety about traffic had made me over an hour early. I was having a coffee and going over some notes when I noticed a handsome, vaguely familiar young man take the seat next to me, but I only knew it was Lukas when he spoke.

"Rosie?" He smiled in what struck me as a falsely self-conscious way. After a moment, he said, "You don't remember me?" I was shocked not just to see Lukas in Orange County, but because I wouldn't have expected anyone who knew me from Regis to approach me at all. These days, I worry about offending someone if I don't recognize them, but back then, I thought it made me seem powerful to act oblivious, to be more known than knower. As adrenaline shot through my body, I calmly squinted one eye, as if I were trying to place him.

"Lukas Van Kampen," he said. Then he smiled. "Dutch."

We talked for less than five minutes, but long enough for me to learn that he had been living in California for three years already, completing an MFA in creative writing at UC Irvine. He was graduating in a month, he said, but life in SoCal suited him, and he hoped to stay. We were interviewing for the same job at the community college, so we had a strained chuckle about that. He suggested grabbing a coffee sometime, which was awkward since we happened to be in a coffee shop already, side-by-side, holding cups, but we exchanged phone numbers, and then he made some kind of excuse for why he had to get going. I didn't think I'd hear from him, and I didn't.

I was the one who texted him. It was a couple of weeks later, the same day I found out I didn't get the job. That night, I went to a party with a girl I knew from college who had gone on to grad school in English. When it got late, a few of her grad student friends started reciting literary passages they knew from memory. Some guy wearing toe shoes—the first pair I'd ever seen—recited the opening lines of *Love in the Time of Cholera*. It was a passage I recognized because I had read it at Regis—it had been one of Dutch's favourites. When I identified it out loud, the toe-shoe guy looked at me with a combination of surprise and disappointment. I had the sudden and distinct feeling that he'd once told himself that he would marry the woman who could identify this passage, and I was not who he had pictured. When it was very late and everyone was getting ready to go home, he came up to me. Drunk, resigned, he said, "And then there were two." His breath held the scent of bitter ale. Under normal circumstances, I might have gone home with him out of boredom, but something held me back.

In the taxi home, I texted Lukas. All I said was: *Curious. Did U get the job?* The next evening, at a more respectable hour, Lukas texted back: *Yes'm. Coffee this week?*

I would have preferred beers or cocktails, but it turned out that Lukas wasn't drinking then. He said he didn't think he was an actual alcoholic or anything but that quitting drinking made him feel a lot happier and more in control. I was disappointed because I was much more comfortable on dates when I was drinking. Getting hammered, actually. And if this wasn't a date, if I didn't know what role I was playing, drinking felt even more necessary to numb the awkwardness.

He made me pick a place, and I suggested an earthy café in a beach city halfway between Irvine and Long Beach. I drank mint tea, he ordered an elaborate smoothie. I had hoped to sit outside in the garden, but it was full, and we ended up on stools at a counter near the washrooms. As we sat, I tried to read his face to see what he thought of my choice of café; I worried he hated it.

"I'm really sorry I got the job," he said.

"That's fine. It wasn't like my dream job or anything."

"Phew," he said. "Because it's definitely mine." We both laughed.

I told him that what I was really doing was trying to make money for baking school. In 2001, the year I should have graduated from Regis, and the year my father died, my mom said that she would pay half my tuition if I got a "real degree" first and earned the rest of the money on my own. The catch was that this had to happen before I turned thirty. But five years had gone by since her offer, and although I now had the degree, I was twenty-seven and very broke. With the job at the college, I figured I could save the second half of my tuition in about a year, but I didn't tell Lukas that, I didn't want to make him feel bad.

"Where's the baking school?" Lukas asked.

"France, I hope."

"Don't move to France! I only just found you!" He smiled in the way I remembered. The way that made me feel I was in on a secret. "Plus," he continued. "My mom used to have a fridge magnet that said: 'Never Trust a Skinny Cook.'"

Lukas was just trying to compliment me. I was in better shape than I had been at Regis, I knew that, but I didn't think of myself as skinny.

"I don't bake things just for me to eat," I said, although quite often I did. "I want to have a bakery someday."

"So that you could bake things for me to eat?"

The possibility that he might be flirting did occur to me, but it seemed just as likely that this had become his way with women.

We talked about Regis that afternoon, but only in the most surface of ways. I asked him who he kept in touch with, and he told me he had kept up with Stefan for a while, but not recently. He said he'd been friends with Sue throughout the four years at Regis, had even lived with her and a few others in senior year, but they had a falling out over a trip to Thailand right before graduation.

"I didn't handle that well," he said, rattling the dregs of his smoothie. "We talked about this amazing trip all year, but I was basically broke and didn't want to admit it. I guess I liked the fantasy. When I dropped out of the plan before we had to buy tickets, she felt all abandoned and betrayed. And then I was super pissed that she was mad at me, like, *Lady, it's not my fault I have no money*."

"Did she go?"

He nodded. "She was there for almost a year. Then I heard she was back in London studying photography at some fancy school. I gather now she's an artist."

This probably shouldn't have been surprising, but it was. Sue was so good at *appearing* to be good at everything that I never seriously considered the possibility that she was truly talented.

Lukas asked me if I was in touch with anyone from Regis.

"No," I said, astonished that he'd even ask.

"Yeah, I made an effort with people at first, but after a while, it's like, do we have anything in common anymore?" This was hardly my reason for losing touch with the Regis crowd.

I gave Lukas a short summary of my life since Regis, but we didn't talk about the circumstances under which I left school. He acted like our shared history was ordinary. It was possible that he thought this was the case. I didn't mind; behaving this way was the easiest way forward for me as well, though I didn't really get why *he* was keen to pursue a way forward at all. What did we have in common anymore?

Lukas told me that, after Regis, he had lived in Toronto for a while, working in event management at a fancy restaurant and writing songs for a band. He started writing fiction somewhere in there and then applied to MFA programs on a whim, which was how he wound up at Irvine, a top-rated program.

"Do you think you'll ever go back?" I asked.

"I prefer it here."

"Why do you like it?" He seemed to want to tell me.

Lukas swept a hand through his hair. "I'm glad you didn't ask if I miss the seasons. Canadians always want to bond over the fucking seasons. Why is it so good for the soul to endure a frigid January? It doesn't actually kill a person to have too much of a good thing."

"So you like the weather then?"

He sniffed. "It's more than that." But he didn't continue, and I wondered if maybe he thought I was too stupid to understand his point, whatever it was going to be.

"I think the no-seasons thing has an evil side," I said. "I think it explains why so many people get plastic surgery here. The seasons don't change, the plants stay the same, so people feel like they should get to stay the same, too. They forget they're even supposed to get old."

"But what's wrong with that?" Lukas said.

"It makes me feel like I can't live here past forty. I'm not a native species."

"Well," he said. "Looks like you're flourishing now."

I mumbled an embarrassed thanks and asked him about his writing. He described the young adult novel he was working on as *Back to the Future* meets *A Christmas Carol*. He was proud of himself for breaking with MFA tradition to pursue young adult writing, which, he said, was where the money was.

"Sounds intriguing," I said, though I couldn't really remember the plot of either story particularly well.

Unlike other writers I'd met, he was eager to elaborate.

"Every year on his birthday, this kid, Billi Bean, has the ability to pick any date in the future, travel there in a couple minutes, find something that's totally fucked up about the world, and then go back and try to fix the problem in the present. He has one day to do *something*. We don't know if it works. But he tries, and he learns all the lessons by trying anyway."

"Can he put an end to greenhouse gas emissions?" I was kidding, awkwardly, but he took my question seriously. He took this book very seriously.

"That kind of thing," he said. "But not that. Not yet. I'm setting it up to be a series. Four birthdays, maybe?"

"I'd love to read it," I said.

"No, you wouldn't." He smiled. "Don't take that the wrong way. People just say that when they want me to shut up." But he didn't shut up.

Lukas walked me to my car when we left. The sidewalk was uneven, broken and raised by the roots of trees. I kept bumping into him and apologizing. At my car, I told him it was nice to see him again. I wished him good luck with the job and the book. "Next time, I'll cook you dinner," he said.

I felt like saying, *Look, you don't have to do this.* I strongly suspected he was motivated by guilt, only being nice to me to pay off a debt for the mean article he'd written nearly a decade ago.

I got in my car and drove off. It wasn't until I was a few blocks away that I realized I hadn't responded about dinner, I just let his offer hang there. My fingers trembled on the steering wheel. My life since Regis hadn't included even a fraction of the intensity I'd experienced in such a short time there. The rapid intimacy, the crushing humiliation. I'd become used to life without those inflections. My relationships—even friendships—were mostly casual. Anything that became stressful didn't last long. Lukas was both what I was looking for and what I didn't want to find.

Lukas didn't cook for me on the second date; instead, he invited me to a student stage production of *Bridget Jones's Diary* at the university, something an old roommate had directed. Men fell for Bridget despite her flaws and missteps, and I wondered if Lukas was trying to send me a message with his choice of romantic comedy.

Our first kiss was after the play, in front of my car in the student centre parking lot. He assumed, he told me later, that I didn't like him because I reacted stiffly and barely kissed back. I remember doing this; I remember hedging. I didn't want to embarrass myself by getting carried away, by letting him think that I thought I had a genuine chance with him. Because I honestly didn't think I did. He was still far too good looking for me.

And yet I wonder. Did *I* like Lukas? Was I attracted to him? I suppose it felt indulgent then to ask myself these questions—my interest in him didn't feel particularly relevant to the outcome of the whole thing because I didn't think he'd actually go for me.

It got easier to be around Lukas. We started sleeping together after a month or two, and although I wasn't exactly sure if he was my boyfriend, he had a lot of the qualities I searched for on dating sites—cute, nonembarrassing clothes, no boring job at a mutual fund—so I took a break from dating sites. I still admired his easy confidence, the way he seemed to belong wherever we went. He took me to buy a Christmas tree that we carried to my apartment because he remembered my *When Harry Met Sally* poster and said that he always liked that scene. When I brought Lukas to my neighbour's party, I got more unsolicited praise for him than for anything else I could remember. "He's so tall!" my neighbour exclaimed, as if that were the most enviable trait to have found in a boyfriend. At dinner once, we bumped into the toe-shoe guy, and I felt smug about Lukas's hand on my elbow. I liked to tell people that Lukas and I were old friends from Canada, and I'd let this trail off on a winking note like, *But who can say where it will go from here?*

It was a story that worked. But, in the end, Lukas hadn't really been a friend. After he wrote about my moral degeneracy, I didn't have a single friend at Regis. But I was prepared to overlook this in 2006. Being with him was like an invitation to reinvent myself, to finally become the person I'd wanted to be. I even had some tremor of an idea that our sordid history would be the thing that could make us work as a couple. He knew I had done some asshole stuff. But I knew that he could be an asshole, too. There was balance and comfort in that.

And Lukas was looking out for me now. He helped me get a lucrative contract in the communications office of the college. On Valentine's Day, he gave me a vintage mixer and a frilly retro apron. He got us tickets to see Billy Joel in Las Vegas and emailed me a picture of us after the concert with the note: "I love this one. You look beautiful!" The impact of this was huge. For so long, "You can look good" still felt like an accurate assessment of my attractiveness. I let myself think that my ship was finally coming in.

We did eventually talk about the ice storm. In bed once, a couple months into sleeping together, I brought up the *Ragged Regis* article because it had been weighing on me. He nodded very thoughtfully when I raised it, said he *kind of* remembered it.

"I was the first-year staff writer," he said. "What could I do? I did whatever story the editor wanted."

I didn't want to press, but I strongly suspected he pitched the story. Why would anyone have assumed there was a humorous angle to a girl going missing? But maybe, maybe, Lukas genuinely didn't remember the specifics. "That article totally derailed me," I said.

He propped himself up on one elbow. "Come on."

"Pretty much," I said, but with a tone that was already reneging on the bitterness. "For a little while."

"The *Ragged Regis* is like the world's geekiest paper."

"Everyone read it."

"Yeah, and everyone with any profile at Regis also got roasted in it at some point. It's a rite of passage."

Passage into what? I wondered. But I shuffled in closer to him. "What did you honestly think of me, though? After everything with Megan? Did you think I was the worst, or like I was responsible for it—"

"Responsible for what?"

"People thought she went crazy because of me. And the thing is, I did truly think she went to Toronto. I know I didn't have clear evidence, but I did believe it was true. People thought I was making it up so I wouldn't get in trouble, but she had been talking about it—"

He shook his head, cutting me off. "Honestly, Rosie? I hardly remember any of it."

"You don't remember what a punching bag I was?"

He punched me lightly on the shoulder. "We were kids, we were all being dramatic. Megan, too, I'm sure."

I nodded, but my chin began to tremble. I couldn't help it.

"Hey." He scooted in closer to me, held my face, and kissed my forehead. "I don't know if this makes you feel better or worse, but I didn't really think about it after it happened. I don't even remember people talking about it. It was a relief when they found her, right? And then, I don't know, she was just gone. And you, too. So is it bad to say we just forgot?"

"It's not bad. It's just not the same for me."

"It must be so debilitating to have such a good memory," he said. "I don't remember shit. If you just forgot about it, you'd be fine."

5

Elaine Ng is on my mind again when I come up from the dock to lie down in my bedroom. I haven't decided whether to talk to her yet. On the one hand, it feels disloyal to Lukas. What if something I say throws off his narrative—and what if I'm wrong? But then I start to feel guilty. After all the selfish things I did in 1998, the least I can do is cooperate now.

If I do talk to Elaine, one thing I could comment on is "flirting." Contrary to Megan's account, I do not remember Lukas flirting with her at the bar. It's true that I was distracted by Adam, but surely I would have noticed if they were genuinely flirting. I was a hawk for that sort of thing. It would have really bothered me. Plus, I can't remember Lukas flirting with anyone other than Sue. And that wasn't traditional flirting, the kind where hooking up is the end goal. They seemed, instead, determined to perform a more elevated intimacy—they were special, better than hooking up.

So if she is exaggerating the flirting, it is *possible* she is exaggerating the rest. But then I think, A letter? I take a deep breath and count to four, which is about the only useful thing I learned in therapy. Why would Lukas write Megan a letter? They *weren't* friends. I was her roommate, and I hadn't even written her a letter. That detail makes him look terrible.

Above me, the ceiling fan turns with its familiar stutter. *The World at Six* drifts into my bedroom from the kitchen radio built right into the wall. Lake water drips from my ponytail and soaks the back of my T-shirt, an old one of my dad's with the words: "Pushing Fifty Is Exercise Enough!" Inside this bedroom, it could be the summer of 1986, the date on the *Architecture Canada* article framed on my wall. Over an aerial image of our cottage, my dad's pull quote reads: "If I had to do it over, I'd do it all the same!" In this momentary time warp, I feel haunted by something else Megan said: *Part of me was erased.*

I can relate to that feeling.

This cottage bedroom is the only place in the world with any relics of my childhood, my adolescence, my early twenties. Mom calls it the Peter Pan room: the room that never grew up. I think of it more as a museum of my pre-Lukas life. It's the smallest room at the cottage, a kid's room, but I gave Benji the sunnier, more modern guest suite when we arrived in the spring because it was a comfort to me to be around my old things: the Strawberry Shortcake pillowcases, the chipped white dresser full of old T-shirts, the wall of ribbons from swimming and paddling contests at the Kendrew Lake Cottagers' Club.

But maybe I can't really relate to what Megan said. Because unlike Megan, who seemed to say that Lukas was responsible for her erasure, I'd been the one trying to erase myself after Regis. Lukas just helped make the process easier.

After abandoning my dorm room at Regis, I moved into my parents' Toronto condo but never bothered to unpack the boxes from my bedroom in L.A. The stuffed animals, yearbooks and *Sassy* magazines from high school didn't feel like the right backdrop to my life as a college drop-out. When I returned to California a year and a half later, I drifted from place to place, from thing to thing, always trying to start over. I deliberately chose housemates who didn't need or want anything from me—fluctuating groups of drifters or couples with a spare room. Friends or possessions didn't stick with me long. I could say that I was trying to find myself in those years, but what feels truer is that I was *avoiding* identity—I was afraid of fixing myself to the wrong places, wrong interests, wrong people. I was afraid to choose who I was in case I chose wrong.

When Lukas and I got together, his plans, his stuff and his fussiness swallowed me up. It didn't feel like a sad process at the time. I had gone so long without feeling invested in my own choices that it seemed false to put up a fight over where to buy our groceries or where to spend Thanksgiving. When it came to our home, I was happy to be told what was good, what made sense. Lukas liked the things he owned to be sources of distinction, high quality. I was honestly fine with whatever he liked. The shoemaker's children go barefoot, the designers' daughter can't express an aesthetic preference. When Lukas moved out a few years ago, I looked around at what was now mine and realized that I had accumulated very little that said anything about me.

The built-in bookshelf across from where I'm sitting on the bed is packed tight with *Archie* comics and *Sweet Valley High* books. Next to those, right in plain sight, there's a stack of old notebooks, most of them bored attempts at diaries. They are largely uninteresting, not for their mundane content but for their avoidance of it: my clear attempts to control my young adult narrative, to present my quiet teenage life in a way that might fool a future me—the me of now—into believing I was cooler than I was. But there are, amid tales of marina boys I never spoke to but pretended to have "exchanged a moment" with, occasional breakthroughs of searing honesty. Take, for instance, an entry from December 31, 1998.

I remember writing it during a rare winter trip up here with my parents when I was nineteen, almost a full year after dropping out of Regis. They'd just had the place fully winterized, and my dad gave us all snowshoes for Christmas, but it didn't snow that holiday. He was sick by the next Christmas and died a year later. I don't think the snowshoes have ever been used.

December 31, 1998.

> *Rules to Try to Follow in 1999:*
> 1. *Do not get hung up completely on Chris (or any guy) unless he is at least partially hung up on you.*
> 2. *Do not lie—not even dumb "white" or "half" lies or slight exaggerations. Lying is stupid, and it gets you into trouble.*
> 3. *Talk to more people.*
> 4. *Be a good friend to Val.*
> 5. *Don't do nothing.*
> 6. *Do not make fun of certain people to impress others (unless they irritate you, you trust that you cannot be overheard, and—most important—you believe what you say).*
> 7. *Continue to watch Buffy the Vampire Slayer, Dawson's Creek, and Felicity— they give you pleasure, you live vicariously through them, and they keep you on top of pop culture.*
> 8. *Eat healthily and scantily.*
> 9. *Learn a "passion."*
> 10. *Fall in love randomly and often.*
> 11. *Use the NordicTrack.*
> 12. *Try to be cheerful and remember when you're miserable that everyone is in that boat, too, or has been—do not be self-absorbed or melodramatic about it.*

13. *Take care to always look and act your best—you never know who you'll run into or who may notice you for the first time.*
14. *Get a job at a café or restaurant??*
15. *Apply to school.*

It's hard to remember who I was back then, other than a lonely person who was desperate to be someone else. It's rules number 12 and 13 that kill me now. I sound so earnest, so unlike my Regis-self when my goal had been to look and act like I didn't care. I suppose I was trying something on, trying to be softer, kinder—at the very least, more likeable. But did I consider how much those rules sounded like Megan? "A smile is the prettiest thing . . ."

At that point, I was working as a nanny for Val, who had recently gotten divorced. Her kids, Julia and Richie, were six and four then. I picked them up from school, took them to the playground, the library, McDonald's. I remember how badly I wanted to trade places with them, to just be little, to have my life to do over again. I was still young myself, but I felt like I'd already ruined everything.

Despite the suggestion of the fourth rule on my list, Val and I still weren't close when I worked for her. My infatuation with Val was similar to my infatuation with Sue, except that it was more obviously one-sided. I would get nervous and tongue-tied when we were alone together, trying to think of cool things to say. I went through her stuff when she wasn't around—just as I used to do when she'd visit when I was younger— looking for things that connected us. I tried on her dainty lingerie and was disappointed, but not surprised, to find it too small. I listened to her music, memorized all her makeup brands, studied the bookshelves in her living room, checked the same books out from the library and left them visible in my bag. When Val came home in the evenings, after Richie and Julia were fed and bathed by me, I waited around the kitchen while she kissed them goodnight, hoping to be invited to stay for a glass of wine. I wanted to bond—about our father, our shared history of disappointing him, anything. I wanted to have a sister, at the very least a friend. We were both only children. But it never happened.

The nannying arrangement went on into the summer of 1999, six months after that diary entry. That August, Val took the kids east to visit a friend for a couple of weeks, and I took a trip to L.A. I told her I was visiting old friends, but really I went to see Chris, the guy I'd had the funnel cake fling with in the summer before Regis and with whom I'd struck up an innuendo-heavy email flirtation in the months since dropping out. He suggested I come down and see him sometime, but in my heart, I knew that I was breaking rule number 1 when I booked the ticket.

A couple of weeks after arriving in L.A., I moved into Chris's room. He lived in a house of five guys near Cal State Northridge, though we—mainly Chris—decided we were only going to be, in the parlance of the time, "friends with benefits." I explained my decision to stay in California to Val in a long email, more words than I had ever said to her in my life, with more details than I even gave my parents. At the time, I was grateful for my parents' laissez-faire take on the whole thing. Their position was that I was old enough to make my own choices, but they wouldn't help me financially until I enrolled back in school somewhere. Now I think, Weren't they worried about me then? I get that "figure it out" was a bit of a '90s parenting mantra, but wasn't I obviously in crisis? In any case, Val didn't appear to care much, either. She wrote back in a short paragraph: *Sometimes the best way out of a shit situation is just to run. Good luck.* I suppose that, in one sense, it was a supportive thing to say. But I was hurt. If she had wanted me to come back, I would have. If she'd seemed mad at me, that might have been enough, too. I wanted to matter, one way or another.

My phone buzzes. Lukas's name appears on the screen.

I may have run, I think now, but I didn't get out of a shit situation. And that shit is still following me.

I return Lukas's call out on the dock where Mom can't hear. It's just before seven, and boats are out for cocktail hour.

"I don't remember you flirting with Megan at the Old Vic," I say. "Just for the record."

"Thank you. I don't remember, either, and that's because all I remember about that chick is that she disappeared."

"But then you wrote her a letter?"

He doesn't answer right away. I can hear the California freeway in the background of his phone. "Didn't everyone? They fucking told us to."

"Who told you to?"

He breathes out; I can tell that he's smoking. "I don't know. That fat girl."

I'm surprised to hear Lukas be that harsh. Not that I assumed he was beyond *thinking* "fat girl," but he's usually so careful with language, especially lately, and even with me. I wonder if he's losing his grip. "I don't recall Bev asking us to do that," I say.

"Right, Bev. I sat in the caf with Sue and what's her face, and we wrote letters."

"I find that to be a very weird part of the story."

"Because any time you do something nice for a girl, you're probably just trying to compensate for attempted rape?"

I have an urge to wipe my cheek, his spittle almost palpable through the phone. "I was just surprised it never came up."

"Ros, it couldn't have been more insignificant to me."

We are both quiet. My therapist, the one time I Zoomed with her about Megan's allegations in March, said the good news was that I was well-equipped to handle this blow. Thanks to the shitstorm Lukas had already put me through personally, I'd become hardy. Was hardiness the same as strength? Maybe not, but she said it would help me.

He breaks the silence first. "How's Benji? Is he around?"

"He's with Ginny and her kid."

"I'm going to be busy with Frankel until eight or nine your time, so tell Benj I'll call him tomorrow night?"

I tell him okay.

"Now that her story's out there, what are your plans for talking to him?" he asks.

"What's *your* plan for talking to him?" I snap back.

"Frankel thinks we should talk to him sooner rather than later. I know it probably doesn't feel fair to you, but Frankel thinks it will be better if you do it. You're in a better position to stay focused on Benji's needs. Plus, you're there with him already, so—"

"Frankel's a lawyer, not a therapist." But I don't disagree with the advice. Back in March, Lukas and I decided not to overload Benji with the story right away; the pandemic was already too much for an eleven-year-old. Let's take it one day at a time, we said, avoiding.

"If Benji finds out from someone else, I'm worried it will come off worse. We've been lucky so far," Lukas says.

I snort. "*So* lucky, Lukas."

"You know what I mean."

"He doesn't know anything."

I can't guarantee this, but I do think Benji would come to me if he heard something that scared him. He's still young enough. And I have made efforts to control the environment. We almost never have the TV on, he is not on social media, and he doesn't have a phone. Back in the spring, he'd see his friends in online school, but now their interactions are limited to video gaming on my iPad. For a while, the video game chat box made me nervous. I thought the question might bubble up at any moment: *Is your dad a rapist or what???* But Benji never said anything about it. And I told myself that even if Benji did see rumours about Lukas online, he probably wouldn't even pay close attention. Lukas is a bestselling author, and Benji is used to seeing his dad in the media. He is even used to seeing Lukas's name associated with sex. He heard a mother reprimand me at the school carnival last spring for giving away signed copies of book five of Billi Bean without first warning parents of the sexual content.

"Frankel have any other great tips?" I ask.

"He says don't call it a *crime*, call it a *complaint*."

"A *complaint*?"

"He's eleven. If you say *crime*, he's going to picture me with a gun to her head."

"And if I say *complaint*, he's going to think sexual assault is about as serious as an overdue library book."

A yellow sailboat cuts past the cottage. A kid about Benji's age is skippering, and next to him is either a grandfather or a pandemic dad whose facial hair has grown in white. I do the token smile and wave. If we were in a skyscraper elevator back in the city, we would be expected to avoid each other's gaze.

I try to recall what I understood about sexual assault when I was eleven. Did I know the term? I recall a T-shirt I had when I was Benji's age with a picture of a salt shaker next to a knife and the words: "A Salt with a Deadly Weapon." Maybe it's in the Peter Pan room. I do remember first learning the words *sexual harassment*: *her-ass*-ment. I remember Anita Hill's picture in the newspapers that we cut out to make media yearbooks in sixth grade English. But I don't know Benji's reference points. He studied Supreme Court judges at school, did they discuss what

Brett Kavanaugh was accused of? All the time I've spent assembling my own memories, I should have also been working on a story for Benji.

When Benji was little, Lukas and I made a real effort to teach him to respect his body and other people's bodies. We used the proper names for his private parts. We never made him hug or kiss anyone he didn't want to, even family members. When he told me that Eunice Ku, who he'd had a crush on since kindergarten, had said that she wasn't going to dance with him at the Valentine's party, I resisted saying, *That's not very kind of Eunice*, as much as the story broke my heart. I explained that neither he nor Eunice had to dance with anyone they didn't want to. No one could force anyone to dance, I emphasized, period. That was as far as we got on consent. Who knows what he's learned from anyone else?

I ask Lukas, "What did you know about sexual assault when you were eleven?"

"I don't know, Ros." Lukas's irritation with a reasonable question frustrates me.

"Do I call it dry humping then? Like what our neighbour's retriever does?" I realize the irony in mocking him for this. It's not like I'd want the image any more violent.

"The main point, obviously, is the woman is fucking crazy. So you can start by saying that."

"Is that what I'm supposed to start with? By calling a woman crazy? No, I don't think I'll do that."

"What are you saying? You believe her now?"

I hear the squeal of glass sliding doors. Mom has come outside, ostensibly to set the table but more likely to eavesdrop.

"I didn't say that," I hiss quietly into the phone. "Relax." These days, every conversation we have involves a request for the other person to relax.

———

Mom, Benji and I sit out on the deck for dinner. Leftover grilled chicken, potato salad. I'm too tense to eat more than a few bites, but the cold wine is calming.

Instead of eating, Benji describes his afternoon meeting Alex and Ginny's prospective dog. "The dangerous part wasn't the dog, it was the owner," Benji says. "He wasn't even wearing a mask."

"Oh, I'm sure it's fine," Mom says. Despite being seventy-one years old and still frail from her injury, she generally seems to think that COVID is not dangerous.

"Alex was *pissed* that Ginny didn't say anything. She just, like, followed him inside."

"It can be awkward to say something," I say.

"It's not that hard," he says.

"Well, did *you* say something?"

"She's the adult."

"Well, there you go."

He blinks at me uncomprehendingly. And I'm also not sure of the message I'm trying to get across. That feeling awkward is a valid excuse for not speaking up?

"Maybe he was cute," Mom suggests. "The owner, not the dog."

"Gross. He was, like, seventy," Benji says.

I glance at Mom, but instead of being offended, she looks amused, primed to make some sort of comment that will embarrass everyone. So I change the subject and tell Benji to eat his chicken.

Benji looks at his plate. He has always been a picky eater, and mealtimes have caused me stress since he was a baby. Starting at five or six months old, he would push my breast away at the most minor distraction and never return. I fed him tensely until ten months in a dim room, staring at the wall.

Before completing his first bite, Benji is distracted again. The yellow sailboat is back, stuck on water that has gone glassy and still. The father—or grandfather—has an oar out. Mom smiles and waves at them with waggly fingers.

"*Knot Today*," Mom says, reading the cursive writing on the stern. "How apt." Her smile returns to its resting position of judgment.

"We should get one of those," Benji says.

"We don't know how to sail," I say.

"Dad does."

Sometimes Benji says things that make me wonder if he really understands that his father and I are no longer together. Lukas knows—or purports to know—how to sail, but that isn't relevant to the discussion of getting a sailboat for this cottage, which Lukas will never return to.

"Your grandfather kept an albacore for a time," Mom says. "But it was an awful lot of work for a little thing, and then the renters pretty much trashed it."

While I was growing up, we spent every summer here except for the one year that it was too much of a hassle to leave L.A. The year of the funnel cake job. To this day, Mom still attributes every problem with the cottage to the renters of 1997.

"About your dad," I say. "He can't call tonight, but he'll call tomorrow."

Benji nods, takes a small bite of potato salad. He talks to Lukas every other day or so. They have talked more on Zoom in the last several months than they ever talked on the phone back home.

"What's for dessert?" Benji asks.

"Five more bites," I say. "Then bird's nest cookies."

Mom winks at me. "Another Cordon Bleu special."

It's a jab, but it's hard to tell the true intention of her comment. This has been our dynamic for the last several months. She mocks me, I take offence, then she says I'm overly sensitive. Her specialty is indirectness, never insulting me straight-on, so that I can't accuse her of anything specific later. In our first weeks here, I took deep breaths and made other concerted efforts to be pleasant and obliging. Beyond the sense of duty that moved me to come here, I did hope that we would get along. She was going through something difficult, especially at her age; it was my job to calmly absorb her irritating comments and agenda-packed inquiries. But we've lost control of things somehow. It seems she can't help herself from cutting me down, and my blood boils hot enough to vaporize my kindest intentions. And in this shitty manner, the days have gone on.

Mom feels she can needle me about the Cordon Bleu cooking school because she paid half of my exorbitant tuition though I have never—at least not officially—used my pastry diploma. Benji was born, Lukas got famous, and working a 4 a.m. job became grossly impractical. I feel guilty about her money, but I'm also sensitive to her treating that year in Paris as another punchline in my life story.

Incidentally, I have been doing a lot of baking since the start of the pandemic. I know I'm not alone in that diversion, as the spring shortages on flour and yeast can attest, but I am taking it seriously. At first, I was baking just to be alone for a few hours at a time and to focus my attention on something other than Lukas or my mother, but then I started taking small orders for acquaintances around the lake: cheerful treats for mostly guestless celebrations. Tomorrow is Ginny's birthday, and I'm making a hot-pink drip cake, at her request.

I do my best not to react to the Cordon Bleu jab. "The cookies are a recipe from *Cozy Christmas Kitchen*, your 1979 edition. I subbed in ground almonds for coconut."

"Interesting," she says, in a distinctly bored way. Then she stands. "I'll get them." It is the first time Mom has worn shorts all summer, and when she rises from the table, Benji stares at her legs, which are a waxy white, purplish and veiny in patches. His face shows a combination of curiosity and disgust. I remember having the same reaction to my grandmother's body when she came up here from time to time. Now my legs will be next.

I clear my throat to stop his staring. Whether he gets the cue or not, he moves on. "Alex and I want to camp over there," he says, shifting his gaze across the lake. "On that island thing."

"It's a lot farther than it looks."

"That's why we need a boat."

"I think it's private property," I say.

"It's not like anyone's there. If it's a problem, we can always just apologize later."

"Where did you hear that?" It sounds like something his father would say.

He takes his last few bites and doesn't answer.

Sailboats, camping trips. Maybe Benji *is* feeling our isolation. He's just a kid on the brink of adulthood, driven by the same instincts that burned in his ancestors: to go somewhere, find something, make something happen. I haven't even taken him to Felsbridge yet this year, the nearest town.

Mom bangs back through the screen door. She turns to Benji with the tray of cookies. "We'll do the cut after this."

"Just a trim," he says.

"Save the curls to catch the girls," Mom says, winking.

"Nana's giving you a haircut?"

He flicks the hair off his face. "A trim," he corrects.

His drive for adventure is clearly more desperate than I realized. Benji's hair has not been cut since March. I ordered a pair of haircutting scissors back in May, but Benji wouldn't let me near him with them, and eventually, I gave up trying. I wasn't doing anything with my own hair, which now has at least eleven jumpy strands of grey in front.

"We discussed it while you were in your room," Mom says, sniffing at a cookie. "Did you have something else planned for the evening?"

I shake my head, feeling guilty relief that my conversation with Benji will need to wait another day, not because haircuts take so long, but because I don't want this bonding moment with my mother to be marred by a terrible memory. Despite my own complicated feelings about Mom, I like seeing her and Benji do things together. It makes me smile to imagine the conversation that led to this plan.

"Are we doing it out here?" Benji asks.

"Kitchen sink," she says. She smiles at me in a self-satisfied way. "I can cut yours, too. If you like."

"I'll think about it."

I turn to Benji. "Let's do something tomorrow," I say. "I have a cookie delivery in Felsbridge, and maybe after we'll get ice cream or something?"

Benji's silent, pleased smile breaks my heart.

6

Lukas texts me the next morning: *How did it go with B?*

I write back: *Don't rush me.*

In my inbox, I find an email from Elaine Ng:

Ms. Fisher,

I hope you have had a chance to consider my proposed meeting. Ideally, I would like to meet by early next week. I am currently conducting most meetings over video conference; however, my office's COVID-19 policy will support an in-person meeting if this is your preference. Given the sensitivity of the discussion, I leave that decision to you. I have copied my assistant, Minerva Brown, who would be pleased to make our arrangements. I am happy to answer questions over the phone. Please be in touch. Warmly, Elaine

Isn't this the sort of manipulation lawyers are famous for? Making it seem like my decision concerns *how* Elaine and I will meet—in person or online—not whether? It strikes me that Elaine probably timed her follow-up to coincide with Bella's interview. She must have known that hearing Megan's side of the story in detail would have an impact on me—my compassion for Megan's situation, possibly my memory.

I do a quick search online for breaking stories on Megan's interview. When the hits fill my screen, I'm reminded of what it was like to flip over a paving stone in the yard as a child—dozens of creepy crawlies, just waiting there.

"Another Day, Another Abuse of Power and Privilege" is a trending story from *The Broad Brush*, a popular feminist blog. Though I often enjoy *The Broad Brush*'s social criticism, this is precisely the kind of reductivism that offends me on Lukas's behalf. The alleged assault happened more than a decade before Lukas was famous—he didn't have any power then, not in the sense they mean.

I scour headlines for news of additional victims—my constant anxiety—but nothing pops up. Several articles reference an animated GIF—Lukas getting bumped all the way to the edge of a cliff by a pornographic blow-up doll—viewed over a hundred thousand times. I don't look it up.

A piece out of the *L.A. Times* skews sympathetic to Lukas with the headline: "Lukas Van Kampen Continues to Deny Assault Allegations, Says, "I Have Always Been a Feminist." The first paragraph begins: "At Regis University, Lukas Van Kampen was president of the White Ribbon Campaign to end violence against women." Yeah, I think, and the next sentence should read: *and this is his most oft-quoted fact about himself*. Even before reading on, I send the story to Ginny with an eye roll emoji. In the comments section, someone called Andrea3000 has posted: *Dear Abusers, "feminism" is not your shield.*

This kind of comment will hurt. Lukas likes to think of himself as one of the good guys. Even before he was publicly lauded for his sensitive handling of teen sex in Billi Bean book five, he worked hard to present himself as a feminist. His efforts often came across to me as cheesy, self-serving. In an interview on NPR, I remember him saying, in response to some question on the subject of feminism, "Like any smart man, I live in fear of my partner and do whatever she tells me." It was such an outrageous thing to say. Lukas was never afraid of me, nor did I ever ask him to do anything. Plus, I told him afterward, being "afraid" of your partner doesn't make you a feminist. The comment just perpetuates the stereotype of women as shrews.

Does Lukas actually care about how women are treated? It's easy enough to look at our relationship and say he doesn't respect them. And yet, I'm not sure that our relationship says anything about Lukas except that he probably isn't made for monogamy. Because he cares mainly about himself.

We were still living together in the fall of 2017 when the MeToo movement really took off on social media. One night as we were getting ready for bed, Lukas asked me why I hadn't posted #MeToo on Facebook. I asked him why he thought I should have: I didn't think I had anything to #MeToo about. I told him that the whole movement was starting to annoy me—"MeToo" had been a powerful message at first, but now it was starting to sound less like a chant of unity to me and more like a playground whine: *Me too, don't leave me out!*

"Come on," Lukas said. "You've received unwanted attention."

"Honestly, not that much."

He shook his head. "I don't believe that for a second."

My body was twitchy with irritation. "Even the way you're saying that, Lukas, like your disbelief should be a compliment to me, is part of my issue with this thing. Like saying #MeToo will affirm my attractiveness, give me membership in this sorority of girls who men can't control themselves around."

Lukas looked at me with a dumb, blank look. But I resented his interest in this topic. I figured he wanted me—his partner and the mother of his child—to be vocal in the movement because it would pave an efficient pathway for him to enter the conversation. He had probably already drafted the comments.

"Don't you think some of these women are kind of wearing it like a badge? 'Yeah, me too, I'm also hot enough, or I was once hot enough, to be the recipient of unwanted attention,'" I said to Lukas.

"Wow. Nope, not once."

"So you haven't looked at an unattractive woman on Facebook with the hashtag and been like, *Really? You?*"

"Are you serious, Ros?"

"Look, I know there's a big problem with men thinking they can do whatever they want. But I think the real stories are getting lost in this onslaught of bandwagony bullshit."

Lukas looked at me. "What's a real story? Is Simon not a real story?"

"That's who I should 'MeToo' about?"

"He assaulted you, so yeah. I think that would be very apposite." Lukas uses big words when he feels threatened.

"I was involved with Simon for months."

"So what? He also raped you, as far as I understand it."

I paused, taking in Lukas's word choice. I hadn't used the word *rape* when I told him about Simon. It wasn't a word that matched how I felt about the story.

"Well, I think how I understand it is the more important issue here," I said.

Lukas frowned and shook his head sadly, like I didn't know what was good for me.

——

In the early 2000s, while I was in school at Cal State Long Beach and trying to earn a "real degree," I started working at a bakery, mainly folding croissants. The work was quiet and easy, and the schedule was compatible with school. Just as Megan had so many years before, I got up before five to go make food. The shop was owned by a thirty-eight-year-old Irish guy named Simon. Half a year into the job, I slept with him.

The first time we hooked up was after work. He took a few of us out for drinks to celebrate the bakery's five-year anniversary, and I drank a lot because that was the only way I knew how to not be nervous around the people I worked with. Toward the end of the evening, when Simon returned from smoking a cigarette outside, he squeezed into the spot next to me. I'd felt awkward most of the evening, and the contact between our bodies was reassuring, hospitable; *sleazy* didn't cross my mind. He offered to drive me home, but on the walk to the car, he suggested we pop around the corner to grab another drink at a bar he liked. When he leaned in to kiss me outside the bar's washrooms, I was too surprised not to kiss back. I thought we'd both just stepped into something unexpected.

Simon and I had always gotten along fine, but we weren't flirty. It simply didn't occur to me to take an interest in him because he was married and had a kid. I also wasn't particularly attracted to him. He was skinny and pale, except where he was sunburned, and he was often sunburned. People said he was funny, but I think it was just his accent. When we stopped kissing, rather than reflect on my own feelings about the kiss, I tried to guess what he was thinking. Did he assume I was interested in him when I agreed to go to the second bar? Was that what accepting the invitation meant?

When we left that bar, Simon didn't offer to drop me off again. We just drove to his place. His wife and one-year-old daughter were back in Ireland for a holiday, and the condo was all ours. The main bathroom was under renovation, so I had to pass through his bedroom to use the ensuite. I remember seeing a wedding photo on his bedroom dresser: Simon standing with his wife on some windswept green-and-purple hill. At the work Christmas party a few months before, his wife had been kind to me. I hadn't worked at the bakery very long, and I felt self-conscious and out of place. She'd taken my hand to shake it, pressed it between hers and said, "Oh, sweetie, are you all right? Your hands are freezing!" The steady, caring look in her eyes reminded me of Megan.

When I came out of the bathroom, Simon had collapsed a futon in the living room. I guess he thought it would be indecent to fuck me on the bed. There was a framed Rothko print on the wall that I recognized from a story I'd overhead him tell a customer at the bakery. He said that holding his daughter in front of "Orange, Red, Yellow" was the only way to get her to calm down when she fussed. It was under the Rothko that Simon took my clothes off. I told him we weren't going to have sex. I'd only had sex with two people before in my life, and I felt too inexperienced to sleep with a thirty-eight-year-old. I told him that I wasn't on the pill, which was true, and that I was allergic to latex, which wasn't true. I gave him a blow job, though. I felt I owed him something.

The next morning, I woke up to his pawing. I think part of me was just grateful that the sobriety of morning hadn't caused him to recoil in guilt and horror. When he got on top of me, I wondered if he'd forgotten what I said the night before, but I didn't know how to remind him of the pill without seeming like a nag. And then it was too late; we were having sex. I took the morning-after pill the next day, on my twenty-third birthday.

It never occurred to me to call this *rape*. It didn't feel like rape. I thought that if I'd explicitly objected to the sex, he probably would have stopped. I felt I had to be accountable for my behaviour, too.

But the other part, which I tried to explain to Lukas, is that I can't really see that night in isolation anymore. After we had sex, I became totally fixated on Simon. I think that I needed to convince myself that I cared about him—that I was really interested in him—so that I could face the idea that I had done this risky, stupid thing. That I had made these choices. I also wanted to believe that his choosing me that night hadn't just been a matter of boredom or opportunity. I tried to get as close to him as possible. I thought that if we had sex again, it would overwrite the first time. If it happened again, and I put myself in the role of a willing participant, I could forget that the first time I hadn't been.

I couldn't concentrate at work; I was perpetually waiting for him, having conversations with him in my mind, angling for moments to be alone. When he ignored me, which was most of the time we were together, I told myself it was just because he felt guilty about betraying his wife. The days felt so long then. In a bad period, after too many days of being ignored, I literally chased him one afternoon. I followed him home after work, trailing him from a distance, then cutting him off after jogging quickly around a corner. "Hello there, Ros," he said, looking mildly amused at our almost-collision, before carrying on and leaving me standing, quiet and rejected, in the blazing afternoon heat.

In the next year, however, I managed to sleep with him twice more. Both times, I felt briefly attractive, but the cold shoulder he gave me after was excruciating. I went to great lengths to appear unbothered. Like I neither wanted nor needed anything more than he gave me. It took him moving back to Ireland to stop me from agonizing about him.

"Post something or don't," Lukas said. "But at least acknowledge what it was. You'll be in good company." He gestured at his iPhone, the endless stream of women and their hashtags.

I'm still not sure if Simon raped me. I don't have a clear read on it. Was he a predator? Was I a victim? I didn't know those words could apply.

Maybe it was the same for Megan. Something dark and disturbing happened, and she didn't know why, or what it meant or whose fault it was. It took her more than twenty years to put language to what happened to her.

7

We pick up Fudgsicles at the convenience store, and then I ask Benji if he'll take a walk with me on the Felsbridge River path. He shrugs his agreement. I heard on a parenting podcast once that conversations about uncomfortable topics are easier for adolescents when you're not face to face. Kids are more open, more vulnerable, when eye contact isn't forced. I feel a little shaky, a touch nauseated, but it isn't as bad as it was two years ago when I told him his dad was moving out. I am getting used to issuing disappointments.

"I want to talk to you about something. About your dad," I say.

"Is he dying?" It's the expressionlessness of Benji's tone, his vacant face, that startles me.

"No, sweetheart," I say. "But he *is* involved in a difficult situation. Nothing life threatening, but difficult."

"That rape thing?"

I try to conceal my shock. "I didn't realize you knew about that. But *rape* isn't the right word here."

He shrugs.

"When did you hear about it?" I ask.

He shrugs again.

"Do you remember who told you?"

"Alex."

I can't tell whether I'm more disturbed that he's been aware of this without my knowledge or that his attitude about the whole thing can be summed up with a shrug.

"Do you know what *rape* means?" I ask.

"Of course, Mom." Benji starts walking faster, moving ahead of me.

I take bigger steps but keep a relaxed pace. I don't want him to feel chased. "What does it mean, do you think?"

"Sex," he says, turning only slightly, not quite facing me.

"Sex?"

"Basically."

"Benji," I say. "*Rape* doesn't mean sex. *Rape* means forcing sex onto someone who doesn't want it."

"But sex, basically." He turns and faces me then, jerking his hair out of his face in a way that felt more dramatic when it was longer. I notice for the first time that Mom's haircut makes him look younger.

"It's a violent crime."

He takes a large bite of his Fudgsicle, and chocolate drips onto the face mask dangling around his chin. We both look out at the river, low and slow moving, more brown than blue.

"Have you looked this up online at all? It's okay if you did. Or if you do. Just remember that the news can be—"

"Fake."

"Yes, that too. But I was going to say *harsh*. What your dad's been accused of isn't rape, but it's related. A woman is suing him, she wants to take him to court . . . because she says he did certain sexual things without her permission."

"Sexual things?"

"Like touching where she didn't want him to."

"But it's not true."

"We don't know what's true, sweetheart. Only your dad and the woman accusing him know for sure what happened, and it was a very long time ago."

"How long?"

"In university."

"What does Dad say happened?"

"He denies it."

"So she's making it up?"

I take a slow breath. This is his father. "I don't know."

"So if it's a crime, will he go to jail?"

"No." I feel relieved to be more definitive on this. "The punishment, if a judge thinks there needs to be one, will be money, not jail."

"That's so unfair." He looks right at me, his eyes slitted with accusation.

You know what's unfair, I think, is that after everything Lukas has done, I'm the one delivering this shitty news by a dried-up river. Carefully, because I'm worried about setting him off, I say, "I'm on your side, Benj. I'm listening. If you have any questions about this, you can come to me." But as I say it, I realize that I am already failing on the one and only question Benji wants answered: Is he innocent or not? I want to know this, too.

Benji takes a final bite of his Fudgsicle and then pulls his face mask over his mouth, hiding whatever emotion might help me figure out what to say next. What damage has this conversation already caused?

What can I do to minimize the harm? I don't say anything, let him take the lead for a bit.

I had imagined a longer walk, but after storming ahead, Benji turns around abruptly at the first of three bridges and begins walking back toward me. "You knew him in university, right?" he asks.

"Yes, sweetheart. You know that."

When Benji was little, he liked to hear the story of Lukas and me. I showed him how to find Ontario on a map of North America, tracing the distance for him to Southern California. *You and Daddy lost each other, but then you found him all the way across the world! Tell me that story!* Five-year-old Benji, the romantic. In his Disney version, some unnamed but banal life circumstance tore us apart, but in the end, it didn't matter because fate had our backs. What does Benji make of this story now that we're no longer together? Did it get filed in the same place as Santa Claus and other childhood disappointments? Somewhere darker?

"If he says he didn't do it, he didn't do it," Benji says.

"I understand how you feel." I regain my place next to him.

He points at me with his Fudgsicle stick. "*You're* the one who was the liar."

I stop. "Pardon?"

Benji's cheeks flush pink; he knows he has crossed a line. More quietly now, he says, "Dad said the reason you didn't finish university together was that you told a lie and got kicked out."

So this is what has become of our romantic story. Details have been added to turn me into a villain, unworthy of Lukas from the start. But what exactly did Lukas tell him? We never explicitly talked about keeping my mistakes at Regis a secret, but mostly that was because Lukas behaved as though he could hardly remember them himself. Had Lukas shared this recently, in anticipation of Benji hearing about the allegations against him? It was Lukas's style to try to deflect attention from his own failings by pointing out the weaknesses in other people. Or were his motivations more troubling? Was he trying to inculcate a kind of skepticism about women in general: *Don't worry about what some woman is saying, kiddo, all the women at Regis were liars. Take your own mother, for example.*

"I don't know what you heard, but that is a very long, complicated story. I promise to explain it to you one day, but I want to talk about your dad right now."

Benji walks ahead again, but I see his shoulders move up and down, dismissing me. I follow quietly until he slows his pace around the parking area. Before we cross into the shade, I notice our shadows. "Look, sweetie," I say. "You're almost as tall as me without even trying." When Benji was little, he would arrange our bodies on the sidewalk to make our shadows the same height. I would blob my shadow over his, pretending to gobble it up to make him laugh. I know he remembers this, but he turns to me and knits his eyebrows in pretend confusion so that I'll think he has forgotten our game. This stings, but the dismay I feel is directed more at Lukas than Benji. How dare he bring me down with his ship, telling our son I'm the liar. Our kid needs at least one steady grown-up. Wasn't Lukas mature enough to know at least that?

I had planned to convey two critical points to Benji in this discussion, both strongly emphasized in my online reading. First, that his dad loves him no matter what. Second, that his dad is not a bad person, even if it does turn out that he did something wrong. But when we reach the car, I say, "Benj? One last thing. No matter what, your dad loves you. Okay?"

Reflected in the car window, I see Benji roll his eyes.

As I unlock the door, Elaine Ng reenters my mind, and I think, Maybe I will speak to you. Lukas doesn't get to tell my part in this story.

8

The cheating started early. Before that, there was incompatibility. The first sign of it came only a few months after Lukas and I agreed to be exclusive, which was about six months after we first fooled around.

I remember being at a diner with Lukas and his friend when a familiar R&B song came on about the singer's all-consuming desire to "make love" and "feel so close." Lukas said, "I hear these songs, and I'm pretty sure they're describing a kind of sex I've never had." His friend and I laughed, but I was unsettled. I couldn't get the remark out of my head. *Never?* It was true, and increasingly notable to me, that all we ever did in bed was fuck. Not necessarily rough or impersonal fucking, just a bit one note. Sitting in that restaurant, I realized that I had been waiting for that to evolve; I'd been hoping we'd settle into a gentler, more tender plain in time. I assumed he was capable of it, I assumed everyone was. What I began to worry about was that if I couldn't unlock that side of him, maybe I wasn't the one he should really be with. But I didn't want him to have the same thought. It was easier to scoff at the corny song than to say anything that might cause him to rethink what either of us should want.

I wasn't worried about our sexual compatibility for my own sake. I didn't love the sex we were having, but I thought that if our sex life had indeed reached its limits of romantic expression, I could probably live with that. Now that we were in a committed relationship, I felt invested and fortunate, and I didn't want a small sexual problem to undo everything. I wanted him to think I was unfussy, unflappable, easygoing. These were the things I figured he liked best about me. Plus, maybe sex wasn't that important to me; there were lots of other things that made us compatible. We both liked Jonathan Franzen, NPR, *The Wire*. We both appreciated a good pun. We respected each other's talents; he loved my baking, and I really did think he was a good writer. There were mornings we spent in bed together discussing Billi Bean, and sometimes he would jot down my ideas on Post-it notes and stick them to his laptop, which thrilled me. We also bonded over our shared dislikes. If someone at a party said something stupid, I loved to catch Lukas's eye across a room, to be the recipient of his secret smile.

Instead of getting better, our incompatibility in bed got worse as the months wore on. Once, Lukas asked me if I had any interest in couples. I told him, quite honestly, that I didn't think so. The idea of hooking up with another couple was terrifying to me; sex made me self-conscious enough with just one person, and I didn't like the idea of performing for, or being watched by, two or more additional people who could later sit around and discuss, in detail, how my body looked or how my moves lacked originality. "No problem," Lukas said. "Just had to ask."

Despite my lack of enthusiasm, Lukas began forwarding me ads from Craigslist: "Couples looking for other couples." He'd write subject lines like: "Sound interesting?" I demurred at first, but not strongly.

Sometimes I said nothing. One Sunday afternoon, after spending most of the day building up the nerve, I replied to one of the forwarded posts with: *If this is something you really want to try, and if I am holding you back, we should talk about it?* Then I waited for two anxious days.

When Lukas responded, he also did it by email. It wasn't a matter of "trying," he confessed. He and most of his exes had been involved with couples. He said it was probably time he told me that he thought of himself as "an individual out of alignment with typical heteronormative practices" and that he'd experimented widely. Groups of all kinds, for example. I didn't know what *kinds* of groups there were, and I didn't ask. He also said—and this was the part I clung to—that he didn't need random, anonymous sex if that wasn't what I wanted. He just needed to know that I wasn't judging him. He explained that he'd gone through long periods in the past of thinking his behaviour was wrong—he'd delete his dating profiles and chat histories—but eventually, he would seek out new, anonymous experiences because it was fun for him, a way to relax and let off steam. He wrote:

> *I just want to be honest about who I am. But I also want you to know that I can and will curtail all of this in deference to you. Being with you is more important to me than being part of any sexual subculture.*

My immediate instinct was to make him feel better. I didn't want him feeling shame or regret. I reassured him, again by email, that I wasn't judging, that I didn't want him to feel he had to hide any part of himself. I said that there were certain aspects of our discussion that tested me, but tests were good. Who wanted life to be completely predictable? Then, because I didn't want him to leave me, I said something I shouldn't have, because it wasn't very honest. I said, "Who knows? I may not be closed to these ideas forever."

At that point, I was mainly optimistic about us. Now that his secret was out, I thought we might grow closer. But months went by, and nothing more was said about what either of us wanted. We moved in together. I tried to forget what I knew. But one Sunday morning, when he was in the shower, I found his computer open to the Craigslist personals. I tried to keep my voice firmly in the register of curiosity, not accusation, when I asked him about what I'd seen. He was honest immediately. He said he just read the ads, from time to time, because women's brazen pleas for anonymous sex turned him on. He even admitted to chatting with them online sometimes, just for the sexy banter. Casually, he said, "Honestly, Ros, it's just masturbation fodder. All guys need to masturbate." He seemed to care more about whether I would judge him than whether or not the behaviour was okay with me. I did my best to be very open-minded, very 2007. "Fine," I said. "As long as it never goes further." He said, "It won't."

I believed Lukas. Then, one spring evening, we drove to Big Bear campground to meet Lukas's friends, and we got lost on the way. I picked up his cellphone from the drink holder between us to call for directions. I noticed a text message from the name "Redhead" and was moved to open it. The message said: *Meet next week? I can't resist your offer of a cock(tail).*

"You have a message," I said to him as calmly as I could. I didn't tell him I had read it.

He snatched the phone from me and put it in his pocket. "Use your phone," he said. "My reception sucks out here."

If you saw this scene in a movie, you'd know what was going on right away. You'd wait for the girl to say something. If she didn't say something in the car, you'd expect it to come out later: a tense, drunk confrontation around a blazing firepit, the other couples backing away into their tents. But we met up with his friends, and I didn't say a thing.

I told myself that "Redhead" was nothing, just a character in his dirty banter. I watched Lukas closely the next week, and he never slipped away for cocktails. So I breathed a little easier.

I was taking lunch at the college where we both worked, eating fries and idly checking Facebook, when I finally got the message. A direct message from a woman called Trista Ames. Her profile was private, and her picture was just a photo of Betty Boop, so I couldn't find out much except that she was from Buena Park. The message said: *We don't know each other, but I feel you should know something. Maybe you and your bf have an arrangement. If you do, that's cool. But if you don't, you should know what's happening with my friend . . .*

I felt so incredibly stupid. Not stupid for being blindsided, stupid because I didn't have any real excuse for calling it a blindsiding—I'd had every reason to investigate after finding that strange text, and I never did. And there were other signs. Lukas was possessive of his phone, he liked to go for long Sunday drives "just to think," and there were nights he left abruptly because of "a Billi Bean idea" that he needed to work out at the late-night Starbucks. What was wrong with me? How had I let things reach the point where I was hearing about them from Trista in Buena Park?

Lukas seemed relieved to be caught. He admitted to feeling lately like his life was a house of cards. Now that the collapse was happening, he saw no sense in holding back. He said, if he had to estimate, there had been about fifty other women since we'd been together. Maybe more. But *just sex*, he said repeatedly. One-offs, for the most part, that had *nothing* to do with me. These were desperate, clichéd reassurances, but they worked on me. What I heard was that I was special. I was trustworthy. Also, that he wanted to stop. He didn't want to live a double life, he said, it made him sick. There was something he needed from these women, but whatever it was, it was not right, and he would fix it. Could I help him fix it? He didn't want to lose me, but he'd understand if I left him.

I was so calm through his confession. I listened as a therapist would. When I did get upset, I immediately dialed it back. I didn't want to be insensitive. I needed to help him. He was ashamed and suffering, and I wanted him to feel safe and attended to.

Lukas found a therapist right away. That therapist, Harriet, said that he could learn to manage some of his sexual compulsions. He set about managing them, blocking the women he cheated with on his phone and Facebook, shutting down his online dating profiles, staying home every night of the week. He tried group therapy. He quit the first group because it was too cultish. He quit the second because he said it just felt like a bunch of nerdy IT guys he couldn't relate to. He quit the third because it had rules against masturbation, and *come on*. Then, after a couple months, he quit Harriet. He admitted to me that he had started to sexualize her when she seemed too interested in the details of his encounters. I doubted she was showing any more interest than was necessary for the job, but I told him I appreciated his honesty. I suggested a male therapist, and he said he'd look into it, but I don't think he ever did. He promised me that he had learned a lot and was already, basically, a different person. For the moment, he didn't need more therapy, he said. He just needed love and acceptance. He needed me.

Still, I applied to Cordon Bleu in Paris. I was short money-wise, but Mom agreed to loan me what I needed, which was far more than half, when the admission offer came in.

The decision to go was mostly for myself, but I also wanted to show Lukas that I could do unpredictable things. I asked him to come with me, but he said, "You know what, Rosie? Maybe a break isn't the worst thing." Nineties TV had taught me that the term *break* meant doomed. I panicked; I didn't want to end things. I begged him not to think that way. He said, "Let's see how things go, see what we learn about ourselves." If he'd asked me to stay, I would have, but instead, I went to Paris.

Lukas gave me a digital camera as a parting gift. I have about three photographs and a bunch of grainy memories of that time. When I see movies set in Paris, I have to remind myself I once lived there.

I thought I was too old for a roommate, so I lived alone; I see now that was probably a mistake. I rented a cheap studio apartment at the edge of the city, and it took me an hour to commute to the school. My apartment had a view of the Marne through windows that opened wide enough to make my heart race. I spent one Saturday afternoon watching a car being pulled from the clay-coloured water; I never found out what happened to the driver or if there were others inside. In another direction, I could see into the kitchen of a neighbouring apartment. In the evenings, I watched the couple who lived there. Once, the man did an odd little dance, twirling a wooden spoon for his girlfriend. They seemed to be in a faraway country that no amount of travel could ever get me to.

I lived close to the veterinary school, which had the depressing effect of making me think of Megan more often than I had in years. What was she doing now? Had she ever become a vet? Had she actually lost her mind that winter? How much was I to blame if she had? I thought of her when I saw happy groups of vet students, or what I assumed were vet students, sitting with tulip-shaped glasses of beer at the brasserie terrace near the metro station. On warmer evenings in spring, I would walk by slowly, sometimes twice, hoping someone might recognize me from around, call out to me, invite me to have a drink. But that's not how things work, and I was too self-conscious to go in and order a drink by myself. One evening, a pretty, fortysomething mother and her son, a boy of about eight or nine, sat at a table in the shade. She had a glass of white wine; he had a large *coupe glacée*. She was telling him a story, her elegant hands tracing a picture in the air in front of her. I heard the music of their combined laughter, and a feeling passed over me, similar to the one I'd experienced my first time on Heritage Street. Maybe this was what I was looking for. Maybe it was the company of a child that I wanted; maybe she was who I wanted to be. And just as soon as I thought it, I worried it wouldn't happen for me.

For the most part, I liked baking school. I learned how to make custard, flan, sweet and savoury soufflés. I liked the impermanence of what I made. Every day, sometimes every hour, I could start again. But I felt very alone. Closing in on thirty, I was one of the oldest students in my group, and while the age gap wasn't that significant, it felt like a gulf to me. I thought that I had to be more serious than my younger peers, but I figured they saw me as a joke: I should be settling down at my age, not starting over. Gilbert, my assigned mentor, a dick in his late fifties, told me there was talent in my fingers, but I worked too much with my head. *Relax, he said. Where do you need to go, Rosaline?* He'd chuckle then, as if he knew there wasn't a good answer.

I spent most evenings watching *Friday Night Lights* on my laptop, eating tufts of bread, cheese and packaged ham. I never baked in the apartment; I didn't have an oven. Sometimes I'd rollerblade home after school to kill time, two hours along the Seine, through the Champ de Mars and past Notre Dame, though I often forgot to look up and take notice. Most of my mental energy was reserved for composing emails to Lukas, but I rarely sent them. Once or twice a week, we Skyped. He laughed at my imitations of Gilbert. He told me what was happening with his writing. Talking to him, I felt the grey fog of my life in Paris lift away.

I returned to L.A. nine months after I left, one week after getting my baking diploma. I had considered travelling around Europe a bit, but I was too exhausted, lonely and broke. Lukas picked me up at LAX. He didn't rush to me, he stood back, smiling a sad little smile, waiting for me to come to him. He touched both my arms, just above the elbows, once I was close enough. My huge duffle still hung across my shoulders; he did not take it from me. "I am so glad you're back," he said.

"It's good to see you, too."

"You look great."

Did I? I'd lost more weight in Paris, all the walking, but I didn't think of myself as looking "great." In Paris, I'd felt invisible. Lukas looked very fit in his thin white T-shirt, jeans and aviators. Very Los Angeles. I almost cried with homesickness for the place I'd just returned to.

His expression shifted suddenly, his eyes sparkling like the terrazzo floor below us. "Billi Bean's going to be published," he said. "You're the first to know. I really wanted to tell you before anyone else."

"That's great!" I said.

I looked at him closely, trying to figure out what he wanted me to do.

"Put down your bag a sec." I obeyed. He took my right hand loosely in his. "I think things could be really good with us from now on," he said. "Everything is coming into place."

When I hugged him, he felt so solid. "I'm so happy for you," I said.

It might seem sad to some that I took him back, but I wasn't sad. I remember driving home with him from the airport, the sun bouncing off the cars on the 405, and the feeling that I was precisely where I needed to be, that I had learned something from the break, after all.

Maybe that's the sad part. That I couldn't imagine anything better.

A few months after returning from France, I was pregnant with Benji. Lukas and I called it an accident, but I think we were purposely careless. A baby was an excuse to stay the course, to stay in the present, think about the future, and not look too hard at our foundation. Still, there were a couple of months in the first trimester when I thought about doing motherhood on my own, because I knew—really, I knew in my gut—that it would end up this way. I thought about the mother on the terrace in Paris, chatting happily alone with her son. I thought about her, and I *almost* considered doing it on my own. That was as hard as I tried to take control of what anyone could see—if I'd let them—was a desperate situation.

As it happened, Lukas and I both got caught up in a wave of fresh start-ism that anesthetized my anxiety. With Lukas's publisher's advance and more money from Mom, we could afford a down payment on a house with a yard, and we found one in a commuter city near the college. With a baby coming, it wasn't the right time to embark on a new career as a pastry chef, so I got another contract at the college, and I baked at home when I was in the mood. I'd never lived in the suburbs, but the dullness and predictability of life in Orange County appealed to me—Lukas could surf every morning to take the edge off, be home by six thirty every night. For a while, he had a little garage band, and that seemed to make him happy. Lukas said that he wanted this life, this stability. I just wanted whatever conditions would make him less likely to cheat.

By the time Benji could walk, Lukas had published another book, and then he just kept going. He gave up his job running the Writing Center, and I took it over. One of us needed a steady income, and I was happy to do my part to help Lukas succeed. In my first few months in that job, I tried to inspire. I sat patiently with students and explained the difference between a comma and semicolon, the importance of topic sentences, and how to frame a quotation. But the students didn't really want to learn. They wanted to look at me with desperate faces so that I would snatch their papers back and fix their work myself. I was disappointed at first, but frankly, this approach was easier for everyone.

Over the next few years, three Billi Bean books made bestseller lists for young adult fiction. Lukas was consulting on a miniseries. And for my part, I felt okay. I felt like I was pulling something off. The job was easy enough and gave me lots of time with Benji. We bought a hillside home in Laguna Niguel with a view of the ocean. I took up yoga and joined a 6 a.m. fitness class in the park. If I didn't always feel alive, at least I looked the part. I met a handful of mom-friends in the years before Benji started kindergarten—kind, generous, available women who could sit in the park for hours and compare parenting doubts and anxieties—*Is he normal? Am I bad? Am I doing this right?* They knew nothing of my past anxieties or my doubts about the future, just a clean, selfless slice of the present. Our connection was straightforward, purposeful and passed the time. It would have been nice to strike up something deeper with one of these friends, to be honest and vulnerable. But it had been so long since I'd tried to have a confidante—a Sue or Val—that I wasn't sure where to begin. Plus, Sue and Val had both rejected me, so my instincts weren't reliable. In the playground, it was easier to keep things pleasant, predictable and focused on the children. And when the kids started elementary school, we mainly drifted apart.

I had considered getting back into culinary work when Benji was in school, but my hours at the Writing Center were very compatible with Benji's drop-offs and pickups, and I didn't want to lose that. Plus, Lukas travelled a lot for book tours. He mostly travelled alone, but sometimes he brought us along. We went to Newfoundland, Scotland, South Africa. I decided that I'd been lucky to find out about the cheating when I did so that we could course correct and arrive at our current, settled stage. Sometimes, I thought about Trista Ames. Did she ever look me up on Facebook and think: Jesus, still together? What a doormat. But I told myself that infidelity was pedestrian, so many couples went through this. The thing was to not let it hijack your whole life. In the busyness of early parenthood, I could put the past out of my mind. And loving Benji so much helped me tuck away the question of what I thought of Lukas.

Then at Benji's sixth birthday party, I picked up Lukas's phone. In general, I avoided Lukas's phone. I told myself this was because I didn't want to live like that—I didn't want to be that girl. Whether this was more for his protection or mine is hard to say—maybe they were the same thing. At the party, I hadn't even tried to look, but the kids wanted to hear Katy Perry, and my phone was dead. I could see there was a message—with a photo—from Miss Carmen, Benji's preschool teacher. Only, Benji wasn't in preschool anymore.

Even topless, Carmen wasn't particularly attractive.

Later, after the paper plates and pinata remains were all cleared away and Benji was asleep with his new lightsaber, I told Lukas what I'd seen and that he had ruined everything for good. I wasn't sure if I meant it, but he nodded and said, yes, yes, he understood my decision. I was enraged. I thought, Isn't this a little too easy for you? Now you just get to walk away?

Lukas didn't beg me to stay. But in the end, I didn't leave. It's funny when I think of it now: he wronged me, but his punishment was that I would cling to him. By then, I felt such shame for having clung to him in the first place, that letting go—having it all be for nothing—was the only thing that would make it worse. I thought the solution was to keep on clinging until I truly got a hold of him.

We started to see a relationship counsellor, Sabrina, who cost a small fortune. We spent most of our sessions searching for Lukas's "trauma story." The counsellor didn't believe that Lukas had never been sexually abused, never been a witness to abuse. Once, when Lukas was caught in traffic and missed an appointment, she said she was glad to have the time alone with me. She said that, on the one hand, I came across as intelligent and rational. But on the other hand—I remember her closing her right fist and then opening her left—I was very naive. She did not say that I "came across" that way, she said *was*. She said, "You need to be watching him. Antennae up for the rest of your life."

I got my own therapist, another two hundred dollars a week, but I needed someone to talk to who didn't call me naive. A close friend would have been better, but Lukas was my only friend. And he had betrayed me.

Even with no one to tell, I worried about people finding out. Lukas had a very public profile, but I also wanted to protect my own reputation. We had the kind of life you could make a bunch of positive assumptions about, and that was what I wanted from people—it was all I had! I was vain about our outward appearance as a couple, proud of my ability to deceive everyone.

I wanted my therapist to tell me what was wrong with me; I wanted her to tell me what I should do. She wouldn't—or couldn't—do that. She was kind enough, but in the end, she felt like another manifestation of my inability to leave someone who took from me without really improving my life. I still haven't officially dumped her.

Lukas and I decided to work on our sex life. We hadn't had sex more than a handful of times in two years and although we knew that sex wasn't the root of our problems, we figured nothing fundamental could ever get fixed if we weren't having sex. I bought an e-book called *Recover Your Spark*. Chapter one suggested sharing sexual fantasies. Just talk, the author said, no pressure. We took an afternoon off work to try it.

"You can't think of anything?" Lukas said, rolling toward me on the bed, resting his head on my shoulder. We were both fully clothed. I was wearing a striped, green T-shirt dress that I thought was flattering. A warm square of light from the window above the bed was hitting the top halves of our bodies.

"Nothing is really coming to mind." I had told him before that I didn't really have fantasies. At some point, I must have stopped bothering.

"What's the last thing you masturbated to?" Lukas said.

I didn't blush the way I would have a few years before. "There's something," I said. "But fantasy feels like a weird word for it. It's more like a revisionist history?"

"I'm listening," Lukas said.

"It starts off with something that really happened in ninth grade."

"Your fantasy is about grade nine?"

"You're not supposed to judge."

"Sorry, not judging." He tucked my hair behind my ear.

"Okay, so it was a birthday party at a water park for this girl named Martha. I wasn't close to her, and she was sort of a tomboy. I'm not sure why I was invited except maybe she felt she needed more girls. Anyway, it was a rare event in that year where I felt noticed, maybe because the girl-guy ratio was way off."

"I'm sure lots of guys noticed you."

"Not really. But anyway, we were playing volleyball in the pool, which I happened to be sort of good at, and this guy Jory told me to get up on his shoulders, which made me very nervous at first, but once I was riding up there, I felt like a chick in a Juicy Fruit commercial. He was tall and had this sandpaper voice. He wasn't, like, the coolest guy in school or anything, but he was well liked. After the waterpark, we went back to Martha's house and hung around in the basement. We were sitting there, and out of nowhere, Jory goes to me, 'This is boring. Do you want to go somewhere and fool around?'"

"What?" Lukas said. "So brazen."

"Yeah, yeah. And I *really* wanted to. I was basically in flames. But I was too scared. I just sort of laughed off the idea. And he was good, he dropped it. I wanted him to ask me again, but he didn't."

"So in your fantasy—?"

"Yes. So in my fantasy, I agree immediately, and we go up to Martha's bedroom, which I've never actually seen, but I picture it with, like, a Michael Jordan poster and a plastic laundry hamper and just, you know, not exactly a hot environment, but maybe that's what makes it hot because it's such an unexpected environment to have sex in. Anyway, we're up there, and I let Jory go all the way with me."

"*All the way*?" Lukas laughed. "And that's exactly what you would have called it."

"All the bases."

"So what does he do to you?" Lukas stroked my arm.

I felt annoyed by this question, like he somehow missed the point. "Nothing super specific. I think the turn-on is just this idea of rocking his fourteen-year-old world."

"So your sexual fantasy is to be some fourteen-year-old's sexual fantasy?"

"It's not about him being fourteen. I'm not, like, *into* fourteen-year-olds. But, you know, when you're that age, everything is so heightened."

"But fourteen? It just feels kind of stalled."

"Well, I'm sorry to disappoint you."

"I'm not disappointed," he said. "I could pretend to be fourteen."

"I don't think that would work. And like I said, I'm not a creep who's into teens. It's about channelling those supercharged teen feelings."

Lukas moved a little closer to me. "Have you looked him up? This Jory?"

"I have, actually. He has a company in Silicon Valley."

"Big shot. So if you came across him again, would you tell him?"

"Uh, no."

"That would be kind of hot, though," Lukas said. "I'd like to find out that some girl still fantasizes about the way I propositioned her twenty-five years ago."

"Well, I don't think the fantasy has anything to do with now," I said. "It probably doesn't even have much to do with him. Plus, there's a good reason my real fourteen-year-old self didn't go off with him. I mean, if I had the chance to go back in time, I probably wouldn't do anything differently. I wouldn't have had the emotional maturity for the aftermath."

Lukas's phone buzzed on the chair across the room. I felt his body react, but he didn't go to answer it. I wondered who it was. I could sense he was wondering if I was wondering, but neither of us said anything.

"That was pretty much how I lost my virginity," Lukas said after a minute. "What you just described. And it wasn't particularly hot." Lukas and I had shared our virginity stories before. I knew he had lost his to a friend's cousin over the summer before high school.

Lukas rolled onto his back. "I guess it would be nice to think she was acting out her desires, like you said. I don't know. But my world wasn't rocked, not exactly. I was just sort of freaked out. I kept trying things, and she just kept letting me, so who was I to try to stop it? My first everything. All at once."

"Did you use protection?"

He laughs. "Yes, Mom. I guess she must have had it on her. Anyway, it didn't matter, I never actually came." This part he never told me.

"You didn't?"

"I know, you'd think I'd come in three seconds, right? But we were at it for maybe forty minutes, or that's what it felt like. I wasn't sure what was supposed to happen. I mean, I knew what was *supposed* to happen, but I didn't get why it wasn't, and I started to panic. Eventually, we just stopped."

"Did she say anything?"

"No, nothing." The sun was in his eyes now, he squeezed them shut and rubbed them with the heels of his hands. "It was weird. But it did give me an ego boost. School started again, and I asked Katrina out."

"Did you tell Katrina about that other girl?"

"No."

"But you two dated all through high school. You let her think you lost your virginity together?"

"I never told you this," Lukas said. He flipped back to face me. "It's actually something I discussed with Harriet way back, but Katrina and I never actually—"

"You didn't?"

"At first, she wanted to wait until grade twelve, which was a long time to wait, but that was the plan. When we got there, we tried a few times, but she always said it hurt too much, so we never—"

"Huh?" I said. "How did I have a totally different idea about the amount of sex you had before Regis?"

"She gave me plenty of hand jobs."

"So what did Harriet say about that?"

"About the hand jobs?" He laughed. "Actually, that's not even totally true about the hand jobs. She gave me a few hand jobs, but then everything kind of died off. I don't know why. We stayed together, but we didn't *do* anything. Harriet definitely thought that was interesting. That was the time I should have been experimenting, figuring it all out."

"Not necessarily. I didn't lose my virginity until I was in university."

"Yeah, but I had a girlfriend. Everyone thought I was screwing her all the time, and of course, I let them believe it. But by graduation, we had stopped even talking about sex. I thought it was wrong to want sex so badly if it could be painful for girls. So I was like, Okay, I'll just try to be happy that I have this cute girlfriend who everyone else wants—I don't need anything more. But I was horny, so I jerked off all the time. Teenage boys do, but I don't know, I was obsessed. I felt really dirty about it, because Katrina would die if she knew. These weren't enlightened times. But then I told myself it was okay if that's what I needed to do to not cheat on my great girlfriend."

"I'm sorry."

"No, I am," he said. "We were supposed to talk fantasies."

"It's probably good to talk about this, though."

"I can't blame Katrina for who I am," he said. "But I think that experience was fucked up. I think it made me feel sort of split, like I had a real Madonna-whore thing going on. I got all freaked out about intimacy with girls I liked, like all girls went reluctantly into sex. I should have had some sort of therapy, but who gets sex therapy at nineteen?"

"What about your girlfriend from out West? The one you dated while you were at Regis. Shauna, right?"

"We had sex sometimes, but I was pretty self-conscious about it. And I only saw her about six times in three years, so we didn't exactly grow sexually, which was the pattern I was used to."

"Did you cheat on her?"

"Yeah, with a few girls at Regis. I liked girls who already had boyfriends, who knew what they were doing so that it wasn't a big deal. There was a grad student who liked it when her boyfriend watched. That was something I was into for a while." He exhaled loudly through his nose.

"But if it was consensual, what's wrong with that? I mean, a lot of people are into that."

But he didn't seem to be hearing me. He took another big breath in, and I thought he might say something, but he went quiet. His hands went up to cover his eyes, and just like that, he was sobbing. I didn't know what to say. I rested my head on his shoulder, stroked his chest. "It's okay," I whispered. Eventually, I got up to get Benji from daycare, leaving Lukas in the darkening bedroom.

After that day, I think we made some progress as a couple, if not in terms of saving our relationship then at least in terms of understanding each other. I didn't feel angry at him most of the time, but I also realized that I didn't want to have sex with him, either. I tried to get in the mood, but then I would think of all the women he'd been with behind my back, and I couldn't figure out why I should be having sex that I didn't want to have. On some level, I understood that not having sex would make it impossible to have a normal, healthy relationship, but I felt unmoved to do anything about it.

My attitude toward Lukas was mainly generous—he wasn't a bad person, he was struggling—but in the next year or so, there were moments when I would look at him brushing his teeth at the sink next to mine and think, How can I still be doing this? What's the point? I did wonder if a moment would come when I decided I was done. Would it be a sudden dawning? Was I waiting until Benji got older? Or was I waiting for a force to push me there? Was I waiting for him to be caught cheating again—was I, actually, *willing* that?

And then one January evening, he came home after a four-day trip to New York with a terrible cold. That night he kept coughing, sniffing snot back up his nose, unravelling toilet paper from a roll he'd placed between our pillows, next to my head. I couldn't sleep; his body sounds were excruciating. This is not what I want, I kept thinking. I don't want to take care of Lukas when he gets old and sick. What has he done to deserve that from me? The next morning, I asked if he thought one of us should leave. Like, *leave* leave. He thought about it a moment, his face unsurprised. "Yes," he said tiredly. "I will."

And that's how it ended. That simple, unscripted exchange. I stayed in our house, he rented a condo in Laguna Beach. He was liberal with money, and we both agreed that maintaining stability for Benji was the most important thing. He took Benji one or two weekends a month, depending on his travel schedule, and I handled the rest. That meant giving certain things up—culinary career aspirations, for the time being—but divided arrangements always meant sacrifice. Though quickly, it began to feel as if those sacrifices were only mine.

But most of the time, I felt self-congratulatory, even sentimental, about our amicable separation. I remained more connected to Lukas than anyone else I knew. He was the reason behind most of my life's design: where I lived, where I worked, what I worried about. That fall, when anyone asked about him, I'd say, "We're still close." And mostly, I believed it.

We celebrate Ginny's birthday at the picnic table on her lawn. It's a warm evening, the mosquitoes aren't too bad, and I am moved when Ginny says that this is exactly where she would choose to be even if it weren't a pandemic.

"How old are you again?" Mom asks Ginny, refilling her wineglass. I'm sure she knows the answer and is simply priming to make some sort of comment.

"Thirty-nine," Ginny says with a downturned, almost shameful smile.

"At least you're not forty," Mom says.

"I didn't mind turning forty," I offer. "It was just harder to get older than that." Turning forty, I'd felt lighthearted and jaunty; I looked the same, felt fine, it almost seemed like I'd pulled something off. But the year sped by so fast, and turning forty-one, in March, was heavier. Age was getting serious.

"It's the ripening decade," Mom says, and this must be the insight she was preparing to unload. "You become an adult in your thirties, but you ripen in your forties. Then all of a sudden, you're fifty, ready to be tossed."

"I don't feel ripe," I say.

Mom looks at me over her sunglasses.

"But not you," Ginny says to Mom. "You kicked off your whole career in your fifties."

"That's when I started my business, yes."

Although Mom graduated from architecture school in her early twenties, it was not until her fifties, after my dad died, that she started her own interior architecture and design business. She's still at it—or was, pre-pandemic, pre-injury. Who knows what the plan will be from here? Before I was born, she was the host of *Insidescapes*, an interior design show primarily aimed at housewives in the pre-TLC era. She helped "real-life" couples remodel their homes, and taught her viewers simple tricks, like how to balance bathroom lighting or exaggerate the appearance of a room's height. She liked the celebrity, but mostly she liked being publicly recognized as someone with talent. She was my dad's second wife, decades younger than his first, and the job buffered her ego somewhat from the icy suspicion of his robust social circle. Women would come up and ask her for her autograph when I was still small enough to ride in a grocery cart, even though the show was already off the air by then. She got pregnant with me in the show's third season, and they fired her before I was born. Ratings plummeted under the new host, and the show was pulled less than a year later. Mom should have taken that as a compliment, and although friends encouraged her, she never went back to work in the industry that spurned her. She stayed at home during my childhood and was susceptible to sudden, almost violent acts of redecorating.

"I admire you," Ginny says now. "How did it feel, starting again like that?" I look at Ginny like, *You don't have to blow smoke up her ass.*

"It just made sense," Mom says. She often frames decisions in terms of what makes sense. I'm not sure if this is because she doesn't think her feelings are relevant, or because she doesn't want to talk about them. I remember telling Lukas that I thought it had gotten to the point where she probably couldn't trust her feelings because she never exercised them. "I wish I'd started sooner."

"I should hire you to make my house in Toronto look good," Ginny says. "At least for pictures. I want to get it up on Airbnb."

"Really?" I ask.

"It's just sitting there. I could be making money."

"So you've decided? You're definitely staying."

Ginny lifts her shoulders. "I think six months, maybe a year. However long this pandemic lasts. If I'm working from home, why not be here? I love it here."

"Smart," Mom says. She turns to me. "Did you ever think of doing that? Renting out your home in California?"

"No," I say, a little guardedly. "It's technically Lukas's house, too. Plus, you've been complaining about *your* last renters for more than twenty years."

"Well. You can stay here as long you want," Mom says.

"Let's both stay forever," Ginny says, taking my arm in hers. "It's my birthday wish."

"It's a nice thought," I say. And the scene, minus my mother, is an easy source of sentimentality. Laughter from the kids on the driveway, a warm breeze, our bare feet in the grass. "Lukas would never go for it, though."

"Hmm," Ginny says. "Did you ever read Judy Blume novels growing up? When parents split up, dads go live in California, and the kids stay in New Jersey with their moms because New Jersey is a normal, practical place."

"Is this supposed to be New Jersey?"

"This is New Jersey."

"If Lukas doesn't like the plan, he's a writer," Mom says. "He could live wherever."

"He *was* a writer. Pretty sure he's cancelled," I say.

Mom sniffs dismissively. I'm not sure she knows what *cancelled* means.

"You know that I do this, too, right?" Ginny says. "I'm *always* thinking about Carl. I'm always like, How can I make it easier for him to see Alex? How can I better accommodate his schedule? As if making life easy for him is the top priority. But I don't even remotely expect him to think about me. And he doesn't. You can really lose yourself trying to accommodate some asshole."

"Screw that," Mom says, holding up her glass for Ginny to clink. Like she's so cool. She turns to me. "I'd be willing to bet that if you rented out your house, you'd make more than your salary in a year." This is a dig at my job, which I know she considers beneath me.

"Much less," I say quickly, though I'm not sure that's true. "And what *about* my job? Am I supposed to quit?"

"You hate your job, Ros," Ginny says.

"I don't *hate* it." Ginny knows I'm bored with my job as director of the college Writing Center; I've no doubt bored her relaying all my frustrations with the students, the administration. I've held onto it all these years because it's routine and easy, and because I'm not sure I'm qualified to do anything else. But, as I told Ginny, it's depressing to imagine all the passing hours there. Nothing to look forward to, nothing surprising left to happen—except maybe getting fired. But I don't want my mother to know about these thoughts; I don't want her to think that all my choices are failing me. "And my job is something real. *This* isn't reality."

"I am loath to sound like a stoned teenager, but what is reality? Why can't this be reality? I'm going to *lean into* Felsbridge, see what it's like."

Ginny picks a shard of icing off the bottom of the cake tray and sucks her finger thoughtfully. "This pandemic is making a lot of people reexamine their lives. Just watch, city people will start moving here in droves. And you know what they won't want? Sheet cakes from the Foodland. *You* could open a bakery."

"You think opening a bakery in a random town during a pandemic is my pathway to a better, more meaningful life?"

"It's not a *random* town," Mom says.

"Felsbridge Thrills," Ginny says. "Call it something like that."

"Sounds like a whorehouse," Mom says. "On second thought, that might make more money."

"So what about Benji's whole existence in Orange County?" I ask them. "All of his friends?"

Mom bats this away.

"Come on. I was a year older than him when we moved to L.A. That kind of upheaval sucks at his age, *by the way*."

Mom shakes her head. "But you were so excited to move to Los Angeles. Movie stars, palm trees, the beach?"

Had I been excited before we left? If I was, I've blocked that out. "I was miserable. Trust me."

I can see Ginny searching for something neutral to say.

Mom looks at Ginny. "Well, I was certainly glad to move," she says. "Toronto was my husband's city. His ex-wife and ex-life were everywhere I looked." I wonder briefly how it would make Val feel to be referred to as my dad's "ex-life." Mom shakes her head. "He still went to the same racquet club, the same restaurants, the same dry cleaner. It was my idea to build this cottage because I wanted our own thing, just for our family. I found the land, the contractors, and the project helped. But when L.A. came up, that was even better."

But you were sad in L.A., I want to say. *Dad thought you might get back into*

TV or work on some cool houses, but you smoked and watched All My Children *and* Y&R *every afternoon with the curtains drawn.* Instead, I say, "We didn't know anyone in L.A. Wasn't that a little isolating for you? It was for me."

Mom turns back to me. "If you disliked it so much, why did you move back the first chance you got?"

It's a fair question. "The problem wasn't California in particular, it's that middle school is a shitty time to move. Did you ever consider that?"

"Please accept my apologies," Mom says.

I turn to Ginny. "We can talk about something else."

She laughs. "No, are you kidding? I love this kind of shit." But still, she manages to steer the discussion to the sunset, moving our attention to some low-hanging clouds that have turned the dirty pink of fibreglass.

After the sun is down, Mom goes back to our cottage, and the kids settle in front of Netflix inside. Ginny and I head to her screened-in porch with a bottle of wine. It is somewhere after nine, but the day's heat still clings to the air. Ginny stretches out on her wicker couch. "How did it go with Benji?" she asks.

"A little surprising?" I try to choose my next words carefully; I don't want Ginny to feel bad. "He knew some things already, actually. He and Alex talked about it?"

She sits up a little. "Alex?"

"It's not your fault. Little pitchers have big ears, as my mother likes to say. Benji seemed sort of unfazed." I pause. "But he used the word *rape*."

"Fuck," Ginny says.

"Does Alex know what that means?"

"She must have some idea, right? I should probably talk to her."

"Maybe. Anyway, Benji is one hundred percent on Lukas's side."

"What kid wouldn't be."

I take a slow sip of wine. "He told Benji I was a liar."

Ginny sucks in a breath. "What do you mean? About what?"

"I mean that Lukas told my son that I am a liar. And does it matter about what? I can't figure it out. Was he trying to get ahead of the Megan accusation by discrediting women in general?"

"Ooh," Ginny said. "That's some pretty Machiavellian shit."

It *is* some Machiavellian shit, and yet, I think Lukas is pretty good at manipulating when he needs to. "*If* he did this to Megan. If everything that happened to her, and everything that happened to me, happened because of him, and still he's trying to call me the liar? *That* makes my head explode."

Ginny nods. "Try sticking with what you know then. Conjecture will kill you."

"Megan's lawyer followed up with me. I can't decide if I should talk to her."

"You're considering it?" She sounds more surprised than I expected. "Why?"

"It's the least I can do. If everything went down like Megan said, I'm pretty much the worst for not letting her into her own dorm room that night."

Ginny cocks her head. "First of all, *you're* not the worst, Lukas is. Or whoever assaulted her. And the '90s. The '90s were the worst."

"I know. But when I was talking to Benji, the whole thing felt different to me. We didn't get into the specifics of the accusation, but one day, he'll know. And I don't want my kid to think that what happened was ever excusable in any decade, in any world. I mean, what would you say to Alex? *Women didn't matter as much back then, so it's not as awful as it sounds?*" I take a breath, let the point sink in for both of us. "I obviously can't fix what happened, but I can at least not ignore it."

Ginny sighs. "I'm just putting myself in your shoes here for a sec.

You and Benji have been through so much already, are you sure you want to get even more involved in this? If everyone says this case is going to settle, maybe just let it do that. Because if any part of you thinks Lukas is guilty, it's risky to talk. I'll bet the lawyer wants your help to fill some specific hole in her story. And she's going to be very convincing. What if you innocently agree to some small detail that seals the deal? What if she sets some trap where you end up admitting that Lukas is a womanizing prick? Because, obviously, he is. And then, oops, now who's paying for Benji to go to university?" She looks at me straight-on. "But it's not just the money, obviously. This is Benji's dad."

"I know."

"And that lawyer is building a case against Lukas. You understand that, right? I mean, look, he might be guilty. I wouldn't mind seeing *him* punished for it, but not you, not Benji. When you look at the whole story, does it feel worth it?"

"Honestly, there's probably nothing I can tell her that will make a difference. Maybe that's why I'm drawn to it."

"So then why bother saying anything at all?"

"It just feels like the right thing to do." This is the first time I've even thought of talking to Elaine as the "right thing."

"Just don't do it because you're pissed at him," Ginny says. "Or because you're pissed at yourself. It's possible you were a shitty roommate. I doubt you were as bad as you think. But even if you were the *worst*, this case isn't about that, right? You're not *wronging* Megan if you genuinely have nothing to say."

"But maybe I'm wronging myself. You know, if I let everyone else speak for me."

"Have you told Lukas about the lawyer?"

I hadn't mentioned it because I knew that Lukas and his lawyer wouldn't want me to talk. There is too much I can tell Elaine that she would love to hear. Being a self-professed individual "out of alignment with typical heteronormative practices" doesn't make anyone a sex offender, but clearly, that sort of information—our relationship information—wouldn't make Lukas look good.

"No, and I don't think I'll tell him," I answer Ginny. "If it's a problem, I'll apologize later."

Before bed, I look online again for Sue's photograph of Lukas in the towel, but the *Globe* has removed that image, presumably because he's cancelled.

I reread the article's description of Sue's contribution to the show:

Verma's images examine both childhood and the environment on the precipice of change. Her images come from the tail-end of the last century, just as the public was beginning to understand extreme weather events as the inevitable consequence of human-induced climate change. These photos were taken in a university dormitory, during that shaky year of transition to adulthood. The impermanence of youth and the fragility of our planet collide in Verma's images. It's dramatic irony that makes these pieces work. We are haunted by what the works' subjects don't yet understand.

I Google Sue. For someone with such a growing profile as an artist, there is surprisingly little personal information about her anywhere. Is she married? Does she have kids? Sue has no Facebook page, only Instagram and Twitter, where she simply promotes her own work and a few environmental causes. I don't remember Sue caring about the environment, but maybe I wasn't paying attention. Or maybe it developed with the fashion.

The dearth of personal details on Sue's social media is incongruous with the fussy collages of good-looking friends she kept on rotation back at Regis. Even then, I didn't think that stuff was there just to allevi-ate homesickness. It came from a need to broadcast the size and aesthetic of her life. But maybe now it's cooler, more powerful, to generate mys-tery by hiding.

I go back to Sue's spare artist website: white background, teeny-tiny font, a selection of rotating images of her work. There are no pictures of Sue, just a lean bio: *Supriya Verma's photographs have been published in the* New Yorker, *the* New York Times, National Geographic, Wallpaper*, Harper's Bazaar, *etc. She lives in Toronto*. There is a contact email. I click it, watch my mailbox open, and then quickly close it again.

I open the tab that says, "Shows Currently on View." Sue's photo of the girl giving head to an icicle pops up immediately with the title: *Power Lines 06/20–07/31*. I try clicking on the picture to see if it will yield more images of Sue's show, but it's a dead end. The gallery, Lara Yang Projects, is in Toronto. I look at the list of summer hours and a COVID policy for visitors.

Then I go back to the image. If the show triggered something in Megan, maybe it would have the same effect on me—maybe I'd remem-ber or see something differently about that week. In any case, I have never seen Sue's work in person, and I'm curious.

I open my inbox again. Then I roll up my sleeves, actually crack my knuckles.

10

As a concession to my mother, I let her cut my hair the night before I leave for the city to meet Elaine Ng.

Mom doesn't know why I'm going to Toronto. I told her I needed to renew my passport and that I hoped it wouldn't be asking too much of her to watch Benji for the day.

"Why wouldn't you ask more of me?" she said. "Leave him overnight! I'm his grandmother!" But if her feelings were really hurt, she didn't bring that up with me directly—she decided to insult me instead. "I mean, look at you, Ros. You clearly need some R&R." I eventually agreed to spend the night at her place in the city.

Now Mom stands over me at the chair in front of the kitchen sink. "I can't do anything about the grey," she says.

"Obviously, I'm not expecting you to change the colour."

"I'll just *try* to give it some shape." Mom starts the water, lets it run for several seconds. "Nice and warm," she says. "Lean your head back."

I do what I'm told, trying to relax against the rolled towel on the edge of the sink. The spray of water isn't particularly warm, but it feels soothing against my scalp.

"Benji seems to have survived. I take it your little talk yesterday went well?"

I should never have told her. "It was sort of a big talk, and I don't think it was possible for it to go well exactly. But sure."

She turns off the water. "I suppose it would be easier if you knew for certain he was innocent."

Is she trying to get me to admit to her that I don't know this? I've not expressed certainty one way or another. I've gotten by so far calling the allegations *hard to wrap my head around*, and she—to her credit?—has not asked a lot of questions. In our last brief conversation about Lukas's predicament, sometime last month, she accused me of misusing the word *modern* when I suggested at one point that his comments did not hold up well to modern scrutiny. In her view, the term *modern* should only refer to the architectural period.

"Kids want to know what side you're on," she continues.

"Benji knows I'm on his side."

"That *sounds* very nice," Mom says. "But he'll want you to believe whatever *he* chooses to believe about his father."

I get the feeling that we are both thinking about the Christmas afternoon almost thirty years ago when the police called our house in L.A.

"He isn't drunk," I insisted after Mom hung up the phone, following her as she collected her purse from the front hall. "He's probably just over the limit." Whatever I thought the distinction was, it was very important to me. Mom turned to me sharply at the door. "No, darling, your dad is drunk. And I'm going to deal with it."

"I know you and Lukas had problems," she says. "I never asked this, frankly it didn't occur to me until I watched the interview, but was he ever . . ." Her hesitation makes my stomach drop. "Violent with you?"

"Not at all," I say truthfully. "Not with me. I can't speak for everyone else." She knows he was unfaithful, I told her that when he moved out—I felt I had to provide some explanation, though I spared her the details.

"Just checking," she says.

"What did you think?" I ask, genuinely curious, though also afraid to know. "About Megan's story?"

She works shampoo into my hair, her fingers sliding hard and fast. "How could I know what happened? I wasn't in that room."

"Yeah, but did her story seem credible to you?"

"Well, I can't imagine making that up. People could say it's for the money, but he's hardly John Grisham. And the attention's not glamorous."

"Plus, she's not the type to lie."

"But what type is she? What I really don't understand is how it got so carried away. Why didn't she scream? You lived like sardines in that dormitory. Even if he didn't stop, someone would have heard her."

"Maybe she didn't want to scream."

"No one *wants* to. But if you're being attacked—"

"Maybe she wasn't sure if she was being attacked."

"I don't understand that."

"If it happened like she said—with anybody, I'm not going to say Lukas—it's believable to me that she might have felt, I don't know, paralyzed?"

"Someone tried to have their way with me once."

"Jesus, Mom." I lift my head and look at her as sudsy water drips down the back of my shirt. It is just like Mom to do this. Normally, if I try to discuss her personal life, she brushes me off completely. But count on her to drop a bomb when she is good and ready, and I am not. "I'm so sorry. When?"

"My first year of university. Same as her."

"What did you do?"

"I kicked and screamed, and then he stopped," she says, an unuttered *obviously* just hanging there. "Lean back, please."

I wait until my hair is rinsed before talking again. With my mom, it's always a balance between giving her the response she thinks she deserves and not rankling her by "overreacting." "Did you tell someone?"

She sighs in a theatrical way. "At the time, no. Your father, eventually."

"Who was the guy?"

"Oh, just a kid." She lathers conditioner into my hair, too much. "He was into politics. An up-and-comer, supposedly. Maybe he forced that idea on me, too." She pauses, as if I'm supposed to laugh at that. "Anyway, I don't much recall him upping and getting anywhere."

"What was his name?"

"Oh, I won't tell you that."

"Why?"

"Because it doesn't matter."

"Just tell me." I want to Google him the second I'm up from the chair.

"It doesn't matter."

"Were you ever planning to tell me this?"

"I wasn't planning it, I wasn't *not* planning it."

"Did you ever consider reporting it?"

"No," she says firmly.

"But he probably did it again."

"I suspect he did. I know he got married, had some children. I saw him once when you were little, at the Ice Capades. "

"Oh God. Did you talk to him?"

"For heaven's sake, no. Anyway, I don't think he'd remember me."

My mother didn't think her assaulter would remember her.

She turns on the tap again and rinses my hair with stone-cold water, but I don't complain, I don't want to rock the boat. I have questions that I need to figure out how to phrase carefully. Is she saying that if Lukas did hurt Megan, she should just get over it? Or that this whole thing was Megan's fault for not kicking and screaming sooner?

I say, "I think maybe the difference between you and someone like Megan is that the line between appropriate and inappropriate behaviour was clearer in the '60s."

Mom laughs bitterly. "In university, I had a summer job as a cigarette girl at the Royal York. Every red-blooded male thought it was his right to pinch a girl's butt if the urge came over him."

"But what I'm saying is that people *knew* that was disrespectful. It just got tolerated in situations where men had all the power and they wanted you to know it."

"Did you live through the '60s or did I?"

"Okay, fine. But I was a kid in the '80s, and everyone taught us that things were different now. Everything had changed, men and women were equal. Women could do anything men could do. We could be CEOs or athletes. We didn't think of ourselves as delicate flowers."

"I don't recall thinking I was a delicate flower."

"I'm just saying that women in my generation—like Megan—might have been slow to clue in to the fact that they were abused. It was confusing in the '90s. We were supposed to be all equal and empowered, so there was this pressure to be *super* casual and easygoing about sex stuff."

"You're saying that when a man who was not your boyfriend crawled into your bed, you were supposed to be easygoing about that?"

"Kind of, yeah. Like, my friend Sue and Lukas shared a bed all the time. That wasn't really considered weird or inappropriate. And they were both dating other people."

"I'm sure you're right that it's my generation that makes this hard for me to understand," Mom says, her tone insincere. I don't even bother saying that *I never said that.* She picks the comb off the counter and drags it through my hair, a tad too roughly. "But you must know this by now, Ros. Men will take advantage. I'm not sure any generation of women can change that. It's what they do."

I think about the question posed to Megan on the Bella show about why she was coming out with her story now. It occurs to me that now is the only time she could say anything. Back then, even if people believed her about what happened, they wouldn't have necessarily agreed it was traumatic or worthy of much attention. They would have likely considered it, at most, to be harmless, garden-variety advantage-taking, not even particularly invasive. And in any case, to them, she should have known better.

A ball thuds against the screen door, causing Mom and me both to jump. Thank God she didn't have the scissors in hand. "Anyway," I say. "I wasn't in the room with them, either. I probably shouldn't say anything more."

"*That* sounds wise," she says, which makes me feel like everything else I've said on the subject is, in her opinion, nonsensical.

Mom lifts a few strands of hair between two fingers. "So about three inches then?"

"Three max."

As Mom snips away, I think about her revelation. In her first year of university, she was just eighteen. Five years later, at twenty-three, she met my dad, a man more than twenty years her senior. They met when he was invited to be a guest critic in one of her studio classes at architecture school. When I was younger, about Benji's age, I had my own story about them. He was a dashing, successful gentleman. She was pretty, looking for someone older and wiser to dance her around a gazebo. But over time, my version of their story developed holes.

My dad really wasn't what you'd call dashing. Plus, he was already married with a kid. And, honestly, Mom could have had her pick, I've seen plenty of photos, she was hot. And she was talented. First in her class at architecture school. So why Dad? Did she feel safer with such a grown-up man? Or was something else pulling her to him, something sadder. Did she feel tainted by the assault in the same way that Megan said she did? Like damaged goods? Or did the whole liaison with Dad just get out of her control, if she ever had any control of it? What, after all, had Dad's attentions been like? He was charming, but charm can be aggressive. Did she try to resist and then worry it would hurt his feelings? It's hard to disappoint a charming man, and they know it. They use that to their advantage.

Maybe Mom had to believe she was the type who knew when and how to put on the brakes, because otherwise, she would have to admit to herself that she hadn't put them on for Dad. When you're the child of an affair, you never get all the details of your parents' story: the leaps of faith, the lies they told, the sneaking around, the hurt and pain they caused other people.

"What did Dad say? When you told him?"

"About what?"

"What you just told me. About what that guy did to you?"

Mom combs the hair straight down in front of my eyes. "Oh, I don't remember his exact words. That kind of thing was not unheard of in the '60s, we didn't exactly pore over the gory details."

"But was he supportive?" Was I being supportive?

"That word wasn't in fashion then. But he didn't call me a 'slut,' if that's what you mean. I really wasn't looking for anything from him."

Benji and Alex crash into the kitchen then. I can smell the bug spray wafting from their sweaty skin.

"We're hungry," Benji says. He opens the fridge and stares inside.

Alex leans against the counter, looking at me. "How short are you going?" she asks.

"How short do you think I should go?" I ask.

"Mom says bangs take five years off," Alex says. Should I be taking five years off?

"I'd love to give you bangs," Mom says. I feel her comb tracing the crown of my head. She uses two fingers to hold out a length of hair in front of me.

"I don't know."

Before I say anything more, Mom twists the hair between her fingers and snips.

11

I get off the highway at Allen Road in time to see a throng of people in masks empty out from the space station that is Eglinton West subway. All these people going to work every day in grocery stores and ghost kitchens, nursery schools and nursing homes—other people's food, other people's kids, other people's elderly parents—while I sit around complaining on a dock up north. My own business here in the city feels suddenly very inessential. It's indulgent, possibly irresponsible. But now I'm here.

I navigate the rabbit warren of Forest Hill, not far from where I grew up, finding comfort in the hushed mansions, the maples and lindens, proud of my memory's grasp of geography. In Orange County, I still struggle to find my way around the sunbaked, freeway-abutting neighbourhoods, but these quiet, leafy streets are hardwired. A masked teenager walks a small white dog across the street, her face tilted down to her phone, a Regis T-shirt cropped to show off her midriff.

In Mom's condo, I crack a few windows and breathe in the dense summer air, redolent with the neighbourhood's chlorine and cut grass. I sit down on the living room sofa and drink a glass of cool water. It's two thirty in the afternoon and strange not to be thinking about dinner, about where Benji has left his shoes, or how much fresh air will counteract too much screen-time. Tonight, for the first time in months, I have plans that actually require me to shower. I emailed Val somewhat impulsively to let her know I would be in town, and she invited me for a drink on her back porch, with three exclamation marks.

Mom's condo is going through a Scandinavian-chic phase: white sofa, white chairs, a low teak table on a pebbly rug. The wall-mounted bookcase across from me seems to adhere to a prescribed ratio of books to blank space: hardcovers are arranged in short lines of three or four, separated by single tasteful tchotchkes. I notice the colourful spines of all six Billi Bean books on the upper shelf.

I am touched to see Lukas's books in such pride of place. Even long before all the scandal, I didn't think Mom liked Lukas. They didn't talk much, even on the rare occasion when we all happened to be in the same place at the same time. Though, to be fair, this was largely by my design. It was easier for me not to mix Lukas and my mother, two people I thought of as belonging to separate parts of my life. They both thought they knew me, but their ideas of who I was were not at all aligned. In Mom's eyes, I was a stubborn and sullen child. To Lukas, I was amenable, easy, eager. It's possible that I am neither of those people. It is also possible that I have always been a mix of both. But who I definitely didn't want to be was someone in between, feeling like both a traitor and an impostor to both of them.

Lukas, whose own mother died in 2010, would often ask what my problem was with Mom. He thought she was fine and that it was strange how infrequently we were in touch.

"She's just not maternal," was the explanation I gave Lukas. It's a Freudian cliché, but it also felt true to me—still feels true, although she's certainly become more meddlesome lately. Growing up, Mom was rarely cuddly, never fussed over me, never asked me about my home-work or personal life at school. She was a responsible adult—I never doubted that she'd sign a permission form—but I don't think she con-sidered my emotional life to be part of her job. At least not after I started elementary school, when so much of life's drama took place out of her sight. Did she think I'd been a happy kid? Not that I suppose I ever reported feeling otherwise—I wouldn't have expected anything helpful to come of that disclosure.

Lukas thought I was lucky to have a mom who respected my pri-vacy, but I don't think it was a choice borne out of respect for boundar-ies; she was simply not interested. It would be a lie to say that this hurt my feelings growing up because I didn't really know any different. I'd see mothers who were more involved in their kids' lives, but I don't remember particularly wishing that Mom would come along on a school field trip or lead my Brownie pack. She wouldn't have enjoyed that; it wouldn't have been fun for either of us. If I was sad or lonely then, I didn't think it had anything to do with her. Or my dad. Looking back at the situation now as a parent, what upsets me most is that I didn't understand that I deserved more attention. I can't imagine not knowing Benji's friends' names or not asking how a school dance went. If he were ever to drop out of university in the middle of a semester, the idea that I would hardly ask any questions about what happened is absurd.

But here are Lukas's books. Mom showing pride or at least interest in my family's life. It touches me in the same way it did when she cut Benji's hair.

I pull book six down from the shelf. Brand new, just out in February. Mom is very precious about books, so it is hard to tell whether she's read it or not. We've never talked about Lukas's books, at least not the content. I consider the cover art: a brown leather pilot's glove, all five fingers held up, plus one from the other hand. The glove is Billi's special time-travel prop.

Book six, which begins on Billi's sixteenth birthday, is different than the others. Instead of going forward in time, Billi is sent *back* in time to fix a past mistake that still weighs on him. This book is inspired by John Knowles's *A Separate Peace*, a favourite of Lukas's in high school. The problem at the centre is about a friend Billi hurt by accident—and lied about having hurt—at a summer camp when he was nine. The story ends on a cliffhanger, and you don't know if Billi lives or dies. We're just supposed to wait and see whether there's another book. But now, how can there be a book seven?

The walk to Lara Yang Projects takes less than an hour, but I didn't account for Toronto's clinging humidity, so by the time I get there, my feet are sliding inside my sweaty flats, and my bangs, which I'd just found a cute way to style, are a clumped mess. I am wearing a dress for the first time since the winter because I'm going to Val's after, and I still have that need to impress her.

On the outside, Lara Yang Projects is fashionably nondescript: a squat mushroom building that reminds me of a portable classroom. The windowless front door is pulled shut, and a masking tape arrow points the way around to the back. I follow the arrow and find myself in front of open barn doors that reveal a gleaming white space. A woman in black denim overalls with a lacy black bra underneath sits at a table and looks up at me without interest as I enter the space. I don't know how old Lara Yang should be, but this woman seems too young.

I hesitate for a moment under the relief of an enormous ceiling fan before entering room B, which advertises Sue's show with an expensive-looking glass sign.

Fewer than a dozen prints line the walls, all fairly large. I glimpse the photo of Lukas right away, but I don't let myself really look yet. I'm not ready. There are quotes stencilled across the four walls, and I make myself read them first: *We were eighteen and insouciant/ There is nothing more electric than the edge of danger/ We try to freeze what we can't keep/ It was not a war, but it looked like one—and is it not a kind of assault, growing up?*

Assault, I think. What a word choice.

Once, at the Los Angeles County Museum of Art, Lukas accused me of reading too much and looking at the actual art too little. I figured that reading first was respectful, the way it is with birthday cards. "Look first," he said. "If you're moved to read after that, go ahead, but you're not here to read. That's not what the artist wants from you." He really could say the most pretentious things.

I start the show in order, beginning with the wall on my right, as if I'll lose something by jumping too quickly to the main event. First, there's a picture that I remember Sue taking: a bagged newspaper, trapped under a lumpy shellack of ice. The date, January 5, 1998, is just visible. This one is clearly intended to set the scene. Next to it, there's a picture of a guy and girl pushing a car down the middle of an icy street. I don't recognize them, but they look like generic Regis kids. The girl wears a short skirt and knee-high black boots—why did we call them bitch boots?—stretching over her broad calves. Her Regis jacket is creeping up her back, revealing a patch of exposed skin.

On the next wall, the blow job girl comes into focus for me as Courtney. That tiny, pretty face. At a glance, she looks like a child kneeling in prayer against a sparkling white background, something you'd see on a First Communion card. In the next photo, a guy toboggans down a roof on a mattress.

On Lukas's wall, the three photos are arranged right next to one another, almost like a triptych. In the first image, two girls in pyjamas sit opposite each other on the bed in a candlelit dorm room. They are sharing a licorice whip—each has one end in her mouth, very *Lady and the Tramp*. I can't place the room, but it has a familiar feel: heart-shaped pillow, beer cans on the floor, a *Pulp Fiction* poster above the bed. But the next photo, I can place. A red-brick house, stalactites of ice dripping from a balcony, a hand-scrawled sign on the door: Cold Beer, Dark Rooms, Hot Girls.

And then there's Lukas.

The photo is artfully grainy, but at this scale, which is at least four feet tall and three feet wide, Lukas is unmistakably himself and unsettlingly young. Young enough to do something stupid, something harmful. I look back over the wall of photos. Was this how the pictures were arranged when Megan saw the show? In this configuration, in this company, is it possible for a young man in a towel not to become sexualized?

I study the image for clues. I want to know what day it was taken. The day the boys moved in? The night we went out to the bar? Sometime after the incident? The photo makes you wonder what he was thinking, staring out that window. Is that what makes it good art?

I move on. The final wall has three smaller photos, black-and-white group shots, kids performing for the camera. A line of girls in high heels on the ice; three guys in Regis jackets pissing onto a frozen fire hydrant. Where was I when she took these photos? We were still friends then, so why wasn't I there?

But the third photo feels instantly familiar. I move in closer, but it's not what I thought it was. It's the upper balcony of the Old Hick, and there are the washroom doors where I stood to kiss Adam, but it's not the photo from the *Ragged Regis*. The focus is on three people I don't know, sitting on a bench. A guy on one end looks directly at the camera, poking his tongue through two fingers. A girl leans into him, laughing, her hand on his thigh. About a foot away, very much apart from them, another girl sits with her head in her hands, an oversized Regis jacket draped over her shoulders.

It *could* be Megan, but it could also be anyone. It's hard to tell what the girl is wearing under the jacket, and in black and white, her hair just looks sweaty, not necessarily blond. A tableau like this was hardly extraordinary for Regis—there were probably a dozen girls passed out at the Old Hick that night, and who even knows if it's from *that* night. It's more likely to be someone we didn't know. Mostly, I just can't see Sue taking this sort of photo of Megan. If it were me on that bench, she might have snapped it to make fun of me later. But Megan was a different story. Megan never acted like a big shot who could hold her liquor, and it would have felt cruel, heartless to take a photo of her in this state. Sue would have tried to help Megan if she found her like this. She *did* help Megan.

I look back around the room. Am I disappointed that there are no photos of me? I had shared in these moments, too. Before Megan went missing, they were some of the happiest days of my life. At minimum, I suppose I had hoped to feel the sort of generic, sentimental pull that made these photos popular in the first place: *We try to freeze what we can't keep*. But I feel freshly severed from the Regis experience. My being there hadn't mattered.

The other thing I feel is something akin to jealousy. While we were getting wasted, was Sue finding her legs on that ice? Did she already know what she was doing, who she would one day become? In time, Sue and Lukas both became famous. As for Megan, she started a non-profit and did something meaningful and brave. What about me? The people captured on the walls here moved on and did things. For them, the ice melted, but I'm still frozen. Frozen in a place that doesn't care that I was there.

12

In my twenties, I imagined a future home on a street exactly like Val's: enormous trees, Edwardians with original stained-glass windows and abundant gardens, a mix of trendy cafés and erotica shops around the block. My Orange County cul-de-sac is more or less its antithesis.

Per Val's instruction, I let myself in through the back gate and onto her deck. She has already set out two wineglasses; two small bottles of Perrier; and two separate plates of olives, cheese and those expensive crackers with seeds and currants.

I hear Val's voice call down from a window upstairs. "You're here, you're here!" A minute later, she comes out with a sweaty bottle of white wine. "Are we doing masks? No masks?"

"Whatever you're comfortable with."

She doesn't have one on, doesn't put one on. I take mine off and wrap it around my wrist.

"I know you need a hug," she says, sitting across from me. "But can you believe I'm sixty-two? I'm practically a vulnerable population!"

Val looks great. Her cropped skinny jeans and linen blouse are consistent with her deceptively casual style (I know her clothes aren't cheap after a year and a half of studying her labels). Her hair is long and still healthy-looking despite her almost immediate apology for not having it "done" in months. I was blond like her when I was little, but she stayed blond into adulthood, whereas my hair went mousy somewhere in puberty. I notice that I am greyer than Val.

At first, Val and I avoid discussing Lukas head-on. I bring her up to speed on the B-story in my life: how Mom's injury is healing, the claustrophobia of Swallows' Point. "She's not easy," I say. I once avoided mentioning Mom around Val, like it would hit a nerve with her, but now that seems silly.

"It must be awful," she says.

Awful feels like too much. "It's fine. I have a close friend next door, so there's a release valve." I realize that I'm proud to be dropping this. Maybe I want Val specifically to know I have a close friend. But I also like saying it because it's true.

"Lucky," Val says. "My friends turned out to be cautious to a fault. I've seen about three people since March." In my mind, Val is always the popular girl; it's hard to picture her alone too long.

I tell Val about the small catering jobs I'm doing around Felsbridge. Val runs her own art consulting business, so I figure she can appreciate my vague entrepreneurship, maybe even offer advice.

"You went to baking school or something?"

"Yeah, in France."

"Right. Your Paris chapter." Is it weird not to be able to read your sister's tone?

I ask Val about her kids. She tells me that Richie, her youngest, is out in Australia. He was running rafting tours in Cairns, though the operation is now closed indefinitely. "He's supposed to come home for the wedding at the end of the summer, but who knows?" Val pauses, studies my face. "Julia is getting married, did anyone tell you?"

"No!" Who exactly would "anyone" be? I try to think of how old Julia is now, somewhere in her late twenties.

"Her fiancé's an ER doctor."

"Wow."

"Thirty-eight. The age gap worried me at first, but now I don't notice it. Or maybe Julia has matured being with Taryn."

Taryn. Was I supposed to know that Julia was gay? Would Julia say *queer*? Or could Taryn be a man's name? "Is the wedding definitely happening with everything going on?"

"Seems to be. Taryn's pregnant. She has a timeline she wants to stick with, so." Val shrugs. "It's going to be very small, which is exactly how they would have wanted it anyway, but now COVID's given them every excuse."

I tell her congratulations.

"Very small," she says again, as though suddenly realizing that I might take offence at not being invited. I do feel a little hurt, but I know it's not fair. The last time I saw Julia was ten years ago at a busy brunch place when I happened to be in town. Benji, who had just turned one, was screaming because he wanted my phone, and I was so self-conscious about how my parenting skills were being judged that I forgot to ask her anything about her life. I lean back in my chair to show how chill I am about not being invited.

"You're going to be a great aunt!" Val lifts her wineglass, then takes a sip. "I was so worried that divorce would fuck them up, but both my kids seem pretty grounded on relationship stuff. I say this in case you're worried about Benji," she says. "Honestly, if I could go back to the point you're at now, what I'd change is all the worrying I did." Did she think I was there for advice? Maybe I was. "Our situations aren't identical, I get that," she says. "But whatever you're doing for your kid is good enough. You've always been good with kids. Richie and Julia were wild about you when you used to watch them. Remember how Julia clung to you? I'd get so jealous." She laughs. "You were young, so energetic. I was exhausted. I was a wreck. We couldn't have gotten through that time without you."

This is genuinely a surprise. It never occurred to me that I could make Val jealous. I want to know more, but asking for details feels desperate. Instead, I say, "I didn't feel energetic."

"It was a rough time for you."

"A little."

"And now? Now how are you doing? You look terrific. I mean, you've always been cute, but those bangs are great."

"Now I'm definitely the one who's exhausted."

Val looks at me calmly enough, but I sense the roiling curiosity below the surface. "How is Benji taking this? What's he now? Twelve?"

"Eleven. I think he's doing all right." Though I've certainly lost confidence making that call.

"Richie didn't talk to me at that age. He talked to Julia occasionally, so I still got to find things out. Do you know he lost his virginity at fourteen?" She throws an arm over the back of her seat. "Jesus, right? So I gave Julia a handful of condoms and told her to fill the bathroom cabinets." She smiles at the memory, and I sense that she loves this about herself. Her liberal parenting. I also wonder if she had a glass or two of wine before I arrived.

"Julia and Richie were lucky to have each other," I say. "I envied them that."

Val looks down at her glass, swirls the pale wine. "I wasn't a great sister, I know."

"Oh, that wasn't what I was—"

"I feel guilty about that."

I shake my head. "Oh God, don't. It was a weird situation for you. Plus, you were much older." Then I add, "I mean, it doesn't feel that way now."

"I was curious about you," Val says. "You weren't the one I had a problem with. But honestly, I do feel badly. I couldn't stand your mother. Jesus, I can't even tell you. I actually shouldn't, she *is* your mother."

"It's fine, it's understandable." But I want her to go on. I am light-headed, giddy. I have wanted to talk like this with her my whole life.

"I was awful to her. Poor thing. And God, she was young! Not even ten years older than me." I don't need Val to do that math for me; I've considered the delta many times.

"Do you ever think about what happened there? Dad was this for-tysomething, and she was his student? That would definitely raise some eyebrows now," I say.

Val tops up her wineglass. "Different times. But I don't blame your mom for what happened. If it wasn't her, it would have been someone else. It's the kind of guy he was." She extends the wine bottle and fills my glass. "I used to swear up and down that I wouldn't marry a cheater, but then look what happened!"

I never officially knew that her ex cheated.

"Happens to the best of us," I say, raising my glass.

"Your mom powered through it, though. It's not the life anyone would choose."

I blink, feeling a burn of shame, of stupidity. Is Val saying that my dad cheated on Mom also? Is this something I should have known?

But it's not necessarily true. Maybe it's just something Val needs to believe: that Dad's behaviour was part of a pattern. Maybe that blunts the sting of what happened to her family.

"I'm sorry, did you not know about Dad?" Val takes in a breath and shakes her head like she's said too much, but I don't get the sense she is sorry. I think that telling me is satisfying something inside her.

"I never really considered it," I say.

"I actually ran into him once with some girl at a supper club in the '90s," Val says. "Incidentally, I was on a date with a much older guy myself. Between our two tables, you'd think it was take-your-grandpa-to-dinner day."

"But just seeing him there, does that necessarily mean—"

Val gives me a pursed look as if she's trying to gauge my naïveté.

"And you think my mom knew?"

"*Your* mother? My God, yes, she knew." How did Val know this? And what was the implication here, what was I supposed to automatically understand about *my* mother? That she was hard-hearted? A martyr? A gold digger? Val's mother, Alice, is so much clearer in my mind than my own.

"Remember all the crying women at his funeral?" she says.

There were many weeping women at Dad's funeral, but I figured that was normal for a funeral—and he knew a lot of people. The woman I watched was Alice; it was hard not to be curious. She sat very still, stared straight ahead.

"How is *your* mom?" I ask, changing the subject.

"Bored as a teenager. She's still in the old house, hasn't been outside since March."

Alice Martindale would be in her nineties by now. She and Dad married in 1952, after they graduated from architecture school. She was ultimately more famous than Dad, and there is an award at U of T in her name. During my time off from university, Dad took me to a retrospective of her work, which now strikes me as a little odd, but she'd been friendly to me there. It was the only time I really met her, but I'd spied on her—or tried to—for a while in elementary school. Her house backed onto a ravine that we often ran through during gym class. She had an Airedale who barked, but I always slowed down for as long as I could, trying to catch a glimpse of the life inside. Looking at that house, which had also once been Dad's, I had the feeling that I was looking at the true centre of his life. Like I could learn something from it. Around the time I was spying on Alice, I saw a birthday card on Dad's desk that he'd written to Val before her thirty-third birthday. It said: "Lord, 33! To me, you will always be ten, your artwork stretching across our kitchen table, your whole life stretching ahead of you." There was so much wistfulness there. *Our* kitchen table. Alice, Val—these were the players in his life's main act, I thought. Mom and I were just something added later to spice up the ending.

"So you're seeing Lukas's lawyer tomorrow?" Val says.

"Not his lawyer, actually. Hers." Val's eyes open wide. "I'm trying to be cooperative."

"But wait—did he do it?" She whispers this.

"I don't know."

"But you want to know the truth."

"I guess I do," I say. And I'm struck by the simplicity of that.

"And *if* he did it?"

"It would be awful, but at least I'd know what to think. I could give Benji some real answers. It's all so murky right now."

She nods. "You know, Julia had a brush with assault at university."

My breath catches in my throat.

"It was at a frosh week event, a concert or something. Some asshole pinned her to the wall, stuck his tongue down her throat, put his hand up her skirt."

I feel a shudder of outrage. "That's terrible, that's more than a brush. Did she report it?"

"She talked to campus security, but they couldn't ID the guy. No one saw it happen. She wanted to go to the police, anyway, but I shut that down. I told her they're going to waste your time and it won't end well."

"You probably weren't wrong."

"I'm not sure. Though, to be honest, that's not the thing I feel the worst about. Here my daughter was, crying on the phone to me, but for the rest of the semester, who did I worry about?"

I shake my head, unsure.

"Richie," she says. "Because he was in this frat down at Western, partying every night of the week, and I was suddenly terrified he was going to get himself in trouble. I did so many stupid, selfish things when I was young. But I was a girl, I couldn't hurt anyone. And I'm thinking, Maybe he has his dad's entitled asshole genes. Or our dad's, right? He was just a stupid kid."

"I think it's normal to be worried," I say.

Val pushes her hands through her hair, giving it volume. "I didn't prepare him. I was so busy teaching my daughter how to be responsible and how to avoid assholes that it never crossed my mind to talk to Richie about how not to be one."

"Richie was always such a good kid, though. You taught by example."

"It doesn't matter. You have to teach Benji all this stuff, I'm telling you. There's no room for mistakes."

I tell her I agree, but I think to myself, I'll teach him not to be a predator because it's wrong, not just because he could get in trouble or be held accountable.

"Oh, I should show you some pictures." Val begins to scroll through her phone. I refill my glass a splash, thinking about her point on genetics. Maybe there is something hereditary about being a cheater. For

Benji's sake, I hope not. But what about marrying one? Tolerating one? Were Mom and I both missing something in our brains that was supposed to signal what to do when someone betrays you? Was it intuition, courage, self-respect—what were we lacking?

"There they are," Val says suddenly. "The brides and their bitches!" The picture she hands me on her phone shows Julia and Taryn with two dogs under a weeping willow.

"They look happy," I say. And I feel a yearning to see Julia again. I don't remember how she "clung" to me because I was too caught up in my own trauma, and I'm sorry for that now. Maybe it was the same problem between Val and me. As a single mom, she was dealing with things I couldn't come close to understanding, she had no room to let me in. If I lived a little closer, maybe now, as adults, we could build a better triangle.

13

Elaine Ng's office is in a historic, four-storey building on the eastern edge of the city's financial district. The lobby is dim and cool with the oak-and-brass decor of a nineteenth-century parlour. I take a minute to fix my bangs in a large, gilded mirror. My face is blotchy, my mascara is smearing, and a dull headache is coming in behind my brow. I take the elevator to the fourth floor.

The elevator doors open right into a modern white reception area that feels incongruous with the lobby. Elaine stands just outside the doors, her hands behind her back. She is a grown-up WILD girl in a blush suit, white cami, and open-toed grey heels. Her mask is pink paisley.

Elaine must have noticed me size her up because the first thing she does after introducing herself is say, "Gosh, it feels like I haven't worn real clothes all year. Would you believe this is just my second time in the office since March?" She smiles vigorously with her eyes, crow's feet darting out from the corners. All this eye-smiling the pandemic demands. I wonder if sales of retinol cream have skyrocketed since the spring.

Elaine leads us across the hall to a boardroom, her hair swishing across her back in soft waves. I am almost certain she has come straight from getting a blowout. Am I worth all this effort? I feel sheepish for asking to meet in person, like I'm making too big a deal.

In the boardroom, Elaine notes the room's new safety touches: air purifier, windows cracked open, a plastic divider in the centre of the table. We take seats across from each other, on either side of the divider. There's a folder on Elaine's side, nothing on mine. Elaine watches me put my purse down on the floor, and I feel like it's the wrong thing to do.

"So you've escaped Coronafornia!" Elaine says. "How did you manage that?"

Her cheerful tone is odd, but I fake laugh as well as I can. I share the broad strokes of what brought me to cottage country this spring. I feel a need to emphasize the fact that this decision had nothing to do with Lukas. That I wasn't running away from him.

"And are you able to work up here?" She pauses. "Sorry, I'm not sure if you work outside the—"

I figure that she's trying to gauge my reliance on Lukas. "I'm a professor," I say. This is a white lie that I've grown comfortable with. Students and parents often start emails to me with "Dear Professor," and I never correct them. "But lately, I've been running a small catering business up north."

She raises her eyebrows as if to say, *Bravo*. "So many people are trying out new things."

"Oh, not that new," I say. Elaine comes across women like me in her line of work all the time—women linked to powerful predators. I know what the world thinks of us: naive, weak, low self-esteem. I can practically smell my desperation to defy the stereotype. To pass myself off as capable, smart and independent.

Elaine reminds me again that this is "just a conversation."

"Of course," I say. My heart is hammering; I wonder how obvious my nervousness is to her.

"Most of what I want to cover deals with a very short window in January 1998," she says. "As my client's former roommate, I'm interested in how you remember that time. But there are things you won't remember, and that's to be expected. Don't try to fake your way through anything. Just do your best."

I recall something my dad used to say to me: *Never tell lies. That way, you never have to remember what you said.* After last night's revelation about him, I'd say it's better to teach kids to avoid the behaviours they'd be tempted to lie about. Unfortunately for Elaine and me, it's too late for that. I remember most of the big lies I told, those aren't the problem. It's the small lies that make things murky, all my attempts to rationalize, explain away, make a long story short. For the college senate, for the police, for Sue, for Lukas, for my therapist, for myself. Each of these tiny, careless refinements have adhered to the memory like gnats on a windshield, gradually specking the view and making it impossible to see past the sprawl.

I tell Elaine fine, great, no questions.

"We can take a break whenever you want." She folds her hands on the table in front of her. I glance at her wedding ring, which looks shiny and grand, but I don't know the first thing about rings. "And I do want to acknowledge, in case there is any question, that I am aware of your personal relationship with the defendant, Mr. Van Kampen, and that's not what we're here to talk about."

I feel myself blush. "Thank you." My hands are shaky when I lift them up to the table to match her, so I put them back on my lap.

"You have one child together? You and Mr. Van Kampen?" I thought we weren't here to talk about Lukas.

"Yes, Benji. He's eleven."

"I have an eleven-year-old at home." She is trying to be nice, relatable. Maybe she actually is nice. She pauses, appearing to want me to say more. I don't. After a few seconds, she picks up her pen.

"Will Lukas know about this?" I ask. "This meeting?"

"There's no reason to raise that with his counsel now."

I'm not sure how to interpret that exactly, but I nod. "That's good."

Elaine's first questions are softballs. When did I start at Regis? What did I study? How long was I there? When I tell her only five months, this appears to be news to her.

"That first year of university is a bit of a weird time, huh?" She wrinkles her nose. "Having a roommate was a very different experience for me. How did you and Megan get along?"

"Fine," I say. "We weren't really in the same social crowd, but we got along."

Elaine makes a sympathetic face. "It doesn't always work out."

"No, I mean, I think it *worked out* fine. We just weren't close." I wonder what Megan has told Elaine about me. Did *she* say it didn't work out? Did she also say I was lazy, thoughtless and a slob?

"Was there any particular reason you and Megan weren't close?"

"We were just interested in different things. She was more serious about school. I was more interested in the social stuff." But that doesn't really begin to sum it up. How to describe the mom jeans? The curled bangs? There are so many specifics. Would Elaine get it if I just said that Megan wasn't cool? It seems like maybe she would, but it still doesn't feel like the right thing to say.

"Regis students have a reputation for working hard and playing hard. Would you say that described Megan?"

I pictured the kids I saw in the St. Patrick's Day video. I shake my head. "Playing hard at Regis meant drinking hard. But Megan and her friends were not big into that. I mean, she *had* a social life, but it was more sort of . . . innocent, I guess?" Elaine writes something down. Probably the word *innocent*.

"I think I know what you mean. How much time did you spend together on a regular day?"

"I probably talked to her every day at some point, but we didn't make a deliberate effort to hang out." I see Elaine write this down, too. "But it's not like we avoided each other. I don't want to give you the impression that I didn't like her. I liked her. We never fought about anything."

"Would you say you were familiar with her habits and routines?"

"In a general way."

"Can you describe what you remember?"

I recall for Elaine how Megan worked at the cafeteria every weekday morning, rising before dawn to be there on time. She worked some dinners, too, and usually studied in the library at night, never in our room. On weekends, she worked at the farm. It strikes me, as I go on, that I can probably account for Megan's time better than my own. I didn't have a job, barely studied, never joined any clubs. I have very little idea of what exactly I did for five months other than follow Sue around and hope for Adam to message me on ICQ.

"And what *did* Megan's social life look like?"

"She and her friends on the floor had TV nights? And she was into musical theatre."

"Was she close with young men as well?"

"I don't remember any guys, but that doesn't mean there weren't some. She had a boyfriend in New Brunswick."

Elaine bobs her head, clearly familiar with this part. "What was her relationship with her boyfriend like, from what you could tell?"

A line from a conversation with Lukas comes back to me: *I liked girls who already had boyfriends.* Another line, my own: *They fuck like rabbits.*

Elaine is looking at me, waiting for me to say something. "I didn't know much about it. It was long-distance," I say quickly. "They talked on the phone a lot, but I usually put my Discman on."

"Discman," Elaine repeats, smiling and shaking her head. She glances down at her notes. "But you had the sense it was a committed relationship?"

"I'm pretty sure Megan thought they would get married."

"That *is* serious. Did she seem to be happy in that relationship then?"

"I think mainly. Maybe he was just a little bit possessive."

"Is that something she talked to you about?"

I try to remember the conversation and can't quite place it. "Maybe I just got that idea from the Bella show. Sorry."

"No need to apologize, Rosalind. It can be difficult to separate our own memories from the things we've heard afterward. That's fine."

I am thirsty, but not sure if it's okay to ask for water. "I do remember Megan saying her boyfriend was a homebody. Like, he never planned to leave New Brunswick. Not even to visit her."

"Did she tell you how she felt about that?"

"She was just sort of matter-of-fact about it. But I thought it sounded kind of . . . limiting." Elaine frowns down at her notebook. "I'm not saying *she* found it limiting necessarily. *I* just remember thinking it was weird."

Elaine leans back in her chair. She puts down her pen for a moment, and I notice a thin gold bracelet shifting on her wrist. "I want to move on to the night that Megan went missing. Can you tell me what you remember about that night? From the beginning."

But what was the beginning? Six o'clock? Seven o'clock? Or was it two days before, in the cafeteria, when Megan said that women have needs?

I decide just to start at the bar, but Elaine cuts me off. "Was it usual for Megan to join you at the bar?"

I back up, explaining the buddy system and how we weren't really supposed to go out during the storm, but if we did go out, we had to be with our buddy.

"And did you truly want Megan's company?" Was this a question Megan wanted to know the answer to?

"Well, I needed her to come, so I was glad that she agreed. And by the time we were getting ready, she seemed kind of into it, so I didn't feel like I was forcing her exactly." I tell her about the clothes Megan borrowed, the makeover. Elaine takes notes, but at one point, I notice her pause to examine her pearlescent manicure and wonder if I'm boring her. I summarize. "Basically, we did some predrinking, and then we took a cab to the bar."

"Was Megan also predrinking?"

"Yes."

"Okay," Elaine says. "So based on what you told me before, that was not exactly in character for Megan?"

"Right."

"Do you remember approximately how much you all had to drink? Or what you drank?"

"Goldschläger. About four shots each."

She smiles. "That's awfully precise, Rosalind."

"And revolting."

She laughs. "I'm not judging." I wonder, vaguely, if Elaine is fun to drink with. Maybe she was once, but now she seems like the type who would hype up a girls' night and then drink half a glass of white wine.

"Your memory on this seems pretty sharp in general," she says.

"I wouldn't swear to any of it."

"Why do you think you remember it so well?"

"I've thought about it a lot." What I don't say is this: I was always watching myself from the outside, watching myself with the harshest, most judgmental gaze imaginable. I was registering every reaction or lack of reaction people had to me. Other people were living life, but I was studying it, trying to find out how to be.

"You thought about it a lot when?"

"Well, back then I had to tell the story quite a few times. You probably know that."

Elaine shakes her head. Did she really not know? Maybe Megan didn't know what happened to me in the aftermath, either. She was gone almost as soon as she was found.

"After Megan went missing," I say, "I was questioned by police and the administration fairly extensively. She was my roommate, so. Like you, I guess, everyone assumed I had information."

"Still, it was a long time ago. A lot of people find it difficult to remember things that far back." Her tone makes me feel like I should be unsettled by my own memory. Or maybe she thinks I'm making it all up. "Did anything contemporaneous help you remember?"

I try to recall what the word *contemporaneous* means. It seems like a word I should know. "What do you have in mind?"

"Diaries? Emails? Photo albums?"

I shake my head. I remember the cops asking me about a diary as well. Was it that normal to keep a regular diary? It did seem like diaries were often being pulled out on TV shows to turn up groundbreaking criminal insights, but who were all these people keeping them? And why assume that they contained authentic thought? Even if I had had a regular diary at Regis, I wouldn't trust it.

"So why don't we keep going. You were telling me about predrinking. What happened after that?"

I describe the ride to the Old Hick with Air Force Mike, who doesn't seem to interest her very much, though the police had been obsessed with him back in 1998. Elaine appears more concerned with what I remember inside the Old Hick. She asks if the night was more or less in step with other nights out at Regis, and I tell her yes and no. Yes, because we were drinking a shit ton. No, because we didn't generally go to the Old Hick. And the power was out everywhere across town.

"Were people on edge because of the storm? Extra cautious?"

"Not most people. If anything, we were extra festive."

"What did extra festive look like?"

"We were probably drinking more, partying more. There was an apocalyptic tenor to the whole thing. You know, *YOLO!* Not that we said that then, but you know what I mean." I tell her about the lights going out and then coming back on again in the bar. I don't mention the breast-grab that Megan told me about. If Megan thought it was relevant, she probably would have told Elaine herself.

"Was Megan having fun?"

"To be honest, my memories of the bar aren't very centred around Megan. I definitely should have looked out for her more."

"Do you say that because of what happened later?"

"Yes. But also in general. I was the one who brought her, and she was a fish out of water. I wasn't very sensitive to that."

"Ah," Elaine says. "Got it."

I feel a stab of disappointment. Had I been hoping for more from Elaine? Reassurance in the vein of, *Oh, Megan and I talked about that, and you're fine, really, don't worry.*

"To be honest, I was distracted because I had a bit of an agenda that night," I say. Elaine lifts her chin like a curious cat. "I was kind of after a guy." This phrase suggests a person with more swagger than I had at the time, but it also seems a fair characterization of what was going on. "My focus was really on him."

"Did you and Megan leave the bar together?"

"No. I left with the guy, Adam, and Megan stayed with my friends." It occurs to me that no one tried to stop me, also a young drunk girl, from leaving the bar with a guy I'd claimed not to know very well.

"How did she seem when you left? Do you remember?"

I remember Adam asking me if I thought she was okay. "She was drunk, but I wasn't concerned," I say, honestly.

"But Megan wasn't someone you were used to seeing drunk, is that right?"

"Yes," I say hesitantly. "But I also wasn't used to seeing my friends at the bar *not* be wasted." I thought of Sue's photograph of the girl on the bench. "She wasn't passing out or anything, not when I last saw her. I mean, obviously today, if someone I brought to a party got visibly drunk, I would definitely watch out for them. But back then, it was normal. Everyone was drunk."

"What about Lukas?" she says after a pause. "Do you remember seeing him at the bar?"

"Yes. Lukas was there."

"And how well would you say you knew Lukas at that time?"

"We were in the same social circle." I avoid saying the word *friend*.

"So, how would you describe his personality? Again, at that time. I know that may not be easy to do."

I've always found it hard to be succinct in describing the people I know best. I try to put myself back in the time, try to remember what I thought of him. "He had this air of sophistication about him, for his age anyway. Maybe it was just confidence." I picture him with his elbows against the railing of the Old Hick's balcony, smoking and looking down at the dancers. Not afraid to be alone.

"What do you mean by *sophistication*?"

This now strikes me as an embarrassingly juvenile word. I am having trouble finding the right words; it hits me that I might be hungover. "He was a couple years older than most of us, and he just seemed to know a lot of things. But he wasn't—he didn't seem arrogant, not to me at the time anyway. People liked him, they wanted him to like them." I don't quite feel satisfied with this picture. How would I have described him then? "He was hot," I say. "I know that's not really a personality trait, but it kind of is?"

"I think I'm getting a picture," Elaine says. "So he was popular."

"Popular isn't quite the word for it. He was above all that."

"Above all that?" She taps her pen lightly against her notebook. "A leader?"

I shrug. "He just kind of did his own thing."

"So more of a rebel-type than a rule follower?"

"Neither, particularly."

Elaine waits.

"Sorry. It's hard for me to pin him down," I say. "I know him too well now. Only now he's less hot." I think she might laugh or smile at this, but she doesn't.

"Did he date a lot, or did he have a steady girlfriend?"

"He had a long-distance girlfriend. A girl out West."

Elaine nods and scribbles. I can tell from her note-taking body language that she thinks this is interesting. Long-distance girlfriend equals sexual frustration.

"And at the bar that night, did anything about his behaviour stand out? How would you describe him?"

"He was normal. Himself."

"Was he drunk?"

"Probably. But not notably."

"And do you recall seeing Lukas and Megan together at all?"

I do. I recall him commenting on her shirt. But there wasn't anything weird or creepy about it. I'm pretty sure that the only reason I remember is my own jealousy. Even though I wasn't into him at the time—at least not in a conscious way—I didn't want my male friends' attention diffused too much. "We were all together, so yes, they probably chatted. But nothing stands out."

"Was Lukas still at the bar with her when you left?"

"He was still there, but other people brought her home. Supriya Verma, a couple others. They talked about her the next day."

"What did they say?"

My heart speeds up here. I don't have my own memory of that part of the night, only what I was told, and I could easily say the wrong thing. "Just that she was drunk, and they carried her to bed. That was it, really. I wasn't there, so I don't know what happened."

She does that patient, staring thing again.

"I can't help on this one."

"Let's put a pin in that then. Let's talk about the next time *you* saw Megan."

I tell her about Megan knocking on the dorm room door and our seconds-long exchange. Anticipating her next question, I say, "Honestly, I was so self-absorbed in that moment, I don't think it was possible for me to notice anything unusual about her or anything that wasn't blowing up in my face. I just wanted her to go away so that I could be alone with Adam."

"Did you ask her to go away?"

"I asked her if she could go sleep at her friend Simone's."

"And what did she say?"

"She said she was going to use the bathroom."

"And after that, no sign of her until she returned on Saturday?"

"Right." My throat feels dry, tickly. "Am I allowed to have some water?"

"Oh," Elaine says. "I'm sorry. Normally, I would have offered you that, but you know, COVID. Who knows what to do?" She goes to a mini-fridge across the room and brings me a mini bottle. I turn away from her briefly and take a quick swig.

"So no sign until she returned Saturday?" Elaine resumes. She doesn't miss a beat.

But "no sign" is not exactly true. There was the purse hanging up in her closet. When the cops found the purse, what I cared about was that it reinforced my earlier position that Megan had come back to our room. Once Megan was found, no one, including me, cared about what the purse represented anymore. But if Megan hadn't come back to the room, how then had the purse come back? Someone must have quietly returned it for her. But why do that on the down-low? And why didn't that person speak up during the search? The only reason I could think of was that whoever returned the purse didn't want to be associated with the whole thing—they wanted Megan to have it back, but they didn't want to be connected with the transaction.

But I don't say any of this, I'm not sure it's safe. I say, "Right."

Next, Elaine wants to talk about any encounters with Lukas that I can recall over the days that followed. I tell her that he was worried about Megan when the news came out, like everyone else. And, like everyone else, he was mad at me.

"Why was he mad at you?"

"People thought she might have been murdered, or killed by falling ice or something, and they thought it was my fault because I kicked her out of the room and didn't report her missing."

"Did that seem fair to you?"

"It was pretty legitimate for people to be freaked out."

Elaine makes a sympathetic face. "Still, Rosalind. It must have been hard to live under a cloud of suspicion like that." She waits for a response, but I don't say anything. "And what was the mood like in the dorm after she was found?"

"People were relieved, obviously. But they still talked about it. There were a lot of rumours."

"What sorts of rumours?"

"That she went crazy. That was the main one."

"Did she seem 'crazy' to you? After she came back?"

"Not really, but I definitely believed it was a possibility."

"What was she like when you saw her again?"

I summarize our meeting outside the cab. "It was awkward," I say. "I was all prepared for her to be mad at me. Also, I had no idea what to say about her running away to a barn."

Elaine cocks her head. "Did you get the sense that she was mad at you?"

"I didn't really. But we didn't talk long."

"And you didn't talk after that time outside the cab?"

"No."

"And after she was found, did you and Lukas ever talk about her?"

"Sorry, no. I can't really overstate the degree to which people weren't talking to me."

"Even after Megan was found, people were still mad at you?" She asks this with an exaggerated sad face, the kind you make for a toddler who has just dropped a popsicle in the sandbox.

"I just think that people were shaken up. The situation made no sense, and they needed someone to blame. People thought I was responsible for her breakdown. Like I precipitated everything by being a shitty roommate and throwing her out in the cold."

"And these rumours—was this why you withdrew?"

"In part. But the senate also kicked me out of residence for violating safety rules." Elaine shakes her head fiercely, as if this is the most unjust thing she has ever heard. "I didn't follow the buddy system," I continue, making the case against myself. "I didn't report someone missing in a dangerous storm. I should have known better."

"I want to switch gears here for a moment," Elaine says. "When did you and Lukas start dating?"

"2006. But I thought that wasn't part of this?"

"Right, I'm just curious . . . Did you ever talk about what happened in January 1998 in the years you were together?"

"Only just to say, like, do you remember that whole thing? Do you still think I'm sketchy, or?"

"And what did he say?"

"I think he was surprised I still even thought about it. I don't think he was aware of how hurt I'd been by everything."

"You don't think he was aware you were hurt?"

"Well, at the time, like, way back, I'm sure he figured I was upset, but he probably didn't think it was disproportionate to what I deserved. I think everyone was so busy being outraged by my behaviour that I became like a nonperson to them. And then I left."

"So you were cancelled," she says. "In a nutshell."

"I don't know if that's quite the right term." Though it doesn't totally sound like the wrong one, either.

"Hmm." Elaine reaches into the folder in front of her and pulls out a printed copy of the *Ragged Regis*. I would recognize the article anywhere. "Are you familiar with this piece?"

I pretend to examine it, as if there might actually be a chance that I'm not familiar. "Yes."

"And you're aware that Lukas wrote for this paper?"

"Yes." I don't bother to say what he would, which is that he was told to write that story.

"In this whole thing with Megan, did you ever feel like you were a scapegoat?"

"No," I say truthfully. "I thought people were overly focused on my role in the whole thing, but I wasn't without fault."

"Okay," she says. "And you never thought there was another reason to explain why Megan did what she did, I mean, outside of her supposed *craziness* or your irresponsible behaviour?"

"Not at the time."

I look back down at the photo of Adam and me, the photo I thought I saw yesterday in the gallery. In my mind, I can still see Dutch pointing me in Adam's direction, encouraging me to make a move. And I remember something else. He had Sue's camera on his shoulder.

This photo isn't even Sue's. And that photo of the drunk girl holding her face at the gallery, was that Megan after all? Why hadn't I looked closer? The thought of Dutch taking that photo of her, of stalking his prey, makes my stomach turn.

"Why did you come in today, Rosalind?"

I look up, try to centre myself, return to where I am. Val had put it one way: I want to know the truth. What I tell Elaine is, "I think I owe her that. Megan."

"But you know it wasn't your fault."

I'm not sure how to answer this.

"Do you have any reason to believe that Lukas assaulted Megan?"

"I don't," I say, surprising myself with the firmness in my voice. "I think that if something happened with Megan and Lukas, I would know. He didn't hide that kind of thing. Not that I'm saying he did this kind of thing, but what I mean is that he was very open about stuff in his past."

"What sort of stuff?"

My pulse is ringing in my ears. I have the sense that I'm losing control of this conversation. "Oh, I don't mean anything much. Just that he was open about his past relationships, that's all." Am I making it sound like I think *assault* falls into the same category as *relationships*? I look carefully at Elaine's face, trying to judge whether *she* thinks I'm sketchy, but her expression remains impassive.

She says, "But he knew Megan was a sensitive topic for you, is that right?"

"Yes."

"Do you think that—is it possible that it was uncomfortable for him to talk about her after what happened to you?"

I translate her question into the suggestion that she is really putting forward: It's not because of what he did to Megan that Lukas didn't tell you anything. It was because of what he did to you.

"I just can't picture it," I say quickly. Elaine purses her lips. I know why Elaine brought me in. She wanted to test out her scapegoat theory: *Lukas called you a liar in a school paper not just because it was trendy to hate you, but because he specifically wanted to keep people's attention on you and away from him. Because he assaulted Megan Main.*

Elaine puts the article back inside her folder. "Rosalind," she says. "If this case goes to court, do you think you'd be willing to act as a witness?"

"I don't—I don't know." I'm overcome by the urge to get out of there. I don't understand what she's asking.

She smiles gently, she knows I'm scared. "You can take your time to think that over," she says. And after a moment, "But I really do want to thank you for coming in today. Please know that you can call me anytime."

———

I walk a block from Elaine's office before sitting down on the empty steps of a deserted office tower. My shirt is stuck to my skin. I have an urge to smoke a cigarette, something I haven't done in over ten years.

I don't know what just happened, what I've done. I can't tell whether I've succeeded or failed at doing the "right thing," who I've helped and who I've harmed. In any case, I don't feel good. I should have known better.

After Megan went missing, that was the constant refrain: *You should have known better.* Known better than to be cavalier about a young woman's safety, known better than to make assumptions I couldn't fully support, known better than to cover my ass at a friend's expense. Lukas was part of that chorus; he carried on like he knew better. And maybe he did know better. At least he knew how to protect himself. He never told anyone about hooking up with Megan that night because he knew that "hooking up" wasn't really what happened. How could he not know? She'd been asleep when it started, and when it was over, she ran away. So when word got out that Megan was missing, he knew to create distance. And when the shit hit the fan, he knew better than to reject the gift of a scapegoat.

I used to think that Lukas would have told me if anything happened with Megan. But Elaine was right, how could he have told me? How do you tell your partner that the terrible thing she *still* feels guilty about—that you made her feel worse about—was actually never her fault, but yours?

I try to calm down by telling myself that Elaine probably wanted to leave me with these sorts of thoughts. It was just as Ginny warned. Elaine wanted me good and mad at Lukas to help her side of things. I can picture Elaine in a courtroom: *He sacrificed you so that people wouldn't sniff around him. Didn't he, Rosalind?*

Did he? But she didn't know Lukas. She has no idea who he was back in 1998.

I pull Sue's website up on my phone, type into the message box, and hit Send before I can rethink it.

14

I wait for Sue at a table in the back patio of Crisp, her partner Patricio's eco café in the east end. I looked him up after she suggested the place; he was the subject of a profile in *Toronto Life* last month on running a restaurant during the pandemic. He said, "Having a patio gives us a lifeboat, but how long can a lifeboat really last?"

I wasn't sure that Sue would even respond to my message, so I was shocked when she suggested coffee the next day. Panicky at the thought of seeing her in person, I offered Zoom, but she told me she'd been "e-toxing" this summer. I resisted pointing out the lightning speed of her responses. When I called Mom to extend my stay another night, she said, with gleeful reproach, "I told you this was a good idea!"

Around me, people drink bright juices and eat from giant bowls, masks dangling from their ears. In our exchange yesterday, Sue assured me that all of Patricio's research says that outdoor dining is safe. She didn't ask how I felt about it.

I have a jalapeno scone and cold-pressed apple juice in front of me, but no appetite, so I focus on the juice. I keep watching for Sue, but I hear her before I see her. That loud, untroubled laugh. I can't imagine being relaxed enough to laugh like that. She steps out into the sun and looks around the patio. I give her a second before waving.

Sue is wearing a flouncy yellow blouse tucked into high-rise button-fly jean shorts. Her mask is jet black with tiny yellow flowers. In my blue surgical masks, I'm starting to feel like an outsider to an important fashion movement.

"Rosalind Fisher! My God!" she calls. That accent. She flips her hair, which she still wears long, but now with an artful Susan Sontag stripe. My students would never call her rude names. She looks like someone they might still try to copy—grey and all.

I smile in the Elaine Ng way: hard from the eyes. So strange to think that at any time in the last twenty years, I could have just done this—contacted Sue. But then again, this isn't any year. People don't have a lot to do right now. Plus, I am a person enmeshed in gossip and scandal—I am a good story, as far as someone like Sue is concerned. *There is nothing more electric than the edge of danger.*

Sue motions to the four-top beside my table. "Let's move? I'd love the extra space." She is still not afraid to ask for what she wants. It's not entirely clear why this bothers me.

Once we're both sitting down, Sue tilts her head and regards me. "How *are* you, Ros?"

"Getting by, thanks. All things considered." It's my standard response these last few months. It feels unseemly to be more cheerful than that in a pandemic. It's also unseemly to be bleaker, even if your child's father has just been accused of sexual assault. If you and your loved ones are still alive right now, you're getting by.

Sue nods with feeling. I notice her forehead doesn't change. Botox. *We try to freeze what we can't keep.* I feel duped. Her grey hair tricks you into thinking she is all about aging naturally, and that way you're left with the impression that her face just naturally defies age.

Sue leans back in her chair. She is ready now for me to begin. My meeting, my agenda. I have never craved anyone's attention as much as I once craved hers, but now I'm uncertain how to proceed with it. I break eye contact, take a sip of juice.

I begin by congratulating her on her show and her artistic success, but she deflects the compliment. "You probably know this already from Lukas. Artists *never* feel 'successful.'" I doubt that she doesn't feel successful, but I am more taken aback by the casual mention of Lukas. I'd expected to take longer to get there. I am also interested to hear her say *Lukas*. I wondered if she might say *Dutch*.

Sue drops her mask to drink from her smoothie. Seeing her whole face, I feel a jolt of recognition. That defined chin, those perfect teeth. The lip ring is gone, but her glow is still there. Had I been in love with Sue? Maybe, in a way. But who wouldn't be?

"Back at Regis, when you were taking those pictures, did you already know you were an artist?" I ask, feeling like some glib journalist.

She lowers her chin, lifts her eyes, and shakes her head. What is this coquettish headshake? I've seen my students do it. It must be in fashion. "I just took photos."

"It was a trip down memory lane." I realize that I have inadvertently quoted her tweet to Megan.

"When I look at those photos, I don't feel nostalgic in any true sense. Because the thing was, I was already preoccupied then with the nostalgia that I *imagined* myself feeling later. I was painfully aware"—she touches her necklace here, a pink crystal pendant—"of how young and free I was and how that wouldn't last. Which made me less free, of course." The speech sounds canned, even the little pause.

"Was that Megan?" I want to knock her out of her little trance. "On the bench with her hands over her face?"

Sue frowns. "I offered to take it down. Megan was unsettled when she saw it at the AGO. But in the end, we both decided it had impact. This vulnerable girl alone in this hypersexed sea of bravado. Plus, no one would recognize her."

Except that I just said I did. "Do you remember when you took it? Like, what you thought you were capturing?"

"I don't think I *could* have known at the time."

"But you did take all those photos, right?"

Sue's look is cold. "Did I take all *my* photos?"

"I just remember that Lukas had your camera a lot? Like when we went out to the bars."

Sue lets out a coarser laugh than normal. "Ros, I would know the difference."

"Yeah," I say. But I'm not convinced, and I wish I were.

An uncomfortable few seconds pass between us before Sue says, "So do you feel at home?" She flutters her hands around, indicating the café. "Patricio and I went to SoCal for research. He wanted that whole breezy, open feeling. I was pushing for more of a cramped Parisian vibe, but thank God we did his thing or we'd be out of business." It is telling to me that Sue is not only shifting the topic but also fishing for a compliment.

"It feels West Coast, yeah." I could tell her that I also lived in Paris, but I don't get the sense it would interest or impress her.

"We didn't do all that California stuff with the menu, though."

"What stuff?"

"All the goddamn choice," she says, piling her hair to one side. "It's all pick a grain, pick a green, pick a protein, pick a *Jesus Christ*. When I pay sixteen dollars for a salad, I want someone to do the work for me. I want my salads curated. Do Americans all think they know how to make the best salads? I'd be a terrible American." She says this smugly, like the truth is that she is too good to be American. Whereas I, on the other hand, must get along fine. "And the portion sizes," she says. "My God."

Shaming Americans on portion sizes is a national Canadian pastime. It's very unoriginal. Sue, at least the Sue in my mind, could do better than that.

"Have you and Patricio been together a long time?" I ask, changing the subject.

"Six years." She flips her hair back again. "No kids." I think she might say, *I'd be a terrible mother,* in the same tone, but instead, she says, "But that's not what you want to talk about."

I fumble for a response to this. "Well, no, I'm curious how you've been—"

"I haven't changed, Ros. Ask me anything."

"It must have been strange to you," I say. "To see that Lukas and I were together?"

It turns out that I can't help myself. I have spent too long wondering what Sue thought of Lukas and me as a couple. I've imagined her coming across that information and being—and being, what, exactly? Awed? Jealous? A question enters my mind: How much of being with Lukas was motivated by some fantasy of Sue's reaction to it?

"These things are a mystery. I was married to a real-estate developer for three years," Sue says, avoiding my question, making it about herself again. "Filthy rich but *boring*. Anyway, I got a couple condos out of it." I wonder if she dumped him because his carbon footprint wasn't compatible with her image as an environmental photographer. She smiles brightly, looks down at her smoothie and stirs with too much concentration. "How's Lukas? I guess not great."

"He's managing."

"Good. I hadn't heard from him in a while."

"I didn't realize you were in touch."

She makes a dismissive hand gesture. "Just on WhatsApp every now and again. He sends me pictures of Benji."

I have a lot of questions about this. For starters, since when? Just since we broke up, or was it more of a longstanding correspondence that he never mentioned? I take a moment to drop my mask, break off a little of the scone. The bread is far too sweet for the jalapenos.

"His career has been so exciting to watch," Sue says. "But the higher you fly—" She clicks her tongue.

"Back at Regis, you and Lukas were so close," I say. "But he said you had a falling out or something? I guess I wondered if—"

"You're asking did he assault me? The answer is no. Lukas never tried anything with me."

"Okay," I say. "That's good to know."

"Seriously. He never tried *anything*," she says, her voice lower now. "And I'm sorry if this makes you uncomfortable, but at some point, I wanted him to. We were both single in our last semester, and everyone kept asking why we weren't together. But it never seemed like that was what he wanted. Maybe it offended me after a while, you know? I was used to getting what I wanted. I thought he was waiting until school was done, until we were travelling alone, but then he cancelled that trip, so."

"He had some emotional issues back then," I say. "I'm pretty sure he was in love with you. For what it's worth."

Sue gives me a look that I can't totally understand.

"Has his lawyer contacted you, by the way?" I ask.

She shakes her head. "Should I expect that?"

"I don't know. You were with him the night that Megan was allegedly assaulted, so I just thought maybe they'd want your side of the story to corroborate his."

"My memory of that time is pretty hazy." She looks at me in a way I recognize, with a slight narrowing of the eyes, like she's peering at me through smoke. I guess when I used to get that look from her, she *was* peering through smoke. It's a look that is searching for agreement, so I give that to her, nodding, urging things along. "I can't say much about that night, Ros," she continues. "But I will tell you that I was extremely surprised by the allegations. That doesn't mean they aren't true, understand? But the Dutch I knew wasn't like that. And nothing about Megan Main's story made me be like, *Oh, wait, you know what? That makes sense.* Like the whole thing makes *very* little sense to me."

"So he never talked about her?"

"Not that I recall."

"The night she went missing, do you remember it? You told me that after you left Megan in Courtney's room, you went back to your room to smoke up with Lukas and Stefan."

"That sounds about right," she says.

"Do you remember if Lukas spent the night in your room with you, or is it possible he went back to Courtney's room?"

"I don't think he went to her room. Otherwise, wouldn't he have been a pretty clear suspect?"

"But there were no suspects then, remember? Because we didn't know about the assault, there was nothing to suspect."

"Look, you're telling me this, Ros, and it is *sort of* coming back, but I really don't remember much."

"You told me that you woke up to Courtney and Stefan hooking up that night." I feel myself blush, both at the memory and the puerility of remembering it. "Was Lukas in the room then?"

"You know Court and Stef dated for, like, ten years or something?"

Did I know? It seems like something I should have known, and yet I'm pretty sure Lukas never mentioned it. I want to repeat the question about Lukas in the room, but I feel too ridiculous. I wait for her to say something more, but she doesn't.

"Do you remember the story in the *Ragged Regis* about me?"

She squeezes one eye shut in a pantomime of reflection. "Remind me?"

"I was crowned the worst person at Regis? The 'Frost Queen'? One of your pictures was in it."

"I don't remember that, but I was always giving Dutch photos for stories."

"It said I was responsible for Megan going missing."

She lets out a breath. "It was a mean little paper. I always said it was beneath him."

"But did it ever seem like Lukas wanted to humiliate *me* in particular?"

"I doubt that was his goal, Ros." Her tone is slightly admonishing, as if I'm the one who is self-obsessed. "He was just writing the story people were hungry for. Someone went missing, people wanted the story." Sue glances down at her phone in the bag next to her. I feel that I'm losing runway.

"But did *you* think it was my fault?"

"What was your fault? That Megan got assaulted?"

"No, before we knew that part." I'm trying not to sound annoyed. "Did you think it was my fault that she went missing?"

"I'm not sure I understand."

This conversation is beginning to remind me of the one I had with Lukas the first time we talked about Megan. I wasn't sure I completely believed him when he claimed not to remember the chronology of her disappearance, or anything about how I was treated in the aftermath. But what Sue seems to be saying is that the whole drama—one that ended with a girl returning safely—was genuinely a passing memory in the grand scheme of four years at Regis.

"Do you remember why I left Regis?"

Sue shakes her head. "Not specifically. I would have probably said it had to do with the Megan thing, but honestly, Ros, I'm barely keeping it together in the present tense."

"I get that it's a weird time to be asking all this."

"Am I meant to be an *expert* on that time period?"

"It's more that you were friends with Lukas."

"Yes, but I'm not sure if our memories are the best way to understand who someone really is." Sue stirs the smoothie again in her pretentious, contemplative way. What a different trajectory I had been following, tagging along behind Sue. What would I have become if I'd stayed in her shadow? I feel deprived of knowing. I feel this even as I decide that I don't like Sue. It could have been my decision to walk away from this pompous person.

"Do you remember why we stopped being friends?" I feel my blood pressure rise as the question comes out.

"Well, you left Regis," she says.

"But before then?"

She looks off at another table. "There's one thing coming back to me," she says. "I don't know how to say it, exactly. Just, like, an inauthentic vibe?"

She sticks that pin so easily. I swallow, try not to look as injured as I feel. "Was there anything specific or—"

"I don't know . . . You just didn't seem to know who you were. Like, didn't you pretend to be vegan or something? Stuff like that."

"Oh," I say. "That was just a silly thing. Lukas told me that Adam Linsky only dated vegan girls, which wasn't even true, but I wanted to date Adam, so I thought it would help if he thought I was."

She glances behind her quickly and then lowers her voice, like there's someone other than me that she could embarrass. "You seem like a pretty normal person now, but that's sketchy."

"It wasn't supposed to be—" I try to find the words. "It was harmless. It wasn't like cultural appropriation or something like that. Not that we really knew anything about cultural appropriation back then." She opens her eyes wide in a way that says, *Don't speak for me.* "Or I didn't. And I think insecurity was part of it, too. The Adam thing was kind of specific, but I always thought that I had to be someone else in order for people to like me. Does that make any sense?"

"Not really," Sue says sharply. "We're all insecure at eighteen."

"You weren't." Hadn't she just said that she expected to get what she wanted? When in my life have I ever, ever felt that way?

Sue laughs. Someone looks over from a laptop a few tables over, and I think this is what she wants when she laughs like that. "Are you kidding? I was just about the only brown girl at Regis, do you think that was easy?"

"Well, you were very confident. You were the coolest girl I knew."

"It was a full-time job. Trust me."

I nod, pretty certain that there's no other correct way for me to respond to what she's told me, but since there's more I need to know before I can finally call off this conversation, I wait for a few respectful seconds before saying, "I'm sorry, Sue. Can I just ask one more small thing?"

"Go ahead." I sense that she is already scripting the story of this meeting to tell people later. Will I be a punchline? Or will her delivery be all head-shaky and sad. Either way, I'm sure I'll be made to look obsessive, unhinged. And quite possibly like a Karen.

"Do you remember that whole thing about Megan's purse?"

Sue wobbles her head impatiently. "Nope."

"The cops found her purse from that night hanging in her closet, but

I can't figure out how it got there since she never came back to our room. Do you remember if Lukas ever said anything about it?"

Sue laughs again. "I don't mean to laugh, it's not funny. But this is so totally beyond what I could ever remember." She motions at the half-eaten scone on the table in front of me and asks impassively, "What did you think?" She's done with me.

"Good," I say.

She looks at me like she thinks I'm exhausting. "But not great?"

"No, I like it."

She doesn't buy it.

"I think maybe a cheese—something like fontina—could really balance it?" Now that I've said something, I feel like an ass.

"Hmm. We don't like to be too conventional."

Is fontina conventional? "Sure." I crumble off another piece.

She lifts her phone from her purse, then puts it down in front of her. "I just have a minute, I'm afraid."

"No worries."

"So, did I hear you work at the college Lukas was at way back? Do you love it?" She asks this in a bored tone. Did she look me up? Did Lukas tell her all this? Does she assume that I lack the imagination for something better than my ex's ex-job?

"It's worked out well," I say, with a forced smile. "But I'm actually making some career changes. I've launched a catering business in Felsbridge. Baked goods, mostly." It's a massive exaggeration to say "launched a business," but she's not about to check for me in the yellow pages—not about to call my mom. It seems like she's barely listening.

"Do you wear a hat?" Sue asks with a lazy smile. She mimes a puffy hat around her head.

I told her about the baking to show off, to convey to her that I am also creative, also entrepreneurial, and that I know a thing or two about scones. Now I see that I'm a joke.

It starts to rain as soon as I get on the 400, and the traffic is backed up beyond view. For twenty minutes, I move at a crawl past an empty Canada's Wonderland and its sloping spines of inactive roller coasters. There's a sign for the Vaughan Mills shopping complex. I wonder if Megan's stables are around here, some patch of throwback farmland tucked behind miles of seashell-coloured subdivisions.

I keep glimpsing my face in the rear-view. Did I look better or worse than Sue expected? My complexion is pinkish and uneven. The hook-shaped crease between my eyebrows is out today, but the new bangs sort of hide it.

CBC Radio is all unsettling news about COVID, with an emphasis on soaring case rates in the US, giving Canadians another reason to feel superior (*I would be a terrible American*). I plug my iPhone into Mom's ancient adapter system and turn my iTunes library onto shuffle. I rarely get to do this with Benji in the car because he claims to dislike my "old" music categorically, all downloaded somewhere between 2004 and 2009. I drive and listen to mournful indie rock—Death Cab for Cutie, Broken Social Scene, the Shins—the last generation of songs I know all the words to. Amazing that I once listed these bands on internet dating profiles, as if they could say anything unique about me at all.

I busy myself curating entertaining scraps from my conversation with Sue to share with Ginny when I get back: *Do you wear a hat?* I think of how different Ginny is from Sue—how much more grounded, and to use Sue's own term, more consistent. I can count on Ginny to laugh at Sue's self-importance, just as I've relied on her to recognize and call out Lukas's bullshit when we talk about him. I can tell Ginny the truth about the last few days and feel seen and supported, not drained and embarrassed like I do now.

The noise from the speaker turns to static, and just as I notice this and am about to reshuffle, the sound of Benji's tiny toddler voice comes through: "No, Dada! Down by Bay sawn!"

Lukas's voice follows a few strums of guitar: "Okay, okay. One more time."

When had I recorded this? Some night, any night. Once in a while, I would slip the phone under Benji's door to record him singing to himself at bedtime. But this was Benji and Lukas together, and Lukas's version of "Down by the Bay" where the watermelons are Benji-melons, and "Did ya ever see a Dada, wearing shoes from Prada?" Benji sings along with Lukas, his voice so loud, so precious.

The pain I feel isn't from longing. I have no interest in returning to a sentimental domesticity that I never truly had. I knew that we were damaged then, maybe irreparably so. But even as I knew that, I still made these recordings, and unlike my twentysomething diary entries, my intentions were honest. I wasn't trying to convince myself my family was something different than it was; I wanted to remember what we were. Benji was adorable, and with him, Lukas could be adorable, too. I remember how I loved the surprise of that when Benji was born. How tender Lukas was with him.

As the phone shuffles indifferently to the next song, I wonder how well Benji remembers those "Down by the Bay" sessions, his father's body nestled against him. If he doesn't remember, and if things don't go Lukas's way, will Benji forget how good his father could be?

The rain lightens on my windshield, and I feel the old hope break open inside me. The hope that Lukas is telling the truth.

15

I let myself in through the kitchen door and find Mom standing at the counter, talking on the landline. She waves her fingers in greeting. I drop my things in my bedroom and then look around for Benji. He isn't in his room, not in the bathroom or out on the deck.

I pop my head back into the kitchen. "Is Benji out with Ginny?" Mom shakes her head, points down to the water.

"By *himself*?"

But I'm outside faster than she can answer, hurrying down the slippery wooden steps. "Benji!"

I can't see anything on the dock except an empty lounger and a pile of inflatables. I rush to the edge, scan the water, the rocks, my heart racing. How could I be so stupid, so selfish? In what world was it a good idea to leave Benji alone with my mother?

"Benji!" The strained sound of my own voice frightens me.

GENEVIEVE SCOTT

"Mom?"

I spin toward the sound. Benji is looking over his shoulder from a lounger on Ginny's dock, turned away from the sun, away from me. His headphones hang around his neck.

"What are you doing down here by yourself?" I can't help still shouting.

His smile disappears. "I'm not swimming!"

"It doesn't matter. You know the rule."

The apples of his cheeks are sunburned, I can see that all the way from here. Didn't I remind Mom about sunscreen? He touches his headphones, and I'm afraid, even as I've found him, that I'm losing him again.

"Please don't turn away again." There's a note of desperation in my voice that's too late to hide, but he doesn't turn away, doesn't lift his headphones. "Sorry for yelling. I was scared."

"You don't need to worry about me," he says.

"You're eleven, my love."

"Thanks for the information."

"If you do feel like swimming now, I'll get my swimsuit and jump in with you?"

He shakes his head. "I'm good."

I kick off my flats and dip a foot into the glassy water, wrinkling the reflected trees. I'm still wearing my dress, but I feel pulled by an urge to surprise Benji and maybe also myself; I jump in.

The cold water makes my lungs constrict, but I duck under the surface and swim toward Ginny's dock.

"You're very weird," Benji says when I pop up trying to catch my breath. But he's pulling his headphones from his neck, getting up, stepping to the edge.

I let my body sink back under and flip backwards to see the column of sunlight reaching down from the surface, but not quite reaching me.

———

Mom comes flip-flopping into the kitchen while I'm making dinner. She pulls a half glass of wine from somewhere in the fridge and wipes the rim with a paper napkin.

"He needs to spend less time in front of that contraption," she says, glancing quickly at Benji who is swiping at my iPad, out in the living room. "Have you noticed he needs glasses?" Of course Mom has found something wrong with him, something I've missed that needs to be pointed out to me posthaste.

"He shouldn't have been down on the dock on his own today," I say. She looks puzzled. "He wasn't swimming."

"It doesn't matter. It's the rule I made. What if something happened? You can't even walk down there."

"All right," she says, holding a palm up to me. "I'm sure you were down there at his age, but—"

"That's not the point."

On the drive home, I made a pact with myself to be gentler with Mom. If it was true what Val said, if my dad was cheating on her, maybe this helped explain why she was so distant. Maybe she was too preoccupied with her troubled marriage to pay proper attention to me when I was young. Maybe she didn't work because she was depressed, and maybe not working depressed her further. Maybe, even though we were home together, she was too miserable to see how miserable I was, or too full of self-loathing to recognize someone else even wanted to be close to her. But then again, I also got cheated on, and I don't use that as an excuse to drop the ball on mothering. Now I'm mad all over again. I take a slow, deep breath. "Thank you for watching him, seriously. Just please follow my rules."

"I heard you."

I throw some onions into the pan. She looks quizzically at the ground beef on the counter next to me. "Tacos," I say, defensively. And then, because I can't help myself, "Another Cordon Bleu special."

"Well, I'm telling you," she says, "he couldn't read the credits on the movie last night. I asked him to tell me who the director was. I knew it was a Canadian, but I couldn't think of his name. Benji couldn't make it out." Was this how it was with my dad? How could anyone stand to be married to such a nagging conversationalist?

"Well, it sounds like you also couldn't read it, so."

"I could certainly read it once I had *my* glasses on. It was James Cameron."

"*Titanic?*"

She makes a small grunt of acknowledgment. "I wouldn't delay on the optometrist. Sometimes these things get worse when—"

"What the fuck, Mom? Am I supposed to do something right this second?"

Mom shoots me an injured look, turning to leave the room with her wineglass. "I know when my advice is not wanted." It occurs to me that I have probably never asked her for advice.

Once the beef is cooking, I call for Benji to help me chop the vegetables. He brings the iPad in and sets it on the counter in front of him. Maybe my mom is right, maybe his iPad use has crept up to problematic levels without my noticing. Or maybe the habit developed over the last few days because hanging out with my mother is insufferable. "You'll cut yourself," I say sharply. "Put that away." He collapses the device in a huff, then picks up the knife and tomato on the cutting board.

"Nana thinks you're having trouble seeing," I say. "Have you wondered about that?"

He rolls his eyes. He looks a little like his father when he does it.

"Can you see what that says?" I point my spatula across the room at a hanging calendar from the Felsbridge Business District.

He barely looks. "Pretty sure it says July, Mom."

"But under the picture," I say. The picture is of a farmhouse bathed in dusty summer light, and underneath it says "Heyman Farms."

Benji looks at it. "Holiday Fair," he says in an irritated tone before returning to the cutting board.

So Benji does need glasses. I feel guilty and defeated at the same time. Why did Mom notice first?

The tomato in front of him is hacked into uneven pieces, rivulets of juice spilling across the white plastic cutting board. "Fine?" he asks, gesturing at his work.

"Very rustic," I say.

He wipes his fingers on his T-shirt, picks up the iPad and leaves the kitchen.

As soon as dinner is over, I phone Lukas from the dock. He asks me how the city was, though he doesn't seem particularly interested in my response, so I ask him for an update on his situation.

"Frankel's feeling good," he says. "I'm going to come up to Toronto."

"Why?"

"We're getting close. It will make certain things easier. Plus, a change of scenery won't kill me."

This announcement irks me. Why should he get to have a change of scenery? Nobody else is allowed. "We're in the middle of a mass extinction event, if you haven't noticed."

He is quiet a minute. "Sorry, Ros, but didn't *you* just go to Toronto for a break?"

I feel a wave of indignation because my trip wasn't remotely restful, and that's entirely because of him. "Not the same. I had errands. Plus, even if it were a break, which it very much wasn't, I'm taking care of two people twenty-four seven."

"If I'm up there, I can help with that. I want to see Benji."

"You're not getting on a plane right now and then hanging out with our son."

"I'm planning to quarantine first, Ros."

"Where are you even going to stay?"

"I'm checking out a few rentals." He sounds like he's stretching, his voice all yawny-yawny. A performance of calm, self-possession. "How's Benji doing?"

"He needs glasses," I say.

"Makes sense. I got them when I was twelve. Huge red ones. They called me Sally Jessy Raphael." He waits for me to laugh, but I don't. "How did it go with your mom watching him, anyway?"

"I don't know. They watched *Titanic*."

"I've never actually seen that."

It feels as if the temperature is plummeting all around me. I can see Lukas standing outside AlCo Hall—his cigarette, his bored expression. He'd wanted to leave town that day, he'd asked if we could stay with my parents. Was he trying to escape? I say, "I saw it during the ice storm. Do you remember? You were supposed to come with us."

"Was I?"

"I can't remember why you didn't come."

"Probably that fucking song?"

"What did you do instead?"

"Seriously, Ros?"

My mind is racing now. "It was the day after Megan was assaulted."

"Your point?" he says.

I don't answer. A jet plane cutting across the sharp blue sky resembles the white underbelly of a shark.

"By the way, I saw Sue Verma," I say. "In Toronto."

"Wow," he says after a pause. "Now there's a ghost of Creighton past."

"Well, not such distant past since you seem to have some sort of frequent texting relationship with her."

Is this how it will be now? Me, finally with my antennae up, trying to expose Lukas in a lie.

"A text or two, maybe. She would have reached out to me after one of the books." *Would have.* He says it like an inevitability. Like anyone who has ever known him would want to reestablish contact after his books.

"How come you never told me?"

"I didn't?"

"You know you didn't."

"It probably never occurred to me."

"But this is *Sue Verma*. She was pretty central to both of our lives at Regis."

Lukas exhales, exasperated. "My bad, I guess. How is she?"

"I went to her show."

"Ah."

"Have you seen those pictures?"

"From the show that pretty much ruined me? Oddly enough, Ros, I really don't want to see them or even think about people from Regis. Imagine that every time you thought of someone from university, you were reminded of the fact that they now think you're a creep."

I choose not to mention that this has been my problem for the last two decades. "I think some of the pictures in the show might be ones you shot, actually."

"What do you mean?"

"I mean that you were taking photos on the balcony at the Old Hick the night Megan disappeared. You should ask Sue about them."

"I'll be sure to accuse her of artistic theft next time we're chatting," he says.

"Like next time you sleep with her?" I'm not even sure where that comes from.

"What the fuck, Ros?"

"Did you sleep with her? It's not a crazy question. Don't act like it is."

Lukas is silent for a long moment on the other end. "Would it be all right if I talked to Benji," he says finally. "Or is there more you want to say?"

"I want you to answer me."

"I never slept with Sue," Lukas says. "I've never even wanted to."

When I turn back to the cottage to get Benji, he's already at the screen door, watching me.

16

When I meet Ginny on her porch later in the evening, I blow right past my meetings in Toronto, even the parts about Sue that I'd been so eager to dissect. I jump immediately to *Titanic*.

"He was supposed to come with us to the matinee. We were all standing outside, ready to go. But he bailed. It's so obvious to me now. He went back to return Megan's purse instead. Something happened in that dorm room, he still had her purse lying around, and he wanted to get rid of it."

Ginny puts on a cardigan. The temperature has dipped, and the breeze rustling through the porch screen borders on chilly. "Maybe he just didn't feel like going to the movie? Are you sure he was even planning to go?"

"Yes! We were all outside, ready to go. But then, when I said Megan wasn't in the room, he saw the opportunity to deal with the purse."

Ginny doesn't look satisfied.

"Look, the whole purse thing got lost in this story, but it's fucked up that someone returned it for her and never said anything about it. Megan said she rushed out of the room after she was assaulted, so that's where she probably left her purse. That room was assigned to Lukas at the time. It follows that he was the one to find the purse and put it back."

"Why wouldn't an assaulter just dump the purse?"

"He didn't need to, like, destroy the evidence. That afternoon, no one even knew she was missing yet. The purse wasn't part of a crime scene. And anyway, you're making the assumption that he *knew* he was an assaulter. What if he didn't quite think of himself that way? What if he just thought he was the perpetrator of a badly blundered hookup? He went too far, he fucked up and made shit scary. I bet he felt dirty and embarrassed about what he did, and he just didn't want to deal with her face to face."

Ginny stares back at me blankly.

"So," I say, "he returns the purse to her closet where she'll find it and realize she doesn't have to go back and ask for it. No need to risk seeing him again so soon."

"But how did he get into your room to return it?"

"Her key would have been inside the purse, I thought of that."

"I don't know, Ros." She glances at me, then looks back out at the lake.

"If you look at the big picture, if you consider what happened before and after, it fits."

"I just don't know if this Agatha Christie stuff is really going to make you feel better."

"It's not about feeling better. It's about knowing what actually happened."

"But you didn't see him do it."

"I didn't have to."

Ginny leans back in her chair, still absorbing. "Okay. You've identified one scenario. But what if Megan left the purse in the bathroom, what if a janitor returned it?"

"A janitor would have said something about that after she went missing. Look, consider the fact that someone both returned the purse *and* said nothing about it when the search was underway. Who had an incentive to be so secretive? Lukas, that's who. He was quiet about his actions because his conscience wasn't right. He knew he'd done something bad to Megan, on some level, even if he was confused by how it related to her disappearance. He didn't want anyone looking closely at him, so he didn't say a thing."

"Ros, all you really *know* is that he didn't go to *Titanic*."

I don't get what Ginny doesn't understand. "I know Lukas, okay? I can put myself in his head better than anyone."

"But it's still a guess."

Frustration ripples through me. "No, there's another thing I know. When it turned out that Megan was actually missing, Lukas turned *me* into the bad guy. I was the scapegoat. He made Megan my fault, my problem, to shield himself. To be honest, I think it's the whole reason we were ever together."

Ginny tilts her head in puzzlement. "What do you mean?"

"He felt guilty for how he treated me."

Ginny lifts a hand like, *Slow down*. "So, what you're telling me is that Lukas wanted to go on dates with you, move in with you, and then have a *kid* with you because he assaulted Megan a long time ago and felt guilty about how you got treated in the balance?"

"Yes. And when we got together in L.A., I sensed that guilt. I did! I just didn't realize the depth of it. I thought it was only the article he felt bad about, because that was a dickish thing to do, especially to a friend."

"But, Ros, if he felt so terrible about what he did, or even about who he was back then, wouldn't he want to, like, rebuild his identity rather than spend time with the people he hurt? Why would he want to get together with a girl who reminded him of his darkest hour?"

"But you could ask the same question of me. What was I doing with him?" But I know what I was doing. In 2006, I still needed approval and acceptance from the same people I tried to please at eighteen. In eight years, I hadn't grown up at all.

Ginny shakes her head. "Is it not possible that he wanted to be with you because you're fucking cool and he liked you?"

"He felt sorry for me, Ginny. And I don't know if it was conscious or not, but he also saw the power in that. It's easier to cheat on a woman who thinks she sucks and is grateful to have you. Who thinks she isn't worthy of anything more. But you know, a big part of the reason I thought I sucked was because of him." I look away from Ginny, flustered by this raw rage.

"You're mad. That's okay. Be mad." She leans over and rubs my arm.

"You know, I wasn't feeling that mad, that's the thing. When I left the city, I was feeling okay. I just wanted this to be over. But now—now I know he's lying."

"Because he didn't go to *Titanic*?"

"Maybe I knew before. But yes, now I have evidence." I ball myself up in the chair, breaking away from Ginny's hand.

"I hate to turn all Judge Judy, but do you know the difference between evidence and a hunch?"

"Yes," I snap.

"So what do you plan to do?" There's a weariness in Ginny's tone.

"I'll talk to Elaine again. I'll go to court and testify against him."

"This is a crazy time for you," Ginny says after an extended moment. "And not just because of Lukas and Megan, either. You've got your mom, this pandemic. Everyone's in a weird holding pattern these days, but for you, it's on several fronts. I get that you want to make something happen but—"

"You think I'm trying to *make something happen*?"

"That's not what I mean."

"What *do* you mean?" My teeth are clenched.

She speaks with a measured patience. "You don't know what's true. Lukas was out of your sight for a few hours while you went to a movie. That's all. He may have done something to Megan the night before, he may not have. I don't see what this purse part actually changes."

"It's proof."

"I just think—" Ginny lets out a breath. "Even if you're right, this is not going to 'set you free' or whatever."

"It's not about me."

"Are you sure? It's at least a bit about you. And that makes sense, you're part of this. He did some really shitty things to you. But this case is about Megan. It's about what he might have done to her." She looks down at her hands and scratches at a cuticle. "If you're sure he assaulted Megan, and if working with this lawyer is what you need to do to live with that, okay. But sleep on it. There might be a better way through this for you." She looks up at me again. "I don't want you to do anything you'll regret."

"I think not doing anything is what I would regret the most."

"Think about the impact on Benji."

"I can't protect a predator just to protect someone else's ideas about him. How will Benji ever respect me in the long run if I don't make that clear? What kind of role model would that make me?" I look over at the trees, too annoyed to look at Ginny. "Do you know what it's like to spend half your life thinking you're a person that no one should ever trust—or even like?"

"It sounds hard." I sense Ginny's effort to be gentler now.

"I was just a kid."

"I know."

I look back at Ginny as she folds her legs up underneath her. "God, you must be exhausted."

"I'm not, actually."

"I guess it's just me then."

"Sorry that I'm so exhausting."

"No, I don't mean you."

Ginny closes her eyes for a moment, and I have the sense that, like Sue, she thinks I'm on the verge, about to crack. Maybe she is less consistent than I thought. When her phone buzzes, she looks relieved, glances at it, then flips it over on the table between us. "What do you think of this," she says after a moment. "There's a broker in the city who says he can rent my house out for way more money if I commit to a year. At first, I was like, *Nah, that's too much.* But then I talked to work, and I got in touch with the principal of Felsbridge Middle School to make sure there's a spot for Alex, and I think it's going to work."

Go ahead, Ginny, I think, change the subject. When I don't reply, she shrugs at her own question. The wind is picking up; I wrap myself in the slightly damp, sunscreen-smelling towel from the arm of the chair.

"Can't Alex just do school online from the city?" I say, wondering whether this small contribution is enough before I can bring the conversation back to where we were before Ginny's phone interrupted.

"Sure, but out here, they're going back in person. Case rates are way lower. She'd be at a new school in the city anyway, and I hate the idea of starting junior high online." She looks at me. "Really, you guys should consider it."

"I don't think so."

"They have colleges here, too. North Shore Community College is actually pretty good."

"*North Shore?*"

Ginny sighs. "Can I just ask why you're so dismissive of Felsbridge?"

"I'm not," I say, genuinely surprised at the accusation. "Staying makes sense for you."

"But not you," she says coldly. "You're too good for Felsbridge."

I look at Ginny, who is staring hard at the lake. Calmly, I say, "I'm sorry I upset you. I honestly have no idea how I upset you, but . . . do you think we could go back to what we were talking about before?"

Ginny draws in a breath and releases it slowly. "About Lukas and the purse?"

"Yes. And I didn't even tell you about Sue's photo show. You kind of interrupted me . . ."

"I was—" She closes her eyes again, and I have a good idea of what's coming before she opens them. "I'm trying to talk about something else."

I had a good idea what was coming because eventually, inevitably, people are done with me.

17

The next two days are cool and wet, and the lake and sky are matching shades of concrete. Alex comes over to play video games, but there's no sign of Ginny. "She's working," Alex says when I ask what her mom's up to.

Alex takes a plum from the refrigerator. It gives me genuine pleasure to watch her make herself at home. I've always wanted to make a welcoming home for Benji's friends, maybe especially because he is an only child, but in our suburb, the houses are too far apart, there are no sidewalks, and no one walks or drops in anywhere.

"What's she working on?" I ask.

Alex shrugs.

"Why are you wearing your swimsuit?" Benji asks, snapping her strap as he saunters into the kitchen. "It's, like, zero degrees, we're not swimming." He pours himself a glass of milk.

Alex blushes. She is a grade ahead of Benji and a couple inches taller. In the last month, I've noticed that she almost always wears a bathing suit under her clothes. I figure it's a kind of compression bra, holding back the realities of puberty. Who is ever ready?

"Benji, you can't do that," I say.

"Do what?"

I'm not sure at all how to put it. "Touch people's . . . swimwear like that."

We all look at one another and then away. I break the uneasy silence by redirecting my scold, demanding that Benji offer Alex some milk as well.

An order for thirty custom cookie boxes comes in from the principal of Felsbridge Middle School. I wonder if Ginny had something to do with it, but I don't text her to ask. The work gives me something to focus on for the next couple of days. Mom's old stand mixer is pushed to the limit, and the work keeps me in the kitchen until 4 a.m., two nights in a row. On the second night, Lukas texts, telling me that he has arrived in Toronto.

Alex and Ginny head to the city for a few days, but I hear about that from Benji. Ginny doesn't even text, and I feel as if we've lost something that maybe she's fine without. I imagine all the friends she'll see in the city, what she'll tell them about the weird sad sack next door.

As I drive around greater Felsbridge, delivering cookie boxes to teachers' houses, my mind turns over the timeline and possibilities of what happened between Lukas and Megan. Ginny's question hovers alongside my thoughts: *Do* I have any evidence to give Elaine?

There's no getting around the fact that I never saw Lukas with the purse. And no, I can't say for sure when the purse was returned. It was clearly *possible* that a janitor returned it, or some girl on our floor who was never questioned by police because she jumped on a bus later that day. I think he returned the purse, but it's a gut feeling. And I can't promise my gut is always right—it's pretty unreliable.

Still, couldn't the purse be useful anyway? Even if it's not great evidence, isn't it precisely the kind of detail that might rattle Lukas on a witness stand? Cases can be won and lost over a little witness stand rattling; I've seen it many times on lawyer shows.

My certainty about the purse begins to wither, but as I finish my last delivery and drive over the Felsbridge River into a blood orange sunset, I'm sure of two things. That I can't prove how the purse was returned or that it even really matters. Also, I know that I believe Megan.

I believe that Lukas assaulted Megan. I believe she was harmed. At the time, neither of them would have used those words. For Megan, it was probably hard to label because it was confusing, even if she knew in her gut that what Lukas did was wrong. She may have had some words early on, clearer words ten years later. But she never changed her story; only the language changed for telling it.

Lukas wouldn't even have tried to name what happened; he didn't want to think very hard about it. It wasn't sex, it wasn't an actual hookup, so he hoped it was nothing. But he knew it wasn't *quite* nothing. He knew he had crossed a line. I think he felt uneasy, embarrassed and— maybe—remorseful about his behaviour. Did he see it as taking advantage of Megan? Did he understand the power play? I don't know. But he knew he'd freaked her out. I don't think he was oblivious to the *possibility* of having caused distress. And that awareness probably grew into worry when Megan suddenly went missing—enough worry to make him panic, at least a bit, about whether that close-to-nothing thing was actually *something*. But once Megan returned, and the rumours about her disappearance fell safely into the camp of "mental breakdown" (set in motion, mainly, by me), he relaxed. Over time, whatever happened just receded, in his mind, into an actual *nothing*. A weirdly tinged noth-ing, but still, nothing to worry about.

So I believe that Lukas *thinks* he's innocent. In the decades since the assault, as Megan got closer to understanding what Lukas did to her, I think that Lukas just got further away from it. Today, Lukas sees himself as a feminist, someone who is good, who just wouldn't have done what Megan is accusing him of because it contradicts too many of his beliefs about himself.

But why should Lukas get to forge ahead believing only good things about himself? It wasn't like Megan or I could ever just choose how we wanted everyone to see us. We were too badly thwarted on the road to becoming ourselves—and by him. How could I, of all people, step aside and allow him to maintain a delusional self-image?

I entertain a prolonged fantasy of myself on the witness stand. "I have a duty to be here," I might say. "Not just as a feminist, but as a parent and a role model. The social cost of ignoring harm like this is scarier than the personal cost of speaking up." Would I be profiled in the *New Yorker*? Rosalind Fisher, the picture of sacrifice? In time, would Benji admire my courage? My choices would become part of his story, too. It would be painful for Benji at first, but the separation had also been hard on him, and he got through it. Kids are resilient; I shouldn't underestimate him. Plus, I don't want to end up like Val, ter-rified of how Benji will treat women down the road. The point is to be strong now. The kind of person who demonstrates the right way to behave if someone is hurt. Eventually, Benji will understand that I was never out to destroy Lukas, but to hold him accountable for what he did. In time, my openness and commitment to the truth could become points of pride for both of us.

But I can't stay rooted in the fantasy long enough to follow through with contacting Elaine. Something else Ginny said is on my mind. *There might be a better way through this for you.* Was Ginny implying some sort of forgiveness?

Alone in the car, I attempt the mental exercise of giving Lukas the benefit of the doubt. I try to put myself in his shoes—in a time, in a mindset, at a level of inebriation—where what he did to Megan was casual, wasn't sex, and didn't require consent. We all make mistakes in college, certainly I did. But I can't get there. I can't put myself in his shoes because I would never force my body on someone like that, even if I had the power.

Val calls me one rainy night while Benji and I are watching *The Great British Bake Off*. Seeing Val's name on my phone brings out a childlike nervousness. It's like running into your favourite schoolteacher at the mall in the middle of summer holidays: something you hope for, but when it happens, your first instinct is to hide because you're not ready. But I don't hide, fearing that it won't happen again. I head onto the deck, leaving Benji watching the show.

Val, without even saying hi first, asks me if I want to make Julia's wedding cake.

She explains that the baker booked for the job is closing shop temporarily to be with her family in COVID-free PEI. "Julia and Taryn are so overwhelmed with everything, they put me in charge of the cake. Anyway, I thought of you!"

It's sweet that Val is trying to throw me a bone, and I tell her how flattered I am, but I haven't made a wedding cake in ages. "Not since Paris, actually. I'm not even sure I have the kitchen space to do it," I tell her.

"Oh, it's just small. Very simple, nothing fussy. But you don't have to say yes now. Take a day or two. The wedding is the weekend before Labour Day."

"Thing is, Val, I'm not sure I'll still be here then."

"Where will you be? You're not going back stateside, are you? COVID is in the air in L.A."

"The college hasn't made a reopening decision yet," I say, although that's not true. An email from the dean last week confirmed what we all suspected: continued remote learning through the fall, all faculty and students working from home. Separately, he asked me to create a proposal for a new online "Writing Lab"—like there's something scientific about a comma splice—since my spring evaluations showed "poor student engagement."

"Let me send the design to you, okay? You can sit on it for a couple days," Val says.

I promise her I'll take a look, but I feel panicked. Wedding cakes are never "nothing fussy." People have expectations, they have dreams.

The first attachment is a scanned drawing and notes for a two-tiered cake: yellow sponge with lemon curd buttercream frosting piped in thin lines like corduroy. Toppings include hand-painted marzipan lemons and a ring of candied lemon slices around the first tier. No fondant, thank God. Still, a cake like this will take me two days to make, more than a hundred dollars in ingredients. Plus, it requires a proper mixer and more fridge space than I have.

In the body of the email, Val's written: *This won't be the first time you save my ass with the kids.* The presumptuous tone of the message could piss me off. I haven't agreed! But instead, I am touched. My whole life I've wanted Val to need me. Plus, there's a PS: *Join us?*

Later that day, I order a few supplies and a six-quart mixer online for five hundred dollars. I tell myself I can sell it later.

The supplies arrive a few days later, and when I return from picking them up in town, Ginny's SUV is in her driveway. She comes outside as I'm sliding my new mixer out of the trunk.

"Need a hand?"

"Thanks, I think I got it."

She walks closer and looks into the trunk. "Does that package say a hundred and twenty cake boxes?"

"Yeah. I thought I ordered a dozen." I expect her to laugh, but she doesn't. "I only need two for a wedding cake," I say, hoping she'll ask more so that I can tell her about Julia, but she doesn't do that, either.

I'm trying to think of something to extend the conversation, but the screen door slams behind me, and out comes Mom with a floppy hat and a basket of gardening tools. I shoot her a look to let her know she's interrupting, but her focus is on Ginny. "How was the city?" she asks brightly.

"We found tenants!" Ginny heads to her car, opens the passenger door, and pulls out a garbage bag with a high-heeled shoe stabbing through the plastic. "It honestly took me longer to clear the closets."

Mom's awkward laugh makes me wonder whether she's picked up on the tension between Ginny and me, but if so, she doesn't take the hint to give us some space.

When Ginny is inside with her bags, I glare at Mom, who is getting down on her knees at the planter box.

"Are you sure you should be on your knees?" I practically hiss. This poorly timed gardening business feels like a targeted rebuke; I've never once volunteered to do anything with her garden while she was too injured to maintain it.

"I need to grow something, I can't stand it!"

"Isn't it too late in the summer for that?"

"Not radishes."

The door crashes again, and now Benji's outside, crossing the lawn to Ginny's house.

"Ah, young love," Mom says.

"They're eleven. They're friends," I snap.

"I suppose now Benji will be scared shitless to even kiss a girl," Mom says.

"I'm not sure that's true. I think that boys have always been scared to kiss girls. Now they might actually be *less* scared because they'll talk about it first."

"How is that less scary?"

It's a good point, but I won't give it to her. Instead, I say, "I made an eye appointment, just so you know."

"You're a very good mother," she says, and for some reason, this annoys me because I do think I'm a good mother, but not because I remembered to do a basic thing like book an eye appointment.

"Does that surprise you?" I ask.

"Oh, I don't know. When you were younger, you always said you didn't want children."

I remember saying that when I was about twelve or thirteen. I'd heard a pretty babysitter say it, and it made her sound interesting—I'd never heard a woman say that before. Once I said it, it apparently became part of how Mom saw me. Why did she even listen to that? There was so much else she could have paid attention to.

"I thought maybe we'd given you the impression that having children wasn't very fun," she says.

"That wasn't it," I say, although she's not wrong about that. "When you're a kid, you just say things." I don't need her to feel guilty, but part of me is glad that this has even crossed her mind.

"I just wonder if Benji might need a little something extra lately?"

I let out a breath. So that's what her compliment was setting up. "Like what, exactly?"

"He seems a little down."

A rush of fury makes me vibrate as I head to the door, leaving my mother in the dirt. "I don't need you to worry about that."

Inside, I pick the iPad off the counter where Benji left it, trying to have my antennae up, but I don't notice anything out of the ordinary. I sink onto the couch and consider texting Ginny, but I'm not sure what to say.

I check my email on my phone and find a message from Benji's school, confirming that his classes will also begin online, that this will continue indefinitely, and with a bump in fees to accommodate a new, higher-quality learning platform. I forward the email to Lukas, since he pays those bills.

Could we still afford Benji's school if Lukas loses this case? His lawyer fees must be adding up, though I've never asked for specifics. I've always relied on him to figure out the financials in our lives, and legal fees are his problem to worry about, though they could hurt us as well.

I thought I'd write Elaine this afternoon. Instead, I write Val to confirm I'll do the stupid cake.

Not long after dinner, before the sun has even set, I find Benji in his bedroom and under the covers.

The door is half-open, but I knock gently. "You okay in there, Benj?"

"Just reading."

I have been nagging Benji to read all summer. "What is it?" I let myself into the room.

He flashes the cover, and I recognize Lukas's third book: "*Billi Bean: Forever Thirteen?*" His thumb holds down a page about a quarter of the way through it.

"Ah," I say. "That's a good one."

Benji sits up. He's wearing a T-shirt and sweatpants. When did he stop wearing pyjamas? "Dad read it to me already."

I sit myself on the edge of his bed. I used to sit with him for at least a half hour at bedtime, but since we've been up at the cottage, I've barely set foot past his door.

"It says right on the first line of Dad's Wikipedia that someone's suing him," Benji says.

"I haven't looked at Wikipedia," I say. "But, yes, unfortunately, it's not a secret."

"I'm going to change it, though. Did you know that anyone can edit Wikipedia?"

"I did. But the news is out there, Benj."

Is Wikipedia all that he's read? Did he stop there? Something Adam said years ago comes back to me, the thing about the internet being like ice in Antarctica. Layers over layers over layers of preserved time. Benji's father's story will be there forever. Whether he digs deep now or later. There's nothing I can do but be here.

Benji looks up at the ceiling. "Alex says his books will be banned."

"I don't think that will happen." His publisher hasn't dropped him yet, neither has his agent. But I am also pretty sure that his books will no longer be welcome at the school fun fair.

"But kids won't read them." Benji looks at me then, his eyes hungry for a contradiction I can't provide.

"I don't know what people will do," I say.

"Alex wouldn't even touch this." He waves the book. "She was like, *Ewww, sick, get that away from me.*"

"People have different tastes," I say, aware that I'm skirting the real conflict. "Did you tell her what you like about your dad's books?"

"What's the point?" He slides onto his back.

"It's hard to have disagreements with your friends," I say. When he doesn't say anything back, I add, "It doesn't feel good."

"Who do you have disagreements with?"

"Oh, plenty of people. Sometimes I say the wrong thing, or I don't act the way I wish I had." I kiss the top of his head. "I promise tomorrow will be better."

"Are they still going to make Dad's TV show?"

"I don't know."

His voice cracks gently, but he doesn't cry. "Is he still going to be famous?"

I'm not sure how to answer that. Because it's not really fame he cares about—at least not in the superficial way. For Benji, fame has just always been part of who his father is. And having a famous dad is part of who Benji is, too. It's not just his dad's reputation, but the damage to his own that he's worried about.

"I'm sorry, sweetie. I wish I had more answers for you."

"Can you read it to me?" He hands me the book but doesn't fully make eye contact.

I swing my other leg up on the bed. "What part are you at?"

I start to read, and it takes a chapter and a half for all the light to empty out of the room. When I ask him if I should turn the lamp on and keep going, he shakes his head. "That's enough."

I lie next to him, listening to the crickets and some distant bird's relentless chant. I need a little more time.

18

Lukas calls the next afternoon, but my hands are covered with marzipan—a trial run on Julia's cake—so I ignore it. Moments later, WhatsApp goes off, followed by FaceTime.

I prop the phone up on a bag of sugar, recoiling at my red, furrowed image on the screen. I've been led astray by Zoom these past few months, taking maximum advantage of its generous smoothing function. I'm a monster on FaceTime.

Lukas's face bobs into view. "What's up?"

"You called me."

He closes his eyes and then exhales dramatically as he opens them. "We're settled," he says.

It takes me a second to make meaning of this. I sit down on a kitchen stool. "What do you mean? The whole thing?"

"It's behind us, Rosie."

"Is it . . ." I don't know what the right question is. "Is it good?"

"It's over." And now he sits, too, collapsing onto a cream-coloured Barcelona chair.

"So what happens now?"

"We make anodyne statements about a satisfactory resolution, and then we move on. We signed an NDA, there's not much else anyone can do or say."

"How does Megan feel about it?"

"How does Megan feel about it? I can't say I give a shit. I mean, legally, she was *way* out of her depth. But if her goal was to malign an innocent person and derail his career, then she should feel pretty victorious."

"You think *that* was her goal?"

Lukas gives me a look—eyebrows bunched, lips pressed into a hard frown.

"I'm just trying to understand what happened," I say.

He sits forward. "Okay, I'll break it down. Some woman who I've had *zero* interaction with—"

"You interacted with her."

"I really didn't, Ros."

"You did."

He pushes air loudly out his nose. "You know, I wasn't expecting you to jump up and down or anything, but I thought at least you'd be relieved."

"I am."

"Really? Because you seem pissed about it."

"I'm not. I'm processing."

But I am pissed. I'm pissed at Lukas for getting away with something. Pissed at Megan and Elaine for letting him. Pissed about the wasted mental energy of the last few months. Pissed that I'm glad to be off the hook about taking my purse theory to Elaine because I probably wouldn't have done it, anyway. Because I am a person of inaction. I don't *do* anything.

"I know you met with Megan's lawyer," he says. "You want to tell me the deal with that?"

I feel my face grow hot. "She wanted to interview me as Megan's roommate. It had nothing to do with you."

"It had nothing to do with me?!"

"I didn't tell you because I knew you'd react like this."

"You all need a piece of the MeToo action," Lukas says. "I get it. You need to ramp everything right up to show how affronted by the world you are."

His phrasing catches me. "What did Megan *ramp up*?"

"What?"

"What did Megan *ramp up*?"

"I'm not talking about Megan."

"But you said, 'You all,' so I thought maybe you meant Megan, too. And since you had zero interaction with Megan, I was wondering what she could have ramped up?"

"Fuck you, Ros."

We stare at each other. He stands up and carries the phone, stalking down the hall, his face swishing in and out of view. I assume he's going to get a cigarette. "Stop twisting everything around. If you girls need an adrenaline rush, then go do something with your own lives. Don't ruin someone else's."

With effort, I speak slowly. "Maybe if you've never been assaulted, it's easy to accuse people of 'ramping things up' for an 'adrenaline rush.' But if you'd had any experience whatsoever being violated, then—"

Lukas chuckles. "Right. So now you've been sexually assaulted, too? That's perfect, Ros. Who's the lucky guy?"

When it was fashionable, when he was on the other side, Lukas remembered Simon.

By the time the call is over, I'm shaking, angry and almost certain enough to pick up the phone and call Elaine. But it's too late now. There's nothing anyone can do or say.

And it's then, realizing this, that I suddenly feel the tiniest bit of relief Lukas expected from me.

19

Ginny knocks on the side door early in the morning. I flipped her the first short article that came out online around midnight: "Van Kampen #MeToo Clash Comes to Quiet Close." I didn't make any comment; I couldn't condense my feelings about the settlement right then, even if I were confident that Ginny was willing to hear them. She may still be done with me.

When I open the door, Ginny smiles apologetically and gestures to a small dog pissing on Mom's attempted radishes. "So we went to a fostering event yesterday. Muddy's owner died in June, I think maybe of COVID?"

"Jesus." I reach my hand out to the approaching dog, who is the unflattering white of coffee-stained teeth. "*Hello*—"

"Don't feel like you have to lose your mind over her or anything," Ginny says. "I'm not so sure myself."

"Alex must be psyched."

"Well, I'm the one walking her now, so that doesn't bode well."

"At least she doesn't bite?" I say, as the dog begins to lick my fingers.

"You never can tell." She looks past my shoulder into the kitchen. "I saw you through the window. I guess you're working? Do you want to take a break?"

"Yes and yes."

We head to the trail in the woods on the far side of the road. The morning sun crossing the tall trees gives the path an oil painting richness.

"Did you have fun in the city?" I ask, not sure where to start.

"Fun? I saw a couple friends." Ginny rolls her eyes. "Everyone's *so stressed out*, it's boring." She unclips Muddy's leash, and she runs along ahead of us. "I owe you an apology, Ros," she says, as if she'd been waiting for the dog to be out of earshot. It's nice to see that, like me, she's nervous.

"It's okay," I say.

Gently, she lifts a hand to stop me. "I miss you. What you're going through sucks. I wanted to help you the other night, but I shouldn't have been so opinionated. Obviously, I should have listened."

"I was hard to listen to. I'm sure I wasn't making sense."

Ginny frowns down at the ground. "You made sense. It's just that—" She waves the rest of her sentence off with a pointed let's-not-do-this-again gesture.

"No, you're right," I say. "The purse stuff isn't rational. *I* think he probably returned it, but I get that I can't prove it or confirm that it's important. I suppose I just wanted something tangible—like if I just had physical evidence, some sort of smoking gun, it would give me permission to do a brave thing, take him down, see him get punished for once. If I could just prove that he hurt her, it would justify all the destruction I'd cause."

"Makes sense. Did you ever talk to the lawyer again?"

"Nope."

Muddy comes back to the trail and sniffs around for somewhere to shit. We stop and wait while she circles, stoops and shudders right in front of our feet.

"But you've talked to Lukas?"

"Yep. He was a giant asshole. He also practically admitted to everything . . ."

"What?"

Even though I brought it up, I'm too tired to translate more non-evidence. "It's complicated," I say. "But he apologized after." I describe the email he sent a few hours later, his aggrieved tone and eye-rolling attempt at a placatory sign-off: *This has been very hard, Ros. I think I deserve kindness now, but I shouldn't be demanding that from you. You've been so patient with me. You don't owe me a thing.*

"Anyway," I say. "I'm taking Benji down to see him for the weekend."

"And that's fine with you?"

"He loves his kid, he's ready to see Benji."

"But are you ready to see Lukas?"

"It doesn't matter. The case is over. Life goes on, and he's still in my life. We'll need to figure out what to tell Benji about the settlement, obviously, but I'm hoping that once we're home again, these last weird, uncertain months in Benji's life won't seem too different from what everyone else went through during the pandemic. It's been a strange time for us, but everyone's had a strange time, so."

"You're leaving?" Ginny bends to bag the shit.

"Soon. When Mom's ready to be on her own again."

"Is Benji's school even opening up?"

"Online."

Ginny looks up at me. "So what's the rush to get back home?"

"We need some stability."

"This *is* stability." She stands and sweeps her arms out in front of her, shit bag waving. Up ahead, Muddy is sniffing the steep bank of the creek, which looks, actually, very unstable.

"It's not practical."

"For who? Lukas? Just because his case settled doesn't mean that *you* have to. Your life doesn't have to go back to being on his terms."

"I know," I say, a little defensive, and I can see now that Ginny wasn't talking about forgiveness before. "But he's Benji's dad, what am I supposed to do?"

Ginny chews her lip. "I don't know," she says. "But whatever you decide, don't you want it to feel like your choice?"

"Obviously." I sound chippier than I mean to, and I try to smooth it over with a smile.

"Good." The smile she gives back is warm, but her tone is disappointed.

And I get her disappointment. But right now, I don't care. Despite all my bluster, all my anger—or maybe because of it—it's been something of a relief in the last twelve hours to contemplate the easiness of returning to our old lives. The idea of some other complicated plan makes me tired and resentful. I could blame Lukas for that, but it's not all him. To be honest, I'm not even sure that he would try to stop Benji and me from staying here. He might not love the idea, but we've managed these last few months apart, and I think he would, at least, consider the pros and cons. I'm the one holding back. If I could go back in time, maybe *then* I'd make better choices. But for so long, Lukas's rhythms have charted the course of our lives, right up to my hand-me-down job. If these last few days have taught me anything, it's that I'm not very good at making decisions or taking any real action on my own.

It's not forgiveness, either; it's just what's realistic.

"You bought a hundred and twenty cake boxes," Ginny says. "And that giant mixer. I guess I hoped that maybe—" She stops and faces me.

"Of course, it's okay to do what you want. You don't have to stay. You don't have to open a bakery. You don't have to do anything. I just want you here. Is that really terrible?"

"That's awful," I say. "But I'm flattered."

And I am. No one has ever wanted me to stay before.

20

Benji stares out the car window as we press deeper into the city. Toronto is not a place he knows well. "Where's Alex's house?" he asks.

"We can drive down their street if you want?"

He mumbles something in a tone that could be interpreted as interest, so I shoot down Bathurst and then west along St. Clair and over to a neighbourhood of shaded, semidetached houses, displaying a full range of owner pride and attentiveness. On Ginny's street, we pass a set of ivy-covered row houses, and one of them has a van parked out front. "Maybe it's that one? Looks like someone's moving in."

He peers out. "Small."

"You think?" What do I expect? This street is so different from the gated, undifferentiated stucco subdivisions and raked gravel lawns that he knows. "Isn't the neighbourhood interesting, though? From here, you can walk anywhere. Subway, corner stores, restaurants." I sound like a real estate agent.

"Alex is moving to the lake."

"For a little while."

"I'd rather live at the lake than here," he says.

I don't answer him, but I see him looking up for me in the rear-view. "We've had a good time there," I say neutrally.

"Obviously. Ginny is your best friend."

I feel a flush of pride; I like him thinking I have a best friend, and I like the matter-of-fact way he says it.

Several minutes later, I am slowing down in front of a loft in Kensington Market. My heart lurches when I see Lukas, already on the sidewalk and leaning against the brick. He looks greyer, older; I suppose that he's also been using the touch-up function. In his wilted white button-down and jeans, the arm of his sunglasses in his mouth, he has the air of an aging rock star, which is almost certainly the look he's going for. Part of me wants to rev the engine, speed away from him, and his ego.

My movements are jangly as I pull up to the curb. But it's too late to change my mind. Benji is unfastening his seatbelt, joy sweeping his face.

"I'll get your bag," I say.

Benji pushes the door open, and I watch as Lukas rushes toward him, folding him into his arms. I know the smell of that hug.

I walk around to the trunk, feeling shaky and strangely light.

"Thanks a bunch, Ros," Lukas says, sidling next to me, pulling Benji's bag from the trunk.

"Sure."

"She's doing a whole wedding cake this weekend," Benji says suddenly. I didn't think he knew anything about my plans, and I am touched that he finds them interesting enough to pass along.

I look over for Lukas's reaction, but he just seems puzzled. I haven't told him anything about my catering work in these last months. We only ever talked about him.

"Julia is getting married this weekend," I say. When the name doesn't appear to register, I add, "My niece." I suppose he never thought of her as his niece.

"Cool, cool. But pickup's still good Sunday?" There's a vague panic in his eyes that he's trying very hard to conceal with a smile. *Yes, you asshole*, I want to say. *After six months of parenting by myself, I wouldn't dare ask for a minute longer than seventy-two hours.*

"Yep."

"I was thinking the three of us could fly back together in a week or two," he says. "I have enough first-class vouchers."

Could we all fly back together? Would I do that? And yet I can see it so clearly.

"I don't know. I'm still looking after my mother, Lukas."

"How's she doing?" I feel him trying to make meaningful eye contact, squinting in a sensitive-guy way that is a little hard to look at straight-on.

"She's all right."

He takes a step toward me. Is he looking for a hug? I turn away, pretending to be distracted by the sound of distant shouting. He has Benji for the weekend, but he gets no part of me.

"Be safe, okay?" I say, turning to hug Benji. But the hug lasts just a second before he skips off, like a much smaller child, toward the front door.

Lukas, who must sense that I'll rebuff another attempt at a hug, gives me a dorky sort of salute.

I walk back to the car, still with that strange feeling of lightness. I take a breath and remind myself that Benji is happy. That's a good thing.

I tell myself that these next few days are a break for me, even though it feels like something is being broken instead. For nearly six months, Benji and I have gotten by fine with me as the only parent. What more will Lukas do or say—about me, about women—to undo my credibility? I figured I could move on without forgiving him, but what if I can't even trust him?

The airless, overwarm car is suffocating, but I'm not ready to drive. I take slow breaths, drink the last of Benji's Big Gulp, try to fill this vacancy in my body. This weightlessness that could be mistaken for relief but feels different, more violent. More like erasure.

Once again, traffic is thick alongside the sad sprawl of Canada's Wonderland. I'm listening to a radio call-in show with a doctor about COVID. Someone asks about returning to school, and the doctor says, for what feels like the eightieth time in four minutes, "You need to make the choice that feels best for you and your family," and once again, the caller thanks her, like this is actually helpful, like anyone ever knows what that is. I switch it off and, for ten minutes, creep forward with the bored rush-hour procession before shifting abruptly to the right lane. I exit onto a small, quiet highway and pull over to find directions on my phone. There are four turns that will take me to RideOn.

Two girls in black horseback riding helmets are pushing wheelbarrows across the gravel parking area as I pull into a spot under a tree. They stop and stare. I roll down my window and call out as cheerfully as I can. "Hey, there! Do you know where I can find Megan Main?"

The girls exchange looks. "She's probably in the office," one of them says. "But people aren't supposed to go inside."

"Could one of you let her know I'd like to speak with her?"

I hope they won't ask my name and they don't. They look at each other again and then walk to a white farmhouse with a wraparound porch and a solar panel on the roof. I can see the stables just beyond the house and a fenced-off riding ring where another girl brushes a rust-coloured horse. The palms of my hands are sweating.

Megan comes down the porch steps. One of the girls trails her, and the other walks slightly in front—a loyal security detail. I consider slipping my mask on before opening the car door, but Megan is maskless. Her face is open, so kindly expectant as she approaches the car that it makes me feel guilty. I wish that I could just be whoever she is expecting to see. I step out onto the gravel.

Megan stops about ten feet from the car and shields her eyes from the sun. "Is there something I can help you with?" she asks brightly.

"Megan?" I say, my voice weaker than I expected. "It's Ros." For some reason, I put my hand on my heart. "Rosalind Fisher."

Megan nods pointedly at the girls, who take a hint and walk off to the riding ring. She turns back to me and lifts her eyebrows. "Is there something I can help with?" The same question repeated, only brusque this time. Something about her tone feels distinctly out of character, performative. She's still a nice person, just on guard. Her eyes move quickly from side to side, as if scanning for other surprises.

I had planned a few openers in the car, but now I can't think of a thing to say that feels right. "I'm sorry to sneak up on you like this," I say. "I know it's been a long time." Although that's hardly the weird part.

She squints, suspicious. "It has."

"I was driving by," I say, though we both know that's a lie. "I thought you might be here."

"Always here."

The noise of a truck coming up the driveway catches Megan's attention. She waves it to the far side of the lot, then looks back at me with an appraising expression that is hard to interpret generously. But which villain am I? The thoughtless coward who didn't report her missing? Or am I Lukas Van Kampen's partner, mostly evil by that association?

"Your farm is beautiful," I say.

She says nothing.

"Well, I just wanted to say"—I often chastise students for beginning sentences that way: *If you just want to say it, then just say it* —"that I really admire what you've done." This is the only prepared line I can remember from the car, and I liked it for its range of meaning. I could be talking about RideOn, but I could also be referring to her courage in a general way. But it comes out wooden. So I add, "It's amazing. After what you've been through."

She tilts her head to one side. The whine of cicadas is sharp in the trees overhead. "I don't think you know anything about what I've been through."

I feel my face flush. "You're right." I let that hang for a second before saying, "But you deserved better."

"I can't discuss the case with you, Ros." She widens her eyes and nods rapidly.

"That's fair," I say.

"Did Lukas send you?"

"He doesn't know I'm here. We're not together, we haven't been for a while." I hope this will earn me an approving sort of response, but it does not.

Megan looks over at the riding ring. "I have a class in a minute."

"Well—" I look helplessly around the dusty, scorched parking lot for inspiration. "Your students are lucky to be here. I hope you turn this place into all you've ever wanted."

Megan blows air from her nostrils, not unlike a horse. "With all my fast cash, or?"

"No," I say quickly. "That's not what I mean."

"Why are you here, Ros?"

"Because I'm sorry," I say, and it comes out whinier than I imagined. "That's it. I was a bad roommate. I didn't help you, and I'm very sorry for that. And I never said so."

Megan looks away, unimpressed. "When I heard you and Lukas were together," she says, "I did think of telling you what happened."

"You did?"

"I suppose I wasn't *seriously* thinking about doing it. But it did occur to me that maybe I *should*."

"Why didn't you?"

"Because I didn't know what the point was. Or what my point was. Was I trying to protect you or trying to spoil your party? If we'd been friends, actually friends, if I thought I could help you, it might have been different. But I decided to mind my own fucking business." She looks down at the ground and then back up again. "I guess if you think about it, I could have saved you a lot of trouble."

I choke a little on my own breath as she turns to signal something to the truck. "Shit removal," she says, without eye contact. "I wouldn't stay."

I glance at the truck, then back at her. "Thanks for coming out to talk to me."

She frowns. "I didn't know it was you."

An hour later, free of suburban traffic, I drive with the windows down. More barns, more horses, fields of bundled hay like overturned soup cans. The bucolic setting is comically at odds with the buzzing of my nerves, a detail I'll include when I tell Ginny the story of my RideOn pit stop. It feels easier to think of it as a story, outrageous and out of character. My brave move, finally. Maybe Sue would call it a "selfish apology," worthless to Megan, motivated only by my own guilt and need for relief, but maybe that was fine. As Ginny said, I am also part of this.

Sue and Megan had said the same thing to me, and they were right. I don't know what they went through at Regis. I only know my own experience, and even that is only approximate—fractured and reconstructed to add up to something that I can make sense of, that I can narrate. What's clear now is that all of us were hurt. It was never up to anyone else to decide how badly. At least now I'd acknowledged my role in Megan's pain.

Though as I drive along, as I come down from the high of my own spontaneity, I realize that I don't genuinely feel unburdened. I don't feel brave. I keep seeing the drop in Megan's face as I said my name. She hadn't wanted to see me. My showing up wasn't closure for her, it might have been the opposite. A rude and unwelcome reopening. Speaking to Megan was no more the "right thing to do" than talking to Elaine.

At a roadside stand, I stop and buy an expensive carton of wild blueberries, still mostly underripe. I devour fistfuls from my lap as I drive, wincing with each tart, tiny explosion. When I bite the inside of my cheek, I'm not expecting to cry. I clench my teeth against the rush of pain, try to stay focused on the road. When the ache in my throat becomes too much, the hard release of sound is startling. Wheezing and gulping that I haven't heard since Benji was the one in tears. I pull over with Benji's purple-red face on my mind—his sixth birthday, running to me when his friend Andrew smashed the pinata before it was even strung up. I took Benji to the kitchen to cry it out in private, forcing the images I'd just seen on Lukas's phone to the back of my mind for another time. My pain would have to wait. And wait.

It's her, that woman kneeling with Benji in the kitchen, who I need to apologize to now. The woman who wouldn't allow herself the space to get upset, who thought she could just live with being let down. Was I betraying that woman still?

21

Mom has been staying out of my way while I work on the cake, but this afternoon she seems hell-bent on getting my attention. She hums loudly and bangs around inside the fridge where I have icing, lemon syrup, marzipan, and layers of sponge cooling precariously on the racks.

"Is there something I can help you with?" I say after the fridge door has been open for a solid minute.

"Nope!" She extracts a half bottle of rosé triumphantly. "Could I pour you a cold glass of wine?"

"I'm working." I avoid eye contact, go back to icing.

"Mmm. It all looks so good," she says, finally closing the fridge.

"This?" I am annoyed by her obsequiousness, which feels manipulative, though I haven't yet figured out to what end. "This icing layer is just to seal in the crumbs. So no, it doesn't actually look good. Not yet."

"All marriages need to cover up the crumbs, don't they?" She laughs, pleased with her joke, and sits herself down on a kitchen stool across from me. I don't respond, but I can feel her eyes on me. "You amaze me. You used to be like your father, so impatient," she says.

"Not really," I say, keeping my eyes focused on the cake. She makes a clicking noise like she knows best.

"Right, I know." I stop what I'm doing to look at her. "I quit ballet. I quit guitar. I quit school. But maybe if you had taught me to be more patient instead of telling me I'm too impatient for everything, I wouldn't have quit all that stuff. What if I tell Benji he's impulsive like his father? How will that work out for him?"

"When did you play the guitar?" she says.

"Never mind."

"I'm only saying I'm glad you've taken this back up again." She gestures at the mess in front of me.

"Because you thought I'd quit this forever, too?" I can't control myself. I'm so agitated, so hot below the surface, so brittle, that if Mom looks at me the wrong way, it will spark a wildfire.

"Because you love it." She reaches across the table and runs her finger along the edge of the cake. I make a motion to clap her hand with my metal spatula. She pulls back, a scalded expression on her face. Her sunhat has gone slightly askew, and it makes her look old in a way that hurts me under the ribs.

"This is a professional job," I say, instead of an apology.

"You're more precious than an architect," she says, but she finally stands up. "I'll leave you be, but can I ask you something first?" I squeeze my eyes closed; I can't help myself. Why is she incapable of leaving me alone? "When you go to pick Benji up on Sunday, could you take me home?"

I open my eyes. "You want to go back home? For how long?"

She pats her leg. "For good? I'm back on my feet now and I need a change."

"But your condo has stairs."

"They don't scare me. I'm ready to get back to work! My clients need me."

I didn't know she was in touch with clients; I hadn't asked. "And what about shopping and things? It's not just your leg I'm worried about, there's this whole deadly disease."

"I'll call Mr. Loblaw if I need to." She fixes her hat. "But I want you and Benji to stay here. For as long as you need to, as long as you want to. You can work on your business without me barging in all the time."

"This is hardly a business."

She heads to the screen door but doesn't quite make it there before turning around again. "You know, it isn't true what you think. When you went off to France, I did believe in you. I didn't think you'd quit."

"Well, I did, so."

She shakes her head. "No. When you got home, you seemed to know what you wanted, you had other priorities. I gave up my career when you were born, so what was I going to say against it?"

"Nothing," I say, though I'm curious what she might have said. "It's fine."

"It's not fine. I should have encouraged you to stick with it."

"Don't worry about it, honestly." I pick up my scraper again, but she still keeps standing there.

"I'm seventy-one years old," she says, abruptly. "Am I going to die without knowing why I make you so angry?" This is possibly the most direct question that Mom has ever posed about our relationship.

"I'm not angry." I look up at her. "Okay? I'm not. Is that why you want to go home?"

"No," she says. "I'm just ready."

She opens the door then, and I watch her find her favourite lounger on the deck and drag it into the sun. The idea of Mom returning to the city scares me. Will she remember to wear a mask in public? Does she know how to do business online? Will she be lonely? But I'm also aware of another tremor of fear, one for me and Benji, because if she leaves, there's no excuse left to stay.

As Mom fiddles to adjust the lounger, I wonder about her assessment of the summer. Her assessment of us. Does she accept that our relationship just isn't good? Like me, had she hoped for something more when we all wound up here? Some opportunity for real conversation, real connection? Was that what she was going for just now? It's impossible to know. I don't know her. Sue's question comes back to me: Are our own memories the best way to understand who someone is?

Mom removes her muumuu-ish swim cover and sits down carefully, looking thin-shouldered and vulnerable in her faded floral bathing suit. She has always been the type to take a swim before eight in the morning—a "polar dip"—and then act sanctimonious about it all day long (*Well, I've had my exercise for the day!*). This year, she hasn't been down to the dock once. I could go offer to help her down there. I could do it right now, take her by the arm. But it's too much, or maybe it's not enough. Either way, it's too late. And I don't know how to do it right.

22

Lukas's lawyer calls me while I'm hand painting marzipan lemon slices with petal dust. I let it go to voicemail and play it several minutes later.

Breathless with irritation, Sam Frankel tells me that Elaine Ng was in touch about my surprise visit to the farm. "Lukas may not have had a chance to explain, but I'd like to be clear now," he says. "This sort of thing can't happen. If we want this settlement to stand, you can't contact Megan Main."

He carries on about legal things, but I press Delete before the message ends. I don't want to blow up the settlement, even if he's telling me I have the power to do that. Whatever move I make next will not be about Elaine, or Megan, even Lukas.

———

I finish Julia's cake just before 1 a.m. It's so clean, so flawless, that I can't stop checking on it, afraid it will somehow cave in or crumble to pieces before anyone has a chance to see. Tomorrow, I'll drive it the fifty miles to Taryn's parents' farm.

Too hot and anxious for sleep, I shower before changing into cool, loose pyjamas. I open my bedroom window to the din of crickets and the vaguely metallic breeze from off the lake. Then I lie down and wait. Normally, I'm not one to get up again after committing to bed, preferring to toss and turn than to acknowledge sleeplessness, but after a half hour, I give up.

I throw my energy into tidying the bedroom, folding and putting away clothes from the laundry, rearranging piles of receipts and other detritus on my dresser and floor. As I pass back and forth across the room, I catch my face reflected in the glass of the framed article on the wall: "If I had to do it over, I'd do it all the same!" In the lower corner of the page, there's a photograph of me at eight years old, climbing the ladder to the dock. It was May when the picture was taken, and the lake was freezing cold. I had to get in and out several times for the photographer to get the right shot. "My hands are purple," I told Dad. "That won't be noticeable in the photos," he said.

I grab a cake box from the corner of the room and then another, assembling them on my bed with an effortless proficiency that makes me feel graceful, fluid, the way I always want to be but rarely am. The paperbacks and comic books go into the first box to take to the Felsbridge Public Library on Monday. I pile the notebooks and half-assed diaries into the second box to drop at the waste management facility for shredding. I empty my dresser of T-shirts and decades-old dust; worn sheets and towels can go to the animal shelter, clothes can go to Goodwill. Back in the spring, this stuff had been a comfort to me—now it's clutter, it's in the way. I don't need these things to prove that I haven't been erased.

Out the window, the sky is growing lighter. I won't sleep now, and for maybe the first time ever, this thought doesn't stress me out. Looking over the emptied room, I feel a satisfied stillness.

Finally, I pull the yellowed article down from its hook on the wall. The wood underneath is a rich caramel. Unfaded and almost like new.

By sunrise, I'm down at the dock with a cup of tea. The lake is quiet and motionless. Ginny will be over in a few minutes to help me load and level the cake boxes before driving out to meet Val. I've decided not to stay for the wedding, it would be asking too much from Julia and Taryn to include me, but I invited them to come up for a weekend later this month, even the dogs.

A canoe glides past, slicing a velvet ripple through the water. The man at the bow points his paddle up at our cottage, showing it to the woman behind him. I wave before turning to take in the property from where I'm sitting. The rising sun washes the concrete box—still beautiful, still a curiosity, after all these years. Mom's brave effort to carve out a new story. Soon she will get out of bed, pack up her things and leave again.

The swallows are queued up on the power lines between our cottage and Ginny's, spaced evenly like holes on a belt. How do they sit there without getting electrocuted? I should look that up. Or I could ask Mom.

I turn back to the water. Perched on the dock pole next to me, a single swallow stares ahead at the distant island. "Your folks are back there," I say. But it doesn't listen, its gaze fixed. Maybe in winter, when the ice is set, Benji and I can use the snowshoes to trek across.

I hear the quiet shuffle of footsteps behind me. I turn, smiling, but it's not Ginny. My mother is on her way down, wearing only her faded bathing suit and her white orthopaedic running shoes. She glances at me, nods, then quickly returns her focus to the path, taking one careful step after another.

ACKNOWLEDGMENTS

Thank you to Gillian, my first reader, whose insight, honesty, and patience helped this story become a book. This effort is, at its heart, a sista mixa.

I am so grateful to the wonderful people who lived through an ice storm with me twenty-five years ago and who cheerfully *relived* those moments when I asked because we're still friends: Jason, Phil, Anita, Angus, Helen, Rob, Sam, and Adrian. And thank you to Carly, Emma, Lindsay, Kath, Al, Megan, Philly, and all the GBC girls for your friendship, support, and the years of conversation that have shaped this book in ways I'm sure you'll recognize. Nola, without our rambling Friday sessions, I may have never finished this. I am so grateful for your friendship.

I'm very much indebted to the friends and colleagues who offered their thoughts on this book in its most vulnerable stages: Cordelia,

Kirsten, the Crupe, and the Imperial gang, whose voices are forever in my head. Your early encouragement made all the difference. For generously sharing specific knowledge on matters ranging from cupcakes to reasonable doubt to horse breeding, I owe a debt of gratitude to Alice, Lisa, Lilia, Wendy, Gillian H, and Carly (again and always). And thank you to Laurie whose thoroughness and last-minute reassurances came at exactly the right time.

To my agents, Stephanie Sinclair and Paige Sisley, thank you for believing in this book and working so hard for it. To my editor, Sarah Jackson, you're frighteningly smart and perspicacious, and I feel so lucky to get to work with you. I am grateful to you and Sue Kuruvilla and to everyone at Random House Canada who believed in this book and made it real.

Thank you to Jesse who doesn't seem to mind living with a writer and is forever furnishing my best descriptions, whether he knows it or not. And thank you to Jarvis for paying such careful attention to words, forcing me to always search for the right ones.

I want to acknowledge the Canada Council for the Arts for their support.

To my parents, I am deeply touched by your tireless curiosity and enthusiasm—I know the effort it takes not to ask too many questions.

And thank you to my readers.

Genevieve Scott is a Canadian writer. Her first novel, *Catch My Drift*, was published in 2018 with Goose Lane Editions. Genevieve's short fiction has been published in literary journals in Canada and the UK, including the *New Quarterly*, the *White Wall Review*, and the *Bristol Short Story Prize Anthology*. Her short films have screened at festivals worldwide, and she was Story Editor for the 2020 Canadian feature film *Jump, Darling*, starring past Oscar-winner Cloris Leachman. Genevieve holds an MFA from the University of British Columbia and an MSc from the London School of Economics and Political Science. She teaches writing at the Laguna College of Art and Design in Laguna Beach. As a volunteer, she mentors at-risk teen writers through the L.A.-based nonprofit, WriteGirl. Genevieve grew up in Toronto and currently lives in Irvine, California, with her partner and son.